Notes
Of
Discord

Paul Lubaczewski

A HellBound Books LLC Publication

Printed in the United States of America

Acknowledgements

Firstly, I'd like to dedicate this to Ralphie Boy from Squat or Rot for helping to bring my band to NYC, and to all the members of the Repressed and bands we played with over the years. Living there in a band is a lot different, and helps form this book.

My family allows me to find a way to keep pushing this boulder up the hill, so Leslie, Morgan, Kaitlyn and Alaric always get a thanks.

Finally, my Beta Readers who agreed to look this over and give me an OK to show it to the rest of you, Mary Pinto Conte, Tim Murr, Kenneth Toglia, Bert Edens, Wissa Raven Ramsey, Alex Havoc, Joy Red Lilly, M. Ennenbach, and Edward Mignot - thanks to all of you for volunteering to look at a book that is well outside the norm.

To Jae Monroe of A.P.P.L.E., we talked about me writing this book, I wish you'd gotten to read it."

Author's Introduction

This, is mostly a work of fiction, based in a very real time that I very real got to experience. My band The Repressed moved to New York right after the Tompkins Square riot. We had been coming up there as individuals for some time before that, call not being one of the ones arrested during the chaos luck of the draw, it wasn't a go to New York City weekend.

That presents a bunch of obvious quandaries in writing the first half of this book, which is supposed to be fiction. How you make a story about that time frame realistic without naming specific names has been the toughest part of it for me. Again, fiction, not biography here. I suppose some of you reading this are going to recognize stories, or even think you're being alluded to, it can't be helped, I guess. At the same time, I tried to keep actual squats out of it, or actual people as well. None of the characters in this are actual people, more combinations thereof. There are specific places mentioned, because you can't totally avoid it, if our hero doesn't go into Alcatraz or the Pyramid...well, it would be bullshit. I name drop some bands as well, because those were the bands, but they don't actually appear in the book as anything but mentions. I didn't want to presume to write my friends or the memories of friends as characters in my book, they are so much more than that. I know there was a Rat running around NYC, there were multiples in fact, but I used the name because years of traveling from scene to scene tells me that Rat is the most generic name I could come up with for a male punk rock character. Every scene had one. Also, for girls, there were at least three Cats for that matter, which I didn't use. I did my best to give the reader exactly what it really felt like, while at the same time not trying to pick fights, or settle scores, or piss off friends. I wanted to give your memories a jostle if you were there, give you a feel for what it was like if you weren't, while at the same time avoiding asking Ralphie Boy what he thought of my fictional account of him.

There is some pure artistic license as well. If Sabotage and the Switchboard seem smushed together, they are. If it seems a bit farfetched to have the band shell running that regularly in winter, it is. We talked about doing just that repeatedly on unseasonably warm days in February we referred to as "ozone summer" (global warming summer would have been more accurate, but what did we know?). If anybody had gotten it together to read a damned weather forecast to know when one of those days were happening on a weekend, we might have gone through with it. So, since we didn't get to do it in real life, we get to do it in the book. Quite a few scenes in here are just things that happened with the actors obscured by fiction. Have fun figuring out which is which. The second half of the book was a lot easier in a lot of ways, it's where most of us are today, I didn't need my memories for that.

How We All Ended Up There; A Primer

A lot has been written about Punk Rock and its nature, its cause, and its meaning over the years by a lot of different people. Call it a cottage industry, has been one for decades. One thing Punk Rock is that most people don't seem to get, at its heart, punk is more reactionary than revolutionary. It is the opposite reaction to external stimulus deep down inside. The yin to the previous youth revolution's "time to grow up now" yang. It was the next generation of kids who felt they had just been sold down the river by the previous generations. The hippies had talked a good game, but what were their real accomplishments in terms of policy? Scaring people into electing Richard Nixon? Twice? Bravo, your kids and your little brothers are so impressed. Worse yet, now the peace and love generation had become the parents, become the politicians, and even more so, the businessmen. They always had that offer from Dad to come to the firm to fall back on which made the revolution go a little easier. You want you some love beads? Come to Honest Moon Child's Love Bead Emporium only 22.50 while supplies last, Moon Child herself is a Reagan

Democrat worth 2.5 mil. The music those remnants were producing by 1975 was even worse than what their politics were mutating into, soulless, gutless, bland, without humanity. Humans have two bases, rage, and joy, sadness is only for when the first two don't work out, and America and Bread and Badfinger reached neither of them. There needed to be a reaction, get a mohawk, a leather jacket, and welcome to the reaction kid.

The really straight Mr. and Mrs. America world didn't even deserve consideration at all in this equation of revolution begetting revolution. Those people didn't even feel real, and they were not to be trusted, nobody went through life with that little soul without all of them having ugly secrets in those ranch house developments. Those were the kid touchers, the wife beaters, the hard drinkers, all of it carefully done behind closed doors where it would stay because polite people don't talk about "those kinds of things" in public. How lucky for them. When the doors were open it was all polyester church suits and McDonald's for dinner like a proper smiling nuclear Christian family. The children of the next revolution already knew instinctively those people were full of shit. Anybody who voted for Nixon with a straight face had the heart of a monster hidden by the veneer of respectability so bright and shiny that its glare cloaked a multitude of sins.

But what really burned, what really set the great punk rock reaction in motion was the betrayal of the hippy wave. Them selling out was the death of your heroes, and in the case of some of them just outright dropping dead. You knew your Bircher neighbor was a cunt, you didn't need telling, you didn't need to learn that the hard way, you just gave him a wide berth until you got the hell out of your childhood hometown. What hurt was how the former world-changers had become weak-willed politicians and toy salesmen or worse prog rock musicians. That was not the promise of Hendrix at Woodstock, this was betrayal. So, if peace and love weren't going to work, how about rage? That's what punk rock did, it was the reaction to the overblown, over-important bullshit of the error, it stripped music right back down and created a lifestyle and a music scene that tapped back into the very primal, the original human. Rage and Joy. Black Flag to the Ramones, right to the root of being human without any pretensions or masks, who cared if the general public liked it? Those fucking people watched Donny and Marie.

Since the general public didn't like it, and certainly didn't understand it, at least judging from the after-school specials and the Quincy episode, the whole thing became its own insular world, chugging along happily without inspection from the outside. It thrived hidden away in the seedier parts of every city around the world. People lived inside that womb, waves after waves, leaving their homes and flooding every city where they had electricity for guitars, looking to escape all the bullshit they had been born into. The media might have packed up their cameras and lights and took the circus elsewhere right after they zipped Sid Vicious's body bag shut, but that didn't stop the kids.

Even when the record industry finally realized they'd never get rich off it, punk just soldiered on in underground clubs without so much as a by-your-leave from the rich and powerful movers and shakers. The music got faster and harder and meaner freed of any constraint from any hopes of "making it big." And while bands themselves would let you down and change their look and sound to sell more records, their replacements were just around the corner playing in some shit hole club, five bands for five bucks and all the booze and fights you could survive thrown in just for the asking.

Chapter 1

It was going nowhere. Straight up nowhere. Andy Weiss thought he had known the reasons he had started this whole thing at first, they were simple enough, and achieving those goals used to be enough to keep him floating through life happy as a pig in shit. He really thought it was all for hot and cold running pussy and a drug smorgasbord every day, for fuck's sake that was the real American dream the one they hid behind the sparklers on the 4th of July. Those were good solid reasons for getting out of bed every day, most people would have agreed, hell when you boiled it all down that's what half the human race woke up for. That magic hope that someone would spread their legs and shoot 'em on up, they might bury it in beer ads, but that was the gist of it. But once he'd had things set up and moving a little bit, he realized that he wanted oh so much more than that. Nobody was as surprised as he was to find out. He shouldn't be dissatisfied, he liked not lifting a finger, people deferring to him in every room of the house, it felt damned good. In this rotten crumbling building that he and his flock occupied, he was God, and who didn't want to be God?

He liked that a lot.

But it wasn't going anywhere. Who knew he gave a damn about or even considered the future? Suddenly he was having those really weird thoughts about his legacy and stuff like that. He wished his flock was growing and going, he tried to make it more appealing, he even tried to preach to people as a last resort. That sure as hell wasn't easy, he had gotten by so far on having really scary eyes and appearing fervent, putting enough words together for a full sermon was a struggle. Sometimes he even washed his clothes and his greasy dark hair so he looked more put together when he did it. Hell, once a week he had his people out there with a fucking vat of soup feeding it to the homeless trying to get attention for the church from the wayward souls wandering by looking for that special "something" to fill the void in their hearts. But for all his efforts the church was still stuck in park going nowhere, most days not even revving its engine, just floating along from one day to another. It had become nothing but a dream deferred and denied, he'd read that somewhere, and it fit how he felt about his little self-made religion. Gods damn it! He needed to make a change in how he was doing things, he needed to find a better song and dance if he wanted to play on Broadway. Andy had tasted power running this little cult, and the problem with power is, it's addictive.

The good Lord helps them what help themselves, so it would only go to figure that the devil would make you beg for it, or at the very least hustle. Andy had come up with an idea that would take him further than he could ever hope. He had been hanging out in an occult shop pretending to browse, with his ears open, and for once he had his mouth shut when it all had come to him. The owner of the shop was talking to one of his long-time regulars when the regular let drop the solution to all of Andy's problems. He had been asking about something that the shop owner knew about coming onto the market, something that was a bit more real than the usual hokey fare in there. Andy made it clear that he was interested in owning that book there and then. It had taken some tricky wrangling to slide into some of Donna's trust fund money in a way that Daddy wouldn't notice, but Donna wanted Andy happy, right? Real creative shit was needed when they needed a larger sum, she had access to a certain amount almost constantly, but there was a lot in there that she couldn't touch, and they needed a bit more. It had taken months to bleed the little bit extra they needed out so no-one would notice, but eventually they had the scratch together.

So, Andy could buy the book he was looking at right now.

Johnathan Morgan, the rare bookseller the occult shop guy had mentioned, was incredulous when Andy approached him to get the book, even with Andy asking for it by name. Andy couldn't one hundred percent blame the guy, he was smelling a bit whiffy, damned water was out at the building again, and even with his hair combed, he knew he looked like a crazed longhair prophet who had just come in from the desert. Andy thought of himself as blessed that somebody else hadn't scooped it up while he was waiting. That was the nice thing about cold hard cash though, it made people listen very carefully to what you had to say. Look at that one asshole developer that was looking to buy up the LES, the one who used to be part of that failed football league, as a for instance. Not one damned word that ever came out of that guy's mouth was true or made any sense at all, but damned if the Post didn't fall all over themselves to print whatever wacky shit the guy said. Guy was a star in this town, not for any reason other than the golden rule we all learn when we're a kid, money talks and bullshit walks.

And today, Andy had the money, honey.

Once he'd gotten back to the squat, he cradled the tome in his hands, amazed even to look at it. Yeah, they'd paid the piper, but most times they don't even let you in the dance hall in Andy's experience. He knew the way forward, at last, after all this time stuck revving his engine standing still. Nobody in this town paid attention to anything short of a miracle, and churches were a dime a dozen down here. He'd make the Church of the Left Eye stand out all right, they wanted miracles, and he'd be the man delivering. Let's see St. Patrick's try to keep up with that! Pious ass rules and regulation nun fuckers wouldn't stand a chance. Andy would give them real miracles, just because the power came from the other side of the good/bad equation, it didn't make it any less miraculous. Ask those hypocrite preachers down south, you give 'em a show and the punters don't give a shit about the moral character of the showman.

Andy had told all of the flock that he was not to be disturbed tonight. The whole floor of the squat that Andy claimed for his own was vacant, most of his children were down on the first floor flocking away. This was one of the first nights in forever that even Donna wasn't wandering around Andy's rooms naked, lithely flowing from spot to spot until he had no choice but to take her on whatever surface proved handy. He was busy making miracles tonight kids, you did want to see the miracles, didn't you? As long as he did everything right, they'd see something special, and for the first time in their dead-end lives, chemical free. The floor may be dirty, the windows were cracked and coated in grime, the carpet reeked of the beer and wine they'd spilled on it, but tonight this rotting hovel would be the hall of the miraculous.

Later that night the body which was known to the

world as Andrew Weiss was assembling the ingredients for soup to be served in the park. But it was less Andrew Weiss than it used to be. It always amazed him, people would put all this preparation into the summoning, the calling up, but at the end of the day, they'd get an important detail wrong. Their hand would shake, a word would be mispronounced, people just didn't realize that the devil really was in the details. Funny how people didn't examine that phrase more closely, old sayings have deeper meanings. He glanced briefly at the magical markings on the wooden floor and allowed himself a smile. Maybe sometimes they didn't consider that in their rush to get started that a raised piece of wood might make the chalk in their hand jump and end up putting a similar looking, but technically useless, symbol on the floor. Funny old world, wasn't it?

He could feel deep inside of his mind a voice screaming in terror. The part inside of him that had wanted that book, mainly for the power, but for something else as well. The part of this mind that wanted what power brought, respect. Well, kid, you wanted miracles? You were about to start to see some stuff that would blow your mind, too bad you'll be watching from a passive front-row view. You wanted power, there was going to be power like you had never dreamed of before with your small petty striving. So shut up in there, you are about to get everything you asked for, enjoy the ride buddy, you punched your own ticket. He walked across to a spot on the floor directly above Donna's bedroom. With the sword cane he favored, he knocked heavily on the floor, the signal for Donna that he had need of her. That girl was an absolute treasure in her servility, Andy just didn't appreciate her properly. But he would now, like he never, ever had even considered before tonight.

A few moments later he heard the door leading to the stairwell open and Donna's soft bare feet padded across the dirty floor. "You needed me baby?" she said. She was trying to sound sexy, but to Andy's new hearing she sounded worn out and used up. A husky sound that already carried the hints of the illness that would rob her of her sex appeal soon enough.

"Yes, my dear. Tonight, I'm making a special soup with a new recipe and I need your help most of all," Andy said, not turning to face her, his hand straying down to something on the counter next to the stove.

"Sure baby, anything you need," she cooed.

The new and improved Andy could hear every sound, every rat whizzing inside the walls, every cockroach scrambling among the food in the cupboards, everything. He used that newfound ability to judge when she had gotten close enough before he whirled back to face her. She barely made a sound, just a small pathetic gurgling around the cleaver he'd put halfway through her neck. The part of him that had opened the book earlier wished she didn't have that expression of betrayal on her face as she sank to the floor.

He reached down and pried the cleaver out of her throat, letting out a sudden rush of blood. How she hadn't noticed the plastic sheet she'd had to walk over to get to him was a testament to the power of drugs and devotion. He took a towel and wrapped it around the wound to staunch the blood a bit before he picked up the body with both arms. She was light, so very, very light. But she would be enough to make a start. She was always willing to make a sacrifice for Andy, bless her for that, she was truly delicious.

It was an hour or so later before he came out of the bathroom tub he had deposited her in. Andy walked carefully not to spill anything from the large metal vat as he walked back to his kitchen area. First, he set some of the meat, carefully wrapped in Saran Wrap and tinfoil, in the freezer for later. Her head he carefully displayed in the refrigerator itself among the beer bottles, almost like a centerpiece, so she'd always be there to say 'Hi' to at the start of each day. Each of his movements was executed carefully and meticulously, he didn't want any off-putting stains on the floor. Andy Weiss liked having people up to party, any sudden change to his behavior would cause questions. Stains in the floorboards would cause even more in conjunction with a missing girlfriend. Soon enough it wouldn't matter, but for now, best to keep up appearances.

Tonight, there would be a feast for just the family, who were busy right now getting fucked up and fucking away downstairs. Soup would be served. The leftovers and he expected there would be plenty, would be given out in the park later. Sometimes to really get their souls, for the real miracles to commence, you needed a communion of flesh and blood. The world would look so much better to them all once they tasted the blessing he'd given them in every muscular fiber they swallowed.

Christ, it was cold tonight. It had been raining earlier before the temperature had dropped, now the wind was moving through the city like a rat in a maze, shoving every bit of moisture in the air all the way past your clothes and into your bones. Rat's bomber was not doing the job tonight, not worth a shit. It was better than his leather in the cold, sure, but since his leather didn't have a lining anymore and it had all those holes where he had haphazardly put the spikes and the studs into it, the bomber would be hard-pressed to do a worse job. The leather was spring and fall wear only. When you lived cheap you had to coordinate with mother nature if you didn't want to freeze your nuts right off.

He was getting close to the friendly neighborhood Anarchist bookstore, if your town didn't have one, it was just a town, not a city in his view. Proximity posed the nightly question Rat had for himself, to stop or not to stop. It WAS marginally warmer than his place and they were NICE people generally, so those were pros. Sincere people made it a point to be nice in public, creepy nice in his opinion, like they were trying to convince someone they were nice, he could never tell if it was you or themselves. But there was only so much NICE the Rat could take in one evening without dying of embarrassment for everyone involved. Self-satisfied and smug NICE was even worse, morally superior NICE made your teeth ache. When you know you're being looked down on, but you can't justify hitting anyone without looking like a fucking psycho because you can't prove it, that kind of nice. If someone would just say something directly condescending and dickish instead of hinting at it and using their college education to dance around it, then he could wallop them or just fucking ignore them and life would be better for everyone. Well, for Rat at any rate, and he was the only one living in his head at the moment so that was ample. It wasn't everyone in there, but there was just enough moral superiority present and accounted for that it needed debating.

No, free coffee be damned, he just couldn't take NICE tonight, and they always served mediocre coffee anyway. It had been a shitbox day at work, one asshole with a big mouth after another from start to finish today, his faith in humanity had suffered. Rat was not open to the idea that people were naturally cooperative and it was just bad people who made us bow and scrape and that we could all work together in harmony if we just throw off these shackles of society, not tonight. Rat wasn't 100% sure what he believed these days, but it certainly didn't involve man's inherently good nature. Eighteen years of life and one hippy girlfriend that he always felt he had to look out for because she never thought to look out for herself had removed those illusions. Best to head for home, such as it was, nobody was NICE there, in fact, they were famous for exactly the opposite.

There should be some wonderful descriptive prose about what this section of the city was like, but once St. Marks hit the park there was nothing wonderful to be said, nothing you should say in polite company. The only wonder left was to wonder how it ever got this bad. While nobody had anything nice to say, everybody had something to say about the place. The city wanted the whole world to know the park was a "war zone," they made sure the papers printed that opinion at least once a week. But if it was battle, it was a pretty passive war, at least in the park itself. Bums and junkies just weren't known to have the kind of energy it took to operate a really "hot" war. A few blocks further east, thirteenth and C, now THAT reminded you of Beirut after a particularly hostile bombing raid. Difference between the "we call it a war" and the actual war as far as the people who owned things was, nobody wanted that block right now, so nobody needed to bring up crack heads with machine guns in polite newsprint. By contrast, the city wanted the park back, it'd go nice with the rat box overpriced apartments developers were already designing, so it was the horror of the park that got press releases. They didn't give a good god damn about the rest of it, so that got ignored unless there was a particularly gruesome murder that gave the Post headline writers a chance to come up with a pun. Rat lived on 7th, near the river but not near enough to see the river. Call it war zone adjacent with a lovely view of the filth, if you liked that kind of thing.

Rat stopped by the bodega on his way and picked up a couple of forties of Midnight Dragon, relishing the enclosed space and the heaters that made it feel almost claustrophobic warm. The rotgut that was being rung up for him was a "tolerate it or absolutely loath it" proposition, with the weird spicing they put in it for God only knew why. Rat had learned to tolerate it out of necessity. If he bought a bottle of Ballantine and took his eyes off the fridge for a minute it would be long gone before he could finish it. Hell, it would be gone before the fridge closed. Roommates were the mother of mixed blessings. If he thought about it, except for rent, he usually had a hard time coming up with other blessings. He was planning to hang out at a bar tonight, so this was just a warm-up beer to get a light buzz going on the cheap, along with something waiting for him when he got home. Cheap, was very much so what the stuff was, the low, low price was the malt liquor's entire saving grace. If they actually paid for water at the homestead he lived in, the Dragon would be cheaper than city water by the gallon.

He took a moment to stop and scratch the bodega cat while his bottles were being loaded into brown paper bags. The big meat-headed old monster slammed his head into Rat's hand repeatedly letting out a great rumbling purr. His own cat was no longer on speaking terms with him since his pit bull had started sleeping in his loft. The fuzzy little bastard would bunk with his roommates for the night and look at him with unspoken rebuke for his betrayal in the form of the dog. Rat was getting his feline love on the street to make up for what he wasn't getting at home. When he looked up from the cat, behind him he noticed some local... well in the 50's they'd have called them hoods, hanging in the back by the coolers. Rat couldn't help but be unnerved by them, which was odd in and of itself. These guys looked damned nigh hostile towards him, which wasn't the usual attitude around here, Rat was a local, he wasn't some junkie trying to score here. It was weird, normally they tried to look inconspicuous so the guy behind the counter would lose track of them and they could pocket some shit.

Not tonight though, tonight they looked like they were itching for some shit to go down. He didn't know why the natives were restless, but Rat was glad he was almost home all the same.

Oh well, it wasn't his goal in life to categorize or get involved in every weird thing that happened in the city. Where would you possibly be able to end once you started an undertaking like that? It would be all you'd ever do with your time. Maybe that was what made some of those guys who panhandled uptown nuts in the first place, the effort of trying to encompass it all overwhelmed their TV expectations for what life was supposed to be like, next thing you know you're panhandling and talking to aliens. Hell, trying to understand the various art installations around the city by guerrilla artists would take you YEARS alone. He gave the cat one more lingering scritch around his neck and under his chin, hugged his bag closer, and headed back out into the night where at least he wouldn't be in a box with the hostile crazy.

The last block home was always brutal, the wind would whip in off the river, and the buildings stood just right to make it an extra special combination of a wind tunnel crossed with an icebox. Rat viewed it as a plus, if you were good and lit coming home after a hard night of getting turned down by every woman in the place, it acted as the bracer you needed for the home stretch. It fought that overwhelming desire to feel sorry for yourself and lay down in a doorway to die, by replacing it with the desire to get the hell inside so you wouldn't die. It turned out that dying hurt, and should probably be avoided, Rat surprised himself some days when he discovered he had a learning curve on that subject.

He was power walking by the time he reached home, digging out his keys just as quickly, fumbling to get the steel door that led inside open. You never wanted to just dangle your keys around as you were trotting up to the door, that was begging to get jacked up and to have your place robbed to boot, or worse. Well maybe not in Rat's case, any would-be robbers were in for a hell of a surprise if they tried it, between the dog and the flat broke. It was always best if you were too skint and dangerous to rob. Once inside and into the darkness beyond, Rat slammed the door with finality. The dimly lit hallway was almost as cold as the street, so he hustled his way along. At least their place wasn't upstairs and just a few quick strides in down the hall placed him standing in front of the next steel door in his path. The one that led to home sweet hell. Rat needed a quick breath to prepare, which steamed out into the cold, creating a little mini fog bank in front of his door for a moment. He never knew what kind of chaos awaited inside, and he wanted to give himself a mental chance to get ready for it.

He could already hear Ralph barking so there was no point in putting it off any longer, he'd end up giving the poor dog a fucking coronary. Rat knew that there were roommates in there, any one of which could be coming to the door to help him in case he was carrying something, He also knew that none of them would be. They had no problem with him making the meals, or him buying the food, or him doing the dishes, helping in any way.... just not punk rock dude.

But who cared about roommates when what did greet him was a burst of doggie love the second the door opened? Ralph crashed up at him in an explosion of limbs, tail, and most importantly, the slobber of love as the hyper-wound canine tried to reach Rat's face with his tongue. Rat knew it was coming and had secured his grip on his forties before opening up. It took a few minutes of fussing to get the dog far enough back from the door where he could even lock it. Looking near the door, he could see the dog log of love waiting for him to come home to as well.

Rat looked up and saw roommate one, and also his rhythm guitarist, Cole sitting on his bunk, "Were you hoping this little gift by the door was going to increase in value, or were you hoping to leave it for Jazz when he gets home to see if he steps on it?" Rat asked as he set down his bottles.

"Really I was hoping it would be Enio that stepped in it. Said it before, not my dog, not my problem," Cole replied before returning his attention back to the comic book he was reading.

Rat sighed and grabbed a paper towel. They used paper towels for almost everything, with the exceptions being one wash rag for dishes, and one for asses. It would never dawn on anyone that in the long run they were spending more on the paper towels than another dish towel cost. Paper towels were cheap, there were a lot of them in a pack, and bodegas sold them, there were no special trips to stores that would sic security guard on them the second they passed inside to be braved.

"Come on Ralph, let's go for a walk," Rat put his beer in the fridge, secure in the knowledge as to its lack of drinkability by everyone else in the homestead, and went and got the leash.

Ralph was almost ricocheting off the walls with glee, forcing Rat to make waving stabs at actually getting him hooked to the leash. When it finally clicked home on the dog's collar he said to Cole, "I'll make some food when I get back." Looking down at Ralph he added, "You know I don't feed you nearly enough for you to shit that much."

Back out into the cold, the encroaching night adding a bit of foreboding to the affair with his big, bad, mean pit bull Ralph. Yeah, nobody messes with somebody who had a pit bull all right, that's why a lot of people got them. And his big tough pit bull needed to take another dump so he could be told he was a good boy. There was a really small sort of a park in front of the housing complex up ahead, the perfect place for an evening crap. Nobody would notice if he didn't pick up after Ralph, except the guy who mowed it come spring, nobody gave a shit. It wasn't like kids played there. With the needles and vials all over the place, dog shit was a distinct improvement over the usual litter anyway, it was practically a public service.

As Rat went by the bodega on that corner, he could see shadows detach themselves from the alcove and begin moving towards them. They moved at a casual pace, they didn't need to hurry, Rat wasn't going anywhere. "Hey, Ralphie! How's the cute boy doin'?" they called out in unison as they resolved themselves into a couple of local dealers coming over to pet Rat's smiling, wagging, useless ass brat of a dog.

After Ralph was finally done being praised and fussed over, Rat dragged the happy beast across Avenue D to shit central. It never dawned on Rat to feel bad about letting Ralph vanish into one of the bushes that somehow against all odds managed to survive all the crap that got done to them there. The people who were good honest working folks who were stuck here because it was all they could afford wouldn't have hung out in this little parkette if you paid them, and who really cares if a drug dealer gets shit on his shoe? Not the drug dealer, it's as good as an excuse as any to get new shoes, they were the only ones here who could afford to.

Rat stood there, staring vacantly into space, the look the dog walker who does not wish to view the goal of the trip in action takes after the dog's ass has hunched towards the ground. To pass the moment he blew a snot rocket, that not being sufficient to fill the time he found his eyes training upwards for just a moment along the windows of the high rise in front of him. But only a moment, anyone who admired tall buildings for too long in Alphabet City got rewarded for their appreciation of architecture by losing his wallet, his coat, his shoes, his keys, and possibly his life. A movement at the top of the building caught Rat's eye, his eyes snapped back up. Holy hell, some spazzoid crackhead was up there on the roof of the building, holding on to something dangling himself over space!

He only got to appreciate the weirdness of the whole thing for a second longer until the evening's roof walker stepped off into the majesty of the open winter air. Rat was already stupidly yanking at Ralph and turning to run like it would do any good at all when the body hit. And at that height whoever it was could only be on their way to becoming a body after they slammed into the turf somewhere nearby. Rat could just as easily have run directly into its path in his flight from the scene. An instant later there was a thud from the sidewalk that led through the park up to the building's doors. A splash of blood just missed Ralph as he was doing a hunched poop walk in the direction Rat was trying to drag him.

"Ho-lee sheep dip," Rat breathed. It wasn't Robert Frost, but it summed it all up pretty succinctly. Ralph was just happy he stopped so he could finally finish his business.

He could hear guys yelling from the bodega and already running over to see what happened. Rat was moving towards them to pass them by. They were going to check the carnage, he had other plans, no way did he feel like being questioned about what he saw. Cops, when they came here at all, gave white boys like him extra special wonder bread scrutiny. The overall feeling was that if you were white and lived here you did it because you were a druggie, not because rents had been going up everywhere, and being a bike or a foot messenger paid for shit. Cops just didn't view reality; they were in power and could have all the irrational prejudices they damned well felt like. The reality, here and now, was if he didn't want to start by being questioned about a suicide and end in the back of a squad car for a trumped-up charge, it was time to get his little punk rock ass the fuck out. He took one look back at the corpse before immediately wishing he hadn't. You can't stop yourself in a situation like that, you have to look, but your instincts are working against you getting any sleep any time soon.

"I seen the whole thing!" a woman yelled as if on cue from one of the doors into the building the jumper had exited this world from. That was the other reason he felt comfortable leaving. For every person like Rat who wanted to keep their interactions with the police to a bare minimum, there were five people who didn't have anything better to do tonight who had, "Seen the whole thing officer!" Whether or not they had was a matter of conjecture, but how much was there to really say? Crazy crack head jumped off a building, he went splat, the end. That more or less covered all the salient details, it didn't have to be Rat who provided them.

So, since Ralph was done with his constitutional, it was time to make tracks. Rat practically had to haul on the dog to get him to even begin to go for home. Ralph was way too excited about all the people suddenly coming out of the rotten woodwork, and how excited they were was telling his canine brain something important had happened or was about to. He wanted to see what all the fuss was about; this was the most entertainment he'd had in weeks. It was kind of funny, the dog had been right next to the excitement when it had happened, but now that it was all over except for the cleaning up he wanted to see what all the excitement was about. Rat understood, even if he couldn't allow it, the animal had been in one room all day, this was WAY more intense than that by far, why in the hell should he want to go inside now?

With enough cursing, and tugging, and yanking, and threatening, Rat was finally able to get Ralph across Avenue D. Resigning himself at last to the fact that he wasn't going to get to meet anyone new or find out what all the commotion was about, Ralph finally started to settle in a bit. He still kept stopping dead in his tracks and looking back hopefully, but his behavior improved a bit overall. At least he wasn't tugging on the lead in the wrong direction now. It improved, even more, when Rat bent over and threatened to pick him up and toss Ralph over his shoulder. Rat had discovered early on with Ralph that being carried outside completely humiliated the dog, he'd do anything, including actually behaving, to avoid it.

He almost gasped with relief once he got the dog back to the homestead and inside.

Jazz had come back for the day by then and was lurking on his bunk when Rat stumbled in the door. Jazz was already in his own little world, wherever the fuck that was half the time, his short hair could barely be seen behind his book. Enio, their other roommate had also made an appearance and was reading an ancient punk mag on his bunk, his lengthy spiky 'do more than made up for Jazz's lack thereof. It was Cole who spotted Rat's face, "What in the fuck happened to you out there that only took fifteen minutes?"

Rat shook his head as if hoping he could shake it from his memory, "Dude, fucking crackhead took a header off one of the towers right in front of me."

Cole eyed him suspiciously, "So why are you not currently having a lengthy discussion with Johnny Law about this occurrence at this exact moment?"

"Are you out of your ever-loving mind? I'm a punker in Alphabet City, I do not talk to fucking cops, man. I booked before the rest of the splatter even finished landing."

"Smart man. Jazz, wanna go look at a crime scene? Bet you the paramedics ain't even there yet!" Cole said hopping up enthusiastically. "The cops should have their hands full with eyewitnesses by the time we get there, they won't give a fuck about us."

"Yeah, sure," Jazz replied in that slow measured tone he always spoke in, before climbing down from his bunk.

"I'm in, I could use some psycho adventure in my life," Enio invited himself getting up and stretching.

"You are someone else's psycho adventure Enio," Cole grinned. "Get your gear mounted up, we depart in five."

Rat had seen it up close and personal already, so instead of a second showing he was going to lose himself in domesticity; letting the three nimrods gather their jackets and run out the door to tragedy gawk. Once upon a time, when he and Rat had first become friends, Jazz would have been horrified at the concept of doing something like that, but there he was fitting into city life just fine. Rat had been worried about whether or not Jazz would be able to acclimate, he didn't want to lose a bassist to homesickness and mental displacement. That wasn't an entirely honest viewpoint, cynical but not fair, he and Jazz were friends and had similar ways of thinking about a lot of things, not everything, but a lot. He'd be losing a friend and an ally in this nuthouse if Jazz split out. Jazz's mental health meant Rat had a holy hope in hell of maintaining his own, safe inside their shared lunacy.

Left alone, he got started on dinner, such as it was. It certainly wasn't exactly haute cuisine, or any real cuisine for that matter, but at least it was edible. Barely. He filled up the pot to get it boiling, and while he was at it added some more water to their heating system. Their state-of-the-art heating system, which also doubled as their bathtub, was an ancient old metal bath basin that they kept full and kept low heat on at all times, providing just enough steam heat that they didn't actually freeze to death. They didn't have a shower or an actual bathtub, so it was forced to serve double duty for attempts at cleanliness to the varying degrees of personal preference being exhibited by the housemates. Where they were pilfering gas from was not Rat's concern, they paid money to their lead guitarist Shane, who kind of served as their landlord (who they all noted lived ten blocks east in a NICE apartment with rent control) and water appeared and the stove worked. It cost a shit-ton less than an actual one-bedroom apartment, so, it was deemed all to the good, even if Shane made them do their own repairs to the place when they could figure out how to do it.

While the water heated, he fed Ralph, who was incredibly enthusiastic over the concept, despite it being the cheapest ass dog food imaginable. Rat considered what he was about to perpetrate in the name of full stomachs for the four of them and found himself envying the dog's ability to be enthusiastic over any food whatsoever. He personally might have wanted something tastier, but Rat knew what he had in his wallet currently, he could go out drinking or eating, and since eating took less time and was an entirely solitary act, drinking had a much higher entertainment potential here.

Rat was just dumping the noodles in when the door slammed open. "Holy shit that was gross!" Cole exclaimed leading the way for the remaining Three Stooges to do the all fall through the door at the same time routine.

"Did I not fucking tell you?"

"Yeah...but....man the cops hadn't even covered the body yet," Jazz added.

"It was fuckin' awesome," Enio gave the final word. Rat wondered what in the hell went on in his head some days, most people who knew the guy wondered about that.

At least Enio was harmless, out of his skull, but harmless.

"Dinner in ten minutes, so clear your heads or go hungry," Rat replied going over to the fridge and grabbing one of his forties.

"How can you drink that shit," Cole growled.

"Correct answer is, I CAN drink that shit. If I left a forty of Ballentine in there I'd barely get a drop," Rat shrugged.

"You're funeral."

"And you ain't invited, so don't buy any flowers."

A horror had just occurred, one that they had all witnessed, but it was over and life went on. Everyone settled right back into their respective roles like pegs on a board that had just been briefly jumbled. Once Rat chimed the dinner bell, and they had all scooped out a bowl of oregano-tofu-mac-and-yak slop it was time for the only ritual that kept them united. The one thing that even more than music gave them a moment of daily togetherness. Batman re-runs on Rat's little black and white TV up in his loft. Yeah, they might huddle around the tape recorder by their one table to listen to old Subhumans records, or up in Rat's loft to listen to actual vinyl he'd pick up from Venus Records, but that was just passing the day. This was tradition, it was sacred, it was Batman. They made themselves as comfortable as they could in a space not meant for four people, even if they were being really, really friendly like, and hunkered in to eat their food-like substance and swim in the nostalgia-driven "quality program like" viewing. Other than masticating and the occasional burst of laughter at the wonderful cheese that filled the screen, if not their bowls, there was silence. This was important. Adam West was God for this half hour a day, and this was church. Ralph, stuck down on the floor, didn't agree. The loft was his spot with Daddy, and now these losers were up there pigging the place up. He whined a bit before curling up and glowering at them about the whole thing from a spot on the floor near the ladder up. Rat's cat was in Jazz's loft, not giving a flying fuck, because cats have it easy like that.

Magic is unfortunately finite if you find it all, and the next show had been deemed as "shitty" by all of them ages ago when the station had first started running it. Beverly Hillbillies might have been able to stretch the moment a little longer, but Dragnet could fuck right off, it couldn't elongate the moment, too straight. The party broke up and they all climbed back down to floor level. Rat decided that he had drunk enough of his horrific malt liquor to have the head start he needed for tonight anyway. He was going to the bar on 13th tonight, one of his regular watering holes on tight money weekends. He still had the week to go until payday, so that made his decision for him.

There were two other bars he frequented, but those were "rock star bars," you drank sparingly at those places. Rock star bars existed for musicians to have a place to whine to each other about how hard it was being a musician, while tourists came in every five minutes to gawk at them hunched over their beers and bitterness. If you got recognized, sometimes you drank for free. Both of his favored rock star bars were also expensive, so Rat went where the little people swilled on his non-pay weeks instead. Where they served dollar dark beer drafts and three-dollar pints of cider all night every night. He prided himself on this type of fiscal responsibility, it was also why he rolled his own smokes most of the time. Just because you had shitty habits was no reason to go broke for them. He preferred the down-home quality of the people's bar, but being in a band meant keeping up appearances and making them on occasion.

"I'm going to the bar, anyone coming?" Rat called out while he laced up his Docs.

"Yeah, what the hell, I'll come," Jazz replied reaching for his leather.

Rat slipped on his bomber, it would be getting chilly, maybe one day he'd get a new leather with an actual lining, but tonight that day was some time off. "What about you two?"

"Skint," chirped Enio his head in a magazine.

"Not in the mood, mind if I watch TV?" Cole added.

"No, but if I come home and I'm not alone get the fuck out of my loft ASAP, or I throw you out bodily," Rat answered.

"Like there's any chance of that unless you count Jazz. I guess I'm sleeping with you tonight then," Cole sneered.

Rat turned to Jazz, "I think that's our cue to get the fuck out of here before I hit him."

Chapter 2

Jazz wanted to buy smokes, so he steered them to the bodega closer to their place on D. Rat wanted to stop at a place closer to the park, where he usually went, but Jazz insisted smokes were cheaper here. This meant they'd be heading up D and down instead of down 7th. They could have backtracked, but spending every day of their life looking for direct routes made it so it wasn't even a possibility in their minds. Rat grumbled about it, "Well hurry up big spender, I hate going this way to the bar."

"It's still early, it won't be that bad," Jazz assured him as he slid in through the jingling door to get his smokes. Rat wanted to point out that normally Jazz didn't go this way at night at all either, but bit his tongue.

While Rat waited outside, his eyes darted constantly to take in his surroundings in case trouble had become a new disease and was catching around here. He grumbled some more to himself while he waited. He wanted to suggest walking back the way they'd come and continuing, but couldn't think of how to do it without sounding like a pussy. Jazz was being naive as fuck, it could easily be that bad going the fastest way to get to the bar from here, it absolutely could be. Some blocks you just don't walk down at night if you had a brain in your head. Even if you lived in Alphabet City you had to have some standards. Between here, and 13th it would only get progressively nastier. No way in hell was Rat walking all the way down 13th itself to go west they'd cut over before then. The shortest distance now was to go up a block and go over and suggesting otherwise would be all but admitting you were scared.

Your neighborhood brand of chaos and insanity all depended on the drug being dealt on which block you were walking down and the high it delivered. People all wanted soma to live this crammed together. Even the wealthy in this city courted madness, even if it cost more, what was the difference between the animal blitzed on high-grade coke and booze uptown and the crackheads here? Location, location, location. Where they were right now, 7th, this was all stoners and dopers. Yes, junkies would steal your shit, no question about that, but facts are facts, junkies don't usually have their shit together enough to be a truly, really real threat. What were they going to do? Nod the fuck off on you? More sad than frightening, you could almost feel bad for them as you made sure you knew where your wallet was at all times. Nobody was giving up their steel doors for lent because shit could go weird when you weren't careful, but in comparison to what else was out there, the neighborhood could almost be considered placid. What else was out there was crack, and crack could be easily acquired on 13th street, assuming you didn't get robbed and killed on your way to making your drug purchase of course. Crack dealers had guns, crack heads had frightening speed sometimes, and were desperate as fuck. Rat was not going down 13th after dark, they would have cut down to the park on 8th which was still shakier than here but at least it was in the mostly demilitarized zone. Even if it was starting to straddle the line.

"Why ain't you got Ralphy?" one of the dealers hanging around on the corner, a short Puerto Rican kid, asked him while he waited.

Rat smiled, "You know, I do have a life outside my dog."

"No shit? I only ever see you wit Ralphy."

"No shit, I'm actually Superman but I lost the reporter gig."

"Maaaannn, you white boys are all out of your fucking mind."

"Must be, I live here," Rat shrugged as Jazz came outside ripping open his cigarettes.

They fell into stride together down D when Rat said, "Gimmee a smoke."

"I thought you didn't want me to stop for them? Now you want one?"

"That was then, this is now, the deed is done and buried and there's no crying over spilled milk. Gimmee a smoke ya weenbag," Rat replied hitting him in the shoulder.

Jazz dug out a cigarette from his pack and handed it over, "Hypocrite."

"I shall salve my wounded conscience with lord nicotine."

As they turned the corner Rat had no problem remembering why he didn't want to come this way. Streetlights only do so much, and in some places, they did less than others, especially since quite a few of them had been shot out. Most parts of the city he couldn't have cared less, but here, know your blocks was a rule of life. On 7th everybody at least knew of him, he wasn't going to get shit from anyone since giving shit to a local could have an unforeseen bounce-back effect. The Avenues themselves were pretty well lit, and the further west you went the safer it would get, especially on the other side of the park. They weren't on the other side of the park though, they were on a block they didn't know anyone, and it was real-assed dark. The kind of dark things can hide in. He almost had to give Jazz credit for being cool about it, the guy was totally oblivious, he was humming as he went. Maybe bass players had some kind of brain damage. Maybe that's why they're bass players and think shit like Rush and Maiden are cool. It explained so much and was the best working hypothesis as far as Rat was concerned at this moment. Rat couldn't take the humming anymore and shushed his friend with a quick wave. When Jazz looked at him with shock flooding his bland features, Rat pantomimed them both being stabbed at him. He was pretty sure Jazz got that. He stopped humming at least.

They were walking in silence after that, they didn't want any undue attention until they finally ran into the park up ahead. Well, Rat sure as hell didn't, since Rat hadn't responded to Jazz's last three comments, and since Jazz wasn't much of a talker anyway, he found it easier to just give up. Rat was grateful for that, he wasn't going to say anything about it, but he was. Swimming in the blessed silence they were passing a squat on the other side of the street. It wasn't an official named one yet, more a proto-squat, one day if it didn't burn down, it might become the real thing, more habitable, with rules to live by, plumbing, and all the walls rebuilt and stuff. It had been opened, someone was inside living there, work was supposedly taking place to fix it up, but...... Well, the line between shooting gallery, crack house, and squat can really come down to the amount of drywall someone's put up versus the amount of spray paint. This one didn't have a lot of drywall up yet.

Lights were lit on the third floor of the building, which was weird, in that none of the other lights in the building were on at all. Not impossibly weird, but the kind of thing that catches your eye when you're walking by. The first-floor windows were boarded, but light would have leaked if they were on, the second-floor windows were dark and uncovered the darkness pulling the eye like the entrance to a mausoleum. Rat had been inside the place once or twice, dragged along by one friend or another when they copped or wanted to meet up with someone. Rat couldn't remember which, he hadn't been paying attention to the conversation and instead he'd spent the entire time wanting to get the fuck out of there. The whole second and third floors were just empty spaces right now, no rooms or anything, just cots and blankets and people thrown around to lay where they landed. He'd gone in at all because someone had instilled some manners into him at some point and he'd felt he should. If you're going to hang out with somebody for the day, you don't just puss out because they're copping, find yourself hanging outside like a psychopath or a narc cop. You go up, you try not to touch anything, and then you start hinting heavily about all the wonderful plans the two of you had for the day the second the transaction or the meet-up was over. Just good manners really.

He had decided to ignore the place and keep his eyes down when a face appeared in one of the windows; blocking the light behind it, causing a sudden shadow to fall where the light reached the street. It caught Rat's eye even without him looking directly up at the window. Rat could see the shadow flicker out of the corner of his eye and his instincts took over, turning his head to look. He didn't want to look, he really didn't, but people tell themselves that they don't like to look at car wrecks either but that doesn't make your commute any shorter for their good intentions and failed willpower, does it? Rat shot a glance, and then almost fell when he stopped looking where he was going and tripped over a raised spot on the sidewalk where the two slabs had pushed up.

Jazz came to a stop a few feet further on before he realized he was no longer walking in rhythm with another set of feet, "What the fuck is with you? You paralyzed or something?"

Rat pointed up at the window by way of answering. Jazz looked up following his finger and his eyes grew wide. Standing in the window, almost, but not quite a shadow with the light behind him was a figure who... was covered in something liquid that ran down his bare chest and arms. The light made it look dark and hard to say with certainty what it was, but that didn't stop Rat from being convinced deep down inside that it was blood.

As soon as the figure saw them looking, he smiled widely. There was no doubt that it was a he since the guy wasn't wearing a stitch of clothing and his cock bobbed as he moved, flopping white in the dark. He looked delighted at getting their attention, whatever he was about up there was now complete with an audience to view it. Even partially hidden as his face was by the shadows created by the light being behind him, the teeth and eyes glowed out of the gloom with an almost idiot grin. He waved at them happily for a second, bouncing lightly where he stood in the window, making sure they had even less doubt about his sex and how much he was enjoying himself. Sure that he had their full attention the lunatic reared back and punched the window out bare-knuckled. The glass crashed down to the street with an enormous cacophony, spraying out as it shattered further, almost reaching them across the street. Rat was positive that right before he did it, the fucking nutjob winked at him.

"Holy fuck!" Jazz barked stumbling back away from where the glass had landed, almost tripping over the steps of another empty building behind him.

When they looked back up a few seconds later the figure had vanished from the broken window only to reappear like a flickering ghost at the next window over. Jazz and Rat made no effort to conceal that they were gawking at the guy now, there was no point, and the psycho was obviously digging the attention. CRASH! And there went another window!

"What in the fuck is wrong with that guy?" Jazz gasped.

"Jazz?"

"Yeah?"

"We should run like fuck."

"Why? I mean, he's on the third floor."

"He's covered with blood, nobody is stopping him, it's not that hard to bolt down three flights of steps, and the most important thing is...."

"Yeah?"

CRASH!

"He just ran out of windows up there."

They both decided to run like fuck.

Ten minutes later they sat on the sidewalk outside the park gasping for breath, and grateful for the somewhat brighter lights of Avenue B showing them anything that might be coming towards them out of the gloom. "We should call the cops," Jazz panted.

"We ain't doing any such thing," Rat retorted.

"But that guy.... he was covered in blood!"

"You go around smashing windows... probably his own."

"But what if it wasn't?"

Rat sighed, hard truth delivery time, "Buddy, your heart is in the right place. Really, good for you, the city ain't gotten to you yet. But the NYPD ain't coming to Alphabet City, after dark, on a Friday, to a squat, for what could be a bad acid trip. For all we know the other fuckers in there locked him up there until he calmed down."

"But what if he gets really hurt?" Jazz pressed, not willing to let this go.

"Then their asses can drag him to St. Vincent's themselves if one of them can sober up enough, not our business. But I do know that if the cops actually do show up at their squat, they ain't gonna give a shit about him either. They'll use it as an excuse to raid the place. Word gets out that we called it in..... Sometimes you just gotta say, not my zoo, not my monkeys, not my problem, and this is one of those times." Rat stared at his friend intently as realization sunk into Jazz's face. Seeing the hangdog expression there that oozed its way into place he patted him on the back and added, "Look, first round's on me. You look like you could use a drink. Shit, after today, I definitely could. C'mon, let's go get shitfaced! It does a body good."

The bar was warm and inviting, the way your favorite local watering hole of choice should feel on a cold winter night. They rolled in and said the superficial hellos to the regulars who hung out by the door like the welcoming committee. Like a welcoming committee that was probably in place to find out if anyone owed them a drink and if that someone had just walked in the door. That was their gig, naturally gregarious people who wanted that superficial continual stimulation of saying all the hellos to the newcomers, and seeing if those newcomers would stand them a round. This place felt like a bar on TV, like an extension of your comforting home, if that home was filled with punk rockers and skinheads of various stripes, so maybe not your home, but possibly Rat's.

It was weird, despite its low rent clientele it also had some of the best beer at the cheapest prices in this part of the city. What it would cost you to get two shitty-ass Budweisers in some club in the West Village would get you well on your way to blotto on imported dark beers and cider here. You had to figure that the owner had originally had dreams of owning an upscale cozy little Irish pub in his head, something he'd experienced on a vacation once, but once his loans came back all he could afford was this place. Alphabet City, more dashed hopes and dreams per square mile than anywhere in America. Still, lucky break for the LES punk scene, right?

Getting served took a moment, they had to fight their way through the greeters to even get to the bar itself, let alone get the bartender's professional attention. Once Rat caught the guy's eye, he just held up two fingers and blurted out, "Woodpeckers." Almost instantly money vanished and cold glasses and change appeared like magic, you barely saw the guy stay still long enough to fill their drinks, but there they were with foam sliding gracefully over the lip and dewdrops already appearing on the side.

Ciders in hand they made a slow steady one hand up weave towards the other end of the bar and the few sparse tables available for conversation and serious drinking. It wouldn't take long before the rest of the night got pretty blurry pretty quickly. Some nights went like that, one minute you'd be saying hi to your pals, the next thing you knew you were saying something really important to a total stranger, next thing you knew after that it was morning. Rat had to go through the highlights and piece it together later as best as he could, which was frankly his normal M.O.in here. The workweek sucked, and if there wasn't a show to be had tonight that you wanted, you were in a city, you were trapped here around all these people...you had to make the week go away somehow.

Shane came into the bar soon after they got there, he stood them for a few rounds, which saved Rat some money. Shane was straight edge, you wouldn't have guessed it to look at him, his hair had grown long since his skinhead days and hung lankly onto his bomber. Nobody wants to sit around at home on a Friday night when all their friends were here, so Shane walked the distance between his place and the bar to watch other people drink. The bartender did not care to see seats taken up by people not drinking so Shane worked around it by buying other people drinks and himself sodas. Which was why both Rat and Jazz were opening up the night with multiple ciders. It cost more than drafts but Shane had way more money than them, so they didn't exactly feel overwhelmed with guilt about it.

Dragging him back to the table they told him breathlessly what had happened on the way over to the bar, not even needing to embellish for once, since this tale of city chaos didn't need any pepping up, it was insane all on its own right. At the end of it, Shane shrugged and said, "Huh! That's fucked up. Well, shit happens ya' know, good thing you guys minded your own fucking business, right?" This was a totally normal reaction from Shane, he was a native New Yorker and not transplants like they were. As far as their lead guitarist was concerned that was just life, the Village had been weird longer than any of them had been alive, it hadn't started getting weird recently just to befuddle them. It would take more than what they'd seen to get any kind of a rise out of him. Maybe seeing the mayor of the city being intimate with a goat....in public.... during the Macy's Thanksgiving Day Parade, but even then, just maybe.

So, Shane's presence at the bar was established as fact for when Rat tried to remember how his night had gone. Within three drinks he remembered wondering where his lead guitarist had gotten off to, but not much else. Jazz left at some point, it probably hadn't been too long after Shane split, Jazz was usually pretty much a lightweight. Rat stayed to keep hanging out with a small group of people they had just met tonight. The part where they decided to join them or they had decided to join Rat and Jazz was a bit fuzzy, Rat couldn't remember if there had been an acquaintance or something. There was a girl, much straighter looking than his "type," whatever that meant, but she was cute and funny, he remembered she was funny. When his eyes partially opened the next morning, he wondered if he had gotten the girl's number, or even what her name was. He was sure she'd told him what it was but he was completely drawing a blank on it.

He sat in his bunk with his eyes closed for a while processing the concept of waking up before he noticed his loft was not occupied by Ralph this morning. It was certainly occupied, but whoever it was had less hair overall and more boobs for starters. His eyes snapped open, she also looked amazingly happy to be sleeping there despite the fact that she must be chilly. The back end of the night came back to him in a rush, especially when they'd gotten back here, they had done something very fun for quite a while it seemed to Rat. Hooray alcohol and the stamina that only booze provides. Throw a parade for not cumming in five nanoseconds because of numbness, but it had to be the exact right amount of numbness, or nothing would happen at all for the same reason. He must have had the dosages just right last night. Rat sat up with a start to find she was awake as well and smiling no less... Well, he wasn't going to have to fumble to get clothing off so that was a plus. He gently pulled her slightly over him, letting her long hair drape down over his face. There are worse ways to wake up. In point of fact, most of them are worse than this.

A very, very short time later they were slowly maneuvering around one another in the enclosed space of the loft pulling on clothing. It had been quite a while since this had happened for Rat, and in the cold sober light of day.... well, a beer or two might have made the whole thing last longer. He escorted her to the door, and they kissed briefly before she was on her way. Rat didn't even need to turn around to feel the eyes of his roommates boring into the back of him as they gawked. The awkward silence was broken by Cole saying, "So, does she have a name?"

There was a longer silence before Rat said quietly, "I can't remember."

"What? You just had sex with a girl twice and you can't remember?" Cole exploded but in more of an amused way than an outraged one.

"WHORE!" laughed Enio from his cot, his voice cracking with overnight phlegm that caused him to follow that with a coughing fit.

"Look, we met at the bar, she told me her name and everything, but we'd both been drinking and....well you know I suck shit at names," Rat shrugged, still unwilling to turn around.

"I, got mugged last night," Jazz said quietly.

"Bet you don't know their names either," Rat retorted. Then he sighed, "Not that it matters, no way she's interested in me now. And I'm sorry you got mugged Jazz, I told you to hang out until I was ready to go."

"What in the hell do you mean? You did it again this morning!" Cole protested.

"Yeah, but I was sober this morning, and you know it's been a minute since I had a girl over... and you know when it's been a while."

"Bad?"

"Probably shorter than a Ramones song."

"UNTALENTED WHORE!" Enio cackled taking a massive amount of pleasure in the diversion this was providing before beginning to cough again as he reached out blindly to find his cigarettes.

"Yeah, she's lost interest," Cole agreed, shrugging and returning to his comic.

"C'mon Ralph, let's go for a walk. Jazz, tell me what

happened with the mugging when I get back."

Big Tom Doyle considered himself to be a bum. The way he figured things, there was a difference between being a bum and being homeless. Homeless insinuated that with a little help, just a little nudge you could be well on your way to a two-car garage and a white picket fence as one more happy rat deeply in love with your maze. You being on the streets was just a little hiccup in the program to be overcome and then everything else would fall back into place like the world had never even broken for you. Tom had stopped thinking of himself that way years ago. He'd lost his job in the '73 recession, and then his place to live. Back then he'd been homeless, back then he was desperate to get back into the game. Even before some two-bit B movie actor had taken on a better role than any casting agent could have ever seen him in as President, Tom had ceased to be homeless.

Really, at this point even if you gave him a house and a job, he didn't think he really had the life skills left to successfully pull normal off. Didn't mean he didn't know nuthin' though, you needed plenty of skills to survive out here, just different ones. He could tell you with minute detail when half the restaurants in the city put out their leftovers, who charged what for booze in a two-mile radius, what the police patrol schedule was for half the parks, he knew plenty. It was just a completely different skill set than what it took to be an upright shiny Reagan Republican. Big Tom Doyle had a bum's skillset down to a t and was proud enough to call himself that if anyone asked. Not that people did, they didn't even want to look at him as he wandered around the city, nobody liked to get a good look at where a bad turn of fortune could put them. The whole reason people gave him what little money ever passed through his hands was so that they wouldn't be forced to look at him any longer and maybe even assuage their secret guilt for the largess in their own life. He was better than confession in that regard.

As a professional bum, he was not going to sleep in the park tonight, he had a secret he wanted to keep to himself and knew the places to go to make sure he did. He had scrounged up a full pint of vodka, and while normally he'd be all for sharing, sometimes you just need to do a little something for yourself. He figured that was the part the commies never got, why they were losing the cold war. It didn't need to be much, but sometimes a body just needed a little treat, a way of feeling even slightly special. It didn't matter if the majority of the city would look at the cheap rotgut he had tucked away in his military field jacket and dry heave at the very thought of drinking it, it was his, and he wanted to get a good buzz on. The nightmares had been getting to him bad this week, and he felt he deserved a little tender lovin' care, that care coming in 90 proof form.

It was a warm night for the winter, he figured he could forgo the normal places of hunkering down near steam venting up from the maze under the city, or a trash can fire and could do it without suffering too greatly for it. Tonight, he had found himself a clear spot in an empty lot not that far from the park itself. The wind went down the streets on either side, but right here up against the building next to the lot it was almost warm. Warmer still once he had taken the first huge swallow of vodka and dug out the hotdog he was saving.

This was fine, this was all right, he could just sit here and listen to the voices chatter among themselves until the vodka did its job and he could fall back into sweet blessed oblivion for a few hours without the cops bugging him. Or someone sitting in the shadows of a fire in the park, waiting for him to drowse off before making off with his little glass bottle of sleep for that matter. And especially not having to worry about those weird kids that kept coming into the park bugging him lately. The soup they served tasted like rat piss anyway. No, on a night like this Big Tom Doyle was happy to curl his long legs under his bulk, spread a couple of greasy blankets over himself, and allow himself to slip into sleep for a little while. The exhaustion of scrambling from one place to another trying to get the few things he needed to make it from one day to the next joined forces with the alcohol flooding his system and demanded their due.

His limbs were stiff and cold sometime later when he was awakened by someone kicking his boot. A voice made its way into his dream, a dream that involved war and fire, like a voice of God echoing over the jungles, "Come on Tommy boy, time to wake up!"

When his eyes snapped open his legs were already scrambling to get himself upright so he could defend himself. A body that doesn't go from asleep to ready to fight in this city was a body that was looking to get robbed or worse. Standing directly in front of him were three figures. Tom was unable to make out anything about them, the streetlights were behind them turning them into menacing shadows and nothing more.

"What do you want? Who are you people?" Tom wheezed out in a voice constricted by fear. The effort forced him into a violent gasping coughing fit.

When he was done hacking the central figure in front of him said, "You've been given a great gift Tommy, my boy. More than once. Yet every time you seem to reject it."

"What in the hell you talkin' bout? Nobody gives me no gifts," Tom snarled trying to fight back more coughing, trying to see who in the hell this was through eyes streaming with tears caused by his previous fit.

"Oh, but you have! All those nightmares, the gift could have taken them all away, all those doubts, gone. You take the sacrament but you never accept the gift, Tommy!" the voice practically oiled at him. He might not be able to see the mouth the words were coming from, but he knew it was smiling at him like it was mocking him.

"Who are you people? I ain't done nuthin' to you! You leave me be!" Tommy cried out, his eyes darting to and fro looking for any avenue of escape from this situation.

"We're your friends Tommy, the last friends you'll ever need."

Tommy tried to dart away still clutching his pitifully few belongings. As he did, even though none of the figures had approached him one step further, it felt like someone grabbed him. Someone had thrown him up against the wall hard enough that all the air left his body as he bounced back forward and fell to his knees before the figures.

"Please...." he gasped, "I ain't done nothing...."

"No, you haven't done a thing with your life, Tommy. But the nice thing is, if a body can't serve on its feet ministering to others, there are other ways."

Tommy saw the gleam, as the city lights reflected off the large object that the figure suddenly raised above his head. Tommy tried to throw up his hands but they refused to obey him, he only got out another wheezing, "Please...."

There was a sharp pain in his neck before he said another word, his vision suddenly tilted horribly, the light of the world was fading out and he could hear hideous gurgling noises from his throat. The last thing he heard before the darkness ate the world like Fenris swallowing the moon was a voice saying, "Oh, you will serve."

Tonight, was practice. Other bands had a good social life, but not theirs, but that was all right in the long run. They really couldn't afford more of one than going to the bar once a week, and MAYBE seeing a Friday show if somebody cool was playing. But if they pooled their scrapings together... Shane still paid for most of the practice space and would passive-aggressively remind them often, usually when someone was slacking at practice. Shane had a business of some kind, Rat never asked more than wanting to know if it was legal, and lived in a real apartment like a big boy. Enio, and HIS band, "Criminal Mischief" went to shows or went drinking or both most of the time which frankly made Rat more than a little jealous. Of course, Enio's band hadn't played in months because they kept forgetting to practice, and when they did practice it usually ended up in a drunken fight, so, maybe there was something to this strong work ethic crap after all.

They biked up to the practice space they had in mid-town as a group, dodging and weaving their way through the evening traffic with instruments on their backs. When all was said and done, Rat would have rather taken the subway, but for some reason, Shane always insisted on riding if it wasn't raining or snowing. Since they kept the better instruments at his place and they were all bike messengers anyway it wasn't like it was a major hardship, it was hard to argue against doing it. Occasionally Shane would spring for a cab if the weather sucked, this was not going to be one of those nights, the clear skies spelled riding. Rat might have preferred public transport, yet secretly he was enjoying himself. The city at night, especially heading uptown had a weird manic beauty to it, all of the lights everywhere, all screaming into the night trying to drag your attention away from all the other flickering illuminations. All of those displays wanting to be your special girl for tonight. It was like Christmas for capitalism, the shining colors giving the whole world a glow caused by the warmth provided by the true spirit of money.

The practice space itself was in a slim building that

looked for all the world from the outside like it would hold apartments. The owner of the building had bought the whole thing years ago and just rented out the studios on each floor and with Broadway and the LES music scene both nearby none of them ever wanted for renting. Every time they went up to their space Rat tried to avoid looking at anyone in the darkened stairwell. It was nothing but musicians and Rat knew for a fact that musicians could be completely fucked up individuals, it was best not to draw attention to yourself. He was a musician, to a degree, he had a solid frame of reference to work from here. He wasn't alone in that conceit, in fact, none of the band looked at anyone. Only Jazz had avoided ever having a serious drug issue in their past, and nobody wanted to see anything in here that might upset or tempt them in any way. Rat drank, Cole smoked weed and drank, Jazz drank, Shane didn't do anything, and if they wanted the band to get anywhere at all they needed to keep it that way. A lot of the bands who had spaces here were has-beens who were just a few more bad decisions away from not even being able to afford this place, Rat didn't want to join them on their way to the bottom. Just because it looked fun from the outside didn't mean it was, that was a hard lesson to learn.

Robbo wasn't waiting for them inside when they got there. It wasn't a shock, the drummer was coming from Brooklyn and he could usually afford to be late, he was the only one that didn't do any setting up when he got here, the kit that was set up in the studio did fine for this. The only thing he insisted on was his own snare. Robbo was almost exactly what you hoped for in a drummer, he rarely talked more than a brief sentence but he could play just about any set you dropped him in front of, a consummate professional. Considering the kind of music they played, that was damned handy, things got knocked over all the time by the crowds, thinking on the fly was mandatory. A drummer who could keep playing through it without missing his cues was worth his weight in gold and more than worth ignoring a few minutes of tardiness here or there. He'd probably be here before they were completely tuned up anyway.

They were just letting the amps warm up, when they heard an enormous sounding growl of a motor outside the building and the screech of tires audible even where they were in the padded cocoon of the studio. Robbo was here. Robbo was a former cab driver and he really LIKED to drive in the city, playing his own game of Serpico wherever he went. None of the band would drive with him anywhere, Cole had once, and if you so much as mentioned the incident to him, he'd pound half a forty and blaze one up halfway down before the shake in his hand went away. Robbo was a lunatic behind the wheel, thankfully being a crazy person meant he fit in with the band pretty well in his way, none of them trusted anyone who pretended to be completely normal. Normal was an act, a lie you put out there, when someone tried it, you couldn't help but spend all your time wondering what they were hiding. Robbo was out in the open, never drive with him, easy to work around, and easier still to forgive.

"Hey," he grunted as he shuffled in a few minutes later carrying his cymbal under his arm like a guy making a delivery.

"Yo," he got back.

They all went back to fiddling with their tuning, Robbo working his stout frame into position at the kit, twisting and turning things until they were to his liking. Finally, he just said, "Well, are we doin' this or what?"

And then they were indeed doing it.

Practice went typically, at least for a Restraint and Control practice. At the start of every practice the first few songs went swimmingly, everybody had their levels set right, everybody could hear each other and pick up their song cues, everything was at a volume where thought was still possible. The main problem that cropped up almost every time at practice stemmed from not having monitors, so no one but Rat really knew what the overall mix was like up front. It was around song three that Cole turned his amp up. What he should have done was take two steps forward so he could hear that it was actually mixed perfectly. That was what he should have done, and every practice he failed to do exactly that. Rat knew from experience that nobody ever did that in any band he knew of, certainly not this one, so to some degree he just expected it.

The war was on by the next song. Rat was positive he was going deaf, his hearing had been dropping in and out for weeks now, and he was positive this was why. Either that or he had a sinus blockage, considering their lack of any real heat and him working outside all day that was also a possibility. Once Cole's guitar went up, Jazz's bass went up, since Jazz was standing right next to Cole and now, he couldn't hear himself at all. As their battle for dominance continued, eventually Shane was affected, so his stuff went up as well. This forced Rat into a position of vocal cord self-preservation and he turned himself up. The war ended where it always did, with Robbo screaming, "IT'S TOO FUCKING LOUD IF I CAN'T HEAR THE FUCKING DRUMS I'M PLAYING!"

Two songs later they wrapped it up. It sounded tight, they hadn't introduced any new songs just ran through their normal set and a few other songs they wanted to keep fresh in their memories in case they needed them for a show. They were leaving with ringing ears, but with the volumes all set back to reasonable spots until their next practice on Tuesday when the process would begin all over again. Punk rock star 101, everything louder than everything else. Nobody had ever once suggested playing quieter until

Robbo freaked out each week, nobody ever would, it was a matter of pride.

The ride back went better than it usually did. One of the multitudes of reasons why Rat hated biking to practice was the additional deafness after practice. It made it difficult to hear all the multitude of sounds around him throbbing away, the cries of an angry city twisting and turning under the humming traffic lights. Any one of those unheard growls of the monster you lived on could send you hurtling airborne to injury or even possible demise. Every bike messenger would tell you, it only took once, until you were no longer employed as a bike messenger, at best you could maybe get a job as a baby food taste tester, at worse a funeral home model. On the subway, on the other hand, ringing ears could be considered a benefit that improved the trip. This way you didn't need to hear the rantings of the various riders who had somehow, once upon a time, gotten on the subway, had a mental psychotic break while down there, and who could never, ever leave now. They could rant and rave to their heart's content, and at worst you only had to hear every third word. If anything, they made more sense that way.

Just getting back to the village didn't mean they were done, their gear still had to be hauled up to Shane's apartment, and that took forever. Mainly because Shane's apartment was on the fifth floor. In theory, Rat could have just gone back to the homestead, since he didn't have a guitar, but it seemed like a dick move. The reason this had to be done after every practice was that it just seemed safer to keep the stage instruments there most of the time, mainly because it was. Shane lived in the village proper and they lived in Alphabet City, it was a simple reality.

Cole had a guitar at the homestead as well so they could write, which technically was a Gibson SG, but in reality, was something they'd been gifted by the widow of a guitarist who wanted to see it played again. That sounded very touching until you realize that the guitarist in question had been a speed freak and an amateur electrician. It had taken Rat and Cole months of puzzling over it, but they considered it almost ready to be played in public again. If they could just get it to the point where it stopped randomly shocking Cole then they'd have it licked. Cole seemed pretty insistent on that point, but it had gotten Rat a couple of times, and Rat thought Cole was being a baby about it. Rat graciously let Cole continue to use Shane's guitars when they played out as a show of band unity and his personal caring nature. It also saved from having the rhythm guitar drop out whenever the SG was feeling feisty.

After saying later days to Shane they were cruising slowly down St. Mark's when they could see the lights. Something was happening in the park tonight. "What the fuck?" Jazz exclaimed.

"No idea, I didn't see any fliers," Cole shrugged.

"Well, we didn't have any plans tonight, did we? Let's go stash the bikes at home and find out."

By the time they had stashed their bikes at home and gotten back, the park was fully alive with people and activity. Enio hadn't been home, so they had to assume he was in the swirl of people somewhere. These spontaneous happenings seemed to be happening more often lately, which was especially weird considered that even if it was a warm winter, it was still winter in the city. Tensions were rising between the city and the squatter community, and there seemed to be some primal urge taking hold of the natives to make sure that the city knew they were still down here and not leaving any time soon. Bonfires were lit in cans all over the park, with not a cop in sight. If it wasn't a planned sweep with heavy presence, cops were leaving the park be, they could feel the tension too, those guys had pensions to think about, no point in heroics. The homeless camps were a bone of contention with the city, but hell, these people had nowhere to go. They'd been left be before this sudden money-driven civic pride, because kick them out of here the depressing fuckers might end up on the doorstep of a donor, and where would you be then?

That had begun to change. Increasingly as developers started looking to own every little bit of downtown, they eyed the East Village, and as they eyed the East Village, they started thinking about what a centerpiece Tompkins Square would be. Every once in a while, the city would make a show of force and stormtrooper their way through the place, but apparently, the budget wasn't there for one tonight. The crazies owned the park tonight, Mom and Dad and apple pie should probably just take in a Broadway show and get out of here. The homeless and the locals really owned the place most evenings, but tonight they were being loud about it, they wanted the world to see them. An act of defiance against a world that had abandoned them to cruel fate, shame this cry against the night was in New York where people step around dead bodies without even looking, so nobody gave a fuck about this. A few squad cars had probably called it in and been told to just make sure it stayed in the park where it belonged and leave it at that. There was already somebody tuning up on the bandshell, meaning this promised to be a full-blown rager tonight.

Somebody else was serving soup out of a huge tureen right near the Avenue A entrance, like a welcoming committee to another country. "Welcome to Scumfuckistan weary traveler, let us feed you!" Rat took one look at them and could see it was those nutfucks from the Church of the Left Eye. They were crazier than a sack of bedbugs on crack, happily being led by their wanna-be guru Andy. Andy dealt drugs, listened to metal, he should be just another village space case with his cult of maybe four. Three girls he was fucking and one guy who wanted to join him in the fucking. Against all logic somehow there seemed to be more of them hippy metal fucks every time Rat looked. Who knew why? This was the Village and Alphabet City, everybody had a church, most of them with the same message, get stoned, get laid, pretend there aren't any consequences for it all and somehow this will make you especially noble and holy. Maybe Andy had found a way to rephrase it to make it sound original this time, maybe he just had better drugs.

"You want some soup?" Jazz asked.

"Oh, fuck no, I took a bowl once, way back when it was just Andy and his girlfriend, it's almost all seaweed. I couldn't even touch a drop, smelled like Battery Park at low tide on a summer day," Cole winced.

"Thanks for the heads up, let's go get some forties and come back to watch the band," Rat said pulling them away from the stoner's suspect tureen of seaweed and who the fuck knew what else.

The bodega they stepped into was on high alert mode when they got inside. Bodega employees never trust anyone to begin with, but when there was something in the park, you could see it right in their eyes. The guy's hand was just HOVERING over the gun or bat he kept under the counter, waiting for the moment that he'd become the next Bernie Goetz, vigilante hero. If you averaged out traffic volume for these events against petty crimes during it, it was probably average, but guys just got overwhelmed by it all. Even the cat looked tense, it was hiding on a stack of titty mags behind the counter and its ears were turned back. Rat's feelings were almost hurt, usually, when he came in here the damned thing wouldn't leave him alone, but tonight it looked like it would take almost zero provocation to get the feline to try and claw his eyes right out.

They had to shove their way over to the cooler to get around people. When they finally stood there staring out the racks of beer luck was on their side, they were able to clear out the last of the Ballantines getting two each. Rat and Cole covered for Jazz who with the mugging and all would have had to have gone without. They could have just left him to watch them sadly, oozing with passive-aggressive energy as they drank theirs but frankly that would have sucked. Oh sure, he wouldn't have said anything, that wasn't his style at all, but they would have been able to physically feel the waves of wistful longing coming off him as he watched them drink. Something like that would have completely ruined their buzz. Some people never say a word, and you get their point of view perfectly, Jazz had a talent. Better to each buy him one and be able to drink in peace.

Making their way back into the park, they were forced to give the Left Eye nutters an even wider berth than their first scouting trip, just to keep a distance forced them off the walkway briefly. A crowd had gathered around the small group of religious lunatics, filling the area they'd parked their table in. Weird, as far as Rat could tell there wasn't anything to separate them from the rest of the tax-exempt hedonists that littered the village, but there were even more of them every day it seemed. Same zonked expression, same filth, same bullshit, just multiplied like roaches, and just like roaches you could never see the individuality of the roach you stepped on, it was only one of many. Maybe it was the stress of being hemmed in with all these people in the city that made people crack and go looking at a joint to find God. When you could feel yourself being pushed directly into the river by the yuppies' slow creep east, it seemed people would believe any old bullshit. Faced with unrelenting crushing forces all around them they get desperate for seaweed slop, pussy, and enough weed and smack to drop a moose, just so they could forget for the time being that in two years or less they were gonna be scrambling for someplace to live when the yuppie infestation took the East Village and Alphabet City too. Maybe you wanted to find God because you'd plum run out of any earthly help to save you.

Cole nudged Rat to keep moving, driving him onward as they pushed their way into the crowd by the bandshell. Where in the hell did all of these people come from so damned fast? There hadn't been any fliers announcing this, hell, they only lived a few blocks from here and they hadn't heard about it. They knew the band onstage personally, an anarcho-industrial-tribal band called Police Tape, you'd have thought word would have gotten to them about this impromptu show. But then again, if this was their typical type of gig, the Tape folks hadn't known themselves they were going to be doing this yesterday. One of them had just said, "Hey let's set up in the bandshell and play until the cops shut us down!" Rat respected that attitude; Cole practically worshiped it.

Rat had heard they had a record out but was in no real hurry to pick it up. Live the whole thing was incredibly powerful, but that was live, that was with it in front of you so it could swirl through your eyes into your soul, so the drums could throb so loud to reset the rhythm to your heartbeat. How in the hell do you translate the excitement of using metal barrels for drums, with fires actually lit inside sending a shower of sparks up with each pounding on to a record? For that matter, who in their right mind would let them into a studio to make that happen? There had to be all kinds of codes against that kind of shit, right? But live, live it was a surreal experience, two guys screaming out at the audience through bullhorns, four guys pounding out rhythm on their barrels, and a guitarist and bassist coming in at random. This was the kind of stuff that legendary political rallies were made of, vicious, primal, terrifying to anyone outside the tribe.

They found a spot at the edge of everything and scanned for people they knew. You always did that first, if nothing else you needed to know where your back up in a fight was sitting. The crowd shifted and swirled as people attempted to slam to what was happening onstage. Rat thought it was pretty dumb, what was on stage was the real chaos, and worth everyone's attention. In comparison, a mosh pit was just some excess youthful exuberance. Kids, sometimes they had just too much damned energy, they'd grow out of it he figured. He rarely slammed anymore, it really started tapering off last year around his birthday. You grow. Rat was also pretty sure Enio was up there somewhere right by the stage, for somebody who drank that much, he had an amazing amount of energy.

Jazz nudged him, "Hey is that Skeev on the other side of the pit?"

Rat squinted, trying to make anything out between the light coming from the stage, the lamps on the trails, and the darkness enveloping the world just past everything. It took him a few moments before he could confirm for himself that it was Skeev, he spotted the bright neon on a leather jacket, "Yeah, that's him, you could spot that damned jacket from Mars. Let's go say hi."

No small efforts were going to get them through the crowd, they needed to work together. Rat tapped Cole and they began making their way working around the crowd. People kept flowing in and out of the action, causing the three of them to have to stop in their tracks repeatedly as someone went in front of them or banged right off of them. At least if they wanted to stick together, they'd stop, if they didn't, one of them was sure to get swirled away into the madness, the crowd was the water, and they were just leaves on the surface trying not to get pulled out to sea. The park was brighter than normal, but it was still shadowy, a bump into a person here, a twist to get around someone there and next thing you knew the trio would be a duo, and then a single, and then they'd spend the rest of the night looking for one another. They'd probably split off from each other as the night progressed, but they all wanted to say hi to Skeev first as a group and see if anything interesting happened from there. They figured he'd been here for a while and would know the lay of the land.

Skeev was paying attention to the band onstage at the moment, so they were pretty close before he looked around and spotted them. He gave a nod and a smile when he spotted Rat first since Rat was the tallest of the three, and at 6'6" tended to loom over the crowd in any event. Skeev waved the three of them over to say howdy, probably thinking the same thing they were, which was, "Well, let's see if they got anything going tonight after this breaks up."

As they approached, a shadow detached itself from the darkness right behind Skeev. Suddenly the figure launched itself at the oblivious punker. They could see Skeev reel from the first blow that struck him in the face. His face was turned into an almost comical expression of shock before the punch even landed. Skeev stumbled back away, only to be pursued by the tall shirtless figure who kept punching him as he fell. All three of them began to run up to see what in the hell this was about, and at least pull the guy the fuck off Skeev before he really got hurt. The guy had already drilled Skeev's prone form repeatedly before they were even close, it had taken a moment to get over the shock to get moving, Skeev was an anarcho-punk crusty, not some big fighter gang guy, so nobody had any real reason to go after him. Rat had to figure this was total bullshit, some drunken mistaken identity. The only way to prove that though was to get the guy the fuck off Skeev.

As they skidded up to the scene Rat recognized the

figure who was facing them, standing over a bloodied and moaning Skeev. He was a black skinhead they'd seen around town at most of the usual hangouts and shows. Rat had assumed when he saw him around that he was part of one of the various gangs that used to infest CBGB's at the matinees and had been forced to look for new places to pollute. Despite whatever affiliations he might have had, normally the guy was all right, Rat had even hung out with him some nights at the bar tossing back a few. What in the fuck was this all about?

"LOOK WHAT I DONE TO YOUR BOY MOTHERFUCKER! LOOK WHAT I DONE TO HIM!"

Before Rat, or any of them, could even consider what to do about it the skin turned and ran off into the darkened parts of the park, repeatedly yelling what he'd said over and over as a vanishing mantra that faded into the night.

Chapter 3

It had been difficult to drag Skeev back to the homestead to take care of him. There were only three of them and he was a wet rag who only occasionally contributed anything positive to their locomotion. No one else moved to do shit but step away so they wouldn't get any on them, and once the beating was over, they lost interest entirely. Some quick chugging on Rat's part freed up a hand to sling Skeev onto his shoulder for the stumble home. Right after he got him hoisted up, he belched loud enough people turned to look back. Rat considered himself good in a crisis, drink the beer, handle the situation, and when he was done, he still had some Midnight Dragon in the fridge. Thank the gods the cops had more or less abandoned the LES tonight, so at least they wouldn't have to explain anything to a pig with too much free time. They still had a sizable amount of beer with them and Skeev looked like shit, it wouldn't be a good story if they were asked, and none of them really felt up for telling it.

Rat passed Skeev off to Jazz before opening their interior door by himself as a precaution. They'd been out for a while, and Ralph was sure to be energetic and happy to see them. The last damned thing that the mumbling wounded Skeev needed right now was fifty pounds of pit bull love lunging up to greet him. No way would he be able to get his face clear of the dog slobber. As expected, as soon as the door opened Ralph was airborne trying desperately to get a good swipe of tongue in on Rat's face as Rat pushed him back into the room. Inconvenient yes, but maybe people would be better people if they felt a bit of love like this once a day, if someone who thought they could do no wrong was waiting when the door opened. While Rat fussed over Ralph the other two got Skeev inside and situated in a chair.

Once the pit bull was convinced that he had been thoroughly missed and that Daddy wasn't going to leave any time soon, Rat turned his attention to Skeev. "Dude, get me a wet rag," he said to Cole. Taking the proffered piece of cloth, a moment later Rat examined the rag for cleanliness and then their friend, deciding what needed cleaning off first. After a few rubs at the still dazed squatter he exhaled, "Man, it looks worse than it is. I think you got a concussion; you definitely got a broken nose but they always bleed like holy Jesus. Here, put a piece of the Post up your nose it's all that rag newspaper is good for anyway. So, now that we're sure you ain't gonna die, what in the fuck was that about?"

Skeev looked thoughtful, or at least like he was attempting cogitation, his eyes were still pretty blank, before slurring out, "I have no fucking clue whatsoever dude. One minute I'm waving at you guys, the next, stars are goin' off in front of my eyes."

Cole said over Rat's shoulder, "It was Rico, no idea what he was even doing there, he lives in Brooklyn."

Rat nodded, "Yeah that's who I thought it was. He was in the bar a few weeks ago, we hung out, guy was cool." He turned back to Skeev and asked, "So what in the hell did you do to piss Rico off?"

Skeev's face registered surprise, his eyes went wide before he replied, "Nuthin' man, not an ever-fucking loving thing! I barely know the guy to say two words to him."

Jazz had been fiddling with his beer looked up enough to say, "Coke man, enough of that will fuck your brain up."

The room went quiet then Cole said, "Yeah, most of those CB's gang bangers are coked to the nines. Who knows what the hell he was thinking?"

"Yeah, probably. We better let Skeev crash here tonight, who knows who in the hell would keep an eye out for him at his squat," Rat said. He wasn't sure about the coke answer, it felt like it was being used as an ex-Machina to explain away behavior none of them understood. Thing was, he didn't have any better ideas short of old-fashioned mental illness, and that just as much of a catch-all.

"I'll be all right man, don't wanna be a bovver," Skeev moaned nasally with his nose stuffed with paper making his words slur a bit worse.

"Oh yeah, you look just swell," Cole quipped, "ready for your Broadway debut."

"More, swelled," Rat added. He handed Cole a ten-dollar bill, "Go get some more forties, we're in for the night."

The workweek started back up, regardless of anyone's preparedness for it, that was its want and habit to do. Skeev had been patched up and dispatched back to his squat on Sunday afternoon and the rest of the day was spent mainly reading or listening to music, all around just fucking off which is all that Sunday evenings are good for. But on a Monday morning commerce beckoned, and when commerce beckoned, the waking metropolis needed swift couriers to make their rounds ensuring the whole commercial wonderland functioned properly. What commerce got instead of swift couriers in sparkly magic uniforms were psychopaths on bicycles. Those members of society crazed enough, deranged enough, unloved enough to plant their ass on a small little toy of a vehicle and to brave the hostile cabbies, the speeding cops late on a donut run, the indifferent or often resentful limo drivers, the construction, the jaywalking tourists and all the rest of the maniacs that made Manhattan's streets unsafe for even walking. There was a secret nobility to the gig, but not the kind recognized on Wall Street, just a hope and a prayer to get home safe for a group that as a whole couldn't find other employment, but could find a bike and who still had the sniff of the wild to them despite being locked in a zoo.

It was a dangerous job that took a special breed, all messengers got into accidents, it was impossible to avoid. Your aim was to avoid serious injury when you had yours. But what else could you do? Very few other jobs were willing to overlook a purple mohawk, and the ones that were willing had occupants squatting there and unlikely to ever quit any time soon, even if they died. It was best overall to convince yourself that you dug the excitement and to just try and get off on the adrenaline, your primal flight or fight caveman free at last. Life would make sure you got tamed eventually, get away with this type of existence before the world noticed and forced you into a uniform.

Before getting on with his day, first things were first. Rat slipped into the deli near his company's office to get breakfast. Coffee and an egg sandwich, Rat had no idea what in the hell the name of the place was, but he'd swear sideways that they had the best egg sandwich in the city. Lots and lots of melted butter just saturating the toast to the point that it would drip onto the sidewalk while he ate.

Massive cholesterol, the key to any good breakfast until you were in your forties and started needing to sweat heart attacks at least. The coffee wasn't special, it didn't have to be, it was better than the cup he'd had back at the homestead this morning, so it was an improvement on his day. In the local bodegas, all they could really afford to make in their little coffee maker was espresso which was the cheapest bagged stuff they sold. Rat had always thought that weird, growing up far from here, espresso cost a fortune and was considered highbrow, but in Alphabet City, Maxwell House was what would set you back. To make it palatable for a first cup of the day, they brewed it weak, which made it taste weird like it was only coffee-ish, coffee-related. So, this deli served him his first palatable cup of coffee in the morning, that made 'nothing special' plenty good to him.

Rat stopped into the office and got his coins for call-ins and his first pickup order of the day. He barely talked to the dispatcher, in reality, he talked to the dispatcher a ton, but not really talking. Words would be exchanged with no humanity, like he'd call in, get his address for the next pick up, talk to him, but neither one of them looked at each other or talked to each other with anything more than robotic tones. You rarely really conversed in the city with anyone if you could avoid it, people talked all the time, but they rarely had anything human to say. Just directions and reactions to orders. Other people were just something you had to interact with enough to have a functional day, nothing more. You could replace most of that interaction with a recording and it would be just as heartfelt. It would definitely be more efficient.

Once you got moving, the day began to blur quickly, you had to figure most people's day jobs went that way no matter what they were. Even for drug dealers, one junkie has to start looking like every other by noon. No day was like any other, but really few days were unique enough to be interesting to him, it was just grinding your time away like the cog you were so you could punch out and live. It just became an endless world inhabited by you peddling a bike around the city, with spots where you took a breather mixed in, you get lost in the repetition of it. Well, that wasn't entirely true, sometimes you got famous people for your deliveries, so those would stand out enough to be worth mentioning later. That was every job as well, maybe not famous people, but trying to find something in your day to talk about so that what you were doing with your life didn't sound so brains dissolving dull.

Rat loved his famous people deliveries, not for that touch of fame, but because those people were so EASY to piss off. It took almost no effort on his part, and if he did it right, he could see that whatever he did would bug those people for days. He was nobody really, and they'd just invite him to live in their heads like that. He'd never do anything malicious or outright obnoxious, just little things nobody could rightfully complain about without sounding like a lunatic. Like the time he had a delivery for a famous Broadway composer. The assistant fretted and floated nearby giving instruction on how the man was to be approached, worrying about anything bad happening because of Rat's uncouth appearance most likely. Like you couldn't ask for an autograph, you couldn't ask for a picture, you couldn't try to start a conversation with him, all kinds of egotistical crap that was supposed to separate this self-important shithead from the human race as if he was above it all because he could hum a catchy ditty. Rat waited until the man flounced over towards them, just as he got close enough that Rat was sure the guy was in earshot, Rat turned to the assistant and asked with his face shining with absolute sincerity, "So what's this guy do again? What is he in construction or something?" The cloud that flooded the guy's face at that moment was so dark the weather service should have been issuing warnings about the storm coming. Rat still smiled about that whenever he was having a bad day, that memory was like a ray of sunshine breaking through the thunderheads every time.

The day moved nicely along, everything said and done, even with the accident. Actually, the accident added some verve to his morning and kept the boredom at bay. Rat was just cruising uptown for a delivery to some faceless building like the ones that were popping up everywhere these days as developers remodeled buildings right into boredom-ville, that's when it happened. A limo whipped in front of him cutting him off, before slamming on the brakes; a bright flash of red taking over his vision. He knew damned well the guy did it on purpose, limo drivers could be such assholes sometimes. The guy could have made the lane switch at any time, he just waited for Rat to be in the line of fire.

It turned out the guy shouldn't have gone for being an asshole, Rat's brakes weren't really good enough to stop in time, for starters. But his instincts were good enough to start the bike turning sideways instead of crashing full-on into the back of the thing. Rat didn't even take a bump from the incident, the limo on the other hand took a brutal set of scrapes across the rear of the car from the pedal on Rat's bike. Best of all, with traffic moving again, Rat was able to just get his bike under control and whipped it up the middle between lanes flipping the guy off as he went. The asshole didn't even have a chance to get the window rolled down to say anything. If you're going to have an accident, make sure the other guy looks worse than you do. Rat told everyone that mottoes were stupid football John Wayne crap, but that would make a good one to have if you had to have one.

After giving the bike a quick once over, Rat called in and got his next delivery. He groaned internally, the West Village. That sucked. The West Village always brought him down emotionally, it was Eden after the fall. When he had first come to visit NYC, the whole village felt like the hodgepodge of drug-fueled artistic madness that he thrived on living here, it was why he wanted to live here. Rat might not be big into drugs anymore, but he loved the inventive lunacy that could come from them when the high was just floating along perfectly in the right-minded talents. Even a few short years ago that had included the West Village. Not anymore, the very yuppie creep they were trying to keep out of the LES, you could see the end product right here, there was a showroom model to view. Big chain stores, the street vendors all sold brand-name chintzy shit just like in uptown, pushing every big movie franchise on t-shirts, there was nothing unique to anything here anymore. All cheap soulless crap all the time.

Even in the former heart of the West Village, Washington Square Park, anymore you'd be hard-pressed to score a dime bag in there, and you'd probably just be getting oregano or busted by an undercover cop for your troubles. If you could even find someone trying to deal, they were doing it for all the NYU students who finally felt safe to wander into the place and wanted to relax from finals. All the cool weirdness, all the street vendors selling books, and records, and the stereo from your car on a blanket, all of that had been pushed east. If the weirdos didn't hold the line at Tompkins Square, where in the hell could they go next? Right into the river? Rat saw the future in the West Village, and it looked corporate and bleak as all hell. Come on down Ma and Pa Middle America, we've scrubbed it off for you, it's still more exotic than your cul-de-sac but you won't see a damned thing that makes you expand your bullshit little universe one solitary iota!

He was heading down Broadway moving steadily towards making his delivery when he had to stop because of a snarl in the street. A crowd of people had gathered on the sidewalks, so many that by the time Rat reached it, it had spilled on to the street itself and traffic was beginning to back up because of the press of bodies. Rat pulled up to a stop at the edge of the crowd and started trying to figure out how to move his bike through people without making any kind of physical contact. Taking in their general mood and makeup, and the way they were all looking up in the same direction, he had a sinking feeling as to what was going on here. His suspicion was confirmed moments later when he heard someone yell out, "JUMP!" which quickly became a groundswell of voices. New Yorkers, always looking out for one another like good neighbors. He got back up on his bike and began to worm his way through stalled traffic away from the crowd. Nine out of ten, they talked the guy off the ledge anyway, and really Rat had no desire to see more of what happened on the tenth time, that image was still fresh enough in his memory. His lack of faith in humanity confirmed it was becoming a long week for it to only be Monday.

The package turned out to be something for a professor at NYU which was a pretty fast and no muss drop off. Back out on the streets, Rat had to take a few minutes before calling in for his next pickup, he needed to piss. Needs must, and the one thing he could say for the corporate hell that was taking over the city was that it meant more free bathrooms. He chose McDonald's specifically because he didn't like them and resented their presence in this part of the city. If anyone should foot the bill for his morning coffee being done processed it ought to be someone he had nothing but contempt for.

Rat had just begun walking to where his bike was chained when he heard a voice behind him, "The mighty punk rock Rat eats McDonald's?"

The mere gravity of what had just been said caused him to stop and whirl towards the speaker to defend himself against such an outrageous accusation. Before he could get a word out his mouth slammed closed again, it was the girl whose name he couldn't remember from the other night. Rat patted himself on the back for recovering quick enough to say, "Not really picking up fuel, more like dropping it off. I gotta pee somewhere and the streets smell bad enough already, let Mickey Dees deal with it."

"You sure?" she looked amused, "I mean I could have a scoop here for scene gossip, THE Rat from Restraint and Control chowing down on Big Macs...I don't know."

Rat squinted at her for just a second before saying, "You're fucking with me, ain't ya?"

"Might be. Happy to see me again?" she actually managed to look cute and coy which wasn't easy to do in engineer boots and fishnets.

"Would have been a lot happier if I had been coming out from taking a piss in a pizza joint instead," Rat managed to force his grin onto his face in a way that appeared devilish. At least a disarming charming smile was what it was meant to look like, he had no idea if it worked. Most people usually thought he was up to something anyway no matter what he did, so maybe it had no effect at all.

She noticed his bike, "So what brings you to this side of the Village?"

"Work, I'm a messenger, see the spiffy overpriced bag?"

"Tres chic, so you gonna be at the bar on Friday?"

"Ooooo, no, but hey, I got a better idea, we're playing the Pyramid Saturday. Come by and I'll put you on as my guest," Rat said taking out a notepad, "what name do you want me to give them?"

"Oh, just Pamela will be fine. Thanks! Hey, I don't want to hold you up from work," she said, leaning in to give him a peck on the cheek before moving on.

YES! Rat was a genius, a stone-cold fucking genius! He had her name! And a peck on the cheek, she had that most wonderful of traits, the ability to forgive a man his first thing in the morning failures. He almost forgot the combination to his padlock on the bike he was so happy about pulling that verbal sleight of hand trick off. He was getting out of everything here, holy shitballs! This almost managed to make up for having to come to the West Village and having to dodge assholes selling *Predator* t-shirts and sunglasses in the middle of the god damned winter.

The rest of the week was only that, another week, a unit of time we use to measure our march to the grave. The drinking was relocated to the Aztec on Friday, which meant that there wasn't all that much alcohol going to be consumed. Rat drank exactly enough to not get kicked out, secure in the knowledge he had forties of Dragon back in the fridge as usual. He was here to mention that they were playing tomorrow night to as many people as he could without seeming pushy about it. He'd get someone talking about their last gig, and then mention their upcoming one causally, or if they were being particularly drunk about the whole thing, just stick a flier in one of the pockets of their leather for them to find tomorrow when they sobered up. Who knew how many of this crowd would actually show up, but it was better than just sitting around worrying about what the turnout would be. Cheap ass Cole was doing the same thing over at their regular bar, lucky bastard. He and Jazz were doing the expensive places, Jazz was at the Alcatraz, which meant Cole would be staggering in while Rat and Jazz would be sipping on bottles and doing some reading later. Assuming Jazz's Ballantine made it undetected by Enio while they were out of course.

One of the five thousand Als that seemed to litter this city slid onto a stool next to him and ordered a beer. In this case, it was Al from Azzault. When they were all sober enough to gig, they were actually a pretty good band, too bad for them that staying away from nodding off during gigs was not one of their strong suits. As far as Rat could figure, Al usually only did smack when he was sure he'd have an audience for it, it fit his Sid/Johnny Thunders image. Of course, you do that enough times word gets out to club owners, and next thing you knew you were finding it hard to get booked. Nobody wants an OD to happen on their stage, most bars and clubs had all kinds of shit tucked away they didn't want the cops asking about, they didn't want the attention. Worse, one day you find yourself indulging in horse riding on your own time more and more frequently.

Rat looked him over, he seemed to be pretty straight right now so he'd be worth talking to, "Hey Al, how ya' doin'? We're playing the Pyramid tomorrow night. You comin'?"

Al got his beer from the bartender and took a long swallow before turning to Rat, "I might just do that. I need a break from all the weird shit."

Rat laughed, "Dude, I do not think that coming to one of our gigs counts as a break from weird shit."

Al shook his short blond spiked head ruefully, "You guys got jobs, steel doors to your place, man I'm out panhandling. The LES is getting weird lately."

Rat snorted, "Al, the LES is where weird flourishes and thrives, it is always weird here. You need to be specific or I can't follow you. That's why we're allowed to live here, we ain't any weirder than anything else. You seen that new art thing on D? Now that shit is weird!"

"Weirder than normal weird. Fucked up weird," Al replied before taking another long drink, his hand was already up signaling for another one.

"How so?"

"Don't know, something is about to blow, that's what I do know." Al turned to look at him, his face deadly serious, "Tell you what bucko, you mentioned art? Go look at that empty lot down on 9th, tell me things ain't getting more fucked up than normal."

Rat didn't know what to say to that. His whole world was so bizarre, what metric would you even begin to use for "fucked up?" There were shootings, druggies, bullshit cults, the homeless, weird artists, and even weirder musicians, and the especially weird, the intellectual bookstore types who looked at all of that and still thought a glorious revolution could be organized in this world. What could be constituted as weird here would be something like the Brady Bunch or the Moral Majority having a picnic in the middle of Tompkins, it would be so unexpected that people would panic.

Before he could say anything to him, Al's second beer arrived. Not standing on ceremony with this one, the scrawny little vocalist tipped back his head and chugged it. After letting out an enormous belch he turned back to Rat, "I'm gonna go get straight back at my squat, I just wanted a couple of cold ones real quick. See you around."

"Tomorrow night," Rat reminded him.

"Yeah, yeah, the Pyramid. Later gator."

A moment later Al was out the door. Rat sat there alone at the bar for a minute puzzling over what Al had said. Maybe Sunday he'd have time to go over there and see what he was talking about with the lot. But now, he thought maybe he'd had enough of pressing the flesh for one night. Suddenly he wanted nothing more than to get home and get behind that nice safe metal door with his large pit bull. All the fun had gone out of this scene after talking to Al.

Show day was a production. It was always a

production to get everything and everyone where they needed to go, so, in that, this wasn't special. Some shows were more of a production than others. They got to headline some gigs, and one of the ways that happened was that they also provided sound. Clubs were more than happy to let you compete for gigs and having your own sound system was a leg up in a scene full of club owners who hated paying for anything. Today wasn't that bad, but it still took a lot of shepherding to get everyone in the right spots at the right time. You wanted to be dependable right now, you wanted to be professional, you wanted to be who the clubs kept booking.

The city was in flux, the hardcore, or as the band liked to refer to it, noo yawk hawd coor, scene was dying down now, most of the bigger bands in that had gone metal and were playing the Ritz. CBs was backing away from the all-ages matinees because of all the fights, so that avenue was limited. Scum rock had never really taken off as big as everyone thought it was going to, it was mainly a big kid, 25–30-year-old thing anyway. So, while there were a couple of big punk bands like Nausea and the Radicts, the door had been left open for some kind of new scene to fill the void. It also helped that New York was large enough to have a fractured many-faceted scene to begin with, there were needs that needed filling if you were willing to play that music. What was happening in the LES now didn't have a name, some people referred to it as Squat or Rot since most of the bands played shows for Squat or Rot promotions at one time or another, some people referred to it as "drunk punk" or "crooked edge" instead, some thought of it as "crusty." All it had in common was a bunch of bands that maybe kinda looked significantly UK82 in style just a shit ton dirtier, and played balls out and bottles up. The Resisturz, Public Nuisance, Al's band Azzault locally, out of towners like The Repressed from Allentown, the Foul

Mouthed Elves from Boston, they all fit into the burgeoning little music culture. Restraint and Control had Marshall stacks and a board, they got to headline some of the bills featuring that sound because the other bands didn't. A leg up.

The downside to that leg up was that those stacks were stored in Shane's fifth-floor walkup apartment. For this gig a miracle happened, thankfully the Pyramid did not involve dragging those down, just practice amps to hook into the overall sound system. Of course, their practice amps were still huge, but easy peasy compared to a stack, ask any roadie the world over if they'd rather move a pre-amp or a stack up and down stairs. Even if they were smaller, it was still five stories, which was a long way on those steep assed stairs, and Shane would bitch and moan about every bump they took on the way down. Add on the instruments, and they'd get a full day's work in before they even got to the gig tonight. It might be winter but everyone would be sweating by the time they got out the door.

Shane was waiting for them the second they knocked, "What in the fuck took you so long?"

"There was a parade of guys that fucked your mom going down St. Marks, it took a while before it passed," Cole said slipping inside to pet Shane's pit bull Humphrey who was busy pushing past Shane to see who was at the door. "Who's my buddy?" Cole said as he swished the dog's jowls around playfully and completely ignored Shane giving him the finger.

"We're only taking practice amps, right? This isn't going to be like the coffee house gig where nobody mentioned we were bringing the stacks and we had to roll them down Avenue A, and then had to bring them right the fuck back, right," Rat demanded with suspicion as he entered behind Cole.

"Naw, the Pyramid has a better sound system than we

do," Shane assured him. "Hey Jazz, how you doing?" he asked the bassist politely. For some reason, Shane was nicest to Jazz, probably because Jazz didn't talk much and also wasn't responsible for writing as much of the music and therefore wasn't someone who annoyed Shane.

"Sup," Jazz responded, heading over to grab his Peavy bass amp.

"I get the Mesa Boogie, and the Les Paul," Cole called out as he began to wrestle with Humphrey across Shane's carpet.

"You can use the Mesa, but use the Ibanez, OK? I barely got the Les Paul playing right again after you hit that guy with it."

"He was on the stage coming at me, it was him or me," Cole protested innocence.

"Yeah, maybe the first time, but you hit him twice."

Most of the stuff was piled near the door. Rat was going to be stuck carrying the t-shirts. That would sound like the better gig all around to someone else, but the box was huge for one, and it was also more duct tape and strapping tape by this point than it was actual box. If it finally gave way once they got outside, they'd end up having to buy back their t-shirts from every crackhead street vendor on St. Marks. While they'd be getting them back for far less than they'd paid per shirt, and they hadn't paid much, especially considering they'd done the silk screening themselves, it would eat up an afternoon and most of the profit margin. And if it was Rat who let the box fall apart, it would be Rat who would be traipsing up and down St. Marks buying them back by twos and threes, and most likely with his own money, while having to listen to everyone bitch about how he'd let it happen. He made it a point of wrapping a few more straps of tape around the thing just to be sure. If he got screwed because he tripped and dropped it, that was one thing, he didn't want it to be critical box failure that did him in.

Painstakingly, one amp and instrument at a time went out the door and began the long, arduous trip down to the ground. Even though he had the lightest thing, Rat considered for the five millionth time that it would be nice to sign a record deal just to be able to have enough cash handy to slip a couple bucks here or there to a roadie. The stairway wasn't heated particularly well, just the random radiator every other floor or so, and lord only knew what the temperature was set at on the things, but even so, all of them were sweating bullets by the time they were huddled waiting for Shane to get down the rest of the way.

When Shane finally joined them on the first floor Cole thrust open the heavy door and pushed out the amp followed by the rest of them. They trundled their amps on their rattling wheels on the actual street since traffic was light. The gray sky made the whole thing feel like the scene should be in black and white, plucky youths lighting up their foreboding world with music. This was it, the rock n roll lifestyle, carrying amps down a New York street like pack mules. This was the part they never asked about in interviews in magazines, but it was every bit part and parcel with doing it in this city. Rat, for one, wouldn't have it any other way, except for maybe having a roadie carrying the stupid box. He was pretty sure he could live without the carrying the fucking box part.

Chapter 4

Rat sat in a booth along the right side of the dark club and watched everything. He was acting completely cool, quiet, and above it all, but that was mainly because he was scared shitless. You couldn't act like a little kid about things, all wide-eyed and exuberant just because you were playing tonight. You grew up the day you left home for good, you had to act the part of an adult, because in this city children were tasty. They had never played the Pyramid before, in fact, he'd never been in the place before, mainly because when it wasn't hosting bands it was a gay dance club and Rat didn't dance, when they had bands, it tended towards bigger bands he couldn't afford.

The place was way bigger than what he'd expected, he wasn't sure what that had been, but this was bigger. Why didn't anybody tell him for the love of fuck? "Oh yeah, this is going to be the biggest gig of our career!" would have worked. It would have been nice to have forewarning, instead, it was sprung on him when they hauled their amps inside. It was probably not that big for someplace else, like even uptown it wasn't like the size of the Ritz or anything like that, but for the Village.... what they walked into was a gaping empty space that they were expected to fill, first with people and then with sound. You could practically feel the void of the place demanding its tribute pulling at you. Rat thought he was going to have a heart attack his nerves were rattling so hard, at least keeling over clutching his chest would get him out of going on stage. He couldn't even really drink much as he sat there, too much he got sloppy on stage and that wasn't what they aimed for as a band. Certainly not tonight. They wanted to scare the shit out of people, make them worry about their sanity for even being here. They were not a good time party band, this was a take no prisoners assault, and you couldn't do that if you were too buzzed. All you could then was break shit with no direction and no focus, like a loser. People needed to see the crazy in your eyes to believe it.

No, alcohol was a relaxant, and he didn't want that, so that was one less thing for him to do during the interminable wait. The rest of the band was schmoozing a bit, so he was left by himself to slowly milk his comped beer under the theory that one beer was practically no beer at all. Jazz's girlfriend Eve had shown up and they were talking, everyone else had gone scattershot. Still, no sign of Pamela but that was OK, Rat would have been barely communicative anyway, this wasn't the side he wanted to show her immediately anyway.

Right now, he was trying to take this little ball of terror he had eating him alive and to condense it down, all the way down until it was just a speck, like the little bit of matter before everything began. He just needed to hold it tight until he could big bang the whole mess on stage in a little while. Rat would never admit to anyone that this was the analogy that he used mentally to get ready, the level of geek there just didn't sound cool or punk rock at all. He also avoided mentioning how much he liked watching old

Doctor Who re-runs for the same reason, or that he had a favorite Doctor (Jon Pertwee). Though he had used that bit of information when he and a skinhead buddy of his had been uptown one afternoon scamming on tourist chicks pretending to be British. It hadn't worked, and he had the decency to feel a little ashamed of himself for trying. More so, because it hadn't worked, he figured if it had worked.... well, use all the tools in your arsenal, including a British accent acquired from listening to so much British anarcho stuff, and watching Doctor Who.

The opening band had started with still no sign of Pamela, but she might not be able to find him. It was dark, and he was in a booth hiding out and had no intention of getting up. He'd left word with the door, she was his guest, her name, her description, that he was expecting somebody, etc. Since Eve was in and that was sure to have been Jazz's guest, he figured that wasn't a problem. Rat knew that he COULD go around and look for her, that was the polite thing, but he also REALLY didn't want to get up from his cocoon yet. Too many people, he wasn't a mingler before a show, too much talk took the edge off. Now was not the time to get pally with people, the audience wasn't your friend yet, you needed to give them something first, you needed to earn their love. He could already see quite a few of their fans sprinkled throughout the growing crowd starting to get rowdy. He kind of felt bad for the first band. They'd run late getting up on stage, and Scumbag, who was A) called that because he honestly wanted to be one and B) one of their die-hard supporters, was front and center. The guy would be pissed because the show ran late and knowing who to blame, he would aggressively be trying to hurry the poor band off the stage as quickly as possible. As if in cue a huge white glob of phlegm arced up through the stage's lights to tangle in the singer's hair. Impressive really, you almost never saw anyone gob at a punk show these days, and certainly not with that level of accuracy, Rat would have to congratulate Scumbag for it later, he'd be pleased to be noticed.

That band was replaced by another, and then another. They were all "pretty good," and Rat was damned thankful for it. Pretty good was optimum, maybe not from the fan who paid to get in standpoint, but from his personal one that was exactly what Rat wanted. Pretty good meant the crowd was warmed up, they were ready, but they weren't already spent from watching something visually arresting. If an opening band tore the lid off, you'd lost the crowd before you even got onstage. The more important part was that "pretty good" did not rev Rat's already frayed nerves any further. "Damned good" caused terror, it put him in fear of not being good enough to make an impression, it made him terrified of the crowd, thinking the band didn't deserve to be where they were, that they were past it, or for new people in the crowd that they were never going anywhere. Rat finished gigs where the opener was "damned good" by falling off the stage bleeding. It might still happen, you never knew what would come into your mind up there as a good idea, but it wasn't a foregone conclusion yet.

The last band stumbled off to a polite, yet enthusiastic sounding applause, they had done an admirable enough job of exactly their job, warming up. The crowd liked them enough to make a good noise, good for them. As soon as they finished their last song and the wave of applause died off, the crowd started to chant "RE-STRAINT" as the openers cleared their gear. Rat grabbed his setlist and his lyric book. Downing the rest of his beer that had gone lukewarm as he milked it, he stood up and headed for the stage that loomed empty again. It was his turn to fill up that gaping chasm, to make them forget anyone had even been there before Rat and his band. Showtime. Time to break the donuts.

The rest of the band was already milling about by the time he got up there. They weren't ready for Rat yet anyway. Everybody had their backs turned to the crowd, plugging in, arguing with one another about sound levels, tuning up, tuning up backup instruments, all the checkdowns it took before liftoff. Rat was as useful as tits on a bull right now, but it still would look too asshole rock star to wait until they were ready to go to get up there. That would look like they were his backup band, and everyone was just wanking around waiting for him so the show could begin. Instead, Rat made a big show of going through his lyric notebook and taping down the setlists. There were only like three songs in the whole setlist that he couldn't recite in his sleep during a drunken dream, but it still looked better doing things this way, a unit preparing for battle, ready to storm the gates of heaven together.

They'd done a soundcheck when they'd gotten in, this was more to not look like asses than anything else. It would look butt assed awful to launch into their big attention-grabbing opening to find out that someone had bumped one of the guitars and now everything sounded off. You could live with it in like song three, but the opening tune had to sound as good as it was gonna get if you wanted to pull 'em away from their drinks and into the pit.

Rat looked up and got eye contact with the rest of the band, everybody nodded. It was time to get on with this, this was the moment where he was so scared, he couldn't breathe except in short little gasps. Finally forcing himself to take that one deep breath that would allow him to release all this pent-up tension. Fight or flight response went through the roof right at this moment, either run off the stage or go on the attack, snarl your defiance to the world or admit that the world owned you. The first step on the million-mile journey and it was up to him to finally put his god damned foot down on the ground.

Rat stood up, mic in hand, his back still to the murmuring crowd, "SHUT THE FUCK UP!" On cue, the lights dimmed. Rat whirled towards the audience and bellowed, "WE'RE RESTRAINT AND CONTROL AND WE ARE ALL GONNA DIE!"

Rat's world exploded in a little neutron bomb behind his eyes. The opening notes hit, the slow intro built, the music paused for just a moment leaving Rat to scream into that empty moment, "NOOOOOOWWWWWWW!" Everything went white again, both in his mind and on stage. The music turned itself up to as fast as it could be played, the pit exploded, kids went flying off each other in a swirling mass, some kids were already getting up on stage to dive. By the time Rat started growling out the stanza he was already on autopilot. His mind knew the words like a wolf knows how to run, his every vocal nuance was so practiced that it came out without volition from his tortured throat. The lack of coherent thought freed his body to thrash about in the spotlights like an animal in a trap, a thing possessed trying to free itself from some horrid miserable pain. He had worn a tux shirt and a vest to go with his normal spikes and belts as an homage to Johnny Rotten and the Pistols, halfway through the song the buttons were gone and his thin bare chest was exposed. He was clawing at it already. It was a normal Restraint show, no restraint at all, and the audience loved it. Blood, sweat, and fury, punk rock on display for your viewing pleasure.

Most of it he wouldn't remember later, he never did, too many self-produced chemicals had been released into his brain to allow for clear coherent memories. Not even the patter between songs which often devolved into train of conscience beatnik diatribes, sometimes even remaining connected to the songs they were between. Nor would he recall many of his physical actions, the faces in the crowd, all of it would blur. Rat knew why other vocalists in other bands would get so mad at the crowd sometimes. If there was a fight, or a bottle flew up, anything like that, it broke the vibe, it brought you back to coherency it made you think about all of this, about the personal exposure to the world you had right now. Rat didn't WANT to think about any of this, he wanted to get this all released as fast and as violently as possible, to just let the spring he'd been tightening his whole life unwind in this sudden violent instance. Thinking about it, thinking about being stripped soul naked up here in this harsh white light, bloody and drenched in sweat in front of all of these strange faces glowing out of the darkness beyond the stage lights scared the shit out of him. He had a brain to write the songs, to practice the songs, but it would only get in the way now. Playing them live was meant to leave him a drooling, exhausted, incoherent mess when he was done and how dare anyone intrude on that? Including himself. That was the bargain he made with himself that allowed him to have the nerve to do this. They were being as professional as they could be, this was a big important club, nothing was getting broken but Rat, but you couldn't allow yourself a second to think, not a moment to contemplate, if you did the whole fragile artifice that he had built up that allowed him to do this at all would crumble in an instant.

He fell off the stage with the hanging final note of their encore still echoing around the club. A voice in the darkness called out, "Barkeep! Let me buy these boys a drink! They damned well deserve it!"

It was Pamela, he recognized her voice even through his mental fog. Rat stupidly thought, "That's nice, she came," before someone picked him up and plunked him into a booth while they forced a beer into his hand.

There were more bands and a DJ to follow, but it was sort of a roving after-party now, especially for Restraint and

Control. Rat had slithered down to the basement section of the club, where there was a buffet laid out inexplicably. Maybe there being a buffet wasn't that weird in and of itself, he'd heard strip clubs always had buffets, but he doubted any strip clubs had a buffet like this. There was more or less one main item, which Rat wasn't eating, and not only because he didn't eat beef or pork. That item was a roast pig, right down to the apple in its damned mouth, and, a riot squad's cop helmet on its head. Rat had meant to just do a cruise through to see who was around, but now he had sat down transfixed by the sight of the thing. It fascinated him, the way the basement's colored lights bounced off the smooth helmet and off the glistening skin of the thing's head. He almost wanted to engage it in conversation as people came through and tore more and more of its flesh away from the body. He wanted to know how it made the pig feel about himself.

Downstairs was quiet except for the thumping coming from above as the rest of the night's activities played out and a light murmur of people. That suited Rat right about now as well, it was softer on his nerves which had been stripped to bare endings by the catharsis he had experienced. Getting the gear completely out of the club would be difficult at the moment, and kind of rude too, the wrap-up bands might have a breakdown of some kind with their gear and need a hand. The nice thing to do was to stick around in case they needed a loaner instrument or amp to carry them through their set. Hell, they'd needed one often enough over the years, and one of the ways you built a reputation as a dickhead in this business was not sharing with a fellow band in need.

Part of him wanted to break away from the deceased swine with disgust, yet this was still the optimum hideout short of backstage, and he always felt like a douche if he went backstage. Like he thought he was a rock star who was too good for everyone. Suddenly he would no longer be one of the crowd, the mass who made punk rock happen. The selfsame everyone who'd just ponied up money to see him, that had bought shirts, bought demos, and who might be forming bands he'd go to see later. But that didn't mean he wanted to hang out in the actual main room of the club either, he was soul sucked weary and not good company. Rat spotted the perfect camouflage for why he was here, Sal the Captain.

He found a spot for him and Angela next to the Captain. "Hey Sal," Rat gruffed pulling out a chair for Pamela.

"Rat! How positively charming to see you!" the Captain smiled, his eyes twinkling in his corpulent face, framed by what remained of his unkempt white hair.

"So, how's every little old thing? This is my guest, Pamela."

For a sweaty, obese old man in a Hawaiian shirt, the Captain did his best to ooze charm as he leaned in and took Pamela's hand which he kissed lightly, "Enchanté mademoiselle. A friend of our little Rat is a friend indeed."

The fat man leaned back, Rat studied his face for a minute before asking, "You look stressed Sal, what's up your ass?"

"Just contemplating the futility of it all, and other pleasant thoughts," the Captain said with a forlorn smile.

"You ain't thinking of offing yourself are ya?" Rat demanded incredulously, "You got rent control in your building, you do that, what the hell hope is there for the rest of us?"

The Captain chuckled, his jowls wiggling as he did, "No, no, nothing like that. I intend to die here in what's left of the Village. But that's what I was contemplating. How long will it even be the Village and not just a collection of street names that used to mean something more than the letters on the signs? I was contemplating the mortality of Greenwich Village, kingdom of the weird and the wondrous."

"What do you mean by that? It'll always be the Village, that never changes," Pamela surprised them both by interjecting.

"Doesn't it? Young lady, you look like a college student. NYU?" Seeing her nod, the Captain continued, "There was once a time my dear, that parents were almost loathe to send their children there. When the West Village and Washington Square Park were the front lines of the culture war and the college was too connected with it for Ma and Pa middle class to send their babies to such a heathen address. In '61 they had the "Beatnik riots" when the cops pounded on folkies. In '69 they picked on the wrong fags on Christopher Street, and there were those riots. But it all slowly got pushed East, didn't it? Now the West Village is tourists and yuppie scum walking around like they built the place from the asphalt up. Now that, my pretties, is a bad influence on all you lovely college kids. Already people like your young beau, they don't live in the Village proper anymore, they live in Alphabet City. Where next, Columbus? The water is calling you, because there's nowhere left on Manhattan after that."

"Jesus, you're in a mood ain't ya?" Rat chuckled before taking a long pull on his beer.

The Captain snorted, "Hmmm, yes I suppose I am. Legal issues, the authorities are always looking to harass the Church over our sacrament. It makes me sour of temperament."

"Weed Captain, your sacrament is weed," Rat sneered.

"Well, it's holy to us, it's certainly more effective at putting one in touch with the almighty than those silly wafers they gave us when I was a child at church," the

Captain smiled beatifically.

"Well, people are organizing, people are fighting back and standing their ground, maybe the line is going to hold at Tompkins," protested Pamela leaning forward, almost like she was enjoying the prospect of a lengthy debate, her voice raised to be heard clearly over the thumping pulse above them.

"Didn't you hear what I said?" the Captain looked at her incredulously, "people have always fought back. But this is New York City, and in New Pork Shitty money talks and bullshit walks."

Pamela surprised Rat by staying with them as they dragged the equipment back to Shane's place. Frankly, Rat only token helped get the gear up the stairs, exactly enough to say he helped, but not staying a second longer. There were other things on his mind and he wanted to get away from the rest of the band so he could deal with them. Most importantly he was intrigued by Pamela still being there, which after the last early morning fiasco was not high on his expectations list. Yet, there she was being personable to everyone in the band and more importantly staying close to him. In all honesty, he wouldn't have blamed her any if she had hooked up with Cole after what happened, if she was that interested in having a boyfriend who was in a band Cole seemed a better choice. Rat wished he could remember what in the hell he said to her that night in the bar because it must have been some primo A-grade bullshit for her to still be interested in him. You need to remember crap like that in life, you might need it later.

Back on St. Marks, Rat assumed he was walking her to the subway, or God help him walk her all the way to Washington Square to some dorm room. "Where in the hell are you going?" she demanded peevishly to his back when he made the left.

"I thought I was walking you home, or...." Rat began.

"Now why in the hell would I do that? I told my roommate she could have the room tonight."

Well, that was all right, wasn't it?

"You sure?" Rat couldn't help but examine this situation further. He should have shown some confidence, he knew that, but it was like a sore tooth, you couldn't help but poking at it until you found the cavity.

"Yes, I'm sure, you dork," she laughed at his discomfort.

"You paid attention to the show, right?" That was definitely been part of what had been bugging, way more than the "Fast on the trigger because of a dry spell," part, that could almost be seen as a compliment in some circles. Rat knew who he was as far as a singer and as a performer, he was part musician part circus geek. Their shows were bloody, they were intense, they were violent, they were in no way sexy. Women tended to avoid him like the plague once he got off the stage, thinking he was a violent mental patient. For the forty minutes they were on stage, those girls had a great case against him. He had figured Pamela was being polite to let him walk her to the train because he comped her, and after that, he'd probably never see her again. That was what he had prepared himself for.

"The way I figure, you just got all your pent-up aggression out earlier, now you can be the normal you. I've met him before, he's kinda sweet in a grungy sort of way."

Rat stopped dead in the street.

When she realized he had stopped, Pamela turned, "What?"

Rat shook his head and started walking again, "No, that was exactly right! Nobody ever gets that right!"

"Well, I'm smarter than most girls," she smirked.

"Must be, you go to a nice school."

"Not necessarily, you'd be amazed at the clueless

levels achieved at just one mixer."

They made their way by the gloomy park. It wasn't really as dark as it should be this time of night, Rat could see a fire burning in a barrel from where he was. It also wasn't really that cold tonight, if anything this was getting close to t-shirt weather which was damned weird in the middle of winter. But that meant it wasn't a huddled for warmth fire. The denizens who spent their lives sleeping and surviving inside the confines of the park itself must have lit the fire more for companionship and comfort rather than warmth. He figured if he was in their shoes, he'd do that too, this city could be a lonely place even with friends, a job, and a place to live.

Rat noticed movement out of the corner of his eye on the bandshell stage. He squinted through the gloom to try and make out what it was and then instantly wished he hadn't. Ho lee sheep dip Christ on a crutch! It was two homeless people fucking up on the stage, really going at it. They weren't all the way naked because of the weather, but enough clothes were removed, and that motion was unmistakable even from this distance. After the shock, the next thought flooded in behind it, everybody needs to fuck, and if you only had so many options, go for the gusto.

"So? What are you studying at NYU," he quickly blurted out, attempting to distract her, and himself for that matter, away from the show that was being performed in the park tonight.

"If I say you'll make fun of me."

"No, I won't, I got kicked out of high school for the love of fuck, I don't have any room to say shit," Rat protested.

"I'm going for film," she said quietly.

Rat was silent for a moment; Pamela's face grew dark as she waited for the joke that she was sure was coming. Finally, he exclaimed, "That is so fucking cool! Most people don't know this about me, but I'm a major horror movie geek."

"What like slasher films?" she looked incredulous.

"Fuck no! Classics, like Hammer, and Lugosi and Karloff, shit like that! Stuff with some plot and some acting. I mean slashers are OK to kill a night, but...."

Rat had no idea why, but Pamela suddenly snuggled up closer to him putting her arm around him. He had to admit it felt nice. As they kept walking, now that he thought about it, if things were different, if he didn't have a bed to go to tonight, why not do it on a stage? If you were forced to go and do it outside like that, why not make it the grandest spectacle of all if you could. It was important enough that most people spent all day every day figuring out ways to do it with as many people as possible after all, it was why we all existed. Why hide something as grand as the muse for most art? They were already living in the park, why hide it in a bush, show the fucking world! Just because you didn't have a roof over your head anymore, just because you had to scramble for every scrap of food and booze and smokes you got, show the world, "Son of a bitch world, you took everything from me, but I can still fuck. I am still here."

Monday didn't seem quite so shitty when it showed up this week. It was always a little better after a show, playing live took the edge off of day-to-day life, but today had a bit more of a shine on it. The sun was even making an appearance, which in the normal New York winter of shades of gray was noteworthy in and of itself. But even if he hadn't played and if it was raining, today would have seemed a little brighter and a bit happier than it would have been otherwise. Rat knew why, and he also knew there was no way he was stupid enough that he was going to vocalize it to his roommates. If he did that, even Jazz, who actually had a girlfriend, would end up calling him a pussy for it. This was the downside of only having male roommates, the sensitivity levels could often descend past caveman right down to rabid dog with a lipstick boner. Men devolved around nothing but other men and did it quickly. Well, there was that downside, that and the smell, oh yeah, and him having to be everyone's mom and cook dinner because......

Putting that train of thought on hold, and despite the degradation of his living arrangements, Rat had a vague smile on his face for walking Ralph. He was even cheerful for dragging the bike out and heading for work, which meant being in a good mood without a good cup of coffee in him yet, only a very bad one. It was a good day to be alive, and he was hoping that nothing out on the streets today intended to dissuade him from that point of view. This wasn't a common good mood, even common good moods weren't so common for him, and damn it, he intended to keep it going for as long as he was able. He knew the city well enough, it wouldn't be very long at all until it intruded itself like a cop at a party demanding people break it up, so enjoy every moment like this when it's presented to you.

Rat cruised by the park slowly, just warming up his legs for the day ahead, keeping loose until he needed to turn it on going on one of the Avenues to go north. As he glanced inside the little pond of wilderness in the grand ocean of gray, he was kind of stunned to see Church of the Left Eye people in there already this morning. What was weirder is he could swear he recognized at least one guy at their table serving out swill and coffee this morning. He forgot the kid's name, Rat thought he might originally be from somewhere in New Hampshire or something, but he didn't think of him as two important things in relation to him being there. Rat doubted he was a morning person, he had habits, and the other was that he sure as hell knew the guy wasn't religious. Rat couldn't help but note the blank spot on the kid's leather as he cruised by, it used to say, "All Religions Are Scum."

It felt like a cloud came over his day to match the shadows of the trees as he flowed onto 7th Street on the other side of A. It felt fitting to flow into deeper shadows between the buildings. Usually, the shaded street felt homey as it moved through the historic village buildings, something quaint and out of time from the rest of the city. Something was off about how many of those Left Eye creeps he'd been seeing. He'd figured them for a cult, but cults were a dime a dozen down here, why in the hell was this one bothering him so much? Because they were always in the park? Did they look like they could afford a real meeting hall, so why not the park? Was it the kid? Just because the kid was a punker didn't mean he couldn't just be a joiner, who knew, maybe if it hadn't been the Left Eye brigade, maybe in a month it would have been some Krishna recruiter that roped him in, the Krishna's would be pissed they missed one. As much as Rat tried to just dismiss it, something about that particular cult had been bugging him for a while now. Maybe it was because Andy, their "leader," barely had two brain cells to rub together, how in the hell was he convincing so many people all of the sudden that he'd somehow, "Found the way to enlightenment?" Fucking Andy would be hard-pressed to find his way back to the Squat he ran on 8th Street without one of his "flock" holding his hand.

He should leave it. It was going to be a long day, and damn it, it was rare he woke up in this good of a mood, he should let himself enjoy things. Of course, thinking that, he had to fight an overwhelming desire to ram his bike into a parked car hoping to injure himself for thinking like some kind of professor positive, new age, crystal hugging twat going on about, "Living and enjoying the moment." He blamed it on worrying about those Left Eye fuck faces, it got him thinking about wacky religions, and it just popped into his brain. OK, maybe he should let himself enjoy things, but find a less objectionable way of saying that. Like, "Dude your show rocked, you got laid, what do you have to be pissy about, you twat?"

Yeah, that would probably work, Hallmark might not buy the rights from him for that, but fuck those corporate sleezebags anyway.

Chapter 5

No matter what your job is the daily grind, grinds, and today was being no exception. Exciting wasn't for the best most days anyway, exciting could easily put you in the hospital. He'd had plenty of excitement for a while with the limo the other day, so he was at his yee-haw quotient for the month. Instead, he got the usual. Corporate suits making their secretaries send packages to other uptown corporate suits, who would make their secretaries sign for them in dingy fake ass little offices at reception desks. Even working there temporarily had to crush the very core being of anyone stuck behind those cheap desks all day. Fake wood, bullshit paperwork, and most likely a package that was only important because everyone forced themselves to pretend it was. If Rat had still believed in any god whatsoever, he would have prayed sincerely to never end up doing something as soul-sucking as that for money. There was giving your time and your body to the machine, nobody got out of that if they wanted shelter, but it was too much to ask for your soul too.

It made you appreciate a job that gave you freedom in

the fresh air, well, as fresh as it ever was in the city. Money was something that existed to provide survival, anything past that, it was only as good as what you spent it on. Rat considered the best usages of the little he had to be cover charges for shows, records, books, and tapes. He didn't consider his booze expenditures to be anything but survival spending, like food and water. He couldn't fathom living in this overturned anthill without it, so it was for everybody's benefit that he didn't try.

The plus side was that a slow day of the same old, same old meant he could mainly daydream and let his feet operate on autopilot as he directed the bike through relatively easy traffic. If you had accused him of daydreaming, Rat might have spit out a witty rejoinder of, "Fuck you, no I wasn't," but he still was. He often let his mind drift off to where it really wanted to be at the moment. He was just letting the rhythm of the Nihilistics record on his Walkman power his pumping legs without much intervention from his brain. It was just him and his thoughts, the music was just bypassing those and making his legs thrash like they were in the pit moshing while getting him from A to B without the world behind his eyes being interrupted any. Those thoughts were on the show, and what happened after the show, and what the next show would be like, and the next after that show. He couldn't help but recollecting what Pamela looked like with just fishnets and a smile, but not too much, it was hard to ride with wood. Rat was having a damned fine day, and he was kind of proud of himself for leaving whatever worries he had about the Left Eye freaks back in the Lower East Side where they belonged.

He was coming out of an office building after another generic delivery to another generic office, this time at a record company. These blessed arbiters of cool on high were indistinguishable from stockbrokers during office hours, same suits, same secretaries, same water coolers. In the time that he had been inside the building where "the music revolution" was being focus-grouped, an enormous crowd had gathered slightly down the street spilling out into the street itself. Already traffic was backing up a bit. Bad luck for him, he had to go that way. Looking carefully, it dawned on him what set this crowd apart from the normal jumper crowd, it was all teenage girls.

Curious, he rolled his bike over to one of the cops that were keeping an eye on it from this side of the street. "What in the hell is all that about?" he asked the uniform.

"Awww some damned rock star is doing a signing or some shit in there, don't know how the teenyboppers found out about it, we barely got here in time to do crowd control," the uniformed snarled.

"Any idea who it is?" Rat asked, curious in spite of himself.

"I dunno' one of them top forty things I guess, considerin' it's all chicks. Maybe that Debbie Gibson, or that other one… George Michael," the cop sneered.

Rat watched the swirling mob of teens for a moment, he thought he could smell all the Aqua Net from here so probably Debbie Gibson. "You know what'd be funny?' Rat said to the cop as he got back on his bike.

"Naw, what?"

"If Debbie Gibson did a punk song."

"Yeah, like that'll ever happen," the cop laughed as Rat rode off.

It wasn't until he turned his bike down 9th street that Rat realized why he had taken this way home. Normally he never would have, it was already getting dark and he didn't want to be caught out here then. He'd tried to put it out of his mind, but what Al had said to him at the bar had been lurking in the back of his brain like a cockroach waiting for the lights to go out. What the hell was in the empty lot that had thrown Al off so much? Al was more of a city vet than Rat was, it didn't jibe. You live long enough in the city, if you didn't go batshit from tension in the meantime, nothing was supposed to get to you.

Gloom was already beginning to overtake the street and the lights were turning on as he covered the block to where the hole in the line of buildings was. They had tried to do a couple of things with it that hadn't taken, art, community garden, they had all failed under the weight of hostility that was a constant here. It wasn't the whole LES, just here it seemed, well maybe not just here, they wouldn't have even tried it on 11th, that would have been just crazy. It was like the gloom from the buildings tamped down any attempt at illumination, even for the soul, like the earth itself rejected anything but rot.

Rat kept his hand on his bike once he slipped off it in front of where the tooth had fallen out from the presence of its cavity-ridden fellows. It was a bit lighter here, the fading light filling the rubbish-strewn lot with dim gray. He walked the bike over the curb and onto the dirt weaving it around the bricks and glass. Looking around he decided that Al must have been seeing things, it was just like every other vacant lot where a building and the lives it contained used to be.

When he turned to leave, he saw the wall of the adjoining building.

Scrawled there in huge letters that appeared black in this light were the words, "And I Shall Be The Ultimate Mocker Of Men!"

Something pulled him forward to look at the words. He gawked at them in shock. There was no art or artifice to how it was painted, it was like someone had just taken a big wall brush and scrawled it out. This wasn't an art statement, or even a graffiti statement, those had style, and class, the way it was done was often as much of a statement as the words. This was thrown up like if the author, had he been able, would have just ground the cryptic statement onto the wall. There was a rage behind this that was palpable. It was like looking at a mind torn apart in just one phrase.

It also wasn't entirely black, up close he realized that the flaking words were tinted with red. Rat knew very well what dried that way. He was on the bike and pedaling as soon as he hit the sidewalk.

Rat didn't say a thing about what he'd seen when he got home, if it was what he thought it was, it would wash away in the next rain, and if it wasn't, it was just shitty graffiti, and who gave a shit about that? What on earth could he even say? There was a tag in a vacant lot that creeped me out? Nobody really wanted to hear it, tonight was quiet time at the old homestead. Everybody had gone off to their own little ventures around the little brick box they called home so that's what Rat did too. Even Enio was in tonight and reading another punk magazine he'd gotten ahold of somehow. Why disturb this rare moment of calm with macabre craziness that quite possibly had no meaning at all?

It was a total mystery to Rat where Enio's magazines came from, he never saw any of them actually for sale. The first time he ever saw them was when Enio was reading them. MRR or Flipside, somebody around here must have sold those, he seemed to recall seeing them at Bleeker Bobs and a few other spots, he thought that even the anarcho bookstore sold MRR. But nobody carried the weird glossies he got his hands on. This was something with Wattie from the Exploited on the cover that had come from Britain. The thing looked like Teen Beat for the mohawk crowd.

Rat had left his troubles outside where they belonged and had settled in at their sole functional table fiddling with soldering something. He refused to say what to the others. Sheer Terror's demo was playing on the little portable tape deck they kept down here. To an onlooker, it might have been funny to have such a violent soundtrack for such a sedate scene, but Rat rarely expected casual onlookers to understand his life. The tapes got played down here because the record player stayed with the TV in Rat's loft. It wasn't that he didn't trust his roommates not to steal anything, it was just that he didn't have many damned records and he in reality didn't trust his roommates not to break anything or scratch his vinyl. So actually, it was that he didn't trust his roommates, it was only a matter of what manner of distrust.

Suddenly an irritating rattling buzz filled the room from where Rat was seated. "ALL RIGHT!" he said slapping the table. "Enio put down the tabloid man, I have need of your services!"

"Huh?" Enio's head snapped out of the magazine that now showed a glossy picture of Bekki Bondage as it flopped open. Looking over at Rat he exclaimed, "Fookin' cool mate! You got the thing running! You got ink?"

Rat's hand came up holding a bottle of India ink, "Oh yes I do, we doin' this?"

"We bloody well are!" Enio had an accent, but what it was, was anybody's guess. Nobody was fully sure where he came from, but he was undeniably there.

"Wash your hands first for fuck's sake," Cole growled before putting his head back into the Kerouac book he'd borrowed from Rat.

"Anybody else want in on this?" Enio said gleefully going over to the sink.

"Nope," muttered Cole.

"Sorry, no, I can't believe Rat is even letting you,"

added Jazz from his perch watching TV in Rat's loft.

"Fooken' pussies," Enio growled as he grabbed the paper towels.

Rat moved his chair around to make room. Right before Enio was about to pull up his own Rat interrupted, "Hey, before we start, give me that punk rag you were reading. It's not like we're gonna talk much, you're gonna be busy, so I'll get bored."

Enio leaned over and grabbed it, "Same thing we talked about, right?"

"Yeah yeah, the Squat or Rot symbol, now, get crackin'," Rat replied taking off his shirt. He mentally tensed up a bit when he heard the homemade tattoo gun rattle back to life. It was a simple tattoo, for a simple machine, wielded by a simpleton, it all worked out perfectly. The symbol was basically a tilted N in a circle with an arrow at the top, even Enio couldn't screw that up. Everybody was relatively sober, so the odds of successful completion went up significantly, all the way to probable. The gun itself was dirt simple, consisting of the motor for a small tape deck, strapped down to a bent spoon with tape. The needle was just a regular needle, wrapped tightly with thread to hold the ink, melted into a bank pen's ink chamber. It had come from a pen that Cole had vicked from a client signing for a delivery months ago. The barrel of the pen kept the needled centered, and another pin held it onto the tape deck wheel.

Rat tried to focus hard on the article about the UK Subs. He could see the date was old, and he was right about the quality of the writing, it was a rag for teens, but he didn't want to tense up and at least it was a bit of a distraction. If your skin was all tight because you were flexing it could fuck up the tatt and it ended up hurting way more that way. He didn't have long to wait for the pain to start anyway, the pin started rattling against and into his skin a moment later.

Now that part was over, he could relax and hunker in a bit. The anticipation of the pain, the time frame where you could have doubts was ended. Every few seconds Enio would have to re-dip the thing and start from where he left off, but the waiting to feel the pain for the first time, the anticipation of the pain, that threshold had been walked over. Now it would be mainly a lot of annoying soreness.

Rat had done this before, he had home jobs like this all over himself. None of them looked professional (except for the actual professional one he'd gotten on his eighteenth birthday) but that was fine. In a world where it constantly felt like you controlled nothing, they were a statement of control over something. Even if it was only the skin on his back, he could dictate something about himself and his life. He could decide on the image he presented to a world he didn't approve of one fucking iota. Too many people suffering, too much easily preventable pain, too many people getting fucked, and too many people uptown in fancy apartments and fancy cars wearing fancy suits, proud to tell you that all those innocent and not so innocent victims of the world deserved it all. No, if that's what being normal and fitting in was, count him right out. Every tattoo put him one step further away from ever being accepted in that world. The pain was just the separation an infant feels from its mamma, it would pass.

He could feel the ink landing cool on the irritation-heated skin as the homemade gun splattered it about. When the mess got too bad, Enio would take a paper towel that had a little water on it and quick wipe the ink and blood away so he could see what he was doing. There had been a small amount of interest from the others when it started, but once they figured out what Rat was getting, and that Enio didn't seem inclined to screw it up bad enough for it to be funny, they both went fully back to their other pursuits. They'd seen people get tattoos before; the possible entertainment was over until it was done. Rat wasn't wincing like a pussy, Enio wasn't making a mess of it, nothing was happening that was worth even cracking a joke about.

"You should get one wit yo' girlfriend's name," Enio said around a hand-rolled cigarette he had wedged in the side of his mouth, before leaning back to take a long drag.

"Only nimrods get a chick's name tatted, and I don't even know if she's my girlfriend yet. Change the tape, I got some Chaos UK over there," Rat responded reaching for the bag of Drum to roll himself one during the brief respite.

"Don't get too cozy, I wanna get this done soon. I'm planning on going out, and it takes forever to wash the ink off," Enio said reaching over the table to fumble with the tape deck narrowly missing the open bottle of ink with his hand.

"Like you give a shit about how your hands look. Also, how the hell am I gonna get comfortable if you keep jabbing me in the arm with a needle ya' fuck?"

Pamela was busy tonight, and the mere fact it was notable to him was not unnoticed by Rat. He had the very beginning of a suspicion he had a girlfriend here. Oh sure, nothing had been said, it was way too early for any "I love you crap" to come falling out of either of their mouths yet. Still, they seemed to be spending an awful lot of time together lately, even after she had seen him perform, which still shocked him a little. She had even said, "COOL!" when she'd seen his new tattoo, which Enio had not managed to fuck up despite the rest of the band assuming he would. Back home whatever girlfriend he'd had would have said some stupid shit about his future after seeing it. He was a high school dropout from a poor family, he didn't HAVE a future to worry about. Nobody cared about what someone like him did, weird to think that they WOULD care about what tattoos he had, which was part of the reason to get them in the first place.

Oh yeah, back "home," more just a place to come from, and then leave. Rat wasn't really from the city originally, but nothing was special about that at all. Nobody was really from here, like even if you were born in NYC, you most likely didn't live in the neighborhood you grew up in anymore. Especially not if you were part of the numerous undergrounds that flourished here. Kids came in as summer stock every year, some of them stuck, some of them were gone by the first snows. Either they ran back home satisfied that they had a little life adventure to tell their kids about, or became one of the unlucky few who snuffed it somehow.

Poor kids came in here squeaky clean and wonderful and ended up as wheat for the thresher. Some little shit comes to NYC to live because they visited once or twice from some fucked up little dink town like Binghamton, New York or some shit and thought it was cooler than their home, only to find themselves in the "All the Drugs You Could Ever Take Land!" amusement park that was the LES. Some of them just couldn't live with that sudden influx of freedom. Freedom can be deadly when administered intravenously, so consult your dealer or clergyman before taking. Not to mention, every once in a while, some of them would just get taken out by poor neighborhood nightmare shit where nobody could have expected that. Well, the perp, he expected it, but nobody else did. Cities are a great place for random violence, there are just so many random people on random trips that may not mesh well with the one you're on, no matter how many times the guy tries to make it mesh with a lead pipe to your head.

With nothing to do tonight Rat was going along to some party Cole and Jazz had found out about somehow.

Rat wasn't too sure how into it he was, this sounded like it would be basically a schmooze fest, which was exactly why Cole was into it. Cole was down to earth most of the time, but every once in a while, he seemed to dig being able to perceive himself as a rock star, as part of some imaginary in-crowd. Maybe it filled some hole in himself, who fucking knew really? Rat was in a band because he never thought he wouldn't be in a band; it was what he wanted to do since he was a little kid. When the other kids said astronaut, he said sing rock n roll. Who knew why all the people that were going to be there tonight had gotten into it? Rat only spoke for himself, and he only did that because nobody else did a good job of it and sometimes people asked.

Cole and Jazz had gone to whatever this was supposed to be early, so Rat found himself standing alone at the open door of the squat it was at. At least he thought it was a squat, it almost had to be, he couldn't believe a whole apartment building would put up with the noise that roiled and echoed down the steps. On the other hand, the place looked so nice, it put the whole idea of it being abandoned in doubt. On yet the other mutant third hand the two skinheads standing guard next to the open doorway made it definitely seem like more of a squat, again, he couldn't see neighbors putting up with this kind of shit. But whatever, Cole had told him the whole band was invited and last Rat checked, he was still the singer.

He steeled himself up for some kind of argument from the skins who seemed to be guarding the door when the one on the right recognized him, "Hey Rat! Good gig at the Lismar last month, spitting that beer on that Nazi was fuckin' cool!"

"Thanks, man," Rat grinned sheepishly, "asshole thought he and his buddy were gonna' jump me after. Fuckin' rude surprise when Shane ran back to his place and used his pittie to roust the fuckers from where they were hiding! Doubt they come back to the city again, we kicked the shit out of them after that."

Both skins laughed at that, Rat was pretty sure they would, Rat could see the SHARP patches on their bombers. These guys were anti-Nazi enough to advertise that they were Skinheads Against Racial Prejudice, and wanted you to know that. For good measure before stepping in Rat added, "Check us out next month, I think we're supposed to play with the Press."

"Cool man! See you there," the skin who'd seen them at the Lismar called out to Rat's retreating back as he made for the noise. Where's there's noise, there's booze, and Rat decided he needed a free drink off of someone for coming to this thing.

All the noise seemed to be happening way upstairs near the top of the building, time to put on his happy face and join the party after a lengthy hike upwards. Put in an appearance, swill some free booze, be sociable... You cut a mohawk, wear a leather jacket or a bomber, tattoo yourself up, just to inform the world you want to be outside of society, so what were you fucking doing now smart guy? Climbing at least three flights of steps to go be friendly like a gutter socialite. Shows how well that worked, maybe for your next trick you'll open a distillery to quit drinking.

It turned out to be exactly three flights past closed doors and silent halls before he got to a floor where all the doors were open and noise was coming forth in a wave of white noise from inside. He stepped through the first door and he could see why all the doors were open, the whole floor had been gutted and re-arranged to form some kind of ultra-studio apartment, almost like something down in Soho put in a former warehouse. Rat couldn't help but wonder how many people were living here, and if he couldn't become one of them, this place was nice. This looked spacious, a concept he missed, even if he hadn't realized it until right then. Even more, there was a set of steps leading up another flight, so this was taking up the entire top two floors of the building! He'd never admit it to whoever lived here but this place was swank.

Rat could see a keg and cups from where he was on the landing, somebody was showing off big time, he wondered who just got signed to a major label. Fuck it, share the wealth and all that, free beer hot on the hoof, all he had to do was find a quiet tucked away place to drink it after he got his hands on some. There were people hovering around the keg, there always were, people who wanted to meet people, or get completely shit faced before ending the night lying in their own puke, often they were the same people. So, he wouldn't have to come back soon, Rat grabbed two cups for himself.

"Hey Rat!" a voice called as he was filling up.

He looked up at Skeev, his face still bruised from the thumping he'd taken, but at least the marks were fading, "Oh hey man! Ain't seen you for a minute, how ya' been."

Skeev's face took on a haunted look for just a brief moment, you wouldn't have noticed it if you hadn't been gawking at what that walloping had done to him, "I'm fine man, fine, thinking about visiting my folks though, get out of the city for a bit. You wanna' tag along?"

"Not me man, I got gigs comin' up and bills to pay. Speaking of gigs, you seen Cole and Jazz anywhere?"

"I think they're up on the veranda sipping chardonnay," Skeev said, his face betraying nothing.

"You're shitting me!" Rat did a double-take and almost overfilled his beer.

"Only about the chardonnay, and even then, maybe not. They got every other kind of booze in here tonight. But go check it out man, they knocked the back half of the top floor off and put in a garden and shit up there. Got all these tables and chairs."

"Whose fucking place is this, and what in the hell are we celebrating by the way?" Rat had to know.

"Somebody just signed a new contract with a major I think, no idea who. I think he was punk in the A7 days and wants to stick it up everyone's asses how big he is now," Skeev shrugged.

"Well as long as the booze is free, I'm whore enough to take it up the ass tonight. Alright, beer's full, I'm gonna go check out this veranda of yours," Rat said cradling his beers for the climb up the steps.

"I'll be here. As long as the tap is still flowing, I'm drinking as much as I can. If it's free it's for me," Skeev grinned.

Rat muscled his way through the noisy throng, he stopped dead when he got to the top of the stairs. Laid out in front of him was something that was indeed a miracle to see in this part of the city. Most of the plants looked dead with the winter, but this looked for all the world like someone's backyard out in the burbs. Lawn chairs, open air, you could tell come summer this place would be full of plants. Somebody had some serious money to waste on a place like this. If Skeev's story had been correct about the guy throwing the party just signing a record deal, Rat was willing to bet hard on one solid fact, he didn't own this place. This place was owned by the record company to impress dipshits into signing away way too much of their royalties. Maybe they gave the "lucky stiff" the place rent-free for a year if he was blessed, and a nice advance which would explain the willingness to splurge on booze. But Rat'd lay down money the place wasn't actually theirs. There had been a land rush on bands comprised of former punkers in the Village playing dirty rock n roll, probably CBS had set this up as an "investment property" to wow their future slave laborers. He might find out in a minute, because one thing the garden of earthly delights contained was Jazz and Cole, and those two loved to gossip like housewives.

"Hey douchebags, "Rat said jovially as he slid up to them.

"You finally made it, took ya' long enough. Give me one of those beers," Cole responded hand reaching up from the lawn chair he was in.

"Fuck you, bright boy, these are mine. You ain't gimped, you know where the keg is."

"Some friend you are."

"You got a head start on me for drinking anyway, it'll do you good to walk off some of it," Rat replied with only a slight shrug to avoid spilling his beers.

Cole got up slowly from the chair, "I'll be right back, don't let anyone steal my chair."

As soon as he saw Cole head down the stairs Rat hopped into his vacated chair next to Jazz who was in its twin, "But I'm not just anyone, said I'm not just anyone, I got my devil machine and now I got his chair. Hey Jazz, how's it hanging."

"Long and to the right," the bassist said with a flat expression before swigging back a cup of something that looked more potent than beer.

"So, who is our magnanimous host here?"

"Not. A fucking. Clue," Jazz shrugged.

Rat gave him a long look saying that he should probably continue.

"I think someone from A.P.P.L.E., was invited and Cole got them to get us invited. Funny thing is, they ain't here. We were invited, by name, but I can't tell you who is hosting this, or who invited us, but since nobody seems inclined to kick us out, I'm staying," Jazz explained after another swallow of whatever he was drinking.

"Well, it's probably good they aren't here, more booze

for us, and less chance at us getting yelled at for embarrassing them by what we do once we've had that booze then," Rat chuckled. "So, the shit talking start yet?"

"Oh yeah, I've heard guys from three different bands all accuse people from other bands of being total poseurs. Funniest part, two of the guys I was standing with the one time were from the band the other called poseurs and didn't know who they were."

"Rollicking, oh well it's a be seen shitdig, and now we're being seen."

Cole came back a few minutes later, Rat didn't budge, forcing Cole to stand there. Rat didn't know too many people here for what was supposed to be an East Village party, so he wasn't feeling too driven to mingle. He often wondered where in the fuck all these people even came from, the show in the park, this, suddenly people just appeared. He at least made an effort to be friendly enough to people he saw at the bar, at shows, in the park, or just around, so you'd think he'd know people here, right? But fucked if every time he went to someone's big time party if it was a nice expensive one like this, fucked if didn't feel like it was taking place in a completely different city sometimes.

Cole broke off from them first tonight, which kind of worried Rat. Cole had issues with harder stuff in the past, he worried after the rhythm guitarist like a brother. They'd written a large portion of the band's material together, so in a way, they felt as close as real kin. As long as the two of them hung out, Cole kept himself pretty straight, beer didn't count, but a party like this... You had to know all kinds of shit was floating around out there tonight. Rat found himself hoping that if Cole did get into something that wasn't good for him that that something was coke. Coke he didn't seem to have an issue with, neither did Rat for that matter. Shit was too speedy, didn't feel to him like you were stoned at all, just felt like you were up for anything. If Rat was imbibing, he was looking to shut down his brain a bit, not kick it all into overdrive so it could find all kinds of new shit to worry him and annoy him with.

Finally, Jazz himself got up to get some more beer and didn't come back. Oddly, people came over to talk to Rat now that he was alone, say hey, talk shit about anyone in a band that wasn't there, etc. Rat was discovering from the conversation tonight that half the bands that played in the Lower East Side were fakes and druggies or fake druggies and all kinds of crimes according to the gossip from the other half of the bands. Rat thought it was funny, a year ago when he came here, these same stuck up shit heels wouldn't have given him the time of day. And a couple of years before that, nobody would have given them the time of day either. They were all former summer stock once, it flows in, it flows out, occasionally it leaves a starfish in the sand gasping for water.

Rat couldn't tell where the chant started from, he couldn't even tell why it got picked up so quickly. But from somewhere in the building, he started hearing something he couldn't make out, being repeated by numerous voices. Eventually, it began to fill the enclosed spaces as it got louder and clearer, "WHOSE PARK? OUR PARK!"

Almost like moths being drawn to a tiki torch at a picnic, the people around him started getting up. Curiosity was a bitch sometimes, because Rat was also on his feet and joining them despite putting no conscious effort into it. You couldn't help it, this was a party and if something sounded almost organized, you had to go see what the big hullabaloo was about. It was like a fight at a show, you weren't there for it, you didn't want to see it, but damned if you didn't watch it while it was happening. That same instinct drove him down the steps to go back inside, despite his better angels telling him to ignore it until it went away.

The irony, that most of the celebrants here had probably not been inside the park itself in years, was not lost on Rat even as he followed along.

People were already moving out the doors, Rat could hear clomping on the steps of boot-clad feet moving their way down. He caught Skeev and Cole who were by the keg, "What the fuck is this about?"

Skeev laughed drunkenly, "I don't know, some shit about 'taking back the park' or something. Cops have done some raids on the homeless in there lately, and I guess everyone's pissed, or at least pretending to be so they can tell everyone what a good person they are."

"Yeah, so now we're apparently all going to march down there in protest or something. It's gonna take a while for everyone to get out, so we're waiting here to keep the poor innocent beer safe from any rioters," Cole added.

Rat looked at the flow of people, he responded by quickly refilling his cups, "Might as well recharge my batteries while we wait. Grab Jazz if you see him go by."

Out on the street, the whole thing seemed even more ridiculous, and it hadn't sounded like a rocket scientist move inside. Rat hadn't even seen a cop on his way here tonight, tonight looked like a "leave the animals alone" night. Who in the hell were they supposed to be even "taking the park back" from? The fucking trees? Certainly not the homeless, this soft mob of wanna-be rebels would get wiped the fuck out if it came to a fight with the people who actually lived in the park. This crowd of purported rock stars had shit to lose, reasons to live, reasons to run when push came to shove. No way anybody in this crowd could manage that level of desperate abandon to get into a fight with the dear theoretical homeless people these people cared so much about. Cared so much about, but never even talked to.

But still, the chant went on, it was being led by someone up at the front that Rat couldn't see. In time with the chant, right at the start, he could see whoever the hell it was thrust their arm up. He was positive it was the same guy every time because while other arms would go up on occasion, the only one going up consistently had a yellow bandanna tied around the wrist. It had to be somebody from the bookstore was his thinking, some guy hopped up on revolutionary literature and most likely tonight he was also full of coke and booze wanting to jump-start "the People's rebellion." Funny how the "people" never included any of the poor fuckers in one-room apartments above them being kept up by this fucking racket. Guess you had to go to the right schools to be included in "the People."

Rat had started to hang further back, Skeev, Cole, and Jazz stayed with him, trusting his instincts on this. They had to practically yank Jazz by the jacket to get him back with them, he read a lot of those books himself and had gotten caught up in the fervor of the crowd. When he protested, Rat had snarled, "Look, if the cops show up in force, I ain't spending the night in a holding cell nursing a lump from a billy club. Thirty people ain't starting no revolution, but they can easily get that many in the back of a couple of vans."

As if on cue, a cop car turned, and made to pull on to the Avenue, somebody in one of those apartments must have called dispatch and they had someone handy. The cop wasn't a total idiot, he saw a street filled sidewalk to sidewalk with extras from a post-apocalypse movie and knew what needed doing in this situation. He did a quick count of who was in the car with him, came up with the number one, did a rough count of what was in front of him, came to at least a rough total, or stopped counting, before hitting the brakes and whipping it back on to St. Marks.

A ragged cheer over this triumph over the "man" went

up from the crowd.

"Fuck that, he's callin' this in," Skeev slurred, pretty correctly by Rat's estimation of how life worked.

"But man! He backed down! A battle won!" Jazz enthused.

"Enjoy it while you can, we ain't letting you get killed either," Cole replied.

The group was already filtering into the park, and now that they were there, Rat could see from where he was that they had no idea what to do next. Really, all they had done was spook a lone officer who had the sense to book out of there when he saw them crowding what he had expected to be a relatively empty street. Now that they were at the park, what now? What had been the real game plan? Already you could see the realization on some of the faces that they had just walked multiple blocks, getting increasingly sober, having left the booze back where they started. They now had to face themselves without chemical assistance, and none of them except the dreadlocked jackass in the green army jacket and the yellow bandanna seemed willing to do that for the revolution.

"I think it's early enough that the bar is open," Cole suggested.

"Yeah, let's get the fuck out of here before the paddy wagons show up. We can hear all about it as free men tomorrow," Rat agreed as they all broke into a light jog heading east.

Chapter 6

This was lame, like totally lame. This was crap you only saw in lame movies that Rat never watched. This was no way in hell are you going to mention it to your roommates lame. How in the hell did he get roped into something like this? Other than Pamela asking, of course, that was probably part of it. Him not thinking of going to a record store or a book store fast enough to stop him from agreeing to do it, that was probably also a contributing factor. God hating him was probably the real reason.

What could he say? He panicked, he'd never been asked to take a nice walk in Central Park before and had said yes before he could stop himself. He'd only ever been in Central Park a few times since he lived here, it was a long way to travel to try and convince yourself you weren't still trapped in a city. You had to stretch your imagination even then, it wasn't like you couldn't see the buildings, it wasn't like there weren't people everywhere, all of them holding on to their hopes of buying that home on Long Island or some Jersey suburb within an easy commute. All of them trying to convince themselves they were somewhere other than where they were, surrounded by concrete and steel and millions of other people stuck in this prison with them.

That wasn't who he really felt bad for in the trapped in the city equation around the park. Nope, that was reserved for the poor damned horses hooked up to carriages. An animal that size had no business spending its days in this city, people built it, people could suffer for it, that was just penance. It wasn't fair to some poor dumb brute who should be running free in the wild, they didn't deserve this. But there they were, innocent victims all around the park, strapped to some stupid medieval contrivance to haul assholes around the place while said assholes tried to get laid tonight by being "romantic." Like it was somehow universally recognized that staring at the ass-end of a horse evoked romance. And if some spore survived tonight's expensive union, then the city would just get more crowded by one. Better for everybody if a taxi just t-boned the fucking thing, killing everyone but the horse. Maybe free of its cruel master the beast would use this unexpected newfound freedom to make a break for the Holland tunnel and to the freedom of New Jersey's pastures. Or it would get shot in Jersey City and sold for meat, but at least its suffering would be over.

Rat was desperately trying to keep these thoughts to himself next to Pamela. This was the kind of shit you said in a bar if you wanted someone to fuck off, not next to a girl that for all intents and purposes you were dating. And a college girl too, she could do better than some scumbag like Rat and he knew it, no need to feed her lines for her future Dear Rat letter. Back home he'd been told by every father of every girl he'd ever dated that he was a drag on humanity and was just a tick on their precious daughter's back that their dad was just dying to pick off and burn. Who knew, maybe she had a dad whose ass she was totally burning by seeing Rat? Totally possible, but for right now it was working out, so best not to dig too deep, too deep was where the bodies were buried.

"Know why I asked you up here?" she poked him gently in the arm as they moved past the big statue of Simon Bolivar.

"No earthly clue," Rat confessed.

"So we could talk where it's quiet."

"We talk!"

"Yeah, but only at night when we're buzzed, or all hushed because of your roommates, or at the top of our lungs at a show. I mean a nice daytime casual conversation," she giggled a bit at that.

"Oh."

Pamela changed the subject suddenly, "Know what you said to make me want to hook up with you? Of course, you don't, we were both blotto and you were just talking without thinking too hard about it, no way you remember."

"Ummm well you were making that decision, so definitely not," Rat shrugged.

"You said you loved Dostoevsky," she replied.

"I do, but I don't get why it matters," Rat looked confused.

"It wasn't a punk rock answer. If you had said Camus, I would have thought The Cure. Kerouac well everybody does that. Kafka same thing because of the bug thing. Bukowski says you listen to Black Flag and Poison Idea. I probably would have thought you were talking shit. Nobody picks Dostoevsky, not unless they really did read it. So now I want to talk to that guy, without Enio yelling something obscene, or some fight breaking out, or anything but the sun and each other. You all right with that?" she turned to look at him carefully.

Rat thought about it for a moment, "Well, now that

you put it that way, I think my brain wouldn't mind stretching its legs a bit."

"Good," she replied putting her arm around his waist, Rat was surprised himself when he reciprocated by putting his arm around her shoulder.

"So, have you read Camus? If you have, I'm betting The Stranger right? That's everyone's favorite," she pressed as they worked their way deeper into the park.

"Not mine."

"OK, Mr. Torn Jeans Smarty Britches, you have another one? What's yours?" she giggled.

"The Plague."

"Bullshit! Nobody ever says The Plague," she poked him.

"I think I just did?"

"Ok, what do you like about it?"

Rat smiled, "There's redemption, there's duty, and when push comes to shove, bullshit is shown to be bullshit. Like bullshit is only capable of being bullshit when things are good, it's a luxury, but at some point, the rubber meets the road and it exposes itself for what it is, false hope and huckster crap."

"Is that stuff important to you? Because it sounded important," her eyes were kind of big like she'd been surprised by the force of his answer.

Rat shrugged, "Stuff like that should probably be important to everyone, I guess. Like no matter how bad you fucked up you can save yourself somehow, like if you take an oath, you stick it out, and if someone offers you pie in the sky, go checking the fucker's pantry, 'cause he's already got all the pies down here."

Rat didn't go into specifics, you didn't bounce around the system when you were a kid, and then on to squats, and panhandling, and all the other bullshit without making some moral compromises. He liked to think that was all they were, compromises, things you did to survive long enough so you could stop making compromises. Maybe he could do what Cottard couldn't pull off, redeem himself without going mad, maybe he could do it by having Dr. Rieux's conviction added to his own oaths now that he'd dug himself a little skyward out of the gutter.

"Hey, that's heavy conversation for a walk in the park," Rat said with a grin to lighten things, "let's talk about something without all that gravitas. Ya' like Vonnegut?"

"For a guy most people are afraid of when you're singing, there are depths to you, young man," Pamela smiled as she gave him a kiss on the cheek. Rat was just thankful he washed his face before he came out here, Enio had opened up a forty after running a block with it to the homestead.

They were both silent for a while as they walked, Rat watched the normal park denizens pass them by, the well-dressed romantics, the joggers, the pleasure bicyclists, the well-heeled and well dressed. This was a different New York from the one he lived in, these people feared his New York and viewed it with revulsion. While they were in the park, the two of them were surrounded by the beast that was going to devour his little New York in its jaws one day.

Tonight, they were playing a squat for New Year's Eve, Rat had only mentioned it in passing to Pamela. There were reasons he didn't want her there, good ones, at least as far as he was concerned. This was a newer squat, it still looked in pretty rough shape outside for starters. You just had no way of knowing what it was going to be like in there. It could be fine, it could be like any other place they played, it might even be nicer than CBs, hell the bathroom would be hard-pressed to be worse assuming there was one. But Rat had never even been in the place, he had no way of knowing that. The fact that needed facing was a squat gets opened up because nobody wants the place any fucking more. It had been sitting vacant long enough that for all anybody knew the guy whose name was on the lease was pushing up daisies in Florida now. A lot can go wrong with a building in a decade or so of sitting empty, a lot of times it smelled and looked pretty fucking gross as well. Rat didn't know why he thought it, but he just thought Pamela was above that shit, too good for it, and didn't need to watch him here. He didn't think he was too good for it, there wasn't much he thought of himself as being above.

Tonight, they were being driven to the gig, which Rat thought was a nice change of pace. The downside was, they were providing the sound system tonight. This meant dragging the stacks down the steps and to the gig itself, which would be horrific. They were planning on leaving early for this, not because the gig was all that far away, it was only a few blocks, but all of them figured they would be so exhausted from hauling their shit down the steps they'd need some time to rest, and maybe get a cup of coffee or something before they could even think about doing anything else.

Rat and Cole were manhandling the massive stack through the front door when they heard their ride, Bob from Police Tape, call out behind them, "Man, you guys got some fucking balls on you!"

They slowly lowered the stack onto the front step before Cole demanded, "What the fuck are you talking about?"

"Dude! We played there last week and it got raided! And you're bringing fucking stacks?"

Cole quickly squirmed past Rat and started running up the stairs yelling, "Stop! Stop right fucking there! Change of fucking plans!"

"Man, I pity him," Bob said leaning against the van.

"How you figure?"

"One more trip up them stairs, he's still gotta come down and help you with that thing."

For the entire trip between Shane's apartment building and the squat, Bob happily regaled them with tales of his harrowing escape from the police raid when they'd played the squat. This included jumping fences with their drums, which would explain his facial expression when he saw they were bringing stacks. Or he was blowing it out of proportion, you never could tell with any of the Police Tape guys, they lived to fuck with people. Even with just practice amps, God help them if the cops raided again. They all were stuck sitting there with worried expressions on their faces for the entire trip, which Rat secretly suspected was why Bob was so happy to give them a blow by blow like that. All of them except Shane that was, who was weirdly enough walking Humphrey to the gig, Humphrey didn't come to gigs normally, but Shane was bringing him to this one. It looked like Shane was a bit thrown off his usual, "I'm an old LES Skin nothing gets to me" game by this gig and the word of the raid.

Good, served him right for not checking it over more before signing them up for it.

When they pulled up to the squat itself, Rat froze up for just a second, like eyes wide, not wanting to get out of the fucking van. The cops had police barricades in front of the fucking place! There was a mobile station right down the street! They were sooooo going to jail tonight, there was no way around it!

"We, are fucked," Rat said flatly.

One of the squatters got up off of the front stoop where he was sitting and came over to the van. He was skinny, and frankly looked younger than they were, his face seemed buried in the hoodie he was wearing like the thing was swallowing him whole. You could see just enough to know that the kid didn't need a razor or shaving cream yet, but his long spiky hair probably desperately needed a shampooing in the worst way. He gave them a smile when the van's side door slid open, "Hey! Restraint! First ones to get here for tonight." Seeing their faces, he added, "Oh don't worry about the cops, it's New Year's Eve man, they all got called uptown! They will be occupied for the duration rousting drunks in Times Square."

Rat burst out laughing, "Holy shit he's right! Shows how much attention I pay to anything. Glad you pointed that out, I was about to shit. Hope they enjoy Dick Clark so we can have a good night of it."

A girl stood up next to the first squatter, she was new to town Rat could tell. Everything about her hadn't got that sheen that gear gets over time in the LES. Her clothes were fashion ripped, not ripped, ripped, and they were mostly clean to boot. You could still see the white on her plaid skirt instead of gray or brown, she smiled sweetly, "C'mon in, I'll show you guys where to set up."

They were beginning to unload and haul stuff in when Shane showed up with Humphrey. Rat noticed he had a big chain on the dog today, it looked like he intended to keep Humphrey with them for the whole night. It did Rat's heart good to know Shane was sweating this more than he was, Shane brought the dog to cover his ass, he was sure of it. As Rat hauled an amp head in, he noticed that Shane was tying the big dog off to a long-broken radiator near where the "stage" was set up. Rat tried to look on the bright side, it meant if the crowd didn't like them, they'd never attack them from that side of the stage. The downside was Humphrey was barking at everyone and everybody as they tried to set up.

A squat by nature smells pretty rough when it's first opened up. Not like anything specific, if it's been empty for too long, those unique and individual smells are gone. It smells like what cold and damp feel like. Like if moist had a smell that would be it. It smells of unchecked mold, it smells of dripping pipes saturating a wooden floorboard, it smells of rusty nails expanding and forcing themselves out of ancient wood. All of the manmade smells are gone, the food, the perfumes, the smells of recent manufacture that we expect out of life, all merged and then overpowered by rot, a stench that tells you the whole place is going to compost. It takes at least a few years of repairs until the smell is gone. Considering there were spots he could see the next story of the building through the ceiling, it was a miracle this place had power. He took a couple of passes around what was now being used as a show hall stomping heavily on the floor. Despite his numerous misgivings about the whole thing, it didn't seem to want to collapse and send them all into the basement, so that was a plus at least.

Nothing to do now but play the waiting game, just like going to war. Long periods of inactivity followed by a frenzy of chaos and destruction. One of the kids from the squat passed him an un-cracked 32 ouncer of Ballantine, so that was a bit of an all right to pass the time until people got in here. As long as he sipped at it, he'd be fine to play, and then he'd have something for when he dropped the microphone and climbed down off the little riser. Rat went and hunkered down next to Humphrey, but not too close, the poor dumb mutt was practically quaking with nervous tension at the situation. At this point he might bite him by accident, just lashing out at who was handy. That was only going to get worse as more people piled in, which they were already beginning to do. Glancing over at the pit bull, Rat scooted his butt a little further away from him. He was pretty sure he was outside of the range of the dog's lead, but he'd hate to be wrong if the fucking thing finally just completely spazzed out. He got along with Humphrey all right, but not well enough to trust him in this situation.

As Rat sat there partially covered by the shadows, people were starting to pour in, the place was beginning to fill up rapidly. To Rat's dismay, he could see the rest of the band out there talking to people. He could use someone to talk to right now himself, but not somebody who was going to be here just to watch the spectacle. He could use a bandmate, someone who had an ounce of an understanding as to the terror he was feeling at the moment. It must be the story of the raid still working on him, normally he wanted to be left alone to let everything build, and he couldn't be mad at anybody, they knew he usually wanted his privacy and were respecting it; they weren't fucking psychic to know that he wanted something else this time. There was a fine line on pre-show nerves, and he didn't want to cross it, get so worked up he froze up right when it was time to go. That had never happened to him, but you know, you read about things.

Rat took a deep, long chugging pull on the Ballantine, it was ice cold, they must be keeping some somewhere with an open window or something. Who knew, maybe they had some rattle trap old fridge tucked away somewhere in a back room somewhere, he'd have to remember to ask once they were done playing. Rat saw a couple of girls come in that he knew well. They'd come up here to the city around the same time he had, they'd sort of come with the band in a weird way, even if he didn't see them much these days. Just as he was about to get up to go over to say "Hi" to Jenna and Terry, he noticed who they were with. Christ, it was Sandy, his ex-girlfriend from back home! This was not what the fuck he needed, Sandy didn't even live anywhere NEAR here, what in the fuck was she doing here? It was a two-hour bus ride for her to get here, why on earth would she be here now?

Great, another shot of adrenaline to the old system, just what he needed here. They were playing in a barricaded squat that the cops had just raided with a spazzing pit bull right near the stage, and to top it all the fuck off, here was his ex-girlfriend.... cool. Rat chided himself and told himself to calm down. They hadn't broken up badly, they just stopped seeing each other, and neither of them made enough effort to change any of that. They hung out one last time, had incredible sex, and then neither of them had spoken to each other for more than a couple of minutes on the phone since then. It was the weirdest not a breakup, breakup in the history of relationships. If she hated him, he was about to fucking find out he guessed, because she'd be up front and center while he was trying to play, he was positive of that... Again, cool.

Whaddya do? You hunker your ass back in and wait, pray she doesn't talk to you, pray she doesn't notice you, pray she isn't here to see you specifically until it's go time. What the hell else could you do? Tell the guys, "Look sorry fellahs I gotta run, my ex is here and we had a really passive-aggressive breakup!" That'd fly swell. No, just put it somewhere in the swirling ball of emotions and let it fester there while he waited to go on. He was pretty sure they were going on first this time, the New York equivalent of headlining some nights, especially with these squat gigs. It was a weird quirk, the big halls, you never wanted to go on first, squatter gigs, often that was the best time to play, people showed up early and wanted to be gone before the cops took an interest. Get the crowd when they're at their most hyped and ready to blow, let the next band try and play for whatever energy they had left. Just stare at your feet, don't look up, and sip on your beer until it was time.

He slipped a Camel out of the pack he had on him and lit it. He'd splurged on a pack for the gig. It was tough to roll your own at these things, too much sweat, too much beer, some nights too much blood, and his hands always ended up shaking. Just wasn't feasible. Rat watched the smoke swirl around his knees and dissipate into the air, he began to find his spot, his own world, nothing else mattered, his mind was going blank. He had no idea how long he sat there, no idea how many cigarettes he smoked, barely even noticed when he capped off the Ballantine for later.

There was a nudge at his feet, he looked up to see Cole staring down at him, his guitar hanging from the strap on his shoulder. "You ready to go?"

Rat pulled himself upright, "Let's rip the lid off this fucking place."

Rat didn't look at anyone as he stalked from the shadows onto the little plywood riser. This was all too close; it was as if he somehow feared the crowd would swallow him whole if he acknowledged their presence. He somehow knew Sandy would be right there front and center in front of the "stage." It would be the perfect passive-aggressive thing to do, be supportive up close in the crowd just for the opportunity to see if she could throw him off by being there. Like this would be some sort of primal scream therapy to get out all the shit that hadn't worked in their relationship out for her every time they finished a song and she "cheered." He was OK with it now, it fed what he needed tonight to give the rest of the crowd what they came here for. Tonight was going to be one of those "tell your kids about it" nights. He was actually glad Pamela wasn't here, there were lines, she'd seen teetering on the edge, he didn't want her to see him taking a swan dive off the board.

The place exploded once they started playing. Once again Rat would never be able to remember playing the first song. His brain was far too poisoned with adrenaline to register what was happening anything more than act and react, they were mid-way through the second song before he noticed that the rest of the band was standing well back from him tonight. Rat had the fear tonight and they recognized the danger, the fear of everything and everyone, it was driving him on to new heights up there. He had a finite amount of time out here in front of this crowd, and he had to get all the terror that came with this life out of him, to just spill it out there on the stage, to puke it out with every lyric. The Pyramid crowd had been treated to the professional version of fear, this was an unruly mob so they could get pure terror. The crowd, he could see it in their eyes, they needed it to splash all over them, most of them were only a half-step away from homeless, they knew terror, it walked by their side all day every day. It was so rare that you could revel in it instead of cowering in the corner from it like a whipped cur. Give the animals what they want. This wasn't a normal night of adrenaline poisoning, this was sacrament, this was communion, this was cleansing baptism, the stink and loathing of the city pouring out as sweat and blood, even the lack of heat in the building couldn't hold it back now. They'd make their own heat.

The second song crashed to a sudden halt the way it was supposed to, the crowd erupted with applause. To Rat's panicked ears it didn't sound like enough, like they still felt they weren't getting their money's worth out of him. Fear was telling him, push the gas pedal until the whole thing blows, we may not get to where we're going but it'll be interesting to find out where we got to when it throws a piston at 120, now won't it? The applause faded, Humphrey's enraged barking grew louder than the crowd, and that just pissed him off, mangy ass fucking dog trying to steal their spotlight. Nobody was getting beer breaks until he had gotten the panic out of himself, go, go go!

By the fifth song, he realized the crowd had started

dragging in the barricades from outside. That was one thing he'd take away from tonight and remember clearly later, having to tell the crowd to stack the barricades closer to the door. They were starting to crowd into where the pit was, and he was concerned that someone would get hurt. That was Rat all over, his chest was bleeding from where he'd tore it open with his fingernails, sweat was dripping from his body despite the cold, and his biggest concern on earth was that someone might trip and fall over a barricade in the pit.

This was all meant to be good clean fun after all! Nobody gets hurt but the lead clown at this rodeo!

Frank couldn't believe it; O'Brien could sleep through any damned thing on earth it seemed. How the hell could you be on the streets on New Year's Eve and fucking snore? Maybe if his partner didn't insist on having the heater in their patrol car cranked all the time the coffee the older man drank constantly when he was awake would do more than make them have to take frequent bathroom breaks.

When Frank had first gotten his assignment, he'd been thrilled. He was a rookie learning the ropes here, and what better way to do that, to learn the ins and outs of the city than to do ride alongs with a twenty-year veteran like O'Brien. Ride alongs had quickly become Frank driving them aimlessly around the city unsure of what to do about anything until O'Brien snorted himself awake and demanded that they look for an open restaurant so he could "take a vicious piss." Frank failed to see how this equated to "keeping the peace" any further than this particular car. Even then, nobody could listen to O'Brien snore and declare that area as, "peaceful."

Tonight, they had the Village, which frankly was a relief. Dispatch more or less didn't want to hear back from them at all unless it was legit serious, and even then, only if they had to call for the meat wagon. The cells were going to be full tonight from the Times Square mess, and nobody needed Frank and O'Brien snatching up anybody for jaywalking or some other minor offense. Half the time Frank had no idea which offenses he should even bother with if they wanted to make any kind of numbers on the night, O'Brien wasn't awake often enough to tell him.

Frank tapped on the brake; he might as well see what was happening in the park tonight. Not that he could do much about it, but it never hurt to see which way the wind was blowing, and around here the wind always blew out of the park, but where it might lead was open to interpretation. He stopped the car in a space between the crosswalk so he could get a good solid look right into the central hub of the place, down the well-lit section that led from directly across from St. Marks Place.

Even from where he was Frank could clearly see a crowd gathered in the center of the park. He wondered for a moment if he should shove the corpulent form of his partner to get his opinion. Just then O'Brien issued a loud snort and shifted away from him to put his face on the glass, probably overheated, which wouldn't have been a problem if the fat man ever let Frank turn the damned heater down to anything short of baking.

Frank kept an eye on what the crowd was doing. Normally just at the sight of the car, quite a few of the rodents would run for their holes, but not tonight. They probably knew as well as he did that nobody was going in the back of that car tonight for anything short of a murder. The cells were reserved for those people uptown who were intent on ruining the shiny happy face New York City put on for the world every January 31st.

It looked like someone running an ad hoc soup kitchen tonight. Normally he and his partner might be tempted to roust the whole thing, just to see if they could get an organizer to let his big fat mouth write out an invite to a holding cell. It was without a permit he was almost positive as to that. It looked like those weirdos he'd been seeing around, all of them wearing yellow bandannas. Rumor around the station house was it was another hippy love cult, like the world didn't have enough of those already. Sooner rather than later he was sure that they'd get them for having something to do with some kind of drug ring, they always ended up that way, but it wasn't going to be tonight. Even if they popped out needles right now in front of him, his partner would personally kick his ass for waking him up for that.

Frank trained his eyes towards where the tables were set up. Might as well get a good look at the ring leaders, that way he'd know who to arrest when he had the time and inclination to do it. His gaze tunneled in on the man behind the big tureen they had on a folding table. At first glance you couldn't even tell why he drew your eyes, he was just another greasy, dirty, longhair in a part of the city that was polluted with them. The only thing he looked a threat to was an all you could eat Indian buffet, the guy looked half-starved himself as he handed out bowls of soup, which Frank found kind of ironic.

As Frank studied the figure it dawned on him what had drawn him in. Even from this distance, even with the light, the guy's eyes gleamed with something approaching religious fervor. Frank noted, it could also be crack, but that crowd seemed more of a downer crowd than an upper one from how they were dressed. He had never believed you could say someone was evil by just their eyes but looking across that distance now... Glancing over the guy's closest associates behind the table, their eyes seemed dull, not just in comparison to the fiery orbs that bulged out of their compatriot's face, but even just compared to the normal denizens of the Village. Not his, not the leader, his eyes twinkled with intent so strongly Frank had to keep from cringing away even in the safety of his squad car.

He didn't even consciously think to do it when he put the car back in drive. If he wasn't arresting it, he didn't need to be dealing with that level of fucked up tonight. A little while later when he turned the car down 8th street, he was surprised to be releasing a long breath he had been holding with obvious relief. Frank made a note, he had to stop letting this city get to him or he'd burn out before he was thirty.

Chapter 7

A few weeks later Rat and Cole were heading to the Aztec, payday had been kind, as had tips during the week from arty types who wanted to show off their success by impressing a lowly messenger. To celebrate his largess, they were going to meet Pamela here. The squat show had gone well, and now they were planning a guerrilla gig at the park's bandshell to show support for the park dwellers in their fight against the city. Everybody had done one by this point, frankly at this point if they didn't do one people would talk. Also, on the horizon, they'd be going into the studio to record their first e.p. to follow up the demo tape they were currently selling at shows. Life was good at this exact moment in Rat's very small portion of the world.

It would be almost perfect if weird shit would stop happening around the Lower East Side. Last week a homeless guy Rat had talked to whenever he saw him hanging around on a corner took a flying run into traffic. That smelled weird to Rat, he knew the guy, and it just seemed off to him. First off, the guy had been on the street since Reagan took office, so it wasn't like he hadn't survived a lot of shit already without going off his nut. The VA cut him off after Nam saying they couldn't treat what was eating at him, despite the fact that the war hadn't left him fit for any job. A guy is on the streets that long and lives, he's way past the kind of depression that makes you jump off or in front of something.

Doesn't mean the guy ain't depressed, but it loses that immediate throb that pushes you off the ledge. You survive that long, Rat guessed for Tommy it was like he was back in Nam, you just worried about survival and that was all you had the time for. You didn't have that part of you turned on that you needed to get wound up, you didn't have that kind of thinking time to wonder if it was all worth it, your physical self was yelling louder than your mental one. The streets made you feral. Secondly, the guy never had psychotic breaks, hallucinations any of those types of mental problems. He understood reality fine, he might not have liked it much, but he understood it perfectly. Rat had spent a little time in Tommy's shoes at different points, he understood Tommy, at least he'd thought he had before the flying car leap. Try as he liked he couldn't rationalize Tommy's suicide with the Tommy he knew.

And that wasn't even the least probable part. No, what really threw Rat off was that Tommy was running right for a cop car with a knife in his hand when the taxi came out of nowhere and sent him ass over tin cups. Rat had never heard Tommy say much of a damned thing about the cops one way or the other. They had their job, and as long as they didn't interfere with Tommy's, which was trying to survive, he was all live and let live. Tommy wasn't a "Kill the pigs" kind of guy. So, what in the fuck had gotten into the guy to turn him into one? Rat hadn't seen a bit of an indication of anything wrong with him when he gave him a smoke just the day before his death, he was the same old

Tommy. "Can I bum a smoke, and you can have a dirty joke as payment." The next day he's a rabid, wanna-be cop killer suiciding out by playing in traffic? Because, even if that cab hadn't hit him, the cop surely would have shot him deader than disco. That takes some deep emotions and hatred....and it just didn't feel right.

Tonight's police mood looked bad already, Rat could see paddy wagons around the park, which didn't bode well for anybody's night. Maybe the incident with Tommy had pissed them off, maybe it was just time for one of their random bed checks, but this was a roust. The cops sold this in the press as saying they were protecting the homeless, getting out "bad elements that prey on them." Like any of these poor tent living fuckers had anything worth taking and weren't wise to most shit that you could try to pull on them, like the cops were the good guys here. What this really was, was an intimidation technique, keep 'em afraid, keep 'em scared. The last thing these poor fuckers had was their freedom, this was to let them know that the powers that be could reach down even here and take even that. This was to encourage them to flee.

Thing was, the cops had played this hand too often, it didn't work anymore. They wouldn't find anything they could hold anyone for, except maybe a dealer or two who was too stupid to get the fuck out of the park when he saw them pulling up. Yeah, they'd break some shit, make some threatening noises, but if everyone kept their cool, they'd fuck off in an hour or two. Just as long as everyone kept their cool. Which was not something that was written in stone or even in the mud with a stick. This behavior had created a lot of resentment, and it was always close to boiling over, so shit could go south quickly. That was the reason why half the cops had their mourning stripes over their badge numbers when they went in there, don't want to have to talk about excessive force to internal affairs, do we?

And you won't have to if nobody gets your badge number, most cops looked the same anyway. Saying it was a fat guy with a big mustache didn't narrow shit down. Thing was, any idiot could see that was just what the cops were hoping for. Give 'em any excuse to call in the riot squad and clear the whole fucking thing in one night and be done with it, hopefully, as per usual, nobody was dumb enough to take the bait.

Cole and Rat were skirting the park, keeping to the shadows and definitely minding their own business here. A small crowd of gawkers was hovering in the lit areas around the park, but Rat couldn't help but notice they weren't so interested in protecting the park now that there looked like there'd be heat tonight. When the police came, the world developed a lot of innocent bystanders. Rat spotted one of the guys wearing one of those bandannas again, a skinny looking crusty, his hair tangling in knotted dreads over his dirty black denim jacket. Alarm bells went off in Rat's head. "Hold on man," he said to Cole stopping suddenly, "let's cross over."

"You're not going to fuck with the cops, are you? You can't be dumb enough ta......"

"See that fucker with the bandanna? I think those are those Left Eye fucks, that's how they're marking themselves. I just wanna make sure he doesn't start any shit. I'm pretty sure it was one of those nimrods that started that crap at that party."

Cole looked at him sideways, "Why bother, so what if he gets his ass kicked by the cops?"

"Cole, look at those cops out there man, they'd love to bust some heads tonight, you think they're just gonna stop with the dumb ass? Keep walking if you want, but I'm gonna go check."

Rat hustled across the street without another word, he didn't even stop to see if Cole was following him.

Something just told him, the guy over in the park was looking to start shit out here tonight. Rat could see the guy was scanning the crowd, shifting from one foot to another like he was waiting for his moment. Almost as if on cue to Rat thinking it the guy reached into his vest and drew out a twelve-ounce beer bottle. Just the perfect throwing size. Rat saw the guy heft it a couple of times by the neck, and then begin to draw back. Rat picked up speed, reaching out with his hand to knock it out of the guy's loose grip an instant before he could throw it.

The air was filled with the sound of broken glass, and the stench of stale piss. The idiot was going to throw a bottle full of piss at the cops!

"What the fuck man? How dare you interrupt my work? My mission!" the freak whirled snarling at Rat. Rat saw a flash of something gleaming in the street light in the guy's other hand as he turned. Rat didn't even hesitate for a moment but came crashing in slamming his elbow directly into the weirdo's face while stomping on his knee simultaneously.

Later, when he thought about it, he would thank God that the elbow landed first and knocked the guy silly because Rat was sure he heard something crack in the freak's knee. If the asshole had started screaming bloody murder about it that would have been unwanted attention. Rat could see what was in his hand a moment before. The knife lay there on the sidewalk glinting at him. He drove his foot into the gut of the prone figure before stepping over him to kick the knife across the street where it skidded under a parked car.

He heard another grunt behind him, when he turned it was to see Cole driving his Doc into the guy again hard enough that it lifted him off the ground a bit. Cole saw him looking and grinned sheepishly, "Sorry I got here a little late."

"Fuck it, share the wealth, enjoy yourself, it didn't hurt me none. Let's go hit the Aztec."

Tonight was going to be weird, no doubt about it, life was weird, the lower east side was weirder than normal lately, so more weird than even that. The band was doing something they'd never done before, play live on the radio. Apparently, somebody at WNYU had a hell of a sense of humor and let punk bands actually play over the air. Rat thought Shane had got them the gig, he wasn't sure, Cole just showed up one day all happy saying, "Dude we're gonna be on the radio!" With an intro like that, you don't question it you just let yourself float along with the excitement of the whole thing.

Rat wasn't totally blasé about it as a concept himself, way back when, before he found other people like himself, he knew they had to exist out there because of the radio. He used to hang wires from his cheap stereo back at home so he could pick up the local college station and get in their punk shows. He'd set his tape recorder in motion taping everything when it was a really good show, instant compilation for later listening. He'd wander around the sticks where he lived with a little hand-held tape deck, it would be an insult to boom boxes to call it one, cranked as loud as he could get it to grind out, up so loud that it crackled with distortion and the batteries died twice as fast. It was his way of telling all the pieces of shit he grew up around, "I am not one of you anymore! I don't think I ever was! This music is a warning! Fuck off!" It didn't work as well as he wanted, but at least it drowned out the "HEY FAGGOT" s being shouted out passing car windows, so that was something at least.

As he stood there looking up at the apartment building, he had just watched a man plummet from not very long ago, waiting for Ralph to finish up his business, he found that he was excited about the prospect of going on the air. Here he was, someone who had been the lowest of the low his whole life, but it was going to be his ass on the radio tonight. He'd be more excited if he wasn't holding a leash with a shitting dog on the other end of it. Still, thinking about tonight was a thought that started the day off right, in a city that had so many thoughts that could start it off wrong.

He saw Skeev hustling up Avenue D, automatically he waved to him. Skeev waved back, and yelled loud enough to be heard over traffic, "I WANNA TALK TO YOUZE GUYS! I'LL MEET YOU AT YOUR PLACE!"

Rather than risk his throat yelling back Rat gave him a thumbs up and watched him scuttle off.

As promised, Skeev was on Rat's stoop when he got back. Rat came up as fast as he could since he was practically dragging Ralph after him. The normal crowd had been on the corner, and Ralph was more than annoyed at being deprived his due of attention. Skeev was bouncing back and forth trying to keep warm while smoking a cigarette as he waiting. "Why the hell didnt'cha knock ya dumb ass?" Rat demanded as he fumbled to get his keys out on this cold morning.

"Aww shit, you're the only one that ever answers the damned door Rat, you know that. Hey Ralphy! You have a good shit?" Skeev replied, before bending down to rub Ralph's big gator-shaped head.

"Well come the fuck in and warm up," Rat grunted as he finally got the door open. Skeev followed him down the almost pitch-black hall to their personal steel door huffing on his hands as he went. Rat unlocked the interior door and let them through that. As expected, none of his roommates had moved more than it took to get coffee, except for Enio, who hadn't moved at all since he was still snoring under his ratty ancient blankets.

"So, what the fuck you have to say that's so important?" Rat demanded unhooking Ralph from his leash and going to get some coffee of his own.

Skeev shuffled his feet a bit, he let out a big gusting sigh before he blurted out in a rush, "Fuck it, I guess I should just spit it out, Jenna OD'ed last night, they found her this morning."

Rat heard his roommates let out various gasps and "no way" s which erupted around the room loud enough that Enio let out a muffled, "Shut the fuck up you cunts, I'm sleeping." Rat didn't say anything, he carefully put the coffee carafe back in its holder, his hand moved in slow motion, he was holding the handle so tightly in his hand he almost wondered if he'd break the cheap plastic. Once the glass clicked into its in place, with equal care he set down his coffee mug.

At last, he turned to look at Skeev, his expression flat but his eyes flashing dangerously, "What happened?"

"Don't know man, all I know is they found her at the 12th street squat upstairs, off to the side of that big open area they got. Ain't heard shit about a note, or any hot batches around lately. What I heard was that she OD'ed. I know you guys were close with her, figured I should let you know ASAP. I didn't want you hearing any bullshit through the rumor mill," Skeev replied, his face was awash with misery, and Rat figured that he looked sincere about it. Whether that was for the loss of Jenna or the discomfort of having to deliver that kind of news, Rat had no idea. Then again, it was a small community, there were only so many people like them on this earth, when one of them died like this their whole world shrank in a way the rest of the world couldn't understand.

Rat's face was tight with suppressed emotion, "I'm going out," he said quietly and evenly, every syllable measured and exact.

Jazz protested, "But dude, we got that gig to-"

Rat cut him off, already opening the door, "I'll be back in time, I will not hurt the band."

"Don't do anything stupid," Cole said, but not fast enough, he ended up saying it to a slamming metal door.

Rat had no idea where his long strides were taking him as the sidewalk flowed by. He was concentrating on his footsteps and where he stepped, it was something to focus on in a world full of endless sights and sounds. He really didn't care where he was going at this point, he just knew he wasn't fit to be around anyone he cared about. He was too pissed off, that was how you said things you couldn't take back, you just let your emotions run the show and they'd find words you'd never say otherwise. Half the time you wouldn't mean them even "deep down inside," it was no Freudian slip thing brought on by a lack of control, you just hurt, and wanted to share that feeling about a bit. Better to get away and to take his pain with him.

Rat turned south on C, he could walk a long way that way and not have to deal with all the chaos of uptown which he didn't need right now, and every block would get him further and further away from anyone catching him and wanting to talk. He knew himself and how long he would be toxic to the rest of the world, if he kept going south with a turn on Houston and another turn south, he'd hit Chinatown roughly around when he'd run out of steam. Rat figured he'd probably be hungry by then. That sounded cynical and cold, he knew it would if he had to tell anyone, but right now he was desperately trying to keep himself as tightly wound as possible. He didn't want to unwind in front of, or worse, on anyone. That was the fucking problem with the city, sometimes you need to howl at the moon, but you damned well couldn't do it here if you didn't want the opportunity to serenade the docs at Bellevue with your heartfelt anguish.

It had been a pack of them that had come here to the city originally, including Jenna and Terry. All of them wanting to shake the dust of their small towns and small cities off, or more likely to flee the nightmares that had made them abandon society in the first place. The shows for the band had gotten bigger, they were coming here to play more often anyway, and one day it seemed stupid to be doing all that driving. You could just live here and have a real shot of going somewhere as a musician, or you could stay out there and be a big local band and see everything you hated most up close and personal every day of your life. A couple of shifts in band personnel to replace those members who couldn't or wouldn't leave, and here they were. Rat, to this day, had no idea how Jenna and Terry figured in that move, but they had. Somehow Jenna ended up dating a guy from a band here, and next thing anyone knew they took half the town's punk scene and transported it to New York City.

Jenna was the first one the city had managed to eat since then.

Probably not the last.

But your first time always hurts.

Funny thing was, Jenna and Terry came from an even more hick-ass place than the band did. When they'd first shown up back home, they took one look at the local scene and decreed Restraint and Control the only real punk band in town. They also set about plotting how to sleep with them. Rat had his eyes set on Jenna at the time, but through a series of wacky mix-ups she ended up dating Jazz for a while, and somehow Rat ended up accidentally fucking Terry. Repeatedly. Any time Rat was stoned, or single for too long, he would somehow come out of his funk to see Terry sleeping next to him nude. Life could be weird like that, they never even really dated, they were more pals than anything. Pals that would occasionally get stark naked and play electric socket together for no other reason than it was fun and they were lonely.

A truism in life is that when you were minding your own business, really trying to stay in your own world because at this time in your life it happens to be a peaceful placid place, there was always an asshole talking shit to you, breaking into your quiet solitude and catching you flat-footed and unable to react. As Rat stalked down the street with fury in his heart just hoping for a confrontation, nobody was coming anywhere near him. It was like the animals in this city could smell that there was a predator on the wind. Someone so close to the edge that the animal that walked amongst them was just BEGGING you to say some shit so it could unleash whatever hurt it was forcing down right onto your face. A more dangerous beast than you, one that pleaded with you to give it a reason to bloody its claws on your tender flesh. No, better to pull up your collar and hide on your stoops until the danger passed.

People just gave you a wide berth on days like that, pussies.

Rat knew Jazz would be upset, for better reason than Rat had, as far as Rat knew it was the first time in his life that Jazz had ever really had any proper loss. It wouldn't be the same for him though, it would be a shock pain that would deaden quickly as it numbed up. They had broken up ages ago, they had made their peace with each other and barely even talked now. For Rat, Jenna had become his little sister. His little sister that he had failed to protect from this evil fucking place and all the filthy fucking needles out there just hunting for your arm, to wound you, to bring you down, to kill you, all the shots in the night that knew the fastest path to your soul and kept that secret knowledge, that inherent truth that if they took your soul first, your body would eventually follow along. Rat had failed, and now Jenna was stone cold, probably in the morgue already. When her parents demanded in the cold air of their hicktown house, "Wasn't someone looking out for her?" the answer would echo back to them, "Obviously fucking not, don't you think?"

Fucking bullshit romantic crap, that's what it boiled down to, her and her junkie boyfriend Dirty playing Sid and Nancy. That useless piece of shit probably hadn't properly killed her by injecting her, but he killed her anyway. He was the one who got her on to that shit. Did she have some personal culpability? Yeah, yeah, whatever. Some kid from some boondock fuckhead little town, like she had any idea what that shit could do to you, like she had watched that movie play out over and over like you do here. She hadn't gotten to smell a long-time junkie panhandling when she'd romantically pictured a junkie in her head and vowed to be one. Of course, the exotic big city nature of being a junkie was probably part of the appeal, Thunders and Dee Dee were still alive, and they were glamorous with their Chinese ditch. Dirty went on and on about how much he loved her, just fucking empty words, real love is saying, "You don't want any of this." Even better love would have been quitting himself. He didn't love her, he loved getting better with someone he could fuck while he was on his run, assuming he was in any shape to do it once he found a vein.

There was no fixing it now, no saving anything from the ashes, no finding a way to send her back home before this happened so she could get clean. It was all over but the funeral, and Rat wasn't going to any funerals out of respect to the parents. People who would finally get to see the great big city, so they could claim the body of their little girl. That was if they even bothered, she didn't talk about her parents, but she'd looked at the city and said it looked better than home. To her it wasn't a cesspool to sink into, it had been a safe haven to flee to. So maybe they'd just slap their hands together on a job well done being rid of her. If they didn't come hopefully some trustworthy local might put together a whip-round for a plot, stranger things had happened. More likely Jenna was heading to a pauper's grave for a punker girl.

It was the bet you made with the city, that this time it wouldn't be you or any of your friends on stainless steel in a cold, clean, city-owned basement. At least not your close friends, buddies don't count. Buddies you see on street corners, or in bars, or at shows, but they weren't your friends. They were just people you were friendly with. Half the time you didn't even remember their name, and when you did, that rest of the time the name you remembered wasn't their birth name. You made that bet that somehow despite everything you saw in the papers, everything you saw on your own damned block, you could at least keep your own safe and clean. Rat was suffering from the knowledge that for every time you won that bet, someone out there had just lost this hand, sooner or later it would have to be you in the barrel.

Rat made it a point of crossing over and heading down 1st Avenue, he absolutely did not want to risk passing in front of CB's. Who knew who in the hell might be hanging about? That was the whole point, wasn't it? To spend some time on his own to calm down? By the time he made it to Delancey, he could already smell Chinatown. Grease, it reeked of cooking grease, the air in this whole part of town felt like the air inside of a short-order kitchen even in winter, thick with animal fats burnt off and left to waft into the air year in and year out.

It got into everything, and everywhere, all of these little restaurants since god only knew when they'd first opened, frying up wok full after wok full of food, it just permeated the world. Soon Rat was looking at the main perpetrator in the windows he passed, the king of greasy food, duck. They just hung there in the restaurant windows like wartime photos of some horrific atrocity perpetrated by Nazi chickens on their hated rivals. The smell did one other thing, it made him hungry despite any residual rage. Rat made it a point of looking for some kind of hole-in-the-wall place, they usually had the best food anyway and cheap. Most importantly, no racks of dead ducks roasting after being found guilty as witches. All Rat was interested in was vegetable fried rice anyway, he didn't eat dead animals, he just mourned dead friends.

Rat supposed he felt better as he walked home, he didn't feel great, but maybe he could stand to be around other people again. If he pulled into himself, he'd get through, and that was the main thing, getting through. It wasn't like he had a choice here, Jenna was dead, not him. Rat still had shit to do whether he wanted to or not, life didn't give a shit, the world didn't come with a pause button for moments of sorrow. He didn't want to die right now, if you had asked him yesterday except for some worries about those bandanna freaks, he'd have said the world was turning in his direction. The band was doing alright, he had what was still not officially a girlfriend, but he knew was kind of a girlfriend. People depended on him to be dependable, and that meant you picked yourself up, you moved forward.

He knew without formulating the words in his head who he wanted to see right now. Pamela wouldn't give a shit if he started bawling when he told her what happened. Girls thought that shit humanized you, not that it made you a pussy, which is what your guy friends would usually say, or at least their eyes would tell you they thought it. They wouldn't be able to help themselves, that was just part of being a guy, weakness belonged to dying animals, in other words, the weak. Girls thought the exact opposite, they wanted you to have a sensitive side, as long as you were willing to deck a guy that got up in their face that was. But behind closed doors, tears and poetry rounded their image of you out some. Even if it didn't, maybe you just had to be who you were?

Maybe after he got back, he'd scrounge up enough change to call her pager, spend the rest of the day before having to play tonight with her. Hopefully, they could even slide up to her dorm room, he really didn't want to put up with anyone's shit at home, especially Enio who just rolled with everything, and if anything laughed about it. Rat could never decide, was the guy fucking dim, or did he play dim as a defense mechanism. Of course, as much as Enio drank, who could tell the fucking difference anyway? He probably didn't know himself anymore and was just as lost behind that grinning facade as everyone else was behind their own.

This part of the Village didn't have much traffic, which suited him fine. St. Marks was the real life's blood of the neighborhood, once you got away from that going south at least, you could be as by yourself as much as it was possible in a city of millions of souls crowding each other out of their own humanity. The question still loomed over him, what was he going to do about all of this? Rat wasn't bringing Jenna back from the dead, but what about everything else? Should he become extra protective of his friends? Should he go hunt Terry down just to make sure she was all right? That was some dangerous fucking ground right there, if Terry was even open to being consoled there was usually only one way, she wanted to be made to feel better, and he was dating someone now. That was major no-go territory. Problem with that was she didn't take no very often, and Rat knew he was a weak-willed little weasel when it came to sex, he had a hard time separating his penis from the equation when it came to feminine approval and touch. Maybe he should just invite her over to the homestead to hang out, and if she got like that, well hell, Cole should be home and he was single, maybe they'd hit it off this time. He'd personally break every single one of Enio's fingers if he touched her.

Rat was so completely lost in thought he hadn't even realized how close he'd gotten to 7th street until it finally dawned on him that there were more people who needed to get the fuck out of his way as he went. Rat pulled his head up to pay more attention, and that's when he saw him. Fucking Dirty was sitting on a bench right inside the park. Even worse the bastard had some chippy of a girl, some out of towner most likely, he was "pouring his heart out" to with her arm around him. Fuckin' Jenna was barely fucking cold and the SOB was looking to make time off her death. Rat power walked the distance, he didn't want to run, running draws attention, he didn't want to be observed.

Dirty saw him a few feet before Rat closed in and stood up, "Rat, ain't it fucking horrible man? You heard ri-"

He didn't finish that thought because Rat cold-cocked him where he stood. Dirty went back, his body bounced off the bench, causing the girl to pull her forty out of the way before he landed in a heap at Rat's feet. Rat stood over him, glaring down at Dirty who was moaning and holding his hand to his face. Already blood was soaking around his fingers from Rat breaking his nose. Rat's hands clenched and unclenched as he glared at him, he didn't even notice his own blood from where he'd caught one of Dirty's teeth on a knuckle. The girl had taken her beer and split, she had come to the city for a party not to get in the middle of a fight, good for her. Sharing a bottle with Dirty was a good way to catch something. But people WERE coming over, Rat already knew that he needed to leave.

"She's dead because of you, asshole!" Rat snarled, "She wanted to make you happy, she wanted to be part of something that was so fucking important to you. Too bad the only thing you give a shit about is dope. She sacrificed herself to the altar of making you happy, just so she could be with you, you piece of shit. Do the fucking world a favor, why don't you fucking join her?!"

Rat turned and began to hurry off. He looked back to see someone he only vaguely recognized helping Dirty to his feet. He couldn't help but notice that the hand that was pulling Dirty up had a yellow bandanna around it. Fuck 'em, Dirty deserved to be mind fucked.

Chapter 8

Rat lay next to Pamela in her dorm room. It was just the two of them and the heat was up so they just lay nude next to one another letting the movement of the air cool their sweat. Sex hadn't made anything go away so it was gone for good and would never torment him again, but it provided a respite. A small island of happiness in what was a sea of misery that had threatened to roll over the ship of Rat's life and drag him under. Right here, right now, lying next to Pamela in her college dorm was one of the few islands he felt he could hunker down on and wait the storm out. This had been the better call, if he had gone to check on Terry, it might have ended up like this, but it wouldn't have felt safe and warm, it wouldn't have felt like he belonged exactly where he was. The second it had ended it would have stunk of guilt and regret. Pamela had held him, dried his tears, and then made him not want to cry anymore, Terry just would have wanted him to fuck her own tears away. She had a right to feel like that, just like Rat had a right to be here instead, he needed to remember that.

"Promise me something," Pamela said softly her finger toying with the few hairs that had sprouted on Rat's chest.

"Depends, don't it?"

"Don't ever do that shit yourself."

Rat was quiet for a second before replying with a rueful chuckle, "You shittin' me? Asking me that after it just graveyarded a friend?"

"You'd be surprised, people feel guilty that they lived, or they want to see what the big deal is, a lot of people who lose a loved one to that shit end up dying the same way," she replied, she was looking at him intently her eyes focused on his own.

"Well, you don't have to worry about me. I already did my time digging a China White ditch, swore it off," he said in what he thought was a humored voice, instead of dead serious one.

"Knowing you had problems with it is supposed to make me feel better how? Exactly?"

"If it helps, you should know I won't go near it. Won't be in the room when it's being done, nothing. It's not even the death rate of it that has me not wanting to touch it. It's what that existence is like, it wipes out anything you want to do, it takes you away, right away from you and who you are. I got too much shit I want to get done with my life, I got the band, I got my poetry... I won't have either if I start chasing any dragons, will I? Just another lump on someone's couch who can barely achieve making it to the train to peddle their ass for money for their next fix. Fuck that, I got plans with my life," he replied emphatically.

She smiled a bit, "Am I one of those plans?"

Rat looked down at her, his eyes looked panicked by what he was about to ask, because he was afraid of her answer, "Do you want to be?"

She put her head down on his chest with a little

snuggling motion, as she rubbed her hair across it, "Yes, I think I kind of would."

He ran his fingers through her hair and replied, "Well, only if it works for you, I don't like to impose on people."

They stood out in front of the building that housed the radio station together. Rat had asked Pamela to stay over tonight, he really didn't want to be alone after they played. Since it was easier, she was just going to sit in and watch them play. Now they just needed the rest of the band to show up. It felt weird standing outside with actual personal business inside of a building like this. He normally made deliveries in places like this, a servant coming in through service doors to do his tasks for his betters. His own life, where he existed was so far under their radar it might have been on a completely different planet. Not tonight, tonight he was the talent to be lauded and celebrated for his appearance within these walls. Weird.

He appreciated that the band had let him go earlier. When he checked in at the place Rat had found them all moping. Skeev was long gone, off to spread the glad tidings elsewhere. Rat had just declared that he'd be no good tonight if he just sat around and moped along with them, as tempting or as understandable as it was. Jazz, bless him, had agreed with him and told him to get the fuck out. As soon as they were done tonight Jazz was going over to Eve's himself to lose himself in someone else the same way Rat had done, so there were no judgments. If Jenna's ex-boyfriend gave his blessings on this, Rat figured it must be the right thing to do here. After Jazz had said that, Cole sure as fuck wasn't going to argue it, Cole offered to walk the dog instead.

It was Cole and Shane who rounded the corner first. They were just carrying their guitars; all the rest of the gear had been set up at the studio yesterday. Shane didn't look fazed one bit, but why should he? He barely knew Jenna at all, actually now that he thought about it, he would bet Shane hadn't even remembered her when he was told the news. Shane was from the city anyway, if he let it get to him every time a friend of a friend died from an OD in this part of the city, he'd have killed himself in sympathy years ago. In reality, unless you were in a small circle of friends and business associates, you frankly weren't in Shane's world, you ceased to exist once you were out of his sight. Cole looked a little sad, but only a little, he had been more acquaintances than pals. Jazz appeared a moment later trailing behind them, Rat could see even from this distance that he'd been crying, so had Rat, so no shame in his tears. Rat only hoped that Enio and Cole hadn't given him a ration of shit about it.

Rat checked his little piece of shit "Swatch" watch that a girlfriend had given him years ago. They had about fifteen minutes, so Robbo wasn't late yet at least. He'd show up five minutes before they were supposed to go in, appearing in a cloud of rubber, at least that was his usual MO. Rat called over to Jazz, "You all right man?"

Jazz shrugged, "Good enough to play over the radio, nobody has to look at us. You?"

"Same." Turning to Shane Rat asked, "You wanna just go up now, or you wanna wait for Robbo?" As the words were leaving his mouth, he heard a squeal of tires and the rev of an engine nearby and more squeals approaching quickly, "Never mind, he'll be here any second."

As they were riding up the elevator to the studio, Robbo looked at everyone and asked, "What the fuck is with you guys? Youse all look like someone fucking died or somethin'!"

Rat couldn't help it, he just started laughing, even after Jazz punched him in the arm, he laughed so hard tears were streaming down his face, again.

When they got to the studio itself the DJ and his engineer introduced themselves, Rat forgot their names almost instantly. He couldn't help it; he was just naturally bad with names. Over the course of time in the band he had been introduced to too many people, so now people got filed where they went. These guys went into the, "most likely never going to see them or talk to them again" file. The guys running the show had bands on, but they weren't scene people that Rat knew of. They were tied to the college, at best the band being here tonight was going to be an anecdote of their wild and crazy days at school after the group packed up their instruments and left. Maybe Rat was being unfair, maybe they went to shows a lot and had hung with all kinds of cool people, but they had just been introduced to him as the guys running this thing, i.e., in the power position, in a building Rat would at best make deliveries to. It was easy for him to make that assumption.

They did a quick tune-up and sound check. Nothing extravagant, just enough for them to set the levels in the booth. It would be just like recording the demo they'd done a while back, the one that Shane had probably passed the station to get this for them. Do a quick intro to the song in the gaps and plow ahead until they got this done. Then he could help Shane load the van and unload the van and once that was done, he was free of his responsibilities to anyone. Except maybe Pamela who would be right beside him on his way to the bar for a couple of beers as a wind-down. Easy.

Right before the light went off to start playing, Rat wondered if Jenna could hear this.

Wrong thought.

A man thinking a thought like that had an animal inside of him, all Rat had to do was release the trap on its leg and let it go for as long as the music played.

Rat finally came down off of his adrenaline cloud to

see the guys behind the booth looking a bit shell-shocked as the last note rang out on sustain. They started clapping but Rat couldn't help but notice that Pamela was giggling behind them in the booth. He checked with the rest of the band, they all looked tired. For that matter, he noticed for the first time that he was dripping with sweat, and his shirt was torn. The important things though, nobody looked actively pissed off about anything he'd done, and now that it was over, he felt better. It turned out what he had needed was to just let it out in the one way he was really good at, yelling at the top of his lungs in a punk band. Hell, it was cheaper than therapy and smack anyway, sometimes you even got paid for it.

Shane grunted as he began to wrap up his guitar, "You sing like that on the ep we should actually be able to sell a few fucking copies of the thing. C'mon everybody, get packed up, I think they want us to cut a few promos for the station before we get out of here."

When they were leaving Shane's after helping haul everything upstairs, Rat leaned over to Pamela and demanded, "So what the fuck was so fucking funny?"

"Huh? When?"

"When we had just gotten done playing, you were laughing your cute ass off," Rat looked annoyed.

"Oh thhaaaattt," Pamela started giggling again, "do you have any idea how many times you cursed while you were playing and during the song intros?"

"Huh? No idea, who cares, they bleep that stuff anyway right?"

"It was live Hun; they don't run a tape delay on live shows. You better pray the FCC never finds out."

"Oh shit."

"Yeah, you said that too, along with a whole host of other words a young boy your age shouldn't know the meaning of. Don't worry about it, nobody who writes to the FCC listens to that show anyway, it's happened before. I listen in when I'm in the dorm. But you, my dear young poet just took the record for potty words per minute, I think," her eyes gleamed with mirth.

"Well, there we go, and people back home thought I'd never amount to nuthin'," he chuckled and put his arm around her.

As they neared the park, Rat pulled Pamela into the shadows on the south side of 7th. She was about to say something when he pointed. At the entrance to the park, two guys were standing there, a white kid with dreads, not a crust punk, but a hippie Rat didn't know, and a guy Rat recognized as being from one of the skinhead gangs that hung around CBGBs. Not natural co-minglers in the wild. But the thing that really caught Rat's eye, even more than two natural enemies standing side by side, was what was around both their wrists, that damned yellow bandanna! He could see inside the park that they were serving that god-awful soup again, but the way those two were at the park entrance looked almost military. Like they were guards or something.

"Creepy," Pamela took the word right out of Rat's mouth.

"You said it, let's give 'em a wide berth here, huh?"

The bar wasn't empty, not by a long shot, people filtered into the place even as the doors opened every day, but on a night like this, it should have been a struggle to get a drink. Instead of the normal press of flesh and fight to get the money on the counter, it only took a minute before Rat and Pamela were moving to a table in the back with a couple of hard ciders. Something was up, something that involved those church freaks, Rat was sure of it, but what? Who knew, maybe with everything that had happened Rat was seeing spooks in every shadow and overreacting, but what he saw at the park tonight... It looked like guards, it smelled like guards, it looked like the church felt they owned the park exclusively. This shit was moving faster than Hare Krishna had a few years back, and back then a lot of those were kids following a fad who were going along to get along. But where was the preaching that was getting all these new converts, the holy book that got all these believers in the pews? Where were the fucking pews for that matter? What was even weirder was that as far as Rat knew, there wasn't any band out there preaching this shit either, selling their message as being cool. For the life of him, Rat couldn't figure out what was driving half of the LES to suddenly be sporting the new wristwear, the whole reason these people lived in the LES was because they weren't nature's joiners, the joiners visited, the weirdos lived here.

First the park, now the bar being half empty. Things were getting so weird Rat was thinking he might have to talk to one of the religious fuck weasels just to find out what the big deal was. As if reading his thoughts, Pamela asked, "So what's on your mind? Still worried about the mean ol' FCC?"

"No, those yellow bandanna weirdos."

"Yeah, I'm not getting that either. Three months ago, I'd never even heard of the.... what the hell is the name of it?"

"The Church of the Left Eye. At least it was before they started wearing colors like that," Rat replied taking a heavenly swig of Woodpecker from his glass.

"What the hell does that have to do with wearing yellow?" she looked perplexed.

"I have no idea, when I talked to one of them last year, they used to just believe in getting stoned and giving that weasel Andy something or other, the first cut of the really good shit. Now? No idea."

She thought about it and smiled, "Well, let's not let weird ruin our celebration of you putting one over on the FCC huh? C'mon, you guys were great tonight."

"Ya think? I don't remember much of it," Rat looked genuinely surprised at hearing her compliment them.

"I'm serious, drinks are on me, and then when you're ready to settle in we can go home, walk Ralph and snuggle up to whatever crap channel 5 is limping out of the stable with."

Riding home from work he slowed his bike near the bookstore. Those Left Eye fuckers were definitely getting to Rat, like irrationally so, he thought he was seeing them everywhere he looked, and he saw at least one solution here. The guys from the bookstore might be dorks holding their breath for a revolution that might never be coming, but they had a store that let people hang out and talk. They honestly might have a better clue than Rat as to what was happening in the park anymore, Rat had to admit that at best he only talked to most people in passing, ghost ships bound for different ports of call. You'd think there would be a lengthy discussion where it would come up with his fellow musicians, but Rat would be the first to admit that while he talked to people, he was more interested in keeping his nose clean of their bullshit. His barroom listening skills were notoriously shitty.

He wasn't waiting for the "people's uprising" or any shit like that, he didn't dream of any great future, he wrote songs that at their root said, "the world is fucked up because people in power act like assholes, and they act like assholes because we keep telling them we want assholes, so maybe we all need to stop acting like such assholes ourselves first." That was paraphrased, but it was a similar message to what got a guy nailed to a cross, but with a lot darker imagery. Jesus hadn't had the nightly news and Time magazine to work with to get inspiration from, he just had the wheat in the field and stuff. But all of that meant that Rat didn't pay a lot of attention to the "mood on the street," what did he care? He'd still have to go to work on Monday, and he'd still have to be at practice on time. If he saw the revolution in action maybe he'd join in to see if there would be refreshments, but until that time, he was too busy to discuss it. Most of the mood on the street was usually pipe dream talking out your ass bullshit anyway. Or it was about what drugs were in good supply, at the end of it all it was all soma.

But maybe it had gone a bit past "if I win the lottery but with taking over the government" fantasy this time, and if it had, Rat wanted to know how and why. He lived here; it was need to know information. They might not be changing the world any time soon, but maybe the bookstore guys would know how the Left Eye freaks were changing the neighborhood so quickly. As a bonus, even if they didn't, it was a little chilly tonight and he could get some free coffee in the process. Win/win situation all around if you asked Rat.

He tromped down the steps to the basement where the store hunkered, barely visible to the passing traffic, and slid in to not let the warm air out, pulling the door tightly shut behind him. Three or four people were inside, Tom was running the place tonight, the other guys he knew by sight if not by name. Tom was fine, if anything he was perfect, the other regular shopkeep. William, creeped Rat out for some reason he couldn't fully define. William was tall and gaunt, and his glasses did little to alleviate the haunted appearance his face achieved at all times. Rat thought the guy should work in horror films and had said as much to Jazz a few times. Tom was the exact opposite, light beard slightly past five o'clock shadow, Jr. Republican haircut, t-shirt at all times to go along with a warm smile, Tom was somebody you could fuck around with a bit, crack a joke. If Rat wanted to press the flesh, Tom didn't make Rat worry so much about eldritch terrors like the ones he read about when he was a kid.

"So, what's the topic tonight?" he asked cheerfully making a beeline for the coffee pot.

"Perfect timing young man, the added perspective of a performer may help us in our deliberations" Tom responded with a grin. Rat could never decide if that grin of his was condescending, or if he was just a naturally cheerful person, or, most likely, he was just fucking with him somehow. It was the way he broke out the college dictionary when he spoke, he had to know nobody around this neighborhood spoke like that normally, and hell if you spoke like that on the street around here you were begging to be mugged, possibly by a priest who might mug you just to relieve you of your valuables in the most humane way possible so you didn't get seriously hurt later.

"Deliberating what?" Rat asked pouring creamer into the steaming cup of joe.

"The Church of the Left Eye to be exact."

He froze for a moment, well that was pretty god damned convenient, wasn't it? Turning to face the room, Rat did a quick scan of the other guys in here tonight, two were artist types he'd seen around, most importantly none of them had a yellow bandanna on. "Guys give me the fucking creeps," he replied flatly.

He couldn't help but note at least one head nod in agreement immediately, an automatic expression of what the guy was thinking. Another of the crowd, an older guy who had probably been a yippie back in the day, probably either wrote poetry or painted now judging from how he looked in his seventies, framed wide glasses and his scraggly curly gray hair, asked, "How so?"

Rat was quiet for a second to compose his response and then replied, "Because....it's like they haven't done anything really bad yet that anybody can prove, but the key is, yet. They're starting to act like the fucking Gestapo around the park. You can see them doing something real bad, real soon. If anything, I'm just waiting to find out what it's going to be."

"But wouldn't that show of force show the police we're serious about keeping the park? Tell 'em we won't be fucked with?" asked the fourth occupant, younger kid. Probably just moved to the city, Rat didn't recognize him as readily but thought he'd seen him around, he had a couple of patches sewn on to his black denim jacket, anarcho stuff.

Rat didn't even blink at the question, "What's this 'we' shit? You in the church?"

"Well no..."

"Well, who the fuck elected them to be their own private army? What the fuck do they even stand for? You got any fucking clue as to what that is? The enemy of my enemy don't always equal friend man. Stalin thought that shit and Hitler tried to knife his ass for it. Come to think of it, Stalin was pretty good at it himself. Naw, people start acting like a gang it's only a matter of time before they start doing gang shit. They start acting like the cops, only a matter of time before they go out and get their own billy clubs."

This was received by some mutters and some glances at the floor, Tom piped up, "And that was the point I was arguing. We have no idea who they really are or who they want the park for. All we know is their leader lives in the area, and they feed the homeless."

"Yeah, and the Krishnas feed the homeless, and I ain't following their asses in to battle either. Anyway, what happened to the "no gods no masters" spiel anyway? It's a church for the love of fuck," Rat growled. He could see the other three people were feeling ganged up on, but at the same time, the Left Eye people did freak Rat out and he needed to say it out loud to somebody. It worried the shit out of him that people might be working themselves up to convincing themselves that this shit was somehow "normal." He had an inkling just in this instant, of how it must have been in 1936 to be the one guy in Germany who was saying, "You know that Hitler really is a stupid psycho fucking racist!" People just convince themselves that it will all work out for the best, and if something bad happens more than a few days in a row, they convince themselves that all of this is just perfectly normal now. Not if Rat had any say about it, cultists putting the park on lockdown was anything but normal, and damned if he wasn't going to say so at the very least.

"Other than putting people around the entrances to the park, it's not like they've done anything any worse than anybody else," the kid said.

"Well, that's not entirely true, I caught one of them getting ready to throw something at the cops the other night when they were doing a shakedown," Rat replied.

"Doesn't that serve the pigs right anyway?" the kid replied hotly.

Rat laughed, "What do you think those cops would have done to everybody in the park that night if he'd brained one of them? How in the fuck does getting the homeless tear-gassed out of their lean to's and then having their shit all torn apart while they're in holding, help them?"

"It'd start a movement."

"My ass, even good liberals barely give a shit about the homeless. It'd be, 'Well they were breaking the rules by taking over the park, and they had gotten violent, good for the officers for doing their job!' and that would be the end of that shit. Maybe some lawsuits, maybe, depending on what the advocates could prove happened. If the cops could even suggest they'd been attacked......well fuck that, all bets are off. The great revolution is a ways off, and it ain't happening in the LES, too many different ideologies, too many chiefs not enough Indians around here. For that matter, so many answers to everything, but never to the important things. How do we house the homeless never comes up, we're too busy arguing about which foods we put out in the free slop pots are the most ethical and spiritual," Rat replied calmly.

"You don't know that! You ain't much older than me, how can you be so damned sure of it?" the kid replied turning sullen by this sudden influx of cold reality into his well-honed fantasies.

Rat smiled, actually fondly, "It's alright, I used to think like that. You sit on some steering committee meetings and see where those go. You watch the cops kick ass with impunity for a while, and you realize that the great leap forward ain't happening right now, not yet."

"So, what? You don't believe in anything?"

"Did I say that? What I believe is that the revolution comes from inside first. We all got to be better to people ourselves before we inflict ourselves on other people. Otherwise, it's like that one scene in Rude Boy where Joe Strummer is talking, we're just changing who gets to ride in the limousines. Most people want to get through their day, get through the next, cash their check, get along to go along. That's how people are. You can't just sloganeer your way into getting them to do shit. But if you change yourself first, if you try to be a threat by example, then maybe you can inspire people to do something about the really terrible shit that needs to end. You can only tell people to fix their shit when you've fixed your own, otherwise, they'll look for any excuse to ignore you."

"Are you?"

"Am I what?" Rat asked.

"A threat by example?"

"No way man. That's why I'm not looking to start the next glorious people's revolution. I've got way too many personal revolutions to win as is."

Chapter 9

None of any of what had been happening was making Rat happy about their next gig. The bandshell in the park itself had seemed like a great idea when he'd been approached about it. That had changed, now it was ground zero for all of this creepy ass bullshit, the epicenter of the future explosion. It seemed like the place belonged to the freaks and they'd be invading into their space. Not the normal freaks either, the ones you were happy to see, the people who might have some issues in the head, but at the end of the day were just ordinary folks somehow trying to survive in this world. And while they were doing it the variety of the individual trips they were all on was what made life interesting and strangely, fiercely beautiful. No, these were the ugly freaks, the ones that wanted to own the park, were the power and rules type of freaks, no matter what they cloaked themselves in. The ones who wanted to be the guys riding around in the limousines. These were the type of freaks that came in the guise of "groovy man we're all one" when what they meant was, "you're all one and I will keep you that way when I sit above you." Little Hitlers, shit heels who had been shoved down and pushed around all their miserable lives finally getting a taste of what it was like to hold the club instead of eating it for once. That was what was bugging Rat about these Left Eye fuckers, they were putting normal people between a rock and a hard place, between encroaching gentrification ugly and a secret army control, neither one of which would give a fuck about all the beautiful freaks on their own trips lighting the doors to magic and wonder. Those poor souls would be crushed under no matter which way they ran. Once someone declared "this is ours" they had also declared, "it is no longer yours."

The rest of the band were having different reactions from his, even without the additional fears Rat harbored. This was a new experience for them that was in and of itself frightening. Robbo was responding best of the bunch by not responding, which was more or less how he handled everything short of nuclear warfare. Shane had set it up, so he was stoked and nobody else's worries were going to knock him off that pedestal, it would have almost been cute in normal circumstances, Shane was actually excited about something. Jazz was sort of in the same position as the kid in the bookstore, he was enamored with the idea of anyone having the numbers to maybe stand up to the pigs, without considering the hows and whys, and he was enthralled with being part of the "resistance" by playing here. At least Cole was feeling what Rat was feeling a little bit, this just wasn't normal, something was off about everything, you just couldn't explain exactly what was so wrong, you just knew it was.

It didn't help anything that they were debuting a new song called, "Followers" they had been rehearsing for a while now that was all about gangs. Rat somehow didn't think that was going to go over well with the Left Eye freaks at all, it read almost like an unspoken indictment to what they were doing. Oh well, what could you do? Not play the song in case they showed up today? Boy that would show the courage of your convictions. If you didn't stand for something you'd fall for everything, they were doing the damned song. Rat just wished they were doing it in a nice cozy club for the first time, he hadn't seen the Left Eye fuckers inside the clubs yet.

Pamela sat with him in what passed as a backstage area. "All right, I'll bite," she said, tilting her head to the side with a look of concern, "you're always tense before these things, but you look like you want to run for the hills. What's bugging ya' babe?"

"Huh!" Rat grunted. A moment later he tried again, this time with a coherent thought, "I guess it's these Left Eye people that have sprouted up like pod people in a horror movie. It's cold out, and it's daytime, but there's bound to be some of them out there. You know how I feel about them, I don't want to play a show for fuckin' weirdos."

"You mean, different weirdos than your normal weirdos."

"Right."

"But you're going to anyway."

He looked at her for a second blankly and said, "Well yeah, I'm always scared when we play anyway and when has that ever stopped me? But this is probably the best reason I've ever had before."

"Except for that one show at the barricaded squat you didn't want me going to where your ex-girlfriend showed up...."

Rat couldn't help it, he laughed, "OK, I see your point. Hey if we ever get to tour, it'll get me ready to play down south huh?"

She smiled and replied, "I don't think you should tour. Especially not down south."

Rat looked perplexed, "Huh? Why not?"

"Well, I'd miss you most likely, I'd be stuck having to date Enio while you're gone, and he doesn't bathe."

"It's finally reached a critical mass where he no longer has BO. I mean he doesn't smell good, but it no longer smells like anything human. You get so confused by trying to figure out what in the hell he smells like you don't even remember to be grossed out."

Pamela shook her head, "I'll just have to take your word for that and forgo the pleasure."

They could hear the band before them winding down, it had been one of those SCUM rock bands that had their moment in the sun last year and now were fading out of sight except for the older crowd. At least that how it felt to Rat, like already that scene was getting ready to wind down. It had that Big Apple record this past year, but the whole thing seemed spent. Crusties and punkers were having a dirty revival in the LES now, and who knew how long that was going to last, things rarely had any kind of staying power in the city. Whole generations of musicians could come and go in NYC and the rest of the country would have no idea about their "movement" ever happening. Especially since Tim Yo at the big national punk mag, MRR hated anything that sniffed of Hawd Coor, by which he meant, New York.

Pamela grabbed Rat's knee, "You'll blow their doors down, you always do."

"Just hope they ain't in a fighting mood is all. Also, we're outside, no doors."

"You take care of what you can control, that's all you can do. Smartass."

Once the stage was cleared the rest of the band slid out into the open to set up. Rat hadn't followed, he listened to the band tuning up, and the crowd already starting to pick up the "re-Straint!" chant. It wasn't a huge show, it was still a bit chilly out, holding down the numbers, but that was made up for by it being the kind that had the magical word, "free," so it wasn't like there was nobody out there. People will put up with blowing on their hands for free shit all day and twice on Sunday. They'd never played the bandshell before, it was kind of a sign you were getting somewhere in a weird way, like a rite of passage. Rat couldn't help but think they'd be more there, wherever there was, if this was happening in the summer instead of guerrilla gig during a weirdly warm winter. Oh well, he probably wouldn't sweat as much today, look at the positives.

Almost on cue, Cole shouted back to where he was, "Will ya' hurry the fuck up before my fingers get numb?"

Rat quickly kissed Pamela before getting up and rushing onto the stage. A cry went up from the crowd and they were off to the races. "We're All Gonna Die" blasted through at breakneck speed, and the pit was moving pretty good. The first thing Rat did was check the cops, thankfully they were hanging back some near the entrances. They weren't happy about them commandeering the bandshell, but it looked like they had decided it wasn't worth the trouble. Rat turned his eyes to the front of the stage. If there was going to be trouble, it was almost always coming from right in front of you. Watch the eyes of the ones who had felt it was worth pushing up. They all looked angry, but there's a difference between letting your anger out through the catharsis of the music, and "I fucking hate the lead singer and I intend to remove his teeth with a fucking bottle." Rat had seen both over the years and knew the difference when he was looking right at it.

They flew right from the opener into "Happytime Fun Zone Death Camp" without breaking stride. The energy was good today, the crowd up front was into it, there were even some regulars shouting along with Rat as he bellowed his way through the lyrics. Rat was feeding off that now, this was his type of crowd, they were digging this so hard right now, it got through even Rat's normal terror at doing this. He found himself moving a bit more smoothly, closing his eyes less, taking it all in. At least what was in front of the stage, what was happening in the park wasn't his problem right now. His only problem was making these people that filled his field of vision happy with being here.

They slammed into a cover, The Kinks, Destroyer. This was Shane's idea, but Rat hadn't fought it too hard. First off, he liked the song, and secondly, it gave his voice a break. He could just pass the mic out to the crowd for bits of it and enough of them knew the song and were thrilled to have a shot at yelling it out for a bit. All you had to do was keep one hand firmly on the mic so you didn't lose it altogether and it was an easy song to play live. At practice it was a hell of a lot harder, he had to remember all the lyrics then.

Rat took advantage of the respite to look away from the people pushing against the stage and out over the rest of the crowd. In the back, the exact people he had hoped not to see at all today were clearly in view, an almost impossibly large group of them. They came from every background you'd expect from people in the village, just not hanging out together, artists, crusties, skinheads, dreadlocked hippies, the clothing on a large percentage of them looked like they were homeless park dwellers. They stood there stock still, their eyes boring into the band with ill-defined malice as they performed. Not interacting with the rest of the crowd at all, just standing there exuding malevolence. It was like having your parent's Baptist church show up at your gig. The one other thing all of them had in common, each of them was wearing a yellow bandanna. The Church of the Left Eye was making a show of force, and they absolutely didn't look like they liked Restraint and Control worth a shit.

Rat came to a decision, a simple one. Fuck em, fuck em all, Rat had refused to back down to rednecks back home, and he sure as shit wasn't going to back down from a fucking bullshit cult here in the city. Destroyer crashed to its end and the crowd that was here for music roared their approval. Rat let it wind down a bit, before speaking into the mic, "This is about all the fuckers in gangs, whether it's on the streets, or a political party, or the Catholic Church. Why the fuck are you so willing to give up who you are just on the say so of somebody else? There is no great wisdom that you 'Just aren't smart enough to understand' there are no gods among men you need to bow down to. Stop looking for gods to grovel in front of and find your own feet to stand up on, put down the knives and the bottles and pick yourself up, this one's called Followers"

He noticed Cole looked a little nervous as his guitar squealed over the audience. Good for him, he must have seen the fuckers and wasn't going to let them stop him either, even if he was scared. Now, this shit was punk rock, it wasn't all playing for your buddies for free beer and pats on the back, not when it was real. They had two audiences, one that looked like they wanted to gut them, and the crowd up front who were into the new tune. Neither paying attention to the other, all eyes on the band. Rat liked this track quite a bit, it sounded like one of their earlier songs, nice and crunchy, all off rhythms on the guitar backed up by slamming drums. Rat could see the Left Eye guys had gotten the message, hell it wasn't subtle, they looked even more pissed with the band's very existence. Good, fuck 'em anyway. Rat was surprised to see they were backing off a bit from the stage as the song continued like they had taken the message. The cool thing was, as those assholes split, some of the real deal homeless, and some of the others who'd been on the fringes of the park listening started to filter in. Now Rat could get back to the business at hand and finally enjoy this set. The enemy had been blasted from the gate, and now it was the time to celebrate.

"Yeah, but even if they are dangerous, what the fuck can we even do about it?" demanded Jazz.

"I don't know, but I'm telling you people are mad enough at the city, they're starting to support those weirdos," Rat replied.

"I mean, fuck the cops and all that, but not so we can just have a church decide what we can do or not do in the park," added Cole. "I've heard they've roughed up some people. I mean other than Skeev. You could have written Skeev off to personal, but now I'm thinkin' it ain't. They're just the same bullies as the Government, just with shittier clothing."

They had been going round and round for days now, even if it was just the three of them today. Rat was pushing the hardest, but even Cole could see something was seriously wrong with this. Jazz was beginning to see his point but it had been like pulling teeth the whole way. Jazz just wasn't a cynical person by nature, you had to work him towards distrust slowly, whereas Cole and Rat started there. Enio had just said, "Fuck cops, and fuck them if they wanna' act like cops." Enio had an almost refreshingly simplistic view of the world sometimes, it was a shame he wasn't here now, maybe he'd come up with a simple solution none of them could because all the thought they were putting into it just confused the issue. Instead of arguing whether the Church was bad, at least today it had progressed to where they were brainstorming on what to do about it. They were filling time while Rat was waiting on Pamela who was supposed to show up tonight. Too bad it felt like it was ending up as more of another brain drizzle than any kind of useful downpour.

"Thing is, this is just like the Nazis skins man, before people started standing up to them, they started taking over everything. Out in the hinterlands, they're still dangerous as fuck, here they get their ass beat. But in clubs out in the little cities, those fuckers are running things. Everybody said the same thing about them when it started, "Like anyone is gonna follow Nazis." Now, try going to a show in Jersey without them cunts trying to jump you, it's not whether or not someone is going to get beat up by them, it's a matter of trying to make sure it isn't you. That's what I'm seeing with this yellow bandanna thing going on. They might have started out as some church and thought they needed to protect the homeless from the city, not anymore, now it looks like they've got aspirations. How long until they start telling the homeless, 'Join the church or get the fuck out of our park?' We don't want the city doing that, we gonna let these fuckers do it because they smoke a lot of pot?"

The door slammed open, causing them all to jump. In walked Enio followed by Skeev who gasped out, "Rat! You gotta fuckin' do somethin'!"

"What the fuck are you talkin' 'bout?"

"Those Left Eye freaks, they grabbed fucking Pamela man," Skeev answered, "me and Enio saw it when we were coming back here!"

The Church of the Left Eye had a squat of its own a few blocks from where they had the homestead. That freak Andy had opened his place up before even Rat had come here, back when buildings were a bit more plentiful. Back before there were mysterious fires that cleared out buildings that Rat figured had been set to clear more space for the gentrifiers. Andy must have had money when he got here because now the entire building was wired for electric and had solid plumbing, which usually took a good-sized group of squatters quite a bit of time to manage. In a homestead like the band lived in, part of what you paid out every month went to fixing the place up, but you definitely had to pay up to live there. The part that made people assume some money had been spent was because the only other people that lived there were the freaks that belonged to the Church, and none of them had ever struck anyone as the great winners for brains in the lottery of life. The idea of those stoners fixing anything boggled the mind. It might have been his girlfriend who had the cash, but nobody had seen her for ages, everybody figured she must have gotten sick of his weird ass and split out.

First instincts say you run right out the door, maybe you think to take the dog as some kind of additional weapon. Rat tried to avoid listening to first instincts because they were often full of shit and got you your head handed to you. He needed to do something, but the important part was that it be the right thing, the get Pamela back thing, not the feel like a big tough guy and fuck everything up thing. All they had been able to get from Skeev was that he'd noticed Pamela walking down 7th, probably coming here when five or six of the freaks from the church grabbed her and started dragging her towards their squat. Skeev and Enio had tried to follow them but with a head start it was like they had just vanished into the city. Doing something like that was bold as fuck, but with the vacant lots they could cross over, and then with general lack of cops, they shouldn't have even have had much of a problem getting to their squat with her without getting stopped.

So, they'd talked about it. They'd come up with the only idea that sounded good, even if it didn't sound great, and now Rat stood in front of their building, by himself. Rat didn't think it was the best idea, but it was the only one they thought might work.

He had left the homestead with Cole, Jazz, Enio and Skeev, but right here, right now, standing in front of the home of the Church of the Left Eye it was only Rat. When he walked up to the door it swung open at a touch, it looked like he might be expected. Not that it mattered, they had probably seen him coming anyway, and them knowing wasn't going to stop him. He looked in to the gloom of the building and took a deep intake of breath of the cool musty air wafting out from inside. He had to go and get Pamela back and there was no doubt that this was where they had taken her. The cops might not come at all if they called, they certainly would not be in time to prevent whatever those sick fucks wanted to happen here. A fact you learned really quick in the city, sometimes you had to handle things by yourself in this crazy old world. He stepped in to the dimly lit doorway.

Chapter 10

He could hear the loose bits of concrete and glass crunching under his feet as he climbed the steps to go inside, every step was like the grinding away of his hopes. Andy might have had money when he set this place up, but apparently, it didn't extend to fixing or sweeping the steps, it was all a matter of priorities. Typical druggie thinking, get the power on, then get that creature comfort water going, then the stoves, the rest of it can go hang. It wasn't like they went outside half the time anyway, at least until just recently. Who needs steps when you ain't going anywhere in a hurry? As he stepped inside the building, he found himself wishing he had a flashlight, the place was dark as hell in here. Their place was dark in the hallway too, but at least you could hear life happening behind the individual doors. Which was weird, he knew they had power in here, he'd walked by and seen plenty of lights from the open windows on the upper floors at one point or another. Maybe the bulb for the hall had burned out and the flake heads had just not bothered replacing it. Still, for a place where so many people supposedly lived, the silence except for what was under his feet was overwhelming; the whole thing felt like he walking into a tomb.

On a whim, Rat reached out and pawed around next to the doorway. It took him a couple of seconds before he found the switch. He flicked the toggle, and low and behold, the hallway lit up like Christmas. The downside to that was unfortunately it gave him a clear view of the two big assed skinheads standing a few feet in front of him, both wearing yellow bandannas. He hadn't even been able to see them in the gloom.

"Andy wants to talk to you." one of them said stepping forward.

"I kinda figured he did," Rat shrugged. He wasn't dumb enough not to expect something like this.

They let him step forward deeper inside away from the door. The one indicated with his meaty paw that Rat should start taking the stairs in front of them, it caused instant claustrophobia. Rat hadn't been intending to turn and leave, but with those two behind him on the dirty steps, it felt like he was trapped here. Maybe he could fight his way through them, but that was a soft maybe, they were big dudes and they were probably expecting him to try something.

The building was dirty, not normal squat dirty, except for the grit on the steps there had been an attempt to clean the place up some time ago, probably when it had been re-wired, but it had already succumbed to fresh grime. This was recent, "Nobody gives a fuck" dirt. Entropy and filth dirt was taking over again, trash bags were in the downstairs hall, rats had ripped some of them apart and strewn the contents around. Rat could smell rotting food in the air, which made him all the more happy none of them ever ate the soup in the park. Enough people did, so many people in this city couldn't wait to get a free meal, even a bad one.

As they clumped up the grimy steps, Rat snaked a rare Camel out from his diminishing pack. In a casual motion, he lit it up and blew a large cloud downwards right into the faces of the skins. "Mind if I smoke?" He heard a grunt from behind him. They were taking that well, if it was him personally, he would have kicked his own ass for that and these looked like the type of guys who enjoyed delivering a good old-fashioned ass-whupping in their spare time, and were probably straight-edgers to boot. That raised all kinds of questions as to what in the fuck they were doing here. As far as them not pounding him right back down the steps, Rat guessed they had orders to deliver him as undamaged as possible. Suited Rat fine, he was perfectly happy with not being damaged in any way, now at least he figured he knew what the goons marching orders were.

As they reached the next floor, Rat couldn't help but notice that all the doors to what were once individual apartments stood open. Most of them had the lights off and the windows boarded up even here on the second floor. It took him a second to figure out what was wrong with that. At first, your eyes filled in what you logically expected until you suddenly realized that the boards were on the inside. It hadn't been sealed off by the city or a developer, these people had sealed the light out. As he passed them, glancing into each living space he finally saw one that had the boards down, allowing him to see the people inside. The apartment was practically overfull with street people, homeless, punks, some skins, hippies, all lying on the floor and couches like they had been turned off by some controlling switch. Like God just had an on/button up there and pressed off on just yellow bandanna wearers today. What kind of dope were these freaks fucking hooked up with anyway? If it wasn't for the honor guard, Rat would be tempted to check if any of them were even still breathing.

It was more of the same in the rest of the building, dark foreboding spaces that he suspected held people but couldn't see into the depths to prove it. In some weird way, he was beginning to feel better, he finally had some kind of logical explanation to give himself, it was just dope. Andy must have made some connection to something extra special and the loyalty had followed. It made sense, if you had the best human trap on earth...well people were beating a path to his door, weren't they? It had to just be dope, if he could get Pamela back and out of here, hopefully, the problem would just solve itself soon enough. Problems involving dope had a permanent solution that was somewhere just down the road.

Rat was practically gasping for air by the time they reached the top flight. He glanced back, the skins were as stoic in the face as they had been at the front door, must have been health freaks before they found religion was all he could figure. Wonder who hooked them up to this wonderful nodding world, or could Andy just afford to hire them as muscle? When they reached the top of the stairs there was only one door for the whole floor. All of the others that had been there had been sheet rocked over and inexpertly painted to make it seem like it had always been just a penthouse suite. It didn't bode well for this meeting, and not only because that limited avenues of escape. Rat had never gotten along with arrogant dickheads, pure mischief always made him look for a way to yank their chain, and it looked like Andy had become one and then some.

While Rat was trying to get his breath back, the bigger skinhead whirled him and pushed him against the wall. He quickly and efficiently patted Rat down before he even had a chance to react, coming up with a lighter, his smokes, twenty bucks, and a set of brass knuckles that Rat always carried. He handed Rat back everything but the nucks which he pocketed.

"Hey, can I get a receipt for those so I can get them back when I get off this ride?" Rat asked the stony face.

The other skin pushed past Rat and knocked. A voice called from inside, smoother and more melodic than Rat had ever remembered Andy's being, "Let the supplicant enter the temple!"

One skin pushed the door open, and the other pushed Rat inside hard enough he stumbled a bit as he went through the doorway. The door slammed behind him with a powerful finality that made him take a step further inside instinctively trying to get away from the noise. It took him a moment to recover his balance before he could get a good look at the place.

As Rat had fully expected, freak show, maybe not the exact freak show he was expecting, but close enough for government work. All of the walls were painted black, matching the furniture which was all black in the living room he was standing in. If it wasn't for the scuffs and tears on the chairs, they would have faded away into the background as only the suggestion of what they were instead of the actual thing. Rather than looking cool like whoever had put it together had intended, it looked like it had been done a while ago by somebody who didn't really know what they were doing, there were streaks here or there where the original white bled through and you could see the brush lines. Rat figured it must have been Andy himself who did it, probably when he first took over the building, hoping to give his rooms a mysterious vibe for anyone who came up here to be so overawed by the spectacle they'd give him money, or drugs, or want to sleep with him.

The same voice called from deeper inside the

apartment, "Won't be a moment, have something on the stove, stay right where you are please, I've been expecting you!"

Rat was at a loss as to what to do here. A hearty "Happy to see you" hadn't ever been part of his thinking here. Being left to just stand and wait, like he was just here for a visit just didn't jibe with the rest of the situation. As far as he could tell what was happening was that he was inside of a building run by a creepy cult, who might be behind some of the disappearances that had been happening around the Village, and were definitely the ones who were stirring up trouble like crazy, and had just kidnapped his fucking girlfriend. Not to mention there were two very large skinheads probably still standing right outside the door who could probably beat him into a red paste. Yet, Andy had made it sound like they were having a long-expected afternoon fucking tea together.

Rat was still trying to square the dichotomy of it all when Andy stepped in through one of the three doorways that opened into the living room. He did not look well. Andy had never looked particularly well, but something seemed especially off about him these days. His skin was pale to the point of being almost translucent, what you could see of it under his formerly white, now gray, poncho-looking thing that covered him. His muscle tone had never been world beater either, now it looked twisted and warped, like he had been put through stresses leading to tension in different directions than life normally demanded of his body, placing bulges in parts of his arms and legs that didn't normally bulge on anyone. This deformity looked even weirder on Andy because of his bone-thin physique. His hair hung lank, long and unwashed, tangling in spots. Dirty hair wasn't abnormal, but he used to at least comb it. He had a beard as well, at least he tried to have one. Andy hadn't been built to have a real beard, so instead, he had patches of a beard here and there on his face looking like he had mange. His eyes captivated your attention away from all of that the moment they caught your own, they looked sunken and crazed, with deep dark shadows around them, belying his previous cheerful mode of speech. Standing near him long enough, you'd get distracted from the madness in his eyes by his breath, which Rat could smell from where he stood. The guy's teeth must have been rotting right out of his head. All that put together, it appeared to Rat to mean that Andy had started smoking the rock, nobody in this neighborhood looked like that otherwise. The man looked like he was decomposing where he stood.

"There you are Rat, I've been looking forward to this meeting for some time now," Andy smiled.

"That makes one of us. Cut to the chase, where's my fucking girlfriend you fuck!" Rat snarled back.

"It would appear that we have started on the wrong foot, let me clarify our relationship for you," Andy said quietly.

With that, he waved his hand almost negligently. Rat felt like he was being pummeled from all sides by invisible fists instantly sending the air right out of him as he gasped in shock! Panic overtook him as he was slowly beaten to the ground by forces he couldn't see. Again, and again concussive blows rained down on him as he slumped until finally, he lay on the dirty floor desperately trying to get air into his lungs. His breathing was impeded further by what felt like an enormous weight resting directly on his back, crushing him into the filthy remains of carpet under him. Animal panic told him to run, to get out now, some deep instinct told him that if he passed out here and now, he'd never awaken again to even discover why this was happening.

"Can't....breathe...." he gasped.

The weight released off his back, but only enough so that he could suck in some oxygen in quick panicked breaths. He could see that Andy was standing directly in front of him, his feet were clad in a beat-up old pair of Chucks that were held together with nothing but the grime packed into them. The smell of the sneakers was not helping his breathing any.

"Sorry about that," Andy said, and Rat could tell by the tone of his voice that he was smiling even without looking up, "I didn't want there to be any doubts as to the situation. I certainly don't want any attempts at heroics that might force me to hurt you more than I have. I don't want us to be adversaries, but mistakes happen. I want you to think of me as a friend, and you need me as a friend right now Mickey Rat. But I didn't want any accidents to happen. An ounce of prevention is worth a pound of cure you know."

"What....the.... fuck? What in the fuck.... are you?" Rat wheezed trying not to study the filthy floor his was face was pressed into, too carefully. If Andy didn't kill him outright, he might still die later from something he caught off the rug.

"Ah, well that's an interesting question, a very interesting ponder indeed. To the law of the land, I am Andy Weiss, the small-time drug dealer and religious crackpot the people around here have come to know and loathe. But I somehow doubt that's what you mean by that question, is it? In reality, I merely wear the shell of Andy Weiss, he was convenient, he gave me a base of operations, and he was foolish enough to play with the wrong things." Andy began to pace a little as he spoke, like he was warming to a favorite topic, "What you're asking is what is wearing this shell, aren't you? I doubt you'll understand, but the answer is that I am one of the Discordia, servants of the real order of the universe, the real driver of your life, the force of raw chaos itself. But mere servants aren't allowed to play with the real nuts and bolts stuff, are we? So, we have to make do with you lot to show our devotion."

"I just want you to know.... that confused me more, and I wouldn't have thought that was possible," Rat gasped out.

"Humans! Silly boy! You poor pathetic seekers of order in the chaos! For millennia you have striven to put some rightness some causation to the whole of your world, so my kind has to come along and remind you who really runs the show. We make the world burn and dance by the glow! We serve what we are born to, chaos of the highest order," Andy hunkered down on his haunches and Rat could just about see his face from where he was glued to the floor, it looked maniacally gleeful as it spoke. Worse, looking into those eyes, there was nothing in there that reminded him of the Andy Weiss he had met before. Those eyes were worse than anything Rat had seen in a human.

"Are you telling me, you intend to make the world burn starting in the Lower fucking East Side? I got news; nobody gives a shit about us but developers. As far as the world is concerned, you're too late, we're already burning," Rat managed to chuckle as he said it.

"And that brings us to you, my dear boy."

"Where the fuck is Pamela?" Rat demanded, he was frightened, but he also knew he was being toyed with. What was the point? He just wanted this to end and intended to push on Andy until it did.

"Here, why don't I let you up, it's more civilized that way, and Andy's mistreated knees are starting to hurt," Andy said standing up.

Rat felt the pressure come off of his back, he quickly scrambled to his feet. He continued to press, "Again, just so you know, I really don't care about your plot for world domination, or whatever the fuck you're doing here, I just want my girlfriend back. So, give her back and you can, I don't know, go on to your next trick, bringing Utopia to the South Bronx."

Andy stood in front of him smiling, "See, I want something in exchange for that, you had to know I would. And it's the one thing I know you have to give. You see, I want you, Mister Rat. This has been an interesting experiment, we conduct them all the time, but the rubber needs to meet the road here. Mankind has to make his world burn for us to show their devotion, and our effective servitude. Chaos is real, something realer than Jesus, and it wants sacrifices and bloodshed, it wants worship here on earth, which is why I'm here. Sometimes we go big, like backing a hack Austrian painter, and sometimes despite all of our best efforts, our efforts stay localized events like the Miami riots in the early '80s. Thought for sure that was going to sweep the nation."

Andy paused just a moment as he pondered that failure before continuing, "But I think I've got something here, the Reagan '80s didn't make everyone rich, there's a lot of resentment all over the country about it. Who knows how big something like this could break? The Lower East Side could be a touchstone, but to really get the message out there, it takes something else. Did you see how big the whole Krishna thing got? And what do they offer anyway? Drums and bad food. I'm offering people a chance to get revenge on a system that hates most of them. With the right soundtrack...."

Rat snorted as realization as to what Andy was asking dawned, "What in the hell makes you think my band would play for you? Hell, half the time I don't even know what I'm going to write myself."

"Well, first, we're going to have some soup."

Rat just looked blank for a moment, before replying, "What in the fuck do wet vegetables have to do with anything?"

"You know, I have found that a good meal can do wonders to change someone's mind. Discovered it quite by accident really, oh those were wild times. But I've found that with the right meat, say, in a good soup, people will do anything you want when they've had their fill, well most people will, there are always holdouts, unfortunately. All through history people have told of the magical powers of the right kind of meat. From the Wendigo to werewolves, people were so close to understanding. You ever notice how many new converts we've gotten since we started serving soup?" Andy said, before turning and walking back towards the room he'd come in from.

"You are out of your fucking mind Andy; do you know that?"

"I would have thought the demonstration of my power would have been sufficient for you to understand. Andy played with things he shouldn't have; Andy isn't home anymore. You know it really is classless to wave the hostage around, but I suppose you want to see the stakes we're playing for?"

Rat felt hands grasp him, and begin to drag him. There was nobody else in the damned room with them, but he was moving anyway, he could feel the hands that had grasped his shoulders pulling him onward, even though he couldn't see anything there. Neither his rational mind nor his animal panic knew what to do, he just couldn't square this with any reality he understood to process a way to deal with it. He didn't believe in God, he didn't believe in Krishna, he didn't believe in any of that crap and regardless of anything Rat believed though, he was still being dragged through the room by hands made of empty air.

"What the god damned fuck!"

"You must practically be an atheist to still be doubting your senses at this point, Mister Rodent. Clearly, there is more than exists in your little world Horatio," Andy smiled as he followed Rat's progress.

Another door leading into the living room slammed open on its own. The light clicked on automatically, at least that's how it seemed. Nobody had touched the door either, so Rat couldn't tell if there might be someone waiting inside, part of him hoped there was. He was pressed forward by the shoulders until he could see there was a bed, and lying on it tied and gagged was Pamela! Her eyes went wide when she saw him, she instinctively tried to yell to him around the gag but only muffled noises came out, as she began to thrash against her bonds. Her eyes were wide and pleading staring out from the depths of the pit her smeared eyeliner and eye shadow had made of her visage.

"If you fucking hurt her...." Rat growled.

"I haven't yet, but you know, it is an option. Maybe those two bald fellows would like to spend some time with her while we talk some more. Of course, they are under my control, so I could certainly suggest that they would want to and they'd certainly agree," Andy hissed right behind him.

Rat went partially limp, he felt the pressure on him go slack, it left him just enough play that he thought he could finally act in this situation instead of being acted on. He violently yanked on whatever held him and was able to jerk his arm back a good foot. He smiled when it satisfyingly crunched with Andy's nose behind him.

Instead of hearing moans of pain, or cursing the way he expected, he heard a muffled sniggering coming from under the hand Andy must have over his broken nose, "Nice! Good show of guts! Doomed, but admirable all the same. Well, you've seen that I have her, and you know what I'll have done to her, so, shall we sup together in brotherhood for a while?"

Rat couldn't see what choice he had, the same

irresistible force that had dragged him to see Pamela bound to a bed, grabbed him and dragged him towards the room Andy had come from originally. He heard the door to where Pamela was slam shut behind them, knowing all the while there was no one there to close it. Why was this lunatic so insistent on Rat eating the damned park soup with him? What had he even meant about the right kind of meat anyway? He tried to squirm against whatever controlled him, but after his cheap shot on Andy the grip on him was like iron, all he could do was twitch his muscles ineffectually as they moved on.

The light turned on in the kitchen and Rat was finally able to see what Andy meant by "the right kind of meat." It was a huge kitchen with the stove off far to the left, but it was what was on the right side of the room... The right side was given over to what could only be called an abattoir. Bones were stacked haphazardly, meat was sitting out, waiting to be trimmed down. Where the slabs of flesh waited it was clear as to what animal had provided it. Only humans had fingers and toes like that. The copper penny stench of dried blood assailed Rat's nose, while his ears filled up with the insistent voracious hum of the flies that came off the meat in a cloud when they entered the room.

Before Rat could gain control over himself, his stomach twisted violently, his head jerked forward and he threw up in front of himself, some of it splattering on his front. The force that held him kept its forward momentum and just dragged him through the steaming mess, his boots leaving lines through the spew.

Andy was behind him still, "Well, now you need nourishment all the more, my boy! If you're going to perform my songs to get my message to the wide waiting world, we can't have you wasting away!"

"This is.... insane!" Rat gasped out through the phlegm that filled his mouth and nose.

"No, no this is all the order in the chaos that you can't understand yet. Once you've eaten, you'll see that. You'll see what a fraud all of the ape's attempts at putting his stamp over the only true order has been. It's like opening your mind's eye to what the truth is, seeing beneath the veneer of civility," Andy sounded almost enthralled himself as he spoke. Even as shaken as Rat was, he couldn't help but think it would have sounded better if he wasn't saying it with a broken nose. It was a survival instinct he had honed back at home before he fled there, when the situation is too big and out of hand, focus on the little things, the ridiculous. The funny shit becomes the only really clear things there are at some point.

"What you don't understand is Chaos is God, it is what we are all born to, it is where you all go. A personality that creates all, and destroys all, and all it wants is you to worship sometimes. You can call me an angel if you like, if that makes it all make more sense to you. I am here to provide the miracles," Andy practically sneered, his voice attempting a pomposity his broken nose denied him.

There was a table placed between the butcher block and the stove, it was tastelessly covered with a stolen tablecloth from some Italian place, including a wine bottle candle. Rat noted that it had suspicious brown stains on it. He couldn't help but notice, especially considering what was so close at hand. Again, with no hands doing it, a chair slid out on the far side of the table. Rat was almost grateful when he was forced down to sit in it, his legs weren't feeling up to much standing at the moment.

Andy said nothing, he just went over to the stove. He began to hum merrily. As Rat watched he took a small spoon and tasted whatever ungodly broth was bubbling away in the huge tureen sitting there underneath the gray frothing bubbles that covered the top. Smiling, he turned down the gas burner and retrieved a bowl and spoon from the drawers and cupboards next to the stove. Rat could only watch entranced as he dipped a ladle in and filled the bowl which erupted with steam from the soup he slopped into it. Andy smiled the whole way back to the table where he sat the bowl in front of Rat.

Rat began gagging and dry heaving at the thought of what those gray hunks of meat that floated among the potatoes and carrots and seaweed had been. His eyes watered and his nose was filled with snot which was dribbling over his lips. The smell somehow made it through the mucus, the underlying meat smell covered with the sweet smell of seaweed. Andy's smile never wavered as he walked back to the doorway, standing there framed by what sunlight came from the living room. He could stand there for eternity as far as Rat was concerned, no damned way Rat was eating this!

"I'll give you a moment to compose yourself. I can imagine it must be difficult, and I must keep this in mind. I've never let anyone see the secret ingredient before, won't do that again I assure you. Seems to put you people quite off your appetite. No idea why, you've been eating each other since you first climbed down from the trees. On your own time. But you will eat, I assure you. Now be a good little boy and eat up, and you can have enlightenment for dessert."

Rat tried glaring at his tormentor through his watering eyes, damn this bastard to hell! Somehow human flesh and whatever fucked up power this thing had inside him controlled people? That was the explanation for all of this? This led to the most important question of all at this moment, could he do it? Could he give up his very soul like that for Pamela? Would he be willing to do something like this to prevent the torments Andy had lined up for her? The plan had been snafu, the bad guy had him, the cavalry had never shown, what was he going to do now for anybody?

If it had been going to work, it would have by now, and when they'd put it together, they hadn't counted on anything like what Andy was now. How in the hell could you account for something like this? He cared about her, but this was his mind, his soul, his very him, that's what was at risk in that steaming bowl in front of him! He looked down at the bowl again, and tried to get control of his stomach, he looked up at Andy as if begging for reprieve from this. A reprieve he knew he wouldn't receive. He was leaving here either under Andy's control or in a stew pot. As he stared at Andy, his face pleading, suddenly Rat's eyes grew wide for just a moment, then he reached for the spoon.

"You've made the right choice, well, the only choice really," Andy smirked, "don't worry so much, you'll feel so much better when I run things for you." Rat couldn't believe what he was hearing, some high-end demon of some kind, and the bastard was low brow enough to gloat.

"Could I have some water or something, to settle my stomach first? Don't do you no good if I just puke it right back up now, does it?" Rat rasped; his voice raw from vomiting.

"Of course, I should have thought of it myself," Andy replied stepping completely back into the room and starting towards the refrigerator.

It worked perfectly, Rat needed to get him clear of the doorway, so the others could come in. The first one behind him was Jazz who started to throw up immediately at the carnage that was presented to him. Cole, on the other hand, pushed past Jazz, his animal revulsion and horror turned over in an instant to rage. Andy turned for a moment, his eyes registered what he saw, but there was no time to react. Cole swung the baseball bat he clutched with all his might. Whatever power resided in the body of Andy Weiss was frozen to that spot before the bat came crashing down on its head with a sickening hollow thump. Andy dropped instantly; Rat felt the force that had held him in place release him the second the bat had landed on the thing's cranium.

Cole was letting out a keening, animal sound, he stood over Andy's body and brought the bat down again and again on the mass that had once been a human head. Had been, but in no way resembled one now. Rat got to his feet unsteadily and grabbed Cole from behind putting some force into it so he didn't accidentally get struck himself. His friend was well past reason and struggled a bit, growling and mewling with horror turned to rage as he twisted attempting to break free of Rat's grasp. As suddenly as the rage had come on him, it vanished just as fast. He blinked at what he had done, finally calmed down enough to stop swinging. A moment later the bat fell with a wooden clank.

"Oh, Christ Rat, what are we gonna do?" moaned Jazz seeing what Cole had done to Andy.

Somehow it was up to whatever genius idea he could come up with on the fly now. Look on the bright side, the idea to have them sneak up the fire escape had worked, maybe he had something else just as good he could come up with to fix this. Rat took a deep breath, "Alright, I am going to kill the flame on the gas, so we're gonna let this place fill up a bit. While it's doing that, we're gonna get Pamela, and we are going back out the way you two came. Oh yeah, where the fuck's Skeev?"

"He's afraid of heights, him and Enio said they'd be a lookout at the bottom of the fire escape," Cole said quietly. His face looked numb like he was in shock at what he'd done.

"All right, first and foremost, we're getting Pamela out, and you too Cole. I think you've seen all you need to see of this shit, am I right? I'll come back and rig it after everybody's out."

Jazz and Rat led Cole out carefully, they both kept

one hand touching the guitarist as they moved him to the living room. "Keep an eye on him," Rat said quietly to Jazz before he went to where Pamela was tied.

Her eyes were wide when she saw him come in before she sank back onto the ancient secondhand bed she'd been lashed to. Rat took off her gag first holding up a finger, "Just be quiet OK, I don't wanna make any more noise than we already have."

"What the fuck happened here?" she whispered as he worked the knots holding her in place free.

"I'm not sure myself as to every little detail, it's all too crazy. But, Andy Weiss was a murderer, a kidnapper, a cannibal who thought he was going to start the next great American revolution right here in our little neighborhood. Also, one of them, whaddya call it, mesmerists, he had some kind of mind control over the whole cult."

"Really?"

"And that's what I can absolutely prove without taking wild guesses," Rat nodded.

"Wait, you said was!" Rat had wished she hadn't caught that part.

Rat was quiet for just a second before he replied, "Cole and Jazz were supposed to sneak up the fire escape and get the drop on him, so we could grab you after we got a three on one knock him down and go. It didn't work out like that, but they definitely showed up in time. Cole saw what the fucker had done in the kitchen and champ just snapped. Don't say nuthin' to him right now, he's kinda hurting bad, can't say I blame him."

"That bad?"

"Fucker deserved to be tortured before he died, shame Cole was so amped up, so yeah, that bad. C'mon, let's get the fuck out of here while we can. We can all have a therapy session about it later."

Once back in the living room Rat said, "Jazz, get

Cole and Pamela started down the fire escape, I'll catch up."

"Wait, what are you gonna do Hun?" Pamela demanded.

"Well, I'm going to turn this entire top floor into a ball of flames in a little bit, so I figured with you and Cole needing some help, you might want a head start," Rat couldn't help himself, he grinned. The madness of everything had seeped into him a bit, part of it was that they had destroyed the evil thing, part was that all that was left was to start burning shit. Burning shit was cool any way you cut it. Bet his old man never guessed that his little boy would become cleansing holy fire, maybe he wouldn't have smacked him so much if he did. Of course, he might also think the beatings were what made Rat an instrument of good and smack him even harder.

He followed them to another room where the window let on to the fire escape. Pamela turned and grabbed him, "Be careful!"

"This isn't going to take me ten minutes, swear to god," he replied turning her on to the fire escape and heading back inside.

Once his friends were beginning their slow clanking descent down the rickety-looking, rusty fire escape, Rat went back towards the kitchen. He needed to take a deep breath before he entered it. He'd seen what was in there already, he'd been stuck in there closer to all of it than he'd ever be able to really get over, knowing to expect it didn't make it any better. He moved cautiously into the room taking care to step around Andy Weiss' corpse and the blood that had flooded out of him staining the tile floor. He tried to not even look at it, but Rat couldn't help but glance at the mangled head, looking at the mashed orb almost with detachment at first, until he recognized a tooth in the bloody mush. He gagged a little again and looked away.

Steeling himself again, he moved over to the refrigerator.

Yanking the door to the fridge open, he had to quickly turn away from what was inside to steady himself. Five heads sat on the bottom shelf staring up at him accusingly with open eyes. He recognized at least one of them, Tommy's buddy Benny. He hadn't seen Benny since before Tommy had killed himself and now, he knew why. Unfortunately, those weren't the only body parts that littered the shelves, but they humanized what would otherwise be just bloody bits and pieces. A hand looks like a prop without its connection to a body, but a head, a head with eyes looking up at you as if to say, "You were too late." There was no mistaking that for anything else than the cruel fact of what it had been.

There was a bottle of ketchup on the door shelf, Rat scooped it up and reached with it to the back, where the light was. With as much care as his shaking hands could manage, he cracked the bulb to the light, praying he didn't fuck this up. There was a slight crack, and part of the glass fell away, but saints be praised, the filament was still lit. Taking the bottle, he used it to prop the door open. Before leaving the frig he saw one unopened forty of Ballantine sitting on the door. "You know what, fuck it," he thought before he grabbed it. Like anybody knew where their beer had been before they bought it anyway, it was still sealed.

Making his way quickly to the other side of the kitchen, he turned off the stove under the disgusting soup, waited a second, and turned all the burners at once. The thing was way too old to have an automatic ignition, it was barely trustworthy to deliver gas, as was attested to by the box of matches on the counter. Beer in hand Rat turned to flee the kitchen as quickly as he could, he didn't know how long this would take, he just knew it wouldn't be nearly long enough.

Just as he stepped over the corpse, Andy's hand shot

out and grabbed at Rat's ankle! Rat let out a scream and pulled his ankle away with a jerk stumbling back towards the door.

The bloody mess that used to be Andy's head rose up, a voice choking and gagging with blood that oozed out of his ruined mouth in clots said, "You think you've won? Only for now.... only for today.... the Discordia are around every corner.... till we meet again Rodent."

The head thudded back down.

"Winning today is plenty good enough for me fucker, I don't plan to live forever," Rat said before rushing out of the room.

He almost ran directly into the two skins that had been standing guard. They stood there dazed until they saw Rat, one of them brightened, "Hey Rat! Maybe you can tell us what the fuck we're doing here?"

Rat groaned; he didn't have time for this shit. He barked at the two of them pointing towards the door they'd come through, "Well none of us are going to be doing much if we don't get the fuck out of here now!"

The authority in his voice must have worked because both of them jogged after Rat as he ran over and climbed out the window onto the escape. Further down, he could see Pamela and Jazz carefully leading Cole down. While the two guys he had with him were just confused, at least they were in the moment, instead of wherever Cole had going on in his head to deal with what he'd just seen and done. The fire escape was rickety and rattled and groaned ominously as they rushed down, but thankfully it didn't seem inclined to come off the wall today, even with the added weight of the two big boys following behind Rat.

They were at the second floor when they heard the "whumpf!" from above. A rose bloom of fire flowed magnificently out of the window as the gas finally ignited. With the windows open, at least it wasn't an explosion, that would have brought the fire trucks too soon. But most importantly of all as far as Rat was concerned, whatever had been in Andy Weiss, whatever had driven all of this, was burning with all the evil it had done to further its fucked-up goal.

"We should probably get the flying fuck out of here now," Rat muttered to the two skins who had stopped climbing and were staring up at the flames coming from where they had just vacated.

Rat reached the ground where the others were waiting. Cole at least seemed to be coming out of whatever trance he had been in, at least he looked more alert, so baby steps. "What do we do now?" he said numbly.

"We go the fuck home, we saved the day, you punished the bad guy, we go the fuck home," Jazz said.

"What about the people in the building?" Skeev asked.

"Tell ya' what, you guys get Cole home, wash him up, buy him a beer, buy him three. I'll go around front and see if they need any help," Rat replied.

"You sure you're, OK?" Pamela asked.

"Right as rain," he winked as he turned to jog around the building. He stopped, cracked the forty, sniffed to make sure it was what it said on the label before taking an enormous gulping drink of it. Then he turned back and called back to where they were cutting through an empty lot for home, "Hey babe?"

Pamela stopped and turned, "What? Do you need help?"

Rat grinned, "Some people have said I need help for years," he called over, "but that's not the important part. The important thought is, I think there might be every evidence I love you. Be careful getting to my place, OK?"

She smiled and called back, "All right, we'll talk about this 'evidence' later then."

Rat nodded and got on with it. That was what you did when you were faced with a situation like this, you grabbed a forty and got on with it.

Interlude

Nice story if it ends there, right? Well, maybe not that nice, but it has a sort of happy ending.

Of course, life doesn't work that way, tomorrow always comes for somebody, maybe not you, but somebody. Things change, and that changes the ending.

The cops investigated, but only a little. Enough that Andy Weiss certainly got called a monster often enough in the New York Post which is a newspaper that lives for that sort of thing, so they were happy. A few people got arrested in connection with the remains they found on his floor that survived the fire, but since nobody could actually remember anything, not even about moving into the building, that investigation got no further than identifying the freezer heads. It was quietly decided to let Andy take the fall for all of it and watch anybody connected to it very closely in case they suddenly had any religious revelations of their own. As far as who killed Andy, when there's numerous heads in the fridge, the cops more or less said it would take less time to figure out who DIDN'T want him dead and work from there. Even then, they seemed more inclined to pin a medal on whoever had done it than arrest them. In other words, another dead end. The city didn't press too hard, another abandoned building vacated of squatters and now open to develop and the people were safe, which somehow, they took the credit for. Like they gave two shits about the mongrels living there before the fire.

Other things happened as well. Restraint and Control

recorded their ep, which had some success. It might have had more, but soon after it was recorded Cole quit the band. He quit so Shane and Robbo wouldn't pressure Rat to fire him. It turned out he was pretty fucking far from all right from what he'd seen and done and had resorted to the Lower East Side's favorite pain eraser to help him cope, shitty brown heroin. He announced he was quitting one practice and just walked out. By the time the rest of the band got back to their little homestead Cole and his shit was gone. Word was he was living in the same junkie squat that Dirty had gone back to after the fire. Nobody saw him much after that and when they did, everybody was too heartbroken to say much about anything important.

Next to leave was Jazz. He and Eve broke up over some trivial shit, or maybe not so trivial, Jazz didn't talk enough for Rat to know how he was coping. Jazz went into a total mope about the whole thing, not a big explosion mope you get over either, something deep-seated. One day Rat got home from work and Enio told him that Jazz's dad had driven all the way out from home and came and got him. Which left only Enio and Rat in the homestead. Shane knew the local music scene and quickly grabbed two guys from similar bands who would be the replacements for the departed rhythm guitarist and bassist. But still, it would take a while to get them worked in.

When the world falls down, it keeps falling. One day Pamela just came out and said it, "I don't think I'm going to be coming over anymore."

Rat didn't even react, he already knew they were just going through the motions by this point, "Yeah, so I guess I'll see you around huh?"

"Yeah."

It was simple enough why it got weird between them. The paradigm of their relationship changed that day in that building. She was going to be the plucky young college girl who finds the diamond in the rough, she was the one who saw something special and unique and poetic in the beast and was going to tame him, teach him tricks, show him to her parents as her science project that she just happened to be fucking. Now she had to deal with him as the hero in the tale, the guy who pulled her out of God only knew what that day. He never lorded it, but as far as she was concerned, he didn't have to. She felt the power dynamic shift away from what she wanted it to be deep down, and they were too young for love, or lust, or gratitude to overcome those emotions. Maybe if they'd both been older and more mature, they could have seen the problem and talked it out. Who knew? And did it matter, since they could only be the age they were?

Finally, the riots happened anyway. On August 6th of 1988, there was a demonstration in support of the homeless, and squatter's rights in the park. The police charged in, intent on cracking skulls, all hell broke loose, violence erupted, most of it coming from the police themselves. Ironically, it was not the torch that the Discordia expected. The city copped full responsibility and tried to look like nice guys who just fucked up here, but would try to do better. They weren't nice guys, by the way, they were bullies and thugs who got caught this time with the cameras running. It worked though; the national media barely covered the thing.

The writing was on the wall though, gentrification was coming. And Rat, he was going, anywhere but here.

Rat, followed Jazz and just went the fuck home. It wasn't much of a home town to go to, but at least he knew more people he could mooch off of there until he figured out what came next.

PART II

Chapter 1

Jim Malloy hated this shit with a deep-felt passion. You had kids to ensure you never had to mow the god damned grass again, that was what made it worth feeding and clothing for the love of Christ! He figured it was in the constitution or something. Not that his kids ever came by the house anymore, both were off at college and already moving towards their own lives. Still, you'd think they'd stop by out of concern and then mow the lawn while they were here. Even if they hadn't come to visit or stay here anymore than was court-ordered even before college had freed them of that obligation. Jim couldn't say he blamed them, if he had to choose between his little, barely in the suburbs, WW2 era brick tract home, and Cindy's McMansion with an in-ground pool, he knew which one he'd have chosen at that age.

Of course, he and Cindy had always had different goals in life, and different skill sets to approach life with.

Hers had landed her a very nice job, in a very nice firm in the city. Once she had cut the dead weight out of her life, god damned if she wasn't pulling in close to seven figures a year. Smart girl in most ways, bit of a blind spot, or at least she had one for the longest time. Jim had been that dead weight the entire length of their marriage. She never said it out loud, she really didn't need to. Maybe he wasn't dead weight anymore, he'd done a lot of work on himself, but six years ago when she had finally said enough was enough, he had definitely been the rope tying her balloon to the ground.

Financially, he was the one getting alimony, despite working. For that matter, she bought his house for him cheap from a friend's firm, strictly so she wouldn't have to sell their mutual one and split the profits. She claimed she loved the place and couldn't bear to part with it and wouldn't he be perfectly happy in this little brick shitbox with a yard and an above-ground pool and just everything. By that point, Jim just said, "Yeah, sure, when can I cash this here alimony check?" In his meager defense in his own head, he had finally gotten better, he was a human being again. But the Good Ship Cindy had already set sail and landed in the port of Todd Baringer. Todd was more her speed anyway, the man had never had a sincere, original thought in his fucking life but he looked good on her arm. He never raised his voice about anything, he just didn't have the depth of feeling to pull that off convincingly. Cindy never had to worry about what kind of mood Todd was in, like a child he could be easily directed to another one anyway. She didn't love him, Jim was sure of it, but she couldn't take being in love with Jim Malloy one second longer, and in a fit of decency Jim Malloy had capitulated completely.

Fuck it, he hadn't done badly to be where he was now, he didn't have enough fingers and toes to count all of his dead friends and yet he had avoided joining them somehow. You mow the lawn, you go inside like he was doing right now, you go in the kitchen, and you grab yourself a beer. A beer, singular, moderation Jimmy my boy, that was the key to everything. And for doing your chores like a good boy, maybe soak in the pool for a bit after. The good life, right? Of course, if it was so good why was he alone for it? That was a poser, he had to admit. He could go out, but he didn't want to, people wanted to drink when they were out, and while he wouldn't say no to a beer, he didn't want to drink. If you didn't know the difference you never really drank in the first place.

Jim popped some kind of expensive porter and sat down in his computer room clicking on the screen. He probably shouldn't keep the tower powered up, but he did it anyway, mostly out of laziness. He couldn't count on keeping a thought in his head long enough, he needed to be ready when he was going to have some genius ass insight into the human condition that needed to be shared on Facebook or Twitter, like, right now. He mainly thought of jokes, but you never knew, one day you could have this genius thought about world hunger or something and forget it while you were waiting for the thing to boot the hell up. He barely touched his phone if he could avoid it, he hated using the damned tiny buttons for one thing. He mainly owned it because people thought they had a right to all your time and all your attention no matter where you were, and having one made them shut up about it.

The AC felt good, damned good. It didn't feel so good when he got the electric bills, but on a day when it was in the 90s and humid as a hippo's ass, who gave a damn? Live for now! He'd pay, and it would be worth every red cent of it. That was life, knowing you'd pay for it later, and then making a decision whether or not it was worth it. Doc Gonzo wasn't minding it either, Doc who had been hiding inside like a coward while the lawnmower was running, big tough pit bull that he was.

Jim popped open Facebook while he sipped his beer, letting Doc settle down at his feet. Friend request, and a bunch of notifications. He quickly scanned through the notifications; they were mainly laughs at some of the posts he'd put up last night. That was one of life's great pastimes now, scrolling through your timeline looking for memes to post so people would think you were funny. It beat having to tell jokes to actual people, you could screen out people on Facebook. He figured if they were on his friends list, they already knew what he was like by now and he could post whatever jokes made him laugh. None of that mentally trying to calibrate if the new person you were meeting on the street had a fucking sense of humor or not. In his experience, people thought they did, and he thought otherwise.

Finally, deciding there was nothing important left to look at, he popped open the friend request. That was when time froze, no it did more than that, it actually went backward thirty years. He had a friend request from a name he hadn't heard in that long, Cole Orvik. Still barely believing it, he clicked open the profile. Alright, the profile pic was a dead clown, but just that alone made Jim suspect it was the right guy. Looking further at the actual tagged pics, that was Cole! A Cole who had had a hard life by the looks of it, but it was Cole nonetheless! Jim didn't even consider refusing it for a second, he clicked accept.

No shit! Cole was still alive, how about that? Being part of the scene back then had so many ways to die, hell even since then, all the damage you did to your body could catch up to you. Not even to mention that the habits you still might have would prove to be stronger than your resilience, somebody dropped that way every year, even now when everybody should know better. For Jim, this moment proved the power of the net. One of the reasons he'd started on social media in the first place was to reconnect with people after the divorce. Being married doesn't always leave a lot of time for "buddies," and for that matter, his temperament for a few years had pushed people away. Yet here he was today, friends with Cole fucking Orvik! Will wonders never cease?

He didn't private message Cole back right away, frankly Jim had no idea what to type. What do you say to somebody you haven't seen in thirty years? Instead, he hopped on a group for Eagles fans and bitched about the draft some with the rest of the Philly faithful which he had found himself becoming by accident at some point. When that got boring, he went over to a punk page he frequented. It was all old farts like him, but it was nice to see people his own age still flying the flag to some degree or another. Jim might not have his waistline, or hairline, or much of anything else left from being a kid, but he had never given up on the music. Sometimes he even managed to play in a band with a few other old farts. It was currently on hold at the moment for a purely old fart reason, guitarist had a heart attack. His doctor said the poor guy couldn't do anything particularly strenuous until he lost some weight. Anarchy! Youth Gone Wild!

Jim also still went to shows sometimes if somebody from one of the boards was going to be there. It was nice to have a face to put with the people he talked to online. Still, it was funny, in his teens, he didn't go to every show he wanted to because he didn't have any money, in his twenties and thirties, he didn't because he was building a life and a family, also ruining it for that matter, and there were just other priorities. Now, he only went every once in a while, because even though he lived right outside of a major city, Christ it was a lot of work to drive all the way down there, go to the show, make sure you were good to drive home, etc., etc. So much easier to just hide in the house with his records and his memories. Sometimes it seemed the only reason he went to shows was to just make sure hiding inside with his memories wasn't all he was doing, like some pathetic old shut-in.

Jim was just about to get up and toss the empty when his messenger pinged. He paused and checked. It was Cole, guess he'd been online and saw Jim was online. Well, conversations had to start somewhere.

Cole: Holy shit, Rat! Is that really you?

Jim: Really me, but for that matter is it really you?

Cole: No shit! Your profile says you're near Philly, how the hell did you end up there?

Jim: Girl. Remember Tara, Pamela's roommate?

After a little bit Cole responded.

Cole: Tall girl? Blond hair?

Jim: Yeah, that's the one.

Cole: You still with her?

Jim: No way, we phone called and wrote letters after I went home, and I guess we were together two months when I got down here to where she lived, but, naw, total art school girl wanted a punk boyfriend to scare her parents. That never lasts.

Cole: So, why'd you stay there?

Jim: By then I'd gotten used to the city I guess, had a job, that type of shit. Met my wife when she was coming down to the Troc regular to see shows, and well, then I had a wife.

Cole: So, how's married life treating you?

Jim: Divorced life now

Cole: Shit, sorry, I just stepped on my dick

Jim: Don't worry about it, it ended on a whimper, I've made my peace with it.

Jim remembered himself, and his manners, which years of marriage had managed to drill into his head.

Jim: So, what have you been doing with yourself
Cole: You know, travel, seeing things.
Jim: You still play?
Cole: When I can, I've been on some things over the years. Ever hear Trilateral Assault?
Jim: Heard of, not heard
Cole: D-beat band out of Frisco, I played on their one ep
Jim: Cool!
Cole: So, what type of music do you listen to these days?
Jim: More or less the same shit I used to. I mean I like newer bands, but, same style and all. Maybe some German stuff, some psychobilly. You?
Cole: More or less the same, a lot of industrial in there. You go to any shows at all?
Jim: Yeah some, I mean my time's mostly my own on the weekends.
Cole: Cool. You ever go into Philly?
Jim: If the show's good enough
There was a long pause in the conversation before...
Cole: All right man, cool talking to you, see you soon.
Jim: Cool talking to you, take care, laters

So, Cole was still alive and, on the internet, imagine that. Even at Jim's age life was full of surprises, good and bad. Despite how things had ended all those years before, Jim was happy for it. Time passes, life moves on, lord knew he'd fucked up enough himself, so he could certainly let Cole's fuckups go. Finding out that anyone had made it through the fires intact was practically the entire fucking point of the internet as far as Jim was concerned. That, and funny cat videos. Sometimes, if enough time has passed you don't wish someone ill anymore, no matter what they'd done, you're just happy with the knowledge that they still exist.

That promised to be Jim's biggest excitement of the day, and since nothing else cool was forthcoming he had some shopping to do. He went to the grocery store most days. No matter what he did there was always something he needed, for one thing, he didn't write down a list, ever. He was fine with being in there almost every day, it kept his head in life. You'd think a job would do that too, but Christ, he worked in a mailroom. He might jabber with some people but that was work. Work wasn't life, it was just what you did to pay the bills, conversations at work didn't count as real-world interactions, they were work interactions where everybody flapped their jaws to pass the time. Those conversations had their own box, and that box closed at quitting time. Really, with Cindy insisting to pay alimony to him, he didn't even need the job to afford this place if he scrimped. With the job, he lived in comfort, if not luxury. No, he did things like have a job, or go to the store just to remain a part of the human race. He knew from experience how easy it was to close the doors to the world and he also knew how unhealthy that was.

As Jim was walking to his car, he noticed something sticking out of his mailbox. Mail had been and gone hours ago so it being out of place caught his eye. He snatched the piece of paper out, looking up he noticed there was one in every box going down the street. Probably some coupons for some new restaurant, but curiosity made him look anyway. When he unfolded it, he discovered, that it was definitely not an ad for Thai. Instead, in a stupid ass German goth band font it said...

"Only The Depraved Join With The Scum Of Our Earth

Cowards Are Happy To Join With The Illegals And Their Jew Owners

Be True To Your Heritage

Be True To Your Race!!!
Be True To Yourself
Join The Aryan Identity Alliance Today!
Free Yourself And Protect Your Children's Future!"

Motherfucker! Jim crumbled the piece of paper up in his hands, his face twisted into a snarl of rage. Fucking actual fucking Nazis were fucking flier-ing HIS neighborhood? The fucking balls that took, especially considering what would have happened if he'd caught the pricks. Not on his god damned watch, no way in hell! Jim looked up, and he saw the line of mailboxes, all of them with a flier peeking out. No, this would not stand at all, not today, not ever!

Jim turned back to the house, storming up his sidewalk to the door. He was so pissed he fumbled a bit getting the right key and getting it into the door. Ignoring Doc, who was acting like he'd been gone a week in that short time, he set the crumpled piece of paper that had been in his box on a table, that shit was getting reported to the police, before continuing into the kitchen to get what he needed to rectify this. Jim quickly fumbled under the sink until he found the box of small trash bags. The rest of those propaganda rags still outside had a date with the fucking landfill!

Back outside and snatching each one from each mailbox, it didn't take long for Jim to make a sweep of the neighborhood. His anger cooled some as he went, repetitive motion and time do that. By the time he was halfway down the block, Jim was worried about one of the neighbors possibly seeing him, and calling the cops on him for fucking with their mailboxes. Still, you couldn't just leave this poison around, there were kids on this block for the love of fuck! What if some impressionable mind got a hold of this garbage?

Jim was beginning to head back to his house when he

noticed Alan in front of his place. Alan was a typical middle-aged white guy, like so damned generic they could use him for JC Penny clothing ads. He had a typical middle-aged beer gut, he grilled, he had two kids in college, and a wife Jim was positive he only spoke to at dinner. Jim assumed they must have fucked twice since the wedding, they had two kids, and they both kind of looked like Alan. He was one of the few guys that Jim had found it impossible to have an opinion on, the guy was just so.... average, nothing stood out about him. It's hard to have an opinion on the status quo because it mainly just exists, it is a false metric of normal taken by knocking off all the bits of real life from the block of stone, it's what's left over after you remove anything of any interest to anybody.

"What's got you so pissed off?" Alan called over to him.

Jim stopped stalking back to his house, "Would you fucking believe it? Nazis came through here stuffing shit in everyone's mailboxes. I just went down the block grabbing them before somebody's kid sees one of the things. Going home to throw them out."

Alan snorted, "Better you than me buddy. What if your trash bag tears open on trash day, they blow around, half the neighborhood thinks you're a Klansman!"

Jim had to admit, he hadn't even considered that. "Oh well, I'll double bag or something, I couldn't just leave them there!"

"Good Samaritan huh? Mind if I see one of them, I assume you already got mine," Alan said with a bit of a grin.

"Huh? Yeah, I guess...." he dug into the bag and pulled out one of the crumpled pieces of paper.

Alan scanned it for a minute before handing it back, "Yeah that is some crazy shit. They aren't totally wrong about the illegals though, I thought I heard something about some billionaire paying to bring them here."

Jim didn't even know what the hell to say to that. Jesus Christ! He'd gone bowling with this asshole once!

The store was sad, which wasn't how most people viewed it, but it was how Jim viewed it some days. He was single, and shopping, which meant it involved light flirting with the various divorcees who read in Cosmo that it was a good place to meet men. Jim had never read the article himself, but from what he had gathered from a woman he'd dated for a couple of weeks after meeting at this exact supermarket, he had all the earmarks that the article had said to look for. He went along with it like a complete weenbag and had since dated more than one divorcee culled from the aisles of the suburban mart. But hey, a guy got lonely, and it was better than being one of the pathetic has-beens who tried to impress 21-year-old punk girls enough to flop into bed with them on the strength of their lengthy punk rock bonafides. There were stories about older men being better lovers and shit, he knew for a fact it was bullshit, if the woman was hot enough, he still came faster than she did, not to mention, he had a bad back. Don Juan, he was not, more Don Juan Step Away in The Produce Aisle.

On the plus note, he reminded himself, it got him out of the house and meeting people however briefly. The house no longer seemed depressingly empty to him, but you spend too long shooting the shit with people online you begin to forget that the majority of what happens on the internet isn't real life. Nobody is who they are on the internet, on the internet you have time to think about it, to craft your personality to the situation. You don't just blurt out the embarrassing story about the time you farted in the elevator next to the judge who would later be hearing your divorce proceedings for instance. At least not right away.

Maybe some guys did, who knew?

He pulled into Whole Foods and let out the same sigh he always did, deep-seated old punker guilt. For fuck's sake, he used to live on nothing but fucking knish's out of carts and Midnight Dragon, now he was buying organic veggie burgers at Whole Foods and nothing but microbrews which he judiciously doled out as a treat for himself. It wasn't where he shopped all the time, but he came in here enough to be a regular, which created that self-same deep-seated guilt about the whole thing nobody in there could possibly understand. Somewhere right now, there was a kid out there living off of Wawa hot dogs because it was all that the spare change he could beg for bought, thinking people like Jim were the enemy. Jim wondered often, in the secret parts of his soul, if that kid wasn't right. Of course, he knew how much it had set him back the last time he had to go to the doctor because his deductible wasn't met, and reminded himself he was just getting by comfortably like a human being, he wasn't the one running this shit. Sometimes he managed to listen to himself and just got the fuck on with his life.

He wanted to get some organic carrots to snack on, that was his mistake. MILFs always prowl the hardest in the produce section, looking to find someone to tell them they're beautiful for a while when it seems the whole world stopped doing it at thirty. Guys are dumb, they think of it as a great time to make stupid double entendres about melons, but that isn't why she's here. She wants to show you that she's healthy, that she cares about her body, and she's looking to copulate with another healthy human. It's simple basic logic. Just primal fucking instincts, the healthy ones aren't going to be in the snack aisle or the beer aisle, no use looking there at all. Who knew, maybe yuppies in their twenties linger over wine selections, it wasn't how he spent his twenties.

He was going over the bags of carrots when he heard a voice next to him, "I see you in here all the time. You must be serious about your health."

Jim turned with an affected grin on his face to match the sultry bass she had put into her voice, something devil may care, but rode hard and put away wet. It was the best expression he had left if he wanted to look attractive. He'd called it right, she looked about forty, maybe as high as forty-five, and had aged well. The dress she was wearing was just tight enough to tell him she had a gym membership and she wanted him to know she had one. A large portion of this woman's time was spent in yoga pants and another large portion was spent getting those blond highlights put in. A quick glance down told him, no wedding ring. He should politely break this off now.

"Well, I didn't use to, I guess I'm trying to make up for lost time."

"Hi, I'm Rebecca," she said holding out her hand.

"Umm, Jim," he replied taking it gently, hinting with the gesture and the hesitation he made before he let it go that he was considering kissing her hand.

"Well Jim, I hate shopping alone. Especially since the divorce. How about you?"

He really shouldn't.

"Yeah, it gets lonely being single after all these years," he replied.

Chapter 2

Rebecca had been nice for a couple of weeks, and when it ran its course, well, that was fine too. They had nothing in common, not music, not upbringing, not movies, not a damned thing, but that was OK. Both of them were using the other for company and comfort, and both of them knew it deep down. You have two weeks where you just fuck and hang out a bit because you're happy that you have somebody to fuck and hang out with before it starts to get old. She had started to pull away first, which was fine as well, he wasn't exactly looking to commit to anything anyway. Jim knew himself well enough to know if something kept going on he wouldn't fight too hard against it, but that wasn't the goal in his life right now, he wasn't quite up to being a giving soul mate yet and he didn't need the emotional validation of having one. So, if she got bored with him, cool, whatever. She'd had a nice life before her divorce and what she really wanted for the rest of it was for it to be nice, not to go to shows on the arm of a beaten-up douche living more off of alimony than his actual job. She was good looking, well put together for any age, and had a pretty decent, if not particularly deep personality. She'd find some stockbroker who was done with his mid-life crisis and wanted to go back to looking respectable with a more refined woman on his arm at some point. She had used him to make herself feel like she'd still got it, and prove that she could get someone kind of dangerous looking and sexy. That was fine with him. Really. Jim was just wasting her time anyway and liked her enough to be happy to see her getting on with her life. She felt pretty and desirable again, which was something else her ex had taken when he left, and being with him for even a little while had put back some. Jim was happy he could make her feel that way.

The slow dissolve of their fuck buddy arrangement meant that Jim had Friday free. He was using that newfound freedom to go to a show for the first time since they'd started seeing one another. It wasn't anything or anybody he was hugely into, some band from England he had a song by on a comp tape thirty years ago, but he was going anyway. If he didn't show up in the city occasionally his friends started giving him shit on Facebook. Worse, they might worry, and Jim sincerely hoped that his days of worrying people were behind him. An ex-drunk, divorced, kids all grown up, living alone... people had active imaginations. He wasn't torn up with despair about himself or the state of his life, hell he jogged a little to keep in shape and had a gym membership so he could potentially live longer. Jim had gotten his emotional turmoil dealt with early, just in time to be the cause of the divorce as he was finishing up with it getting his mind clear of the past, of childhood, of all the bad things that had happened to him had turned him into an emotional wrecking ball for a while, anybody close could only hope to take shrapnel while avoiding the brunt of his lashing out. But it was behind him now, he was better off for it, the kids were better off since he wasn't quite such an embarrassment now, and frankly Cindy was better off. She was with her own people at last, where she belonged.

He wasn't exactly enthralled with driving to the city, but he hated taking public transport from that far out even more. You lost control if you had to rely on transit, you were stuck somewhere until the next train or the next bus and that was that. It allowed for exposure to an increasingly crazy world that he could take a pass on. Not that driving in was any dance through the daisies on a lovely day in spring. Looking for parking in Center City always bit the big one, there was always the chance of a break-in if you had to leave it at night, assuming you found someplace that still had parking. Mainly though, it was that the traffic sucked ass and left him wanting to punch someone dead in the mouth. Not that he would, those days were behind him as well, that trapped anger became frustration and annoyance instead. He was adult enough to know the consequences of just hauling off and drilling someone you deem worthy of a busted nose. It was funny, at nineteen you didn't even hesitate, which was stupid if you think about it, you had a whole lot longer to live with the consequences. Now with the clock winding on to the second half of your life, you just knew better.

Jim was shocked to find a spot only two blocks from the actual hall. Like, he had such a level of surprise that he had to walk around the vehicle twice to look for any signs or markers indicating the space might be illegal before he was willing to hit the alarm on the truck. Another of life's little jokes at his younger self's expense was that he drove a truck. When he was a kid, he thought everybody who drove a truck was an automatic redneck, because that was all he saw in his hometown. Now that he was an adult, he thought being able to haul any damned thing he wanted was worth its weight in gold. Priorities, so many shift with the sand going out as time washed away from the shore.

There was the normal crowd out front as he walked up. Kids, mainly trying to shake down friends for enough money to get in, or just hanging out to see what the evening might bring. Even if you couldn't get in when you were that age, it was worth being there since you knew all your friends were going to be there anyway. Placing yourself in position for the before and after drinking, so vital, not being there for it was a rookie mistake. Jim had a ticket, and would not be partying, before, or after, so this was not his scene. He slid through the kids, and they parted almost in shock, he was an obvious adult now and just not part of their world. Even with his hair spiky and bleached, he looked like he existed in this place solely to tell their dads if they misbehaved. Which was hilarious, even if they didn't see why, they were all there to see a band that was even older than Jim was tonight. He'd first heard them when he was younger than these kids were now.

Just because he was no longer someone named Rat, and just because he was part of the adult supervision in the room didn't save him from reacting like he had done going into every show since he was a kid. It was an instant transformation once he handed over his ticket and stepped into the room. Jim started scanning immediately taking stock of his surroundings instinctively. If you had walked up to him and said, "What are you looking at?" he might have muttered something about seeing who was here or something. That wasn't the full description, or even a truthful one. What he was doing was scanning for trouble. Who looked like a problem, who had made comments about kicking his ass recently, where the fight was going to be, and which direction to move to get the fuck out of it. Nobody had threatened to kick his ass in ten years now at the least, but old habits die hard. In the case of this particular habit, Jim figured it was one of the things that had ensured he hadn't died for so long.

Jim spotted some people he knew from the local scene who was working one of the merch tables in the back. He took a deep breath and told his apprehension and social anxiety to go fuck itself before he headed over. It was Billy and his girlfriend Alicia; they were selling merch for Forensic Blind which was one of the local openers. There was another band of kids opening before them who Jim had never heard of, but Blind had been around for a while so they earned further up the bill.

"So, he actually snuck out of suburbia to have some fun!" Billy said when he spotted him.

"Yeah, well, your mom was sore, so I had to give her a night off," Jim replied gruffly shaking the shaggy looking slightly younger man's hand. "Hey Alicia, I see you still ain't developed any taste in men."

"Nope, but if I ever decide to get into lemon parties, I'll call you," she grinned behind the mop of fuchsia that hung over her face.

"We all caught up on insults now?" Jim asked.

"Yeah, I think that covers the normal ground," Billy replied, "you going anywhere after this tonight?"

"Doubt it, I'm old, we get cranky if you keep us out too long."

"Oh, you are not that old," Alicia huffed.

"Old enough. Naw I'm just here long enough to make my hearing worse, and then it's off to the land of Ensure, to my health."

"You were more fun when you were a drunk," Billy chided.

"Maybe, but I don't call you at three AM crying about bullshit anymore because drunks can't read a fucking clock."

"True."

Their witty repartee was interrupted by the first band

plugging in something. Jim turned to see them climbing on stage, they looked almost like they were trying to sneak on. Somehow in their heads, even though their name was on the flier somebody at this late stage might still pop up and yell, "What in the hell are you doing up there?" He knew the feeling; he'd been in the new band once upon a time himself. In a way, Jim kind of envied them, this was all new, exciting, something they'd talk about when they were his age. Assuming they got to be his age of course, never a good idea to assume something like that in punk rock. But whatever the future held for them; it did his heart good to see that kids were still out there as a new generation of misfit toys. Even if to his eye they dressed like the fucking homeless these days, but who was he to judge? Last thing he wanted out of himself was to be some cranky old man bitching about, "these kids today" and their fashion sense.

There were a couple of crunches as the guitarist checked to see if he was in tune, the bassist began throbbing away through his notes as an undertone. The drummer hit the skins a couple of times, no one was completely sure why drummers did this except for other drummers, they'd just set the kit up just moments before, maybe they just wanted to feel included. A few members of the crowd started to drift to the front for the sacrificial lamb opener, Jim took it as his cue, nodded to Billy and Alicia, and began to drift a little closer himself. He made it a point of checking out new bands, you never knew, it could be a "You could say you were there," moment. At the very least it didn't cost you anything to be supportive of the youngsters.

The singer went meekly to the mic stand, grabbing the microphone itself almost delicately, "Hey, thanks for coming out. We're Needlenose and this is called 'Our Parents Lied,' hope you like it and stuff."

Whatever social anxiety issues the kid was dealing

with in the rest of his life vanished the moment the band started. The band, the crowd, and most importantly the singer erupted from the opening note. Jim was surprised, the kid had a higher pitched scream/yell than most bands went in for these days. He liked them, it sounded old school, like real American hardcore. He could taste hints of Life Sentence, that offset the bouquet of Anti, they even occasionally downshifted into some hearty whiny snotty Crucifucks, early Dissent sarcasm. He'd have to make a point of drifting over to the merch table when they took a break to see if they had anything for sale. If you wanted to keep on living you had to surround yourself with the living, just having your heart beating didn't count.

The heat in the hall went up drastically as the crowd began slamming. Jim figured the band must have played around a bit and had some kids who knew them and he'd just missed them before tonight. Nobody gets the crowd, even as it was still filling in, moving like that first time out of the gate, no matter how good they are. Oh well, he could afford to be behind the curve on things like that, it wasn't like he wrote a zine or anything. You do enough time in the scene, you can afford to be out of date, your punk points remained stockpiled.

Their set was twenty minutes tops, they probably played fifteen songs in the time they were up there. Jim was definitely going to have to see if they had something for sale. Short and sweet and to the point, he even clapped for them as they left the stage, something he rarely did anymore. As they toddled off the stage to make room for Forensic Blind, who was next up, Jim made his way over to the table again. He wasn't alone in that idea; it had gotten a bit crowded already by the time he made the distance. Totally deserved, they'd put on a solid set.

Tucked away on the side he spotted a 45 and a t-shirt, thankfully his old guy card was working and Alicia dealt with him right away. It wasn't a large crowd of people, but Jim hated lines and crowds at all, for that matter. Which maybe some people would find odd considering a lifetime of shows, but people lining up to buy shit had a different, impatient, and aggressive vibe to them that people standing around watching a band play didn't. It might be tightly pressed and all, but watching a band still felt like a solitary action, the wall of sound cut you off so completely from everyone else that you were just touching them, you weren't really next to them in any real way. Even the pit with bodies flying everywhere was more about what YOU were doing, not them, other people were objects to bump off of, not actual people. When one of the bodies forced itself into your consciousness it was usually a precursor to a fight.

The place had a refreshment stand sort of thing which was weird to him for some reason. Sugary soda, potato chips, and Raisinets for the revolution. Despite that, or maybe because of it, for a moment Jim considered going over and getting something. After he saw the un-ironic line forming, he dismissed it quickly. The crowd for tonight's gig had officially arrived, it was getting steamy and tight, so he angled his way down one wall to get a bit closer to the stage to get into position to snap a few photos. He didn't slam, hadn't for years, slamming was for people who were young and bent better than he did. How fucking humiliating would it be to have his back go out in the middle of the pit?

Forensic Blind took the stage as he found his spot to be in the crowd but remain as extra alone as was possible. There was a repeat of the brief crunches as the guitarist plugged in and hit a chord. Ben the lead singer didn't say a word to the crowd. He just stalked up to the microphone looked back at the band who nodded imperceptibly to indicate readiness before he turned back to the crowd and screaming, "1,2,3,4!"

In an instant, the crowd was moving well enough to the wave of thrash that followed that Jim was getting stumble-backs into him even at the side of the room where he had stashed himself with his camera. He still dug this, the energy backlash that shook you to your toes from a room during a show. That crackle that bounced from the band to the crowd and back again. As long as there weren't any fights, this was the moment where the entire crowd became a single organism to an outside viewer. They might be in their own heads but the body had joined into something pulsing, throbbing with energy, screaming out to the entire uncaring universe, "RIGHT HERE AND NOW WE ARE ALIVE!"

One of the things he liked about Forensic was that they never let up, no lengthy pauses, no big diatribes to introduce the songs, no anything that would hamper this moment, or put any kind of pause to this organism's life cycle. If they had been around back in the day and had managed to get a couple of albums out, they'd be the ones headlining a gig like this. These days, well there were still kids, but with the internet and everything, it took some of the event feeling out of a band releasing an album. You couldn't feel special or unique discovering a band from half a world away for the first time when all it took was a decent internet connection to discover every band on earth in a second.

Since it was nonstop it could only last so long, the human body had limitations. They were around Jim's age or maybe a little younger, but not much, so good for them lasting as long as they could. Forty-five minutes doesn't seem long, but at that pace, and that age, it was a triumph. It wasn't like they just stood there or anything, these guys moved around and really went for it. They might look absolutely exhausted and older than their years for it, but at least when they fell off stage at the end of their set, you had no doubt whatsoever that they had given you everything they had in them. To the kids that had gotten to witness it, they were gods right now, and rightfully so.

As the band left the stage, music was turned on from the hall's sound system. Almost as soon as Forensic had vacated actual roadies swarmed on to change things around for the next act. From the looks of it, the headliners must have had some big gigs lined up in some other towns, or some major guarantees along the way. No other way they could afford the swarm of ants that were making everything just perfect for them otherwise. Maybe there was some big festival coming up that had paid everything to get the band on tour, that's the only way these bands could afford the time off to come to the states half the time. Jim had no idea; he wouldn't be caught dead at something like those huge monstrosities. At no point in his life had he had any interest in seeing a "punk rock Woodstock" no matter who the fuck was playing. Punk rock happened in halls like this or smaller, once you got to arenas it might look the same, it may sound similar, but it wasn't really punk rock anymore. If the kids in the audience couldn't picture themselves up there doing it for themselves, it was just rock n roll. Jim supposed that was all right for some, but that didn't mean he wanted to go.

It humored Jim that even with the lights up, and them hiding in the shadows, he could still see the headliners standing back there sipping on water and beer waiting for their cue. They didn't look like Burning Chaos anymore, they looked like some genial old duffers dressed in jeans, docs, and t-shirts. Loads of tattoos covering their sagging arms though, relics of when they lived up to their name and then some. Somebody, he had no idea who, actually walked out front to grab the mic and announced, "And now, all the way from Birmingham, England! Burning Chaos!"

The crowd erupted with a cheer, pretty good for a band who had one well-known song on a compilation record back in the day and some stuff almost nobody in the states could get their hands on when it came out. Good work if you can get it. He vaguely remembered that they had put out some mediocre sounding reunion album a few years ago. It wasn't bad per se, it was just uninspired and half-assed. Something to tour on, but not really anything that had the fire they might have had in their youth. In their defense, at least it wasn't just one member, usually the singer, and some hired band playing in a totally different style than the original band had. Jim had seen that scam pulled often enough.

The crowd might have reacted young and energetic but the band that came out to greet their applause looked old. Well, the three guys who were really from the band that was, since that record had come out it looked like they had gotten a second guitarist and a new drummer to add some life to the proceedings. The new guys looked like they were young enough to be the kids of the original band. Who knew? Maybe they were. A Van Halen sort of deal, keep the royalties in the family.

The band cruised through the two albums they had recorded before breaking up in the early eighties more or less going through the motions. Every once in a while, though they'd slip something from the new record in, or something that might be a totally new song to keep the crowd guessing. It felt like.... like all the shit that Jim used to make fun of the boomers for back in the day when there were like three different versions of The Byrds and they all played Vegas. The crowd loved every second of it, but to Jim, it looked like the original band in old man suits. Or maybe like they had been skinned and their pelts had been hung on to robots programmed to play all the old favorites. It was competent, enjoyable enough as a light diversion, but it had no immediacy. There was no feeling like this was some great moment that you were privileged to witness, more like it was all a reenactment of the great punk rock revolution being put on by the local playhouse. It beat sitting around at home all night, but only because he didn't drink like he used to. Jim felt like he was a ghost on a lake shore watching the last few ripples from where the cannonball had struck the placid water years ago, during the war he'd died in.

Then they left the stage. Since they hadn't played their big "hit" everyone knew this was just to beg for applause for the encore. Such a time-honored rock n roll cliché to finalize a set built on being one. Say any damned thing you wanted about the UK Subs, but Uncle Charlie never stopped cranking out music, he never went through a new wave or metal phase, he never went away for thirty years. These guys did, and what they had come back as was a lounge act. A fast and loud lounge act, sure, but they were going through the motions every bit as much as Wayne fucking Newton did. Jim only prayed that they didn't remind him to tip his waitress before they got off the stage.

You had to know when your youth rebellion was over. It may have left a permanent stain on you, but no more great changes were forthcoming from that quarter. It had made whatever mark it was going to on the world, along with the one you carried around. That whole time it had happened in had fucked right off somehow. The kids had bigger problems now. His generation didn't want to end up mindless drones punching the clock, this generation was afraid of starving to death while they did it. The machine they were raging against was uglier and crueler than it had been when he was a lad, maybe if they had just killed the thing then and there...... It turned out the Dead Kennedys were right about everything, what had seemed to be hyperbole at the time seemed sunny cock-eyed optimism now. Considering the DKs were also a lounge act these days maybe it was just Jello who had gotten the advance copies of today's online readers polls.

When you were young and first found punk, it articulated what you felt. That you were a child, and all the words on all the billboards always went on about how precious children were, but you never felt like that once. If anything, you felt like your school, your parents, their god, and your government all actively hated your guts with an almost religious passion, an almost biblical disdain. Punk said that there was someone out there that understood that they were assholes. You might have been lied to about being the precious future, but at least you had company.

If you didn't accidentally fuck up and become your domineering dad one day, and you were still in this with gray hair, you still had ample reasons to be pissed. You had discovered that there were so many things, so many unique moments, and people, and places and they were all so precious and all these years later there were still plenty of people that constituted the powers that be who'd happily tear them down, person, place, and thing, to slap ugly modern asphalt and concrete over every inch of them and call it "gentrification and progress." Progress of course being rich white guy slang for money being made. For all that it was declared to be progress, it never seemed to make anyone any happier. So, you were every bit as pissed but robbed of your youthful fire, you went around with an aching sore spot in your gut that throbbed dully with irritation every waking moment of every waking day. You were Jacob Marley unable to change the world of the living anymore, that time had been squandered.

Your goal in life now was reduced to finding enough precious things to appreciate and to try and protect for this precious moment until you finally had the good grace to drop dead. Live fast, keep on living, holy shit, keep on living, leave a wrinkled corpse. Put it on a t-shirt, we'll all make millions.

The oldies revue ended the way it had been planned, with the big song from the comp, and the crowd chanting along happily. Jim guessed he was happy enough that he'd come out, even with all his bitterness about old age leaving a bad taste in his mouth at the end. He'd seen a few people, and he couldn't say these guys had been bad. It was just easy to remember what they'd been and want to compare the two unfavorably. Most of these kids didn't have the baseline for comparison that he was cursed with, good for them. But now, it was time to gather his new shirt and single, and head home to post his pictures on Facebook. He knew the well-being he got from the likes that pics like that got was totally artificial, but what wasn't? Enjoy your hot dog.

Jim had just slid out the door to head for the truck when a voice behind him said, "Rat?"

Jim froze, he knew the voice, he just hadn't heard it for years. Turning, he saw the owner, "Cole?"

Standing behind him was, well he was older, his hair was receding, and he had gone in for the dirtball crusty look in a big way, but it was definitely Cole.

"In the flesh man!" Cole's face broke into a broad grin. They did the only thing they could do in the circumstance, they hugged for a long moment.

Finally, Jim broke off first and said, "What in the hell are you doing in Philly?"

Cole just shrugged, "Passing through man, that's all of my life it seems, just passing through."

"Well, where you staying while you're in town?"

The shrug again, "Hadn't procured a place to crash yet, I saw something about the show when I got into town this morning, and....well priorities."

Jim laughed at that, "Well, fuck, it ain't in the city, but

you can crash at my place tonight man. Can't have you sleeping on the ground, the worms will crawl in your ears."

They both laughed, it was a good clean laugh of friendship that time hadn't ended as much as put on hold. Jim started walking, and Cole fell in to step beside him.

As they approached where the truck was parked, adulthood reared its ugly head. He hadn't seen this guy in decades, and frankly, Cole looked like he'd spent most of his time sleeping outside these days. Looking at it logically, the guy just magically appeared here? With no place to crash lined up? There was an entire subset of "hobo-punks" out there, and Cole might fit that bill. Some kids, but quite a few adults, people from the scene back in the day, a lot of former crust punks, a lot of people who just never found a way to make their peace with society. They just hitched rides, they snuck on to trains, they found the holes in the great big system like rats, and just like rats, they found there were more than enough scraps falling off the table to at least get drunk and high and hopefully eat sometimes. The only doubt that Cole hadn't become one was that he didn't have a scruffy ass looking dog, those guys almost always had one. Having things, adult things you actually owned, meant distrusting people, and Jim hadn't had a lot of trust for people to spread around when he had been called Rat.

But what could he do about it? He'd said Cole was crashing at his place, you couldn't be a dick about it now. Thankfully he didn't have much in the place that was worth much to him if he lost it except amps and his records. The place had an alarm that had to be turned off once it was set, what was the guy gonna' do? Try to smash through the bay window with his hands full of records and try and run off through suburbia? If anything, he began to feel a bit ashamed of himself for thinking like that. You get ripped off enough times when you're squatting you start wondering if it was feasible to actually nail all your shit down, but still, this was Cole he was thinking about.

He looked hard at Cole, old Doc Martens, bottoms probably slick as glass, threadbare looking black jeans, a Nausea t-shirt that had little holes eaten into it everywhere, and an elderly looking black bomber covered in patches. He made a decision, "I wanna stop at a diner on the way back to my place and get some food, my treat."

They didn't talk much on the ride. The stereo in the truck was cranked playing Conflict's "Ungovernable Force" album, so if they had ever been able to afford a car back then, it would have been just like old times. Neither said much at the diner they stopped at on the way to Jim's house, either. Cole ate like a man who hadn't seen food for five years, and who was afraid that if he didn't devour what was in front of him now, it would be taken away from him. Jim was so bemused by the spectacle he sprung for another slice of pie for his old friend just for the reflected pleasure he got watching someone enjoy food that much. At least both of them had enough manners to not talk with their mouths full.

As they pulled up to his house Jim was grateful for two things, he didn't have to work tomorrow, and that he had just stocked up on beer from the distributor last week. You don't see somebody for 30 years, it's going to be an all-nighter, no way you're getting around that. Just because he didn't drink drink didn't mean he couldn't cut one loose on occasion, as long as it stayed an isolated incident. Nice thing was, when those occasions happened, he was a way cheaper date than he used to be. There's a difference between having a few and drinking and it had taken him years to know the difference. Having a few is when you're with friends or you've had a long busy day, you might hair of the dog to make the headache go away the next day, but it ended there. Drinking, on the other hand, is when you never want to stop, when you're positive you won't survive if you stop, when you feel like deep down like you had reduced yourself to a pathetic drunk and this was all you were now. It's an unconscious desire to drop dead being manifested in the foolhardy attempt to just poison the source of your pain senseless. It had taken Jim a long time to decide he wanted to live, that whatever happened to him growing up wasn't his fault, he wasn't the worst person available on this planet, and that there was no good damned reason he had to die for the world's sins. It might have been too late to save his marriage, but it hadn't been too late to save his life.

From the looks of him, Cole hadn't come to that conclusion yet. Good thing Jim had a lot of beer in the house.

When he parked the truck in his driveway Cole whistled, "This your place? I'm impressed."

Jim snorted, "Don't be. My ex's place is huge, she bought this to buy me off in the divorce. My lawyer said some shit about reason to believe that she had left long before she left if you get my drift. But fuck it, I'd done enough, she was more than fair."

"Surprised you didn't take her to the cleaners," Cole replied unbuckling.

"Didn't want the cleaners, this is fine. It's too much really," Jim replied getting out.

Doc was already living up to his Gonzo name as they made their way up the sidewalk to the house. Jim'd be cleaning up some torn-up cardboard after they were settled in. If Jim was going out at a time that was unusual, he always made it a point to toss some empty boxes in the living room to give the poor panicked beast something to do with his time while he worried about where in the hell Jim was. Jim had barely made it in the door before he had a brindle rocket of joy launched at him.

He swatted at the dog trying to avoid his slobbering tongue as it jumped in the air while it tried to lick him, "Jesus Christ ya' dimwitted fool! I've only been gone for a few hours!" Jim saw Cole standing back a bit warily, "Don't worry about him, he's a big fuckin' baby. If you don't want him jumping on you, just shove him down. I know everybody says that about their dog, but I don't think Doc can even growl, he's a complete wuss." For emphasis, he bent down and played with Doc's jowls and said, "Ain't ya? Ain't ya a big food snorking wuss?"

Jim stepped by and let Cole make friends with the joyous pit bull while he disarmed the alarm. He didn't care for the thing, but Cindy had insisted when they bought the place, and fuck it, who was he to argue? So, he just kept it. Cole eventually made it the rest of the way in, trailed by Doc who was eager to learn more about it his new friend, like if his new friend might have any treats about his person that he didn't feel he needed and wanted to share with a nearby dog, and barring that, if he could pet Doc some more.

"Want a beer?"

"Oh yeah, cool," Cole said hesitantly. Jim could figure why, Jim had streeted a bit too. These situations were uncomfortable and frightening. You want to hope everything is cool, you want to hope your safe, on the surface you are as far as you can see, but you can't see far enough yet. The guy who isn't looking around every corner for the unwanted sexual advance, the ass beating, the serial killer shit, sooner or later that guy ends up in a landfill. Way too many people out there rifling through societies refuse bin looking for hapless victims they can find some way to make use of. Use was the operative word there.

Jim went to the fridge and grabbed a couple of cold local micros out. He paused for just a moment and took a six-pack out of the case and put it in the fridge. Walking back out to the living room he saw Cole was still standing there petting Doc and looking around bemused at his surroundings.

"For fuck's sake, take a seat all ready, hell, sit on the couch and get to know it, you're sleeping there," Jim said handing him a beer.

"Oooo hoity toity beer huh? Too good for Ballantine?" Cole said with a grin.

"I don't even think you can get it here, and yes, yes I am," Jim said plopping himself into his recliner. He took one of the remotes that lived there and turned on the .mp3 stereo that lived next to the TV. The Subhumans "Day the Country Died" album started up, Jim turned down the volume so they could talk.

"You've done all right," Cole said taking a swig on his beer.

"Yeah, I guess, can't say I approve of how I came by it, but it's acceptable. Keeps the rain off my head," Jim shrugged.

"Still, not bad for an old street kid," Cole replied.

"I suppose it isn't at that. So, how about yourself, what brings you to our fair city?"

"Well, I wanted to see you."

Chapter 3

The printing press whirred away in the building set aside for it. Thumping in perfect continuous rhythm as leaflet after leaflet dropped into the delivery tray, each one as vital as the last. The younger recruits nattered at him constantly to just buy a printer or to just get stuff done at Kinko's, but Howard Calvin Fillmore wouldn't hear of it. He informed his well-meaning underlings that God damn it, didn't they realize that the government kept track of all that crap? They had no idea who owned this printing press, it had been sold and re-sold so many damned times by now the little AB Dick was most likely thought to have been junked years ago. Most of its brethren had been turned to rust or spare parts decades ago, and while buying supplies created a paper trail, it was an easy one to bury, especially if you paid cash.

He kept after them all the time hoping it would finally sink in, it was about self-determination and control. Control was not buying little ink cartridges from China where the commies could turn off the spout at any moment. It sure as hell wasn't about leaving a paper trail for the government to find by going to some store to get copies done. This was about a revolution, and revolutionaries who got sloppy got to keep the dirty towel heads in Guantanamo company. So, while it was nice that they had ideas, and were trying to move the movement forward, their opinion didn't matter much. In the eyes of the world, once they dug down through the alt-right noise and the web pages, and the layers upon layers of the onion they'd find that Howard Calvin Fillmore was the movement. And Howard Calvin Fillmore didn't wish to discuss shit with any federal agents until they had enough of their people in power that when the race wars finally came the powers that be would be on his side anyway.

Howard tilted his head back and enjoyed the trance inducing rhythm of the machine, each thump was a potential new recruit.

"So, what about you? What have you been doing for the last thirty years?" Jim asked, now that they were settled in some. Doc was hunkered down at his feet, but he'd get up on occasion to wander over to Cole to get pet. Jim took that as a good sign. Doc was a sucker for petting, but if he hadn't liked Cole at all... well, it was a good thing he liked Cole.

"Bounced around, I mean, I guess I just never grew up. There were other things... I mean, I'm clean right now, but heroin is really good at fucking shit up. I'd settle some place for a while, get in a band, whatever, and then I'd start using again," Cole replied, his eyes were almost blank as he said it, like he was repeating a litany he'd told many people over the years. Then a smile flashed over his face, "But it ain't been all bad. I mean I got to be on a few records, went on some tours, I've seen almost all of the country, and I ain't dead yet. Who knows, maybe this is it at last and clean takes for good this time?"

Jim shook his head, "I never understood why you started with that shit in the first place." As soon as he heard what he'd said he shook his head, "Look I apologize for that, I don't have any right, 'specially figuring how I spent a decade swimming in a bottle."

Cole gave a smile, almost like a Buddha in its soft perfection, "Naw, it's OK. I get it. We always think of booze as being lightweight compared to smack. I guess, maybe it is, you seem to have it under control now even without completely quitting and going to meetings and shit. I don't think you can do that with junk, no shit about that. Not many social junkies, at least not for very long. But it's actually all right, I can tell you stuff, talk about things, which is a weight off my mind. Having to go to counselors over and over again without ever being able to tell the full story of why? Shit like that will eat at you. But you get it, I bet that day in that squat with that sick demon had a hand in pushing you over the lip into the bottom of a bottle too."

Jim was quiet for a long moment. He should have known that was going to come up tonight, but the thing was, he tried not to think about it. He thought of Cole as an ex-bandmate, not someone who had been with him when he'd experienced the unthinkable. Cole was good memories of their times on stage together, not.... not that. So, there it was, all out on the table. Jim got up and went out to the kitchen without saying a word, before returning with two more beers.

"Fuck this melancholy shit, life didn't turn out perfect for either of us, it was never destined to. Instead of sitting around moping, shit we should be happy we're still here. Wanna watch a flick?" Jim said gruffly when he came back.

"Anything but Suburbia, I mean speaking of mopey, that ending man," Cole responded as he took his beer.

"All right, *Straight to Hell* then," Jim said heading over to the rack of DVDs and Blu Rays he had accumulated over time.

"Which one's that?"

"You shitting me? Directed by the same guy who did *Repo Man*, stars Joe Strummer and the Pogues, funny as hell," Jim looked at his old friend like he'd grown another head by not knowing that vital piece of punk rock history.

"Perfect."

They had tossed in *Repo Man* itself to make it an Alex Cox double feature and had reached the point of feeling no pain. Not sloppy drunk, not the "I love you, man...let's fight" stage. Not even the stage where Facebook should be avoided, just warm and cozy. Ain't goin' nowhere and that's a good thing. They'd already taken a couple of selfies on both their phones to put up on their pages. They even put one of them up on the Restraint and Control page Jim ran. He ran it because if you didn't have an official page somebody out there was going to put up an unofficial page, and letting that happen that way, lay madness.

"You still think about it much?" Cole asked as they watched Duke get shot on the screen during *Repo Man*.

"What?"

"Don't bullshit me, you know what!" Cole snorted.

"I try not to. It was horrific, but it was the only thing that could be done there. If there were other choices, I don't know what they were. I've run it through the processor a million times and I always end up the same way," Jim said flatly.

"You know what I think?"

"About what part?"

"About what it was, what it claimed it was at least," Cole replied before taking a pull on his beer.

"You mean an agent of chaos? Helping man hurt himself?" Jim replied. He'd run this part through his head numerous enough times himself to know.

"Yeah."

A second later Jim demanded, "And?"

Cole started as if he'd been daydreaming, "I think it's happening again. Just bigger."

"Fuck you."

"No, I'm serious. Let me ask you a question, in the nineties and thousands how many times did you see racists around, like being taken seriously?" Cole sat up and looked intently at Jim as he asked.

"That could just be that there have always been assholes out there, and now they feel empowered. Like somehow, they feel they're finally winning. We don't need no supernatural forces to act like douchebags, people are totally capable all on their lonesome to take it into their heads," Jim replied.

"True, that is true. But it usually takes something to get them past the saying it quietly under their breath, to the we can actually rule the country phase," Cole looked at Jim intently, almost like he was trying to burn his thoughts into Jim's mind. "I traced it down to a single source."

"Yeah, Trump. Thank fuck he's gone" Jim laughed.

"No, he was just a tool, he always was for that matter. Even back in the old days, Trump was nothing but a willing tool. When we were fighting the developers, there he was being the perfect cartoon villain, but that problem started before him, and it ran deeper. Same now, we think he's the problem, but really, he's just the symptom, the guy who was willing to pander to the ones that were already there just waiting for a political figurehead that could finally win anything. No, I traced it down to one guy whose been writing the books that the real hard-core preachers of the cause read." Cole paused for a moment to let it sink in before continuing, "I think it's another one of them. It's why I came down here, to talk to you about it in person. The guy is holed up in a compound, and doesn't that sound familiar, out in Lehigh County."

"Is that where you were? I mean before you came here?"

"Yeah, I only scouted around it a bit. I read about the guy online, on some of the more out there chat boards," Cole shrugged.

"What in the fuck were you doing on there? 8Chan will give you brain rot," Jim asked with a raised eyebrow.

"Know your enemy and all that. I'd taken part in a few scuffles over the years with these psychos, I wanted to know what in the fuck made them tick. Like why would somebody be that way, you know? I mean I don't want to get all hippy-dippy and shit, but life is easier overall when you don't waste so much time hating on people who ain't your problem. In a country as fat and lazy as America, it seemed weird to me that this was the kind of thing that would get these guys up and mobile, especially since it doesn't even help them worth a shit. I mean kill the boss helps them a lot more, but they hate the idea, preferring to bitch about people who have less than them instead," Cole explained quickly.

"OK, yeah, actually I can see that. It wouldn't have occurred to me, but it makes sense. If you know the guys are going to show up, well you can't help yourself really, next thing you know you're curious. Yeah, I'll go with you there, but fucking casing the place?"

"Like I've got somewhere better to be? I needed something you know? Something to keep my head busy. Before you go there, don't think I was just obsessing about what happened. I was obsessing, sure, but it was about why anybody would still be that hung up on race. It was after what I saw at the compound that I started thinking about what happened back in the day."

"So, stop stringing it the fuck out, what did you see?" Jim demanded. But then he put up a finger, "Hold that thought, I'm just gonna bring a sixer in, I tossed a couple in the fridge a while ago."

"Look at you, thinking ahead like a big boy," Cole chuckled.

Jim came back into the room setting the six-pack on the glass coffee table and opening one with a can opener from the kitchen, "So, why are you so sure it's the same thing we saw in New York and not garden variety nutjobs?"

"That's the thing ain't it? You used to get to be an expert on fucking loonies living in the Lower East Side, didn't you? Godheads, artists, junkies, mental patients, we got 'em all. You became a connoisseur of all things out of its fucking skull. But Weiss's psychos had their own look, you ever really notice it? Like not all there and totally there at the same time? Somebody else was totally running that show, and once we figured out what, then it all made complete sense, I mean the look in their eyes when you ran into them. Well, the thing is, everybody that this guy has around his compound up there, they all look like that. Every single one of them. Normal people sometimes go in and out, I guess at this point it realized that going big-time meant not controlling every single adherent, but everyone in that compound, he's running them just like before," Cole explained in a rush like it had been pent up, like it's one thing to talk about it online, and Jim bet he had, but another to actually confess your thoughts to another human being. Now that he had, the dam had broken, and the waters rushed forward.

"So does our new Andy have a name?" Jim said with kind of a sneer. It wasn't that he could completely discount it, this had happened before, but he just thought it too unreal that it could happen to him specifically twice now.

"Howard Calvin Fillmore, he wrote some book, about twenty-five years ago called 'The White Lambs Are Slaughtered' it's some kind of bible for the new alt-right, militia, white-power, psycho movement. *The Turner Diaries* but without the laughs. He was smart this time, he started by building off the remains of the skinhead and the militia movement, kept his press in house, and when the net finally started exploding with chat rooms, he made sure his followers were everywhere. That book is probably the most famous thing that most people have never heard of."

"Doesn't sound like Andy's M.O. at all, that happened pretty fast."

"Not really, he'd been building on that for a while before he started escalating. Who's to say the thing couldn't learn from its mistakes and develop patience. It took credit for some lengthy burns in the past," Cole replied his face radiating sincerity.

Jim could kind of see that, even if he didn't really want to, a slow burn using something as bedrock American as good old-fashioned racism actually wouldn't be a terrible idea. He also realized that he was getting a buzz, and he might be willing to think this way because of inebriation, not good, equally old-fashioned, common sense. He decided he wanted this tabled for the night. He dealt with it the only way he could think to, he changed the subject.

"So, how long you gonna be around Philly?"

"No idea? I guess that all depended on what you'd do," Cole shrugged.

"You play guitar still?"

"Well yeah, that never leaves you totally."

"Except for us getting buzzed tonight, you think you're sober enough to swing a hammer without hurting yourself most days?" Jim asked gruffly staring straight ahead at the TV rather than Cole. He didn't look at Cole because he was formulating something in his own head, and he didn't want distractions. He wasn't truly paying attention to the TV either, it was just a direction that his eyes were dragged to by the flashing scenes.

"Well yeah, like I said I'm clean now."

"Good, you can stay here for a while, I know a guy who does roofing who always needs somebody, and I've got a band down a guitarist for the foreseeable future. Even if this attempt at adulthood doesn't take, it'll give you a chance to squirrel away some cash. Now could we please put this debate on the shelf until we're both stone-cold sober? Let's either watch another movie, or talk about shows, or some shit, alright?"

"Yeah, totally cool, we got time to talk later now," Cole smiled sincerely.

Mornings happen, they're scheduled and nothing can be done about it now. Jim had prepared for this eventuality but it didn't make it suck any less. His mouth felt like it was filled with mold, his head hurt a bit, and his stomach lurched warningly when he opened his eyes. Frankly, he was too old for shit like last night and knew it. He'd been excited enough about seeing Cole to give himself a day pass, but that didn't make it hurt any less, or make him want to do it again any time soon. Jim sure as shit wouldn't be getting out of bed no matter what time it was if he didn't have to piss and had to do it God damned now, but that was the agenda at least if he didn't want to buy a new mattress. Funny, when you drank you just accepted this as life, when you only had a few on occasion you spent your morning wondering what in the hell you could have possibly been thinking to get here.

As Jim hovered over the bowl, he heard Cole snoring from the living room. Something began to natter at him from his subconscious as he emptied his bladder, something about what they talked about that was important. Thank God almighty they'd only gotten illegal to drive levels and not hammered last night. Today hurt bad enough as was. A breakfast beer, some aspirin, and some coffee, maybe a nap, he might just survive.

Tucking himself back into his pajamas, his brain still functioning on very basic levels. Jim was hit with the aroma of fresh brewed coffee, thank fucking god, he'd set it up last night. Opening the fridge, he got out a beer and some milk for his coffee. Poured himself a cup, popped open the beer, before first taking a sip of the coffee and then a deep pull on the beer. His stomach calmed down, he sighed at the stupidity of it before assessing the day.

Which is when what had been nagging at him finally got through. For the foreseeable future, he had a roommate. Fuck. It seemed sensible last night, Cole was an old friend who needed to get off the streets, and he had made an offer that he had been sure was the right thing to do after four beers. Jim certainly had no intentions of backing off it now, he'd said he'd do it, but Jesus, all the things he hadn't thought of. How Cindy would react, how the kids would, shit, could he even get him that job, the extra food... Oh, well. Fuck it, it would probably seem like a good idea again after waking up all the way, so why not work on that?

Cole was still out like a light, so that was all right, he could just toddle off to the library and open up the desktop computer. Jim had put some things out of his control with his big mouth, so screw it, time to see what the big old world wide web was up to, and did it involve funny distracting videos. As far as he was concerned that was the net's real purpose. He knew what a clusterfuck the government was, he didn't need the internet for that, he knew how mean-spirited and cruel the country had gotten, no great revelations were forthcoming there. No, what Jim needed was something adorable, and, or funny to pass the time. Or, if he had to do politics, he could just about stomach something that made fun of the giant steaming mess like Maher or Oliver or Colbert. If it couldn't be fixed, at least someone out there had the decency to make fun of the assholes making it worse.

He was watching the monologue of last night's *Real Time* when he heard rustling coming from the living room. A few moments later Cole stood in the doorway looking like Jim had felt. Jim was by no means out of the woods yet, but felt just coherent enough to say, "Coffee, or beer, or both?"

"Coffee, dear god how can you drink a beer?" Cole practically whimpered.

"Settles my stomach, and it needs settling. Coffee is hot and, in the kitchen, milk in the fridge, if you want sugar, I know there is some somewhere, where would be anyone's guess."

When Cole came back a little later, he got right to the point, "You mean what you said last night?"

"I said a lot of shit last night, which part in particular?"

"About me staying here?"

Jim nodded and took a pull on his beer, "Yep, I mean if that's what you want. I mean if you don't, I'm going to have to give you directions to get to the bus, because I'm fucking useless for this morning. Just a heads up, last night was a one-time rarity. One of the reasons I don't drink can be summed up by this morning. There's the night one fun drunk, and then there's the next day recovery. Too fucking time consuming."

"Cool, I get it. Well then, I just want to say thanks," Cole smiled softly.

"Don't thank me yet, I'm still an asshole, so that hasn't changed."

He might have gotten himself into this as a reminder to not drink, and he might have had immediate regrets about it, but Jim was surprised at how easily things settled into place going forward. It turned out that the job was the easiest part, Phil always needed people, especially these days when it seemed like almost every week ICE was scooping someone off his work crew. The band was only marginally more difficult, first he had to call Alan to tell him at length that he wasn't looking to replace him, it was just stupid at their age to miss gigs because he was currently on the shelf when they could find somebody to fill in for a little while. Anyway, if Cole worked out long term, a two-guitar sound was what they'd had in Restraint and Control, and it wouldn't hurt any of the new band's originals to have a little beef added. Alan surprised Jim by saying he was all for it, his logic was slightly different, if he wasn't fully up to speed when his doctor let him play again, at least there'd be someone to cover the missed notes.

Hates of Gray, the name of the band, was comprised of a group of adult men who just happened to also be scene vets who had been in some moderately successful bands of their own. While they did write original material and had even managed to eke out a little 45 ep on a local label, everybody in the band viewed it as more of a hobby, the way other people viewed jogging or hiking. Thankfully they had the songs from their old bands to draw from to pad out their setlists to as big or as short as they needed it to be. It was an enjoyable diversion for all of them, because they knew that's all it was. When you're 19 or 20 you have dreams, you want to be the next Clash, or Germs, or Exploited, some voice of your generation shit that Rolling Stone has to write about after you break up when they do one of their punk history pieces. When you're middle-aged, all you're really hoping for is to have a good time, and gas money would be nice. The stakes were so much more reasonable now.

What had taken the most time was trying to find a day to practice after the lineup change had been broached with the rest of the band. Three middle-aged men let out of a weekly obligation immediately find something to do with that time. It may appear to the casual observer that what they're doing is nothing, because it is, but it has now become their scheduled nothing, and they are loathe to give it up. Reading, watching football games, all the nothing's you fill your day with at that age suddenly feel prioritized because frankly, entropy becomes so much more attractive when you have a series of aches and pains that are the result of years of having an interesting life.

It had taken serious wrangling to get all of those ducks in a row again. Everyone responded with enthusiasm to having a new guitarist, especially one that not only knew the old Restraint and Control material but actually helped write it, but finding a time of vast empty nothingness each of them was willing to give up again every week had proven to be more of a challenge. Finally, after a lot of phone tag, they had agreed on Sundays at 11 AM, unless somebody was able to score tickets to an Eagles game. The revolution would have to be put on hold if someone had good seats at the Linc.

All of which led them to where they were now, in a basement, standing around awkwardly. Cole had been introduced around, everyone had done the manly handshake ritual and now three of the four people standing around were trying to remember that they were in a band together, while the fourth one was forced to wait until they got around to it. He was forced to do it silently without giving any input as to how to make that work because he was the new guy.

It was Teddy who pointed to Cole, "So whaddya want to do first. Try and get through a song you know, or do you want to try and learn one of the new ones first?"

Cole thought about it a second before replying, "I listened to your single, I think I've got how it goes." He went over to the amp and guitar that he was using. It was

Jim's, but he barely played the old SG unless he was trying to write riffs, so it was dusty even with Cole playing it lately. When he clicked the amp on there was still a bit of a crackle of dust. "You guys want to try, 'The Mistakes We Repeat'? I think I've got that one down pretty good, I've even played with it a bit to maybe see if I can punch it up. If you don't like what I did, let me know."

Everyone got in their mutual positions ready to go. There was a long pregnant pause before Jim finally said into the mic, "Umm Benji, you're kinda supposed to click this one off with the sticks dude."

There was another pause of only a moment before the whole band started laughing. The tension that was there while working a new member into their little private world was broken, you could feel it move out of the room. You couldn't very well sit there and be judgmental about the new guy if you'd just blown it like that. Now everyone in the room had shared a moment, they had one little instance in time they could joke about later if they wanted, now everyone could be friends.

Once everyone settled in a bit, Jim said into the mic again, "Benji if you would be so kind?"

Benji clicked his sticks four times and the band started off. Cole and Teddy were looking at each other to keep in time with one another, neither fully trusting the speed they practiced the song at. Cole played it with a slightly different rhythm putting in D-beat chunks where they hadn't been before, but they never moved off of Teddy's hammer blow bass line. Jim almost missed his cue to come in with the lyrics he was so shocked by how well the intro was going since they'd never played together before. He found himself playing catch up the entire first stanza and wasn't able to get back into rhythm until the chorus kicked in.

The sound crashed to a halt as it was supposed to, and everybody had some variation of the same grin on their face, the joy that came with the knowledge that this was going to work. If anything, the song sounded a bit better, a bit harder with the little extra's Cole had slipped in. It was Teddy who first said something, "Well, if the rest of this goes like that, we might be able to book a gig for the first time in forever."

"Well, let's get through the set list huh? I still got plenty of time to blow this," Cole said demurely.

Chapter 4

The first practice went amazingly well, if anything most of the screw ups were on the regular band members who really hadn't so much as touched an instrument since Alan had gotten sick. Music ceases to be your life when you've got a wife and kids and a real job to worry about. Finding the time when you aren't actively gigging gets impossible. It just gets harder and harder to justify taking the time away from everything else you have to do to dedicate time to practicing. Cole had only been sitting around learning the tracks for a couple of weeks and he had them down pretty well already. Like he had just been patiently waiting on this chance to play with them. Of course, some of their songs he'd actually written, but definitely not the majority, they had gone pretty deep into their mutual catalog and he hadn't had a problem with anything presented to him.

They were all sitting around Benji's basement winding down before packing up and leaving. "So, you sound tight dude, what's between the days of playing with this guy before and playing with us?" Teddy pointed at Jim.

Cole shrugged, "I travel a lot, being able to play's a good way to make friends, you know?"

"So how long are you gonna be here bailing our asses out?" Benji asked from the couch he was sprawled across.

Cole shrugged again, "No idea, long enough to get you gigging again. Who knows maybe longer, things seem to be working out all right so far, and Christ, I've seen everywhere else already."

"He saved the worst for last," Jim joked.

"Well, it's good to be playing again, I know that," Teddy nodded. Turning to Jim he added, "So how soon until we can book something you think?"

"Shit, we did more than a setlist today, I can see what's coming up and book us something in about a month. I mean hell, what we did today would only be considered 'a little sloppy', a month to practice we might not suck that bad."

Frustration. That was the only feeling he had at the moment, every other feeling had been overshadowed by that one, had drowned in the sea of it. They were so close, what he had worked so hard for was almost there... But goddammit! The drones kept fucking it up! Not the ones on the compound, they were too close to him to get ideas, but the converts, the believers, the ones out there in the world… It seemed like they couldn't go a week without screwing one thing up or another. They'd let someone into a private chat, they'd give an off-the-record interview, and boom, there's an expose in a magazine and online. Even the ones that had gotten close to the real power circle, or the satellites they were influencing would say something stupid to the press. Rallies became riots in these moron's hands. Yes, he loved a good riot as much as the next man, but they had to be strategic, they had to put fear in people's hearts, not outrage. You couldn't let the sheep know there was a wolf among them, plain and simple.

No matter how many times he tried to tell them, fly under the radar to get young converts, build to get power, then you make the weakling public fear you when you had all the power... some would just find a way to screw it up. When you were one half of a riot and a ragtag group of undisciplined rabble can stand up to you, you don't look like an inevitable force anymore. You don't look like something to be terrified of, to hide from, to bow to. What you end up looking like is a bunch of crackpots playing dress-up who got beat up by street people. And on days when people he thought he had trained well enough to not screw up did, that's what they were as well, rabble.

Well, no more. Tonight, he was making an example of someone. He had to. Without message discipline people would have time to react against them, they would know that they had to. Without discipline in every aspect, when the time came, he wouldn't have storm troopers ready to take the world by force, he'd just have a lot of bodies being taken out by a disciplined military. He needed all of his pieces in place for this to work. He did not have the time for this bullshit, this life was nearing its conclusion, maybe not soon, nothing terminal that he knew of, but still, he was an old man. He didn't have all the time in the world to wait to try again if this project and plan failed, and he had worked so hard, and now they were so close to making his dream a reality.

Discipline, it removed the broken part and made sure that all the other cogs polished themselves until they gleamed.

These were the times you had to make an example of someone to create that discipline in the ranks. You needed an object lesson in what failure looked like. He looked at himself in the mirror, made sure that his hair was perfect, his clothing was exact. Howard had an image he put forth, not a military leader, but as a rugged visionary. Uniforms at this stage marked you as a frothing lunatic playing make-believe, what did the kids call it? Cosplaying? It told people you were not a serious intellectual with thoughts that needed to be respected. Howard generally dressed as he was now, blue jeans, a flannel shirt, and most importantly a holster carrying a Walther P38 so polished and oiled that it gleamed in the light of his cabin. He had camouflage outfits, but he only wore those at the firing range. The rest of the time he presented himself as a normal man, only smarter and more manly in every way, even at this age. Perfect for a reclusive messiah of the race.

He stepped out of his cabin into the light being given off by the torches and the fire pit the men were assembled around. The night was dark and clouded over, the only light was coming from earth not from above, the heavens could not see them now. The men fell silent, the only noises were the animals that were kept at the compound making various grunts and snorts in their sleep. There was a raw electricity among the men, that sweet morass of fear for themselves coupled with the excitement to see another suffer. Numerous of the splinter groups he had secretly founded were represented here, in different dress or uniform, they all needed to see this. He found it useful to disseminate information and infiltrate the world outside by having numerous public faces, people who could act independently of him and his storm troopers in the compound, people he didn't have absolute control over. If one face collapsed it was only a minor setback to the overall movement, and in some ways that benefited him. It let the fools who knew little of the movement he'd help foster think the boogeyman had been defeated when that cookie crumbled. Not that Howard tolerated any setbacks whatsoever when dealing with the men, as everyone would learn tonight.

The men parted for him, making a path that led to the

example that was going to be made tonight, the man on his knees, his hands bound behind him and duct tape over his mouth. Everyone in range could smell the stench of his fear, the reek of sweat and adrenaline the moment he'd been dragged before them all. Howard would tell everyone who would listen later that he didn't enjoy these moments, but that was a lie. Howard secretly relished them; it was one of the few moments where the mask of stoicism could slip even a little. It was the purpose he had been built for finding release. He fought to hide his anticipation as he walked forward. A wooden stump next to tonight's object lesson held a hunting knife and pair of pliers, you had to look for the slight tremor in his hand as he reached for them.

He stood straight and said loudly, "I think more than a few of you already know why we're here." Howard looked down at the bound and wide-eyed man and smiled slightly, "I know you do Hunter; I know you do."

Harold turned and addressed the assembly, "Without your ego, you aren't much of a man. It's your ego that makes you stand up for yourself, it makes you fight back against the injustices of the world, it is the base of all that is manly. But as much as you need it, it can get you in a world of trouble, can't it? It can make you pick fights you shouldn't with people. Get you all beat up and bloody when the smart thing to do would be to find them when you had superior numbers. You can hurt yourself; you can hurt your relationships with others, terrible thing the ego if it is not nurtured correctly. In some cases, it can make you so braggadocios that you forget yourself."

Harold, for all his age, moved like lightning, grasping the ear of the terrified man in front of him with the pliers and pulling it out away from his head, "It maybe means you don't listen when I tell you to keep your communications on the damned interwebs restricted to approved things,

Hunter! When I tell you we got to keep a low fucking profile? Well since you don't like listening, I guess you won't need this anymore!"

Harold brought the knife up with his other hand, placing it where the ear joined on to the head. He leaned in and began to saw the blade back and forth slowly while putting pressure on the blade, dark looking blood began to run down Hunter's face in the firelight as the old man cut away at him. Harold forced himself to keep his face implacable as the younger man's muffled screams practically vibrated up his arm from where the knife was doing its work. He knew what the faces of those watching would look like. Some of them would be barely concealed grimaces, they were who this little object lesson was for. He'd have his main companion Jake give him a rundown later of the ones who maybe had a little glee in their eyes over the whole thing. Maybe he'd have to add a few more troops to the compound on a permanent basis, outside of the world's prying eyes. Wild dogs often brought attention.

When the last bit of gristle gave way to the knife's attentions, Harold held the ear aloft for all to see. He had no trouble ignoring the pleas being cried out by Hunter that he could almost make out through the gag. The knife was razor-sharp, he could have cut off the ear easily, but he'd had no problem making Hunter suffer either. Suffering made sure that all eyes were on what was happening here tonight. Once he knew that he had the attention of everyone, he tossed the ear into the fire pit. All of the troops gathered for this could hear the brief sizzle it made as it landed on the coals. Harold thought he heard a few stifled gags at that. Good, those boys would remember this important life lesson well, especially when they were alone in bed tonight in the darkness.

He waited until Hunter's screams had run out of steam. That spot in his agony where exhaustion took over and it became a low continuous sob. Then, he leaned in close to his former soldier. "See the problem with you son, is you forgot that this is all supposed to be a secret. So, you get to braggin' on one of the chat boards about what a big shit you are. The feds pick up on it and remote hack your god damned email, hell your whole computer. Now they have cause to see who you've been talking to, they start picking around a bit, and damned if they didn't walk right in on two brothers in the movement who THOUGHT THEY COULD TRUST YOU. The feds scoop them up on the synagogue plot. We lose momentum, we lose two soldiers, we lose an opportunity, and all because you couldn't keep your fucking mouth shut Hunter. Do you know how much those new computers we had to buy cost us?"

Harold yanked at the duct tape. "Please sir, please, I didn't mean...I didn't expect," Hunter babbled thickly through the snot that clogged his nose and throat."

Harold shook his head, "No, no I expect you didn't." He nodded to Jake who moved forward and grasped Hunter's jaws forcing his mouth open.

Harold leaned in as Hunter tried to pull away only to find that Jake was far too strong for him. Harold forced the pliers inside Hunter's mouth and pulled back dragging the younger man's tongue out into the light. "See, your problem is that you like to use this thing too damned much. We're here for you Hunter, we can fix that."

Hunter tried to thrash away from the hands that held him as the knife bit into his exposed tongue. He gasped out throaty "Nnghs" of pain as the older man forced the knife to dig deep like he was letting the sharpness of the blade and the weight as he pressed down do the work for him, like a knife through butter. At last, the man came up holding the offending tongue aloft in the pliers. With a flick, it went into the fire. Jake let Hunter go and he just slumped forward moaning, blood pouring from his ear and mouth onto the ground where it fell like rain on water creating splashes and pocks where it landed in the dust.

"Now that we've taken care of your punishment, what shall we do with you?" Harold sniffed at the air, "Jesus boy, you shit yourself! You actually fucking shit yourself in front of all these people!" In one smooth motion, the Walther came into the old man's hand, "Man doesn't have any reason to live without some dignity left to him, and that was just humiliating boy."

A single shot rang out.

All eyes were on Hunter's body as it tumbled back and lay flat on the ground from the force of the shot, his eyes still open staring at a sky that the clouds had made look as dull and lifeless as he had just become. All except for Jake and Harold, they were watching the rest of the men. Harold motioned for Jake to come close, he whispered to the other man, "Kill a pig, make sure they all hear you do it. But, wash the boy up tonight too. We're gonna have some BBQ tomorrow, we'll talk later about who gets what portions."

It had been strange at first having Cole live there, and that was really an understatement. Jim had gotten more than a little used to being a curmudgeon and a misanthrope and you did that alone usually. He had the place, he had his dog, and he had the internet, and the occasional fling with "lonely single women in his area." The point being, that was fine, it was enough for him. That had all changed dramatically. Now, now it would be weird if Cole moved on. He'd gotten used to having another person actually in the house instead of somewhere out there only connected to his life by bundles of wires.

It was different in person, you put some thought into what you were about to say to someone's face. If he was being completely honest with himself, the more time he spent online, the less able he was to just converse with people face to face. You had a buffer of time to reply on the net, a chance to polish what you were going to say, to cut out all the dumb bits, or the angry and unreasonable bits. And even if you were blasting someone, who gave a shit? It wasn't like you'd ever see them anyway, blast away. You could remake yourself on the net, not as some hero, or tough guy, though a lot of people did that, but how you wanted yourself to be. You could be smarter and more well thought out if you took a second to think. Life didn't give you that, it demanded a reaction now, immediately. When you did most of your talking online your brain got lazy, it got used to being able to slow down and reword stuff. Having Cole around made Jim feel like his brain was quickening if for no other reason than to not look like an ass to someone he lived with.

The band was moving along at a great pace as well. They'd even slipped into the studio once to record some new stuff off the board, and had brought an 8-track to a couple of practices as well. If they recorded this stuff for release it would hopefully be down the road as a five-piece. But recording even this much gave them something to put on YouTube as proof that things were moving along, that this was a working band, not some stupid pipe dream. Jim was pleased, the new stuff was getting very solid buzz from their fan base. Life was going along kind of well right now.

They were sitting around playing video games, it was a dumb time consumer with no actual value to reality, but sometimes that's just what your universe called for. Something with a reset button and unlimited lives. It was a racing game, no racing games have many cut scenes that are truly vital to anything, you got to the next scene and you hit the gas. It left the door open for conversation so it made for a perfect game to play with someone else in the room.

"So, you never wanted to get married again?" Cole asked out of the blue.

"What the fuck dude? You gotta lead up to questions like that, not just spring them on people," Jim protested leaning his body as he tried to get his car around a nasty corner.

"Sorry, not sorry. You didn't age that horribly, you got a band, you got a house, you almost never drink, no drugs, OK the vaping is a bit obsessive, but in some circles, you'd be a catch. Why'd you never get back up on that horse?" Cole pressed.

Jim grunted as he had to slam the brakes on his pixilated car to avoid crashing it, "Why the fuck would I inflict myself on a woman. Hard enough to be female in this society."

Cole chuckled, "Dude, you got to work on your self-esteem issues, Jesus, I thought I was bad."

"Has nothing to do with self-esteem bubba. I know who I am. I am cynical, bitter, and easily irritated. I work on it, I don't just lie back and wallow in it, but I know who I am. Any woman you'd want to be with long term, even the mopey ones who listen to goth and won't admit it, they have a bubble to them. Something that shines through and is just wonderful. It takes real strength to give a fuck about puppies in this world. But you can watch a woman whose been through the wringer in life come to adorable life if you hand her one. Why in the fuck would I want to tarnish that by saddling it with me? My head is singing the Descendents "Everything Sucks" the moment I get out of bed. Short-term cynical quid pro quo relationships are for the best, that way I don't hurt anything," Jim expounded on his relationship philosophy.

"That is either the most noble or self-serving thing I've ever heard," Cole grinned.

"Let me know if you figure it out before we play live.

There's usually a couple of moms at these things, and since we don't scare the shit out of them like we did back in the day, they actually will sleep with the lead singer."

It was funny, if anything Jim buzzed even more in the days leading up to a gig. Back when he was a kid, you were in a band, you played gigs, it was just...life. But now, yes, he was technically in a band, but if they did one show a month, they were practically on tour. So, each one had time for you to get yourself worked up and psyched out about it. He had started supplementing his nightly melatonin with Benadryl just so he could get some kind of sleep before work. Cole on the other hand just had the same relatively happy-go-lucky attitude he always did. Jim supposed that made sense, Cole had been getting by on his ability to play a guitar in every city he'd lived in over the years, there were no huge gaps for marriage and kids for him. For Cole, this just was life like it had always been.

Jim wondered if Cole was amused by his constant going over gear and the set list, his constant sitting down with practice tapes and singing along softly to get his rhythms correct. If he was, at least he had the decency not to show it. Jim didn't even know what he was nervous about exactly. The songs had been perfect the last practice, most of them they'd performed dozens of times as a group live, except for Cole who was more or less a professional when he was straight like he was now. He could say that it was because they were debuting a new member he supposed, but that didn't feel right. Jim suspected it was all about comfort zones. He had gotten old one day, and the older you get, the more you find the things you're comfortable doing, and the more you hate to do anything that takes you away from that. His nervousness was the moaning and dying old person inside of him trying to take control of the situation away from the remainder of his youth. Punk rock was over, at least his version of it, and Jim could live with that. They were just the shadows that the cleansing light hadn't been sufficient to dispel. Time would, sooner or later, and Jim had to learn to be comfortable enough with that as well. But that didn't mean he wanted to stop just yet.

The day of the show it was just like nothing important in the world was happening for everyone but Jim. He almost sleepwalked through his whole routine for the day. Which was easy enough to do, he liked routine, routine didn't need him for anything, he could just put his mind on coast for routine. His nerves thrummed as we waited for the day to end, causing him to keep hitting droppers full of CBD oil just to take the edge off himself, that crap was a godsend. As he got older, especially after he stopped drinking, anything too far out of his comfort zone caused panic attacks. They were nonsensical, it could be something he was looking forward to in reality, but suddenly he'd be convinced that his breathing was restricted. He would keep going through the warning signs of a heart attack in his head like a record on repeat. CBD nipped that shit in the bud, it wasn't a real drug, it didn't cause any mood changes or anything, it just skipped the record of his panic attack before it could dig in a groove.

When it was time to start to load the gear up, he was almost calm. Not completely, not really, but at least he felt like he was even-tempered. Jim felt good enough to joke with Cole, "So all those bands you been in, you ever reach the point of not having to roadie for yourselves?"

"Oh yeah!" Cole grunted hefting his amp. "Yeah, we got so big we'd just borrow instruments so we could play, cause all ours were in hock," Cole winked as he stood back up from setting the amp down.

"You're a funny guy for an old fart. C'mon, let's get a moving."

The place where the show was taking place was an old church which was pretty cool. Benji and Teddy's vehicles were already in the lot when they pulled up. "Alright, do me a favor, run in and tell them we're here. I don't want to leave the gear in the back of the truck at all if I can avoid it. Band got their shit jacked out of their van here a couple of months ago," Jim told Cole.

"Righty ho!" Cole replied hopping out and heading for the door. There were already kids hanging around outside even though the gig wasn't for hours. There always was, usually kids from out in the burbs who took the train in with nowhere better to go, or crusties looking to scrounge up enough spare change to get in or for beer or whatever. Nobody that looked like trouble specifically, but there were enough of them that Jim wanted one of them hanging tight outside.

A few minutes later the door burst open and Cole was heading out with the rest of the band. The cool thing was that it was the entire rest of the band, even the one who wouldn't be on stage tonight. Jim hopped out and went over to greet them, grabbing Alan in a big hug. "Fucking all right, the wife decided you were well enough to come out and see us at least," Jim grinned.

Alan was still a bit overweight, even though Jim knew he was dieting now, but he looked healthy as he grinned back, "I got news, doctor says I won't drop dead if I go on stage. So, after this, I can start practicing and we can work on putting solos and shit as a five-piece now!"

"That'll be awesome, we can trade off," Cole said with real enthusiasm. Jim could have kissed him right then. Any awkwardness that could have been there was diffused at that moment. Alan was still in the band he had helped form, and both of them were fine with the other being there.

"Benji said you fiddled with some stuff to make it sound a bit beefier. Looking forward to hearing it," Alan replied.

"It'll sound even better with another guitar. We recorded some stuff, some new stuff as well, so you'll have a good chance to listen to it to get it down," Cole replied.

"Well, if you two are done sniffing each other's butts, let's get this shit inside so we can sound check," Teddy cut them off as he headed towards the back of the truck.

Chapter 5

There was a band up on the stage running through their own soundcheck when they got inside the club. This wasn't the same place that Jim had run into Cole but if not there he'd have run into him here. There weren't that many clubs to choose from for punk on the best of days. Maybe in New York still, but not here. It was always amazing to Jim how many people got in early to these things. Between the various band's merch people and significant others, there was already a small club's worth of people inside milling about or setting up stuff. While they waited for the other band to finish off what they were about, they piled their shit up next to the steps that led onto the stage. Tonight's lineup was kind of funny to Jim, the band that were headliners were some ancient Noo Yawk Hawd Coor band that used to wear hoodies and have big Xs on their hands, not a band he had much time for, but the mix and match nature of the oldies circuit had thrown them together. These days the headliners while they still had shaved heads, it was more because they didn't have any hair and didn't want to look like tough guy accountants.

One of the other bands must have already sound checked and were hanging around with their girlfriends or wives or whatever, and they made Jim laugh inside just as hard as the Ben Gay tough guys, if not harder. They were some scum rock band back in the day, and man, they were going out of their way to show everyone that they were still living that rock n roll lifestyle. They probably weren't during the week, they probably all had straight jobs, but everybody was supposed to go along with the dress-up here tonight. Jim had to wonder how you got eyeliner to go on right around that many bags under your eyes. It also told him the promoter must be a kid and didn't know any better. While all three bands technically had something to do with New York, especially now with Cole in the fold, they couldn't have been more different, or have had more different fan bases.

Once the hawd coor band had finished blitzing through a couple of songs, their roadies scurried over the stage breaking down whatever would go back to their dressing room with them. Dear god, these pompous shits had a full road crew for a drive down the highway gig. Amazing. Not one act on this bill had made enough book back in the day to fill up a place like the Ritz on their own, and yet these guys thought they were important enough to rate a full crew. These guys hadn't even been fucking rock stars when they were rock stars, yet here and now in the land of the oldies review they still thought they rated the royal treatment. Jim made a mental note, no matter what else happened, he was blowing these cunts off the stage tonight, even if he had to go to the fucking hospital with a heart attack afterward.

Their soundcheck just took a couple of songs which they chunked through handily. They knew the songs, and the guy working the board knew his business. Once they were done most of their gear could stay tucked away to the back of the stage. Since it was a "triumphant return" gig and debuting a new member and one from Restraint and Control no less, the promoter had them right under the headliners. Further down the bill, you had to set up on the fly a lot of the time, your marks and tunings didn't matter worth a shit to the promoter or the crowd, so you had better be ready to go at the word go. Once they were done, they just unplugged and toddled backstage. Benji's wife was working their merch table since she was the most tolerant spouse tied to the band. Benji headed right over to hang out with her leaving the three of them to take their instruments and go live the rock and roll lifestyle. The cramped dim area was more or less deserted, the hawd coor fucks had commandeered the only private dressing room for them and their "crew." Jim had no fucking clue what they were doing in there, either tar heroin or blowing each other was his guess, most of those straight edge groups ended up having some really fun secrets.

Teddy leaned in, "So, no matter what, we're crushing those assholes right?"

"No doubt," Cole replied with a grin.

"I fucking hate straight edge," Jim agreed.

The way these shows were set up, the bands hung out of sight, backstage was there, and it was expected so the kids out front would think of them more like rock stars instead of elderly never-had-beens. They were soon joined by the scum rock band and their entourage of aging women. What Jim guessed was the lead singer waved to one of the girls who held up one of their records so it was laid out flat in front of the guy. The guy pointed and the pair of them went over to a spot near the door of the private dressing room. Jim couldn't see exactly what they were doing, but he could pretty easily guess, especially when the air was torn by an enormous snorting noise with the guy hunched over the album. It would have been kind of funny, doing it right in front of the former straight edge heroes dressing room, except the whole thing seemed so contrived. It was why those bands didn't have a long shelf life with Jim, or much of anyone else really, the whole thing seemed so phony, a rock 'n roll' Vegas act with marks to hit on and off the stage. Everybody involved in it seemed to be trying too hard to be rebellious and degenerate, it all seemed too tied to society. If society says it's bad, well then, we'll do it, but only because society said so. It wasn't rebellion so much as it was contrarian, and that seemed like too much work to Jim, just double-checking what polite society was offended by each day. Fuck the lot of them, and get on with your life was how he had always viewed it. He might have gotten into punk as a negative reaction to the world around him, but he didn't have to do everything that way.

They could hear the opening band starting up so Jim went over to the door and looked out. The crowd was already filling in, people were showing up kind of early for this. Thank God he didn't see that much of the headliners crowd in there. He wished he could remember their name, something monosyllabic that was supposed to sound masculine but sounded kind of sexual, like Thrust or something like that. Their crowd would be the old guys with the full sleeves of tats who dug their Fred Perry's out of mothballs for this. There were a few, but not enough that they'd suddenly want to relive their youth by jumping somebody twenty on one. They probably didn't have good enough joints for it these days anyway, Tiger Balm and PMA can only do so much.

Just like the last time he was at a show, the openers were solid enough to warrant a trip to check their merch later so he made a point of putting their name in his phone in case he forgot. It was amazing how a small action like that could liven up someone's world, in a minute, tiny way it made the world slightly less awful for them, and you got a cd or a 45 out of it to boot. Jim would have been paying even more attention to them but his heart rate was running high. He wanted to be where they were right now, and every song they played was keeping him from what he wanted. The call to arms had been sounded, and now he wanted to plunge into battle again while he still could.

The rest of the band was loose, goofing around with each other. Teddy was bitching about his son in college which was his favorite complaint on earth, and Cole was going along with it. Benji was out at the merch table being personable, which he was good at. Jim on the other hand felt like he'd gone back in time thirty years to when he was an angry young man, just centering it all into a ball right next to his heart so he could release it all on stage on an unsuspecting audience. Jim let out an audible gasp of relief when the band on stage crashed to a conclusion at last.

Jim was practically tapping his feet with impatience as the other band broke down their gear. He could feel the good vibe and kind feelings he had for them evaporating with his need to get up there and just go. It wasn't their fault, he chided himself for his irritation. Hates weren't supposed to go on until after the scum rock band anyway, so there he was being frustrated with a bunch of kids who had no idea why. Hell, nobody except him expected what he was hoping to deliver tonight, the crowd was expecting them to deliver competent at best. He might know all that logically, but it didn't matter to his racing emotions. Jim quickly hit himself with a dropper of CBD oil just to keep himself from working himself into a panic attack. Right now, he was just raring to go, but he could feel where it would and could get away from him quickly if he wasn't careful.

Finally, the younger band cleared the way and let the next band on, the scum rockers. Jim almost laughed as he saw two members of the band carrying up bottles of Jack

Daniels as they clambered up the steps. How absolutely, marvelously cliché of them. They were out of hearing range, thank God because he did laugh when two of the women with them stripped off their pants to just panties and high heels. The whole thing might have originally been meant as a parody of Sunset Strip hair metal lifestyles but too long playing the role had made the joke age every bit as poorly as the latest Motley Crue farewell until the rent's due again tour.

Jim walked to the back, near the closed dressing room, and took a seat. What was going on up there promised to be a sloppy set, and frankly he had only liked a couple of bands on the fringes of that whole thing anyway. The older, uglier, we've begun to actually believe in this shit, sloppy drunk version he could take a pass on. Bereft of anything useful to do he checked his phone and his messages. There were a ton of posts on the band's Facebook page wishing them well tonight, which he thought was nice, so he scanned through them for a minute. His face froze at one of the names, Jasper Williams. Holy shit it was Jazz!

He was about to say something to Cole, but as he began to speak, he heard the band on stage falling to a train wreck of a finish out there. Jim would just have to mention it later, right now it was time to get his shit together, it was time to break the donuts.

The whole thing blew up when they stormed the stage. Sure, it wasn't the explosion of force that it had been in the old days, but Jim was still aiming for over the top even if he couldn't climb as high up the mountain as he used to. And he was sure they'd get there tonight, for an oldies act that was. The other guys picked up on it, so did the crowd. There was no screwing around tonight, none of the playfulness their sets usually held. Most nights they knew what they were, a nostalgia trip, and just went with it. There was no real fooling themselves that this was a career, or that they were dangerous in any way, they had kids in college who thought they were old and out of it. Maybe it was the wait, maybe it was just disgust at being sandwiched between one band that was still aping the rock n roll lifestyle and the group of fifty-year-olds that would mention the "kids" and "youth" in at least three songs tonight, hard to say. For tonight at least, they were a dangerous band as they plowed through their set.

Jim looked over to Cole and saw him playing like a pro. Gone was his usual lackadaisical demeanor, his befuddled good nature that he tried to face life with. Tonight, his houseguest was a fierce hardcore guitarist again. This might only last for tonight, God only knew they couldn't do this two nights in a row, but right now they owned this stage. Life was fleeting, any one of them could keel over from a heart attack tomorrow like poor Alan almost had. This was the best thing for it, take life by the horns and wring everything you could out of it while you still had the chance. Worry about how bad it was all going to hurt tomorrow if you got to tomorrow.

Sweat poured down Jim's face in the hot lights as he poured himself out to the world. Maybe he had been faking it with the band before, just going through the motions because it was "a thing to do." Not tonight, all of his upsets, his pent-up anger with himself and the world had an outlet. The crowd could feel it, they didn't usually have a serious pit for their sets but they did tonight. Faces lined up in front of him, from his peers, to kids his own kid's age. They wanted to be able to say they'd seen it later. How long had it been since anybody in the group had been "must-see" instead of simply entertainment?

It felt like before it had really even had time to get going, the last song ended with a reverberating explosion of noise. The crowd erupted, and Jim appreciated that, but he was already sinking into himself when the lights dimmed. Whatever he had let loose on the stage had to get put back wherever he kept it before he faced the world. You can't walk around like that every day; you'd end up in jail or worse. The lights were off and it was time to remember how to be a normal human being while you packed up.

"Fuckin' hell," Teddy said as he unplugged his bass and put it away in its case.

"That fuckin' rocked," Benji agreed.

Cole was grinning widely at Jim, "Just like old times huh?"

Jim nodded numbly, "Yeah, but speaking of old, let's get our gear stowed before my body remembers how fucking old I am, huh?"

The hawd coor band was finally beginning to emerge from their dressing room as the Hates were just stowing the last of their gear back in the dressing area. The scum rock band was already gone, off to their hotel to party most likely. It was funny watching the baldies just standing there waiting for their gear to be set up. They hadn't watched anyone else play, they hadn't interacted at all with anyone in this hall tonight. In their minds, they were rock stars and they were above it all. Benji chuckled to himself before he split to check on the merch table, leaving just the three of them.

"Well, that went well," Teddy grinned.

"You know, I think it did," Cole added.

Jim didn't say anything, he was watching the other band. They weren't nervous, they didn't have "it." He was sure they'd give a professional showing, like professional musicians, but nobody would be talking about them later except maybe a few kids who had always wanted to see them and thought even existing in the same room as those guys was some huge honor. Maybe if they had been less self-important, they would have checked out the other band's sets. They'd know they needed to bring their A-game tonight, they'd have some of that fire in their guts right now. Instead, they looked bored.

"Let's get paid, and get out of here. Nothing interesting happening now," Jim grunted just loud enough for the other band to hear as he picked up an amp.

The band pretty much went their separate ways after the gig. That was the thing at this age, it was more a hobby the wives put up with, like golf but with more leather involved. That left Cole and Jim sitting in the living room alone drinking a beer. Both of their moods were light, but now that the adrenaline was gone Jim's body was starting to remember how old he really was. At least he was smart enough not to try and chide himself, like maybe if he'd worked out more, ran more, etc., etc. Middle-aged was middle-aged and even if you were in great shape for your age, it was still only, for your age.

"You happy?" Cole smiled over at him.

"Fuck yeah I am. That shredded and you know it," Jim grinned tiredly his head back on the couch and his eyes half-closed.

"Yeah, that felt good. I'd ask if you wanted to celebrate tonight, but...."

"The old man is tired and looks ready for bed," Jim finished for him.

"Just want to note, you said that, not me."

Jim chuckled softly, "Duly noted, it will not be held against you on your quarterly report."

They had a couple of more beers, Jim noted that Cole was still pretty wide awake, even fidgety. He figured that he probably was still wound up from the gig. Jim kind of wished he was, it hadn't felt that good to play after so long on the shelf. Try as he might to stay up though, he could feel his eyes beginning to drift closed. All things considered; he knew he needed to make an effort to get some sleep by choice before it became by force.

"All right you crazy kid, don't stay up all night watching the horror movies. You and your mom are sick of you climbing into bed with us," Jim said as he got up.

"Gee whiz pops, I won't," Cole grinned back up at him. As Jim was getting ready to head back to his room, Cole added, "Hey, I don't know if I've said it before, but thanks for everything man. I almost feel human."

"But not quite human?"

"Hey, look what I have to work with," Cole joked opening his arms as if displaying himself.

"Anyway, no problem. We've been friends for a long time, it's what friends do."

With that Jim headed off to his room. He got on Facebook briefly to give a breathless, well maybe not that effusive, but a glowing report about how he felt the gig had gone. He made it a point of liking some of the pictures people had taken with their phones, he had been so in the zone he hadn't even noticed them flashing away. Or, the other possibility was that phones were just such a part of a gig these days he just ignored them, he could ignore most things when he was completely wrapped into that wall of sound. Somebody said they had video and they'd have it up tomorrow, so that would be cool. A couple of people said that the mosh pit band had kind of sucked in comparison to the band and was a distraction, so that was nice. For a moment it actually felt like he still mattered to the world.

It was a good feeling to close his eyes with.

"Jake, god damn it, why is he backing out now?" Howard demanded petulantly slamming his fist on the table they both sat at.

"The good Senator is afraid of getting outed," Jake shrugged.

"The son of a bitch has more or less taken marching orders from me for five fucking years now, and now he gets cold feet?"

Jake sighed, "He saw what happened to that State Rep Thomas when the press got a hold of communications between him and one of our satellites. He cares more about his career than the white race. I've said it before Howard, the problem with owning a politician is that they're a politician, they're like cockroaches, born survivors."

Howard knew Jake was right. Jake was almost always right about things like this. It was one of the reasons he left his second in command retain that much of his autonomy. The man was a good thinker, and even without Howard's power over Jake, Jake was committed to the cause. Jake had come to him years ago on his own, it hadn't taken much on Howard's part to get him to bow to his master. It was Jake's fervent beliefs and the depth that he felt them that made Howard so sure that he was on the right path here. That depth of feeling could be mined, it could be expanded, it could lead to greater things, battles, and chaos truly worth the price of admission, instead of just squabbles on street corners. Riots in the capitol building were all good and well, but he wanted to see the whole damned thing burn to the ground.

And after Howard had met Jake and taken him to his bosom they had expanded dramatically. They had built a veritable army of foot soldiers and underground networks together that went further up the ladder than people wanted to believe. Unfortunately, over-zealousness on their parts and some of the flock wanting to start the war early had set them back recently. That capitol mess was shooting your wad early and had generated no sympathy from the greater nation. Too many racists still didn't want to identify themselves that way, were afraid of the censure of their neighbor for their beliefs, the torrent of hate that flooded them on the internet once it came out. They were cowards, but in a way, they were right. When things came out into the public view, the larger public had time to prepare and defend the body politic against the virus. Howard's main hope was that the disease was far further spread along than people realized, like a lump on your chest that is the first warning you have before the doctor tells you your lungs are littered with cancer and you should write a will.

Everything was so close to working, the hatred between people was almost at a fever pitch. If only, if only he could find that one thing that would tip it over. But what? The problem with the outrage society was that there were so many of these outrages people just moved on to the next one the next day. He needed something special. Something that could be sustained, something you'd want to have a war over, something that once it was sent in motion, even God himself wouldn't be able to stop.

"Call in the boys, it's time for that something big to tilt this all the rest of the way over."

"But what? We've done plenty it seems," Jake asked.

"Give me a few days to come up with the details, but I think I know now. All a race war in this country is going to take is the right push, and I'm feeling ready to shove," Howard grinned.

"I'm surprised you don't just..." Jake wiggled his fingers.

"If I could do those sorts of things on the scale I'd need to, I wouldn't bother with people at all," Howard grunted.

Jim's eyes opened slowly. He had one brief moment of dull and empty bliss before a wave of aches and pains reported in from all over his body. He closed his eyes again in the naïve hope that the world would just go away and take all those aches with it if he denied its existence long enough. His bladder absolutely wasn't having it. He tried tossing one way or turning another to see if he could relieve the pressure enough to go back to sleep but the entire operation was no go, he had to rise from his own ashes like the pissiest, grumpiest phoenix in history.

After relieving himself with his eyes open exactly enough to find the toilet, he briefly considered returning to bed. No, he was up, and if he slept too long it would screw up his sleep patterns for the week. Instead, running on auto-pilot he went and got a cup of coffee. Cole was still asleep he guessed, but then again, he'd looked like he'd still be up for a while when Jim went to bed, so no real surprise there. Nothing that needed to distract himself from his overall goal, java.

Slumping into his chair in the computer room, he booted the tower up, the damned thing had needed updates last night and had powered itself off. He could have used his phone, but he preferred the bigger screen on the computer, sign of old age and bad eyes he guessed. His Facebook message alerts had blown up overnight, all about last night's show. Everything seemed positive in a scan through of what was being said. There was video, there were pictures, there were plenty of atta' boys from people who had been there and friends who had heard about it third hand alike. It was so bizarre to him, last month most people had already forgotten about them and their little ep, but if you read the descriptions of last night's gig it was like gods had returned from Olympus. People, so delightfully fickle.

Screw letting him sleep, he had to show Cole!

Jim walked out to the living room and froze when he saw the table by the couch. There were works there, a needle, a spoon, a lighter...

"Oh, Cole...no, man," Jim moaned, feeling pain somewhere deep in himself for his friend's lost sobriety.

He rushed the rest of the way to the couch. They were

going to have this out right now, he'd do what he could for him, but no way was this shit going to fly! Jim reached over to roll Cole over and wake him up. When his hand touched the cold flesh, the world felt like it shattered in that frozen instance, shards flying away from the spot where his hand had landed on Cole's shoulder. Like the whole world they'd been building this time was fragile crystal and this was a hammer blow.

"Fuck," Jim breathed, summing it all up.

A half an hour later he was out on his front porch. There was an ambulance, there were cops, there was a scene. He had lived here quite a while without there being a scene, but there sure as fuck was one now. A big muscle-brained, jarhead of a cop stood there asking him questions, there was already sweat beading on his testosterone, and probably steroid, poisoned forehead.

"So, you don't know where your roommate got the drugs?" he asked holding out his little notepad to write it down the second Jim incriminated himself.

"How the fuck should I know? I wouldn't touch that shit myself!" Jim snarled taking a drag on his vape.

"And why is that sir?" the fucking asshole thought he was being clever.

"Because the results of fucking with that shit are currently being zipped up in a body bag in my living room! Because that is how that shit always ends if you fuck with it."

The cop actually managed to get his bulldog face into something approaching a thoughtful expression before saying, "Good point. Well, if we have any more questions, we can call or email you. Do you have anything you want to add?"

"Yeah, don't be a junkie, because sooner or later you're going to leave a fucking mess like this for a friend.

Now if you'll excuse me, I'd like some time alone to bawl my fucking eyes out for the poor dumb son of a bitch."

275

Chapter 6

He had just heard the doors on the ambulance slam outside with a devastating finality when his cell phone rang. Jim looked at the number. Fuck! It was Cindy, he absolutely had to take this, and he absolutely didn't want to.

"Yo," he said, his voice husky.

"Jim, one of the neighbors called, are you all right?" Cindy's voice came through with a tinge of panic to it.

"Me? Yeah, I mean, I guess. I'm not the one that left in an ambulance that wasn't running its sirens."

"What the hell happened? They said there were police and ambulances," she said, her voice retaining that edge despite being able to talk to her ex-husband. He wanted to make a point of asking why the neighbors had her number but left it alone, no point.

"Well, you know how I had a friend staying here?"

"Yeah, I thought it might be good for you."

"Yeah, it was, and I think it was good for Cole too, so imagine my fucking surprise finding him OD'ed this morning," Jim practically sobbed.

"Oh, Jesus Christ...I'm so sorry Jim," Cindy said softly.

There was an uncomfortable silence before Cindy said, "Jim, I'm worried, I'm coming over."

Jim was caught in his swirl of emotions as he felt them pull him down, "No...no Cindy, you don't have to do that. I'll live, I have to. Certain kids would never forgive me if I wasn't there for their graduations, I couldn't bear doing that to them."

Jim could actually feel Cindy smile through the phone, "Very noble, and I'm coming over anyway."

"No, Cindy, Todd will have an absolute shit if you did that. Don't do that to your thing."

"Todd is on a business trip anyway, probably fucking his secretary, which weirdly I don't mind. But even if he was home, he could suck a dick, this is important," she replied adamantly.

"Nice language, I approve. So, I got no choice in this?"

"No, you don't, I still love you, dumb ass, I just can't live with you. I'm going to make sure you're OK, and then you can go back to talking shit about me after I leave."

"I don't talk shit about you Cindy," Jim chuckled.

"You don't talk shit about your ex-wife? You, sir, are a fucking weirdo, I'll see you in a bit."

Jim hung up.

He opened up messenger and started composing a message to Benji. He stopped after typing the words, "*Horrible news*"

He stared into space and dialed Benji's number. A moment later Benji picked up, "Yo, Jim I'm surprised you're able to move."

"I got some shit news man," Jim replied in a quiet even voice.

After a moment of silence, Benji finally said, "And

that news is."

"No nice way to say this, Cole's dead, I found him dead on the couch this morning," Jim said in that same weirdly unemotional voice.

The line was silent for a long moment before Benji breathed, "Fuccccck."

"Yeah, that's what I said," Jim agreed.

"You all right man?"

"No, no I am not all right. Somebody I have known for over thirty years was dead on my fucking couch this morning." Jim caught himself, he heard his tone getting tight and angry, "Look, clearly I'm not straight in the head at the moment. Don't worry about me, OK? Cindy is already on her way over to keep me company whether I want her to or not. Just, could you do me a favor?"

Benji replied instantly, almost like he was waiting for it, "Sure, what do you need?"

"Tell the rest of the guys, if you've got the energy put something on our page, or I'll do it later tonight. Yadda yadda, died in his sleep, yadda yadda, we aren't over, we don't think Cole would have wanted that."

"We aren't done?"

"You think that's fair to Alan? Cole played on a bit of recording time, wrote a couple of songs, and played live with us once. Alan was our guitarist before that for years, and he's busted hump to get healthy enough to play again."

There was a pause. "You're right. Alright man, sure, I can handle that," Benji replied with an almost exhausted tone of voice. He might not be exhausted yet, but his tone showed that he expected to be by the time this had all run its course.

"Thanks, man, I owe you."

"Do you know what it was?" There was the question Jim had been dreading, but he wasn't gonna' fucking lie. Cole did that in his house, he owed Cole a lot, but not a lie.

"He OD'ed."

"Fuck."

"Yep, that's still the right answer."

Jim made love to Cindy that afternoon. He hadn't planned to, and he was sure she hadn't either. It didn't change anything, it didn't mean anything, except that Cindy still had a very loving side to her and went with the quickest path to making him happy. It wasn't even the first time it had happened, but for something that didn't mean anything long term, maybe it meant more to Jim today because he needed it more. Cindy had a marriage that she liked on paper, it was empty and tolerable, and that's what she wanted now. Jim and Cindy had a passionate relationship once upon a time, that due to Jim, often became intolerable. When she missed passion too much, she saw what Jim was up to. If he was free, he obliged, because he still loved her in his way. Today, had a tenderness that was kinder than just fucking to feel something again. Fucking just so she could feel passion for a few minutes was fine by him usually, but it didn't have a lot of depth.

But that wasn't what today was about.

"Thank you," he breathed as she snuggled up against him.

"What for? I enjoyed myself too you know," she giggled softly, her perfectly dyed blond hair splayed out over his chest.

"You didn't want me to feel alone, and now I don't. We make a lousy couple, but I have no trouble remembering why I love you," he said.

"Thank god we don't still live together," she agreed, "if we did, we wouldn't even have that left. Of course, if one of these days you figure out that you aren't a bad catch and let some other woman grab you, we won't even have this."

"Naw, I'll still love you for days like this and more."

"And we'll still have memories, some better than others."

"At least this way we've stopped making those other memories, the ugly ones we told the therapist about," Jim said kissing her on top of her head.

She raised her head and kissed him lightly, "If only the world stopped at the bedroom door."

Cindy went home after they'd made love again, after he'd assured her he'd be all right by himself. Which left the other part of his day, the other part that he didn't want to touch but had to anyway. He called the hospital. After talking to the first nurse on call, his call was transferred.

"Records, can I help you?" said a male voice that sounded harried and tense.

"Hi, umm I'm calling about a recently deceased, Cole Orvik. I was wondering if his next of kin has been notified," Jim asked in as professional a voice as he could manage in the situation.

"And who am I speaking to?"

"My name is Jim Malloy; he was living with me when he passed away. There are things, and really, I'm not even sure if I should touch his stuff."

He could hear tapping, someone punching things up on a computer before the voice on the other end sighed, "Look, Mister...Malloy, was it? In my experience, nobody claims these bodies. We put in a contact to the only living relative we could find, a cousin, but they told us they didn't want his remains. So as far as I'm concerned you can touch any of his stuff you want."

"They won't claim him? You mean like no funeral?" Jim asked shocked.

"Yeah, county crematorium is probably where he's headed," the person said, at least having the decency to sound somewhat sad about it.

"Do me a favor, call the cousin back, see if they'll let me claim the body. He was a... friend...I can't let him not have a funeral, that's just not right," Jim said trying to fight back tears as he considered the concept of that happening to Cole.

"If you're willing to pay for a funeral, I'll call them. I can't see them having an issue with it."

"Thank you, let me give you my number."

That left social media. Jim didn't want to, but he had grown up enough to realize that people cared about him, that people expected to hear from him. Especially in this day and age when everybody's lives didn't even seem to exist if they weren't posted about on Facebook. If he didn't at least post something, they'd worry. Not to mention Cole had friends out there, maybe he even had some relatives connected that might want to have his remains who didn't know where he was. Jim checked the band page, true to his word Benji had put up something brief, more or less word for word what Jim had said without the yadda yaddas in there. The page had blown up with condolences and idle speculation, which frankly he didn't want to read right now. They meant well but saying you're sorry now felt hollow, like echoes in this empty house. He also understood the curiosity, when these things happened, he felt the same way, the great unwashed masses could stew in it for a while longer.

Instead, he opened up his own page and typed slowly and thoughtfully.

"This morning I found my friend of over thirty years Cole Orvik deceased. If he has any family out there that will see this, please contact me. If no family comes forward in time, I will take care of the funeral arrangements myself. He was my friend, and it seems the least I can do as a way

to say thank you for our friendship. And that is something we owe all of our friends, thanks for what they bring to our own life. I'm not going to be on here much tonight, I intend to get drunk watching movies. I am very upset, obviously, but I'm also a grown man and know that this is how we all end up eventually. So, there's no reason for anyone to worry about me. If you try to call, you'll most likely get my voice mail. I just want to be alone for a little bit to put my thoughts in order, and then disorder them a bit, and then try and put them back in to order again later. I love all of you, and I'll try to be more sensible tomorrow, but it's been a long day and guys don't cry in public. -Jim "

First, he checked his beer supplies and found them way more than ample. Since there was no way to know if the rest of the band would want to come over to celebrate the gig last night, he'd stocked up like they would be. It was a long shot, but he'd learned his lesson from previous gigs, it could happen, and he never wanted to be forced to make the beer run that late in the evening to be the happy host. Jim left the lights off in the living room as he tossed on *Reform School Girls*. It was high-end dumb exploitation cinema, it wouldn't ask anything of him, it had no deep emotional feeling or memories attached to it. If he left the lights off, he wouldn't see Cole's shit. The drug crap was already gone, it had left with the cops as evidence, but there was still his friend's life stacked in the one corner of the room. The bag he'd had when Jim had first run into him, and some stuff he'd had sent here from his last lengthy stay over before he'd gotten here. Jim didn't want to be reminded of it, but he was too mentally exhausted to move it right now.

Part of him was mad at Cole, it wasn't fair to be, but he was anyway. How many people had to crash and burn like this until the rest of them figured it the fuck out? It killed us back in the day, so why would it become forgiving just because you got gray hair? They should have known better right from the start; they had the evidence available. The mid and late-eighties punk scene had been a bunch of lost kids combing the beach, building something new out of the detritus left behind when the big kid's boats crashed and sank out on the high seas. All these years later, just when you thought everybody had either crashed to the bottom or found some placid waters to drop anchor in, it turned out there were still squalls out there yet to be weathered.

Two beers in, and he found himself legitimately empathizing with the characters in the movie, which definitely took alcohol. After the fourth beer, he was looking at the dark shape in the corner that constituted Cole's earthly possessions. Jim wanted to write his curiosity off to just being nosy, because that was nice and safely human. People rooted around in other people's shit. Deep down, he knew that wasn't it, he needed to know what in the fuck Cole was thinking. He'd been clean the entire time he was here, Jim was fucking sure of it! Did Jim do something? Was there something he had no idea about happening in Cole's life? If it was a moment of weakness, that was fine, well not really, but understandable. Jim needed to know he didn't do anything to cause this. Every time he told himself that he wouldn't, his insecurities told him to look to prove them right or wrong.

There were some boxes, so he opened those first since they felt the least private for whatever reason. There were a lot of old tapes, some CDs, various mementos of bands he'd seen or been in. Under that were fanzines, if Jim was going to guess, probably ones Cole's bands had been reviewed in, he'd probably look through those later out of curiosity. What came next caught his breath, there were fliers for shows. He gently lifted them out of the box to find they were all held in individual sheets of plastic. Lying right on top was one for the show they had just played. Jim quickly went to the bottom of the stack. There in his hands were the fliers for every show Restraint and Control had ever played, sometimes multiples if there had been different designs. Somehow Cole had managed to hold on to all of these!

Jim quickly wiped away a tear, and gently set everything back in the box. To distract himself for a second, he tossed in another movie and sat back with another beer. This one was newer, but had still been out for a while, a werewolf film called *Dog Soldiers*, the sergeant in it cracked him up, so it made for safe viewing. Jim tried not to think about the fliers in there, and what they represented, the memories of when they'd just been two friends in a band together. He didn't even have most of them, he'd moved around too much to hold onto things. Maybe he had a couple, but certainly not all of them like that. For Cole to have lived the life he had and kept all of them like that, there was evidence, proof, he might have left the band back then without so much as a protest, but Cole had cared about those times.

As Jim sat there trying to watch the movie, he was forcing himself to ignore the elephant in the room, Cole's backpack. The same one he'd been carrying when Jim had run into him at that show all those weeks ago. He knew Cole kept a notebook in there, Jim had seen him scribbling away in it often enough. It was like a catch-all journal; he wrote down notes about whatever music he was working on but Jim was pretty sure he also kept notes about whatever life he was living at the time. The answers to the questions Jim had about everything that had happened were most likely sitting right over there. The thing was, Jim was afraid to look, he was afraid he wouldn't like the truth of what had happened.

Yet, he already knew he'd look, he was just steeling

himself up for it. This indecision was just a game that needed to be played out before he could get on with it. He needed to lie to himself that he had struggled with the decision before he made it.

The movie ended and he got to his feet. The theory was he was putting on another movie, that was what he told himself when he got up and moved in that direction. Jim looked over at what loomed in the lengthening shadows of the night, made blacker and deeper with no picture on the TV. The monster that hid and lived in those depths needed to be faced down, why not now? Jim debated it with himself while he tossed on another film, the punk classic *Rude Boy* a semi-fictional film about The Clash. His way back to the couch could have taken him on the far side of the table, instead, he stood in front of Cole's bag. He froze, staring down at the bag containing all that he had left of Cole. Fuck it, rip it off like a band-aid. He unzipped the bag and took out the notebook he knew would be there.

Jim sat back down on the couch with it and took a long pull on his beer. His hands almost moved of their own volition as he thumbed it open to the last entry in there. His body felt at war with itself, his peripherals vanished and his hands had gone right to the spot, but his brain refused to direct his eyes to look down and read what was written there in a neat cursive hand. Finally, with a wrench he forced himself to man up to read his friend's final words.

"June 5th Man my mind is a mess, pulling in so many directions. First off there's the gig, and I'm completely stoked for it. Last few practices have been tight. I just wish I wasn't thinking about doing what I'm thinking about, but Christ, that offer. It's like offering a wine expert a vintage Chardonnay or some shit. I figure if I straighten up after I'm done Jim won't notice, I hope he doesn't, I don't want to fuck that up like I've fucked up everything else this way. Just a taste won't be the end of the world, right? I've gotten

away with tastes before, and shit, I have a lot more reasons to put it down after just this once. I'm sure it will be fine."

Jim sits quietly for a moment to take that all in. Now he knew. It was an accident, a stupid fucking accident. But that's just the way life is, isn't it? Just a series of one dumb fucking accident after another, dozens of kids going to bed every night without their mom because of a dumb fucking accident, lovers standing by graves because of them, and him here reading the last words of one of his few real, true, and oldest friends. Nobody meant for anything bad to happen, nobody expects anything fucking bad to happen, but it does anyway. Everybody thinks that the consequences of their shit will never catch the fuck up with them, but somewhere out there right now, somebody's shit just parked itself down to stay, just like it had right here.

Fuck!

Would he have preferred he'd driven Cole to it? This wasn't nice, but if he was being honest...

He took a long pull on his beer, seeing it was empty, he put down Cole's notebook and went to the fridge to get another one. When he finally found his way back to the couch he was torn. The desire to see Cole's thoughts was still there, it almost felt like reading them would make it feel like he was still here in some way, and if Cole was in some way, then this miserable ass first night alone in the house would pass that much faster for it. Then there was the anger that made him not want Cole here at all. All of this, this whole fucking miserable ass day was caused because Cole fucked up doing something he knew damned well was dangerous. Like he thought he could keep dancing with that devil forever and the devil would never ask to settle up the bill!

And here's the guy who used to have a drinking problem that was so bad it cost him his marriage with a beer in his hand being judgmental. Jim laughed at himself, it wasn't the same, it wasn't even close to the same, after tomorrow he probably wouldn't touch the shit for months, and he'd have tomorrow to do it with, but still... Hypocrite much? He knew he was still drip dropping poison into his brain tonight to make the owie go away, even if it was only for tonight, that didn't change the what and the whys, now did it? Fuck it, at least he could hang out with Cole a little while longer, he figured at some point, SOME relative is going to want his shit, they'll smell money from his music once they realize that they've got a dead rocker on their hands with a juicy back catalog. Hell of a shock for them when they found out there isn't any money in punk rock, but it'd be funny to watch. In the meantime, might as well take the time he had here.

He flipped through the notebook a couple of times trying to decide on where to start. An entry caught Jim's eye, it was the way that it's splotched with water, the ink running a bit. Like someone was either crying or caught out in the rain when they were putting it down. Either way, it was the kind of thing that caught a scanning eye.

"July. 10th Well, I wanted to see the big bad wolf for myself so here I am. Sitting on a rainy ass hill overlooking a psycho compound with a set of binoculars. My curiosity is going to get me killed one of these days, and good work too, it won't be the greatest loss to the world. The place is weird, I mean weird even for what it is, there's a bunch of people, but other than a few people moving around to do basic maintenance you'd think the place was a ghost town. Are they all on the internet all day trolling or some shit? From the shit you see on the news you'd think they'd be out at their rifle range all day, but not a thing. Just weird quiet, broken up by some occasional hammering, not the militia I was   expecting.

July 15th Finally some action, if not some weird action. Someone who didn't look like they were dressed for the film, "Gomer Pyle And the Worst Unit in The Marines" like everyone else here, showed up today. Guy was a total suit and tie guy, and even more, he had a fucking bodyguard if you could believe it! Slipped in through the gate in a plain-looking Toyota and practically ran to Fillmore's cabin which is towards the back of camp, like he was afraid even in here behind the walls somebody might see him. Actually, guess that fear was pretty well-founded after all, seeing as I saw him. Thing was, I was positive I recognized the guy, so I got out my phone for when he came out. The zoom isn't the best, but when I checked it later and did an image search it came up that State Senator Aston. The one that got made fun of on the Daily Show for saying something kind of racist a while back! Seems like these Nazis have some political clout here! Maybe they want to start a professional BBQ joint and need the zoning permits, the fuckers keep pigs on part of the property and they have a bunch of those big-time smokers on the grounds. Ze Fuhrers Down Home BBQ!

July 23rd OK this has gotten both fucked up and familiar. Too familiar. Late in the afternoon two of the thugs came in with a third dude. Guy didn't look that much different than me, figure he was homeless, younger, carrying a backpack. The two guys he was walking between were talking him up, that leaning in style so it looks like they're being friendly if you don't know what they're really doing, hemming you in so you can't bolt for it. Out of the house steps the man himself, Fillmore. He's smiling at the sight of the kid, which should have been a warning, nobody is happy to see you when you're streeting it, nobody. But here this fucker is smiling like he just won the lottery. He's just standing there with this other guy next to him, I guess *his right-hand man, and he's really talking the kid up, the kid is smiling like he thinks he's finally found someplace, and hooray, happy Aryan endings all around, right?*

I figure the kid hasn't been out on the streets too long, he went into someone's power place, he's way outnumbered, he doesn't have a clear escape route. Worst of all, he didn't pay attention to his peripheral vision and the moving parts. Because while he's having the nicest conversation you ever did have with Fillmore, his right-hand man has slipped behind the kid, he's surrounded. I know something bad is going to go down! I want to warn the kid, but if I say a peep, my knees ain't good and I'm out in the woods outside of an armed Aryan compound, and I don't want to die here.

Which makes one of us, the kid barely makes a peep when the right-hand man drags that hand across his throat holding a knife. The kid just drops like a rock with a shocked look on his face. And the fucked-up thing? Compound full of people, nobody even fucking blinks, not even a shocked expression in the entire joint, most of them don't even bother to glance over as the kid is lying there bleeding out!

I can only say I've never seen part of what happened next before. I've seen what a human being looks like chopped to bits before, hell, that might even be what set me off to find my lifelong little China White helper in the first place, but I've never seen the process before. While I watched they stripped the poor kid out of his clothes and hung him up like a rack of meat. While they were doing that another one of them came from the back with one of the pigs these people keep for food. A moment later two carcasses were hanging there, both of them were gutted out in short order. In just as short an order both bodies were loaded into a smoker.

I want to be wrong about this, but this is way too

fucking familiar.

July 25th A bunch of new recruits were brought in to see the grounds. They got some stirring speeches from the man himself. You could tell they were into it by all the one-armed salutes they did. Then everybody sat down for a filling meal.

They had BBQ which was doled out from big vats of the shit, enough to feed an army. Everybody ate.

The smokers they had stuffed with the pig and that kid were both standing empty.

None of the new recruits left, they all got up calmly after their meal and went over to one of the empty barracks without a peep.

I have definitely seen this shit before. Fuck me. I need help, and I especially need it from someone who might actually believe me, somebody else who has seen this shit before! For now, I am getting the fuck out of here and not coming back, I don't want to be anybody's mystical fucking brainwashing meal. I've got to get some people together to do something about this, and I can't do it as part of a happy meal sloppy joe that's half Cole, half pig"

Jim read over the entries repeatedly. No matter how he read it he got the same message. Cole wasn't being hypothetical or bullshitting him that first night. He'd lived with Cole for a while now, Cole wasn't batshit from being on the streets too long. Other than his addiction he had seemed to have his shit together. How he'd managed that was beyond Jim, but he did. He had really seen something up there. He'd even done the most sane thing a person could do, when given a choice between settling into a nice decent life with Jim, or going demon hunting, he had let the demon drop and enjoyed his couch and three squares.

Now the million-dollar question was, what in the fuck

was Jim going to do with this knowledge?

Chapter 7

What had been handed to him in that notebook by Cole felt like a priority, but it wasn't. Not yet anyway, real life was a priority, and in the real-world Cole was dead, that was immediate and had right now things he needed to do attached to it. After a day of recovery around the house, Jim had more immediate things to worry about than mystical Nazi entities threatening America, they were all the way up in Allentown and he had shit to do here. The mind works that way, we put off the great big issues until we can get the immediate things we HAVE to do out of the way. Somehow the nuts and bolts of the world always take priority over the epic, we take out the trash and double-check our messages before we climb into the lion's den. Maybe we just don't want to have to worry about it during a key moment later, distracted by the thought of whether we left the oven on when we should have been dodging a claw.

In this case, Jim would have thought what he had on his plate that needed clearing was huge no matter what else was happening. The coroner had called, the family didn't give a shit, in fact, less than a shit, they told the guy not to call again. Frankly, Jim wasn't that shocked, when he croaked most likely it would be Cindy who was stuck with his body, and even that was chancy. His birth family wanted nothing to do with him, and the feeling was more than mutual. Welcome to the wide world of how so many punk kids ended up being street kids in the first place, it was because they had families who told them by their own actions that adults were all douchebags early on, and that as bad as it might get on the streets, they were better off on their own. Those ties had been severed by life too long to be renewed by its absence. Those wounds had never healed.

He'd never planned a funeral before, hell, his wedding was something he was only vaguely involved in, mainly in the form of showing up moderately sober and able to stand on his own two feet. Planning things like this had always been the domain of the women in his life, when there was one. When there wasn't, shit happened if it happened, except of course gigs, which he micromanaged after the early days of letting Shane pick their gigs. Jim had been happy to leave the better half of the species to it, they were more sensitive and would consider people's feelings better than he would anyway. But with no women handy to take the reins here, there was just him trying not to make a butchery of everyone else's grieving process.

He had to take every step of the process in the order it presented itself, otherwise he'd be completely out to sea. His messages, for starters, had blown the fuck up on him. He expected it and he had started plowing through the pile during his slow casual day after. Once Jim had gotten a little tired, he put it aside, no point in getting emotional on Facebook, what the fuck was that going to help? Worrying people hundreds of miles away like that? Jim used social media to get away from shit, now when he needed an escape, all anyone wanted to talk about was his shit.

Jim took a break and called around to funeral homes to get an idea on pricing. Also, how big each funeral home was. It turned out that a bunch of people had expressed interest in being there, Cole would have been shocked. Somehow Jim wasn't at all surprised by it, Cole might have been practically homeless, but he was a likable guy deep down. Not to mention he'd made a lot of music over the years, and that stuck with people long after your fuck ups. Jim decided to plan for a hundred, and expect twenty. He needed a place that had a big room, and then smaller rooms if people stopped thinking with their emotions and realized they weren't going to make it after all, no matter what their well-meant statements were saying today. He also checked out the websites extensively and their ratings, deciding that it was fucked up reading reviews of funeral parlors. It almost felt like the dead themselves had returned from the grave just to bitch about the service at some of them.

They each asked him to come in and make the final arrangements in person when he called, which he supposed as a real adult he could do, but he damned well didn't want to. Cole was gone, he was doing the right thing by a body in ritual, this was just a way to make sure that he wasn't just thrown out like trash. Cole deserved better than that. What Jim didn't want was some douchebag in a suit working him over trying to hard-sell him something other than something simple and to the point. Jim just wanted to get this shit the fuck over with, not create an expensive dog and pony show out of the whole fucking thing. Service, box, hole, stone, everyone's off to the wake.

He was just about to pack it in for the night when he noticed that he had a message request on Facebook. Someone he wasn't friends with wanted to talk, curiosity got the best of him so he clicked it open. Holy mamboing Christ on a pogo stick, it was from Jazz Williams! He opened it up and saw that he had another message under it as well, Pamela Shineman. He didn't recognize the last name, but he had a strong suspicion that he knew what Pamela it would be. Checking her profile some, more or less confirmed those suspicions. Nothing like a corpse to bring people back together it seemed.

Hilariously, both messages were almost exactly the same. *"Hey, how are you? I heard what happened,"* being the gist of it.

He responded identically. *"Well, I'm alive, so I guess that puts me ahead of the game. How are you?"*

Then Jim carefully turned his computer off and went for a walk with Doc. He had too many things swirling in his head, and when he walked, they could all be blotted out to nothing. Just him and what he was listening to on his earbuds and the dog dragging him onward. He had checked in with Cindy, checked in with the girls, made sure that they knew he was fine and that he didn't need them for anything. After freeing them to have a non-him life again, it was time for him to just check out for a bit of non-anyone time.

When he got back, he saw what he should have expected, two more messages. He checked Pamela's first. *"Hey, I'm coming down for the funeral if that's all right. I've missed you guys and, well I want to say goodbye to Cole."*

Jim felt a bittersweet thrill at that. It would be nice to see her after all these years, it really would. He checked her Facebook profile a little further almost automatically. She honestly didn't look that different than she had once upon a time in the magical world of New York's Lower East Side. Oh sure, lines and a bit of gray hair here or there, but he had more lines, and if it wasn't for the vanity of bleaching his hair who knew how many grays he'd have of his own. No doubt about it, she was way ahead of him in the aging gracefully department. It was nice to see time had treated her kindly. As he looked over her profile, he saw that maybe he'd spoken too soon about time being kind, it also said she was divorced. Well, then again so was he, and he didn't feel that terrible about it. Maybe she made the mistake of finding another project like she thought he'd been back then when they first started dating. That was indeed the kind of thing that could lead to a reverse trip down the altar, here he was as proof.

"Let me know where you're staying. I guess I might have a few people to the house after to reminisce, or whatever you do after a funeral." he typed back.

He was happy to leave it at that, he hoped she would too. Right now, he had a lot of weirdness in his life, and getting into his whole life story with his ex-girlfriend online was too much. Jim was sure it would all come out in the wash, it sounded like he was seeing her soon anyway, but it didn't have to be right here, right now. That way he could trade off with her in a game of "twenty questions of how we both fucked up our lives and ended up being divorced," with the pleasure of seeing the person you were talking to.

Anyway, he still had Jazz to deal with, which all things considered also promised to be weird. Weirder, than talking to Pamela at any rate, they hadn't exactly parted amicably. It's hard to be amicable with someone who is sleeping with your now ex-girlfriend, only you didn't know she was your ex-girlfriend before that conversation started. He just sat and stared at the second message that was waiting for him.

"Alison and I are coming down. Are you gonna be OK with that?"

Well, that was polite of him. Jim considered it for a moment, was he going to be OK with it? He looked deep inside of himself and realized something that surprised even him. He couldn't care less about Alison, not to say he was looking forward to seeing her, but she was a non-issue. Yeah, sleeping with a guy's girlfriend is weak sauce, but Christ they were barely legally adults back then. Hormones and shit. Life was too short to worry about it, it wasn't like he hadn't been attached to and dumped by numerous women since then. Hell, he'd married one, she was gone and he was fine with that. No, he knew deep down how he felt, and how he felt was that staying mad forever was too time consuming. And anyway, it looked like it worked out between the pair of them, clearly, it wasn't going to work out between Jim and her. If it hadn't been Jazz, it would have been somebody.

"Yeah, sure no problems there. That was all a long time ago."

Jim just stared off into space for a moment. The sudden swirl of conflicting emotions and memories froze him to the spot. He needed the time to get a hold of all of it so he could wedge it back into the box labeled, "Ancient History: Who Gives A Shit?" in his head. His reverie was broken by the ping of a message hitting his inbox.

Jazz again.

"If you don't mind, I'm going to help pay for the funeral. Just let me know what it tallies up to."

Oh, come the fuck on! It was one thing to come down for the funeral, it was even fine to bring Jim's bitch ex-girlfriend with him, but to act like he was going to ride in on a white horse and help save Jim financially from this horrible burden he'd taken on... Jim caught himself in mid mental tirade. He didn't need to say it like that though. Maybe he wanted to, sure, but he was too old to act that immature. He hadn't talked to Jazz in thirty years almost, and Jazz should be at Cole's funeral, that felt right. Jazz might not be if Jim didn't rope his shit in right now.

Jim: *"Look, dude, I got it covered. I'm going to finalize the arrangements tomorrow it's no big deal."*

Jim had almost begun to think it was settled when his messenger pinged again.

Jazz: "*Yeah it is, we had to have one for my dad last year. It isn't cheap. Look, don't take this wrong, but he was my friend too. He even stayed up here for a while about a year or so ago. Not everything has to be a burden for you, I know you have a habit of expecting life to be constantly kicking you in the ass, there's no reason this has to be more of the same. I just want to help, I can afford to help, as his friend I deserve to help. Please, don't block me out of this, I'm begging here dude.*"

That froze Jim in his tracks. Did he have a persecution complex? He'd had a bad childhood, kids from that kind of background learn real early that life is indeed out to get them. Being paranoid was the path that didn't end up with you getting physically hurt so much or dead much too young. Had he been pissing on the heads of his guardian angels even when things were good? Did he spend so much time looking for the black widow in the dozen roses that he never bothered to smell the damned things? It bore some examination, hell maybe there was some truth to it. He'd be sure and tell his therapist all about this theory if he ever bothered to get around to going to a personal therapist like Cindy had asked him for most of their marriage. In the meantime, he could see no real reason that he could justify for freezing Jazz out like that. He had reasons, plenty of bad ones, but not a single one of them that he could put into a coherent logical thought.

So instead, he just typed, "*Cool, no problem. I'll let you know what it comes to when you get here.*"

That must have frozen Jazz's brain a bit, he had probably been gearing up for the big fight that was about to follow. Instead, he was just forced to type,

"*Thanks.*"

Well, there it was, they were going to have a great big

punk rock family reunion. Cool. Perfect timing considering what Jim thought he'd have to do once Cole was buried. All the other original players on the stage present to bury one of their own.

The funeral was in three days. By this point, Jim's grandest wish was to get this the fuck over with. He'd made his peace with Cole's death as much as he could, maybe it wasn't some placid deep Buddhist understanding, but it was as good as he was getting. As much as he could was the operative phrase, he wasn't over it, he doubted he would be any time soon. Jim had been alive long enough to know that you never just went, "Yay totally over it!" when someone died. There were a million useless fucking platitudes about remembering the good times and feeling blessed that you knew the person, and frankly, they could all suck his dick. Some of that was true, but there would always be the undercurrent there of missing them and wanting them to still be alive. Platitudes didn't fix that, time did most of the heavy lifting. But even then, not enough to say you ever got over something as final as that.

Until Cole's "big day" Jim was more or less cooling his heels. In deference to the situation, he more or less had the week off, his overlords had seen the papers and wanted to look human by giving him, "Time to grieve." Jim hadn't taken full advantage of it; he'd put in some hours just to not be sitting here alone in the house like he was now. Doc did his best to try and cheer him up, but you could only do so much with a dog's vocabulary. He'd gone in, gotten some work done, and got back out before the breakdown and the tears started. Still, embarrassing as it was to have to leave like that, it beat the flying fuck of sitting in the house by himself and watching that last show they had played together on YouTube over and over.

He was surprised to hear his cell phone ring. Who the

fuck actually called anyone anymore? He took out his phone and gave a grunt of surprise, it was Pamela. "Your dime," he answered gruffly before he could stop himself.

"Wow, that is so dated. Who are you a Humphrey Bogart impersonator?" she replied.

"Naw, Marlon Brando, a later film 'The Bloated One,' didn't do that well in the theaters," Jim joked.

"Nice to see your sense of humor is intact at least. So, what are you up to?"

"Not much of a god damned thing, it is the wonderful week of waiting to host a funeral, which frankly wasn't a lifetime dream of mine."

"Good, text me your address. I got in yesterday, I'm bored witless, I barely know this city at all. Not to mention we won't really have a chance to catch up at the funeral. I have no idea if you're still doing anything after, but even then, that's not exactly catching up when you have to yell to be heard," she said in a perky-sounding rush.

What the hell, "Alright let me get off the phone and I'll text it right over. I'm just sitting here, so that sounds nicer than just doing nothing."

"Boy, you make it sound so appealing. I feel the love."

"I didn't mean it like that," Jim protested quickly.

He could almost see her eyes twinkling with mischief as she answered, "Oh I know, I'm just fucking with you. Alright, I'll see you soon. I've had enough of this hotel."

"Alright, bye."

"Bye!"

Jim didn't want to become a nervous wreck waiting for her, that was acting like a child in his eyes. The problem with that was that simply put, even in the oldest man there's a lot of little kid still hanging about. He hadn't seen the woman in thirty years, even if they had dated and broke up, he didn't hold any ill will about it. In fact, he'd thought of her fondly more than once over the years. Even back then he saw what was going to happen even as it was happening, he couldn't fully say he blamed her for the way things had been going. He'd just been too young and inexperienced in life and emotions to do a damned thing about any of it. He could only watch it like a casual observer, which is a weird experience to have if you're also in the driver's seat of the crash simultaneously.

No matter how it had ended, he looked forward to seeing her now. Despite how life had gone the last few months and looked like it was going to stay for the foreseeable future, he tried not to live in the past, at least not anymore. One of the reasons he'd spent so long trying to find the crackerjack prize at the bottom of various bottles was from spending too much time looking backward. So, he wanted to see Pamela now, not thirty years ago, because he was happy to see an old friend today. Not because he wanted to rehash and re-litigate something they'd both been too young to fully control. It'd be interesting to compare notes on how they'd changed. It was clear to him that one thing that hadn't changed was the fondness he felt for her.

Jim laughed at himself as he straightened up the house. He was acting like a teenager bringing a girl home for the first time. Still, it was a nice enough house, in a nice enough neighborhood, what was the point in having a guest who was an old friend over and having her find your dirty ass socks? It wasn't that the place was a sty, he kept things relatively clean, he could feasibly have left it. A mental sigh crowded in, it was the ADULT thing to do when you expected company, and despite his best efforts, he was an adult sometimes.

His heart froze for a moment. All of Cole's stuff was still out in the living room. Leaving it there seemed weird now. Almost accusatory. Yes, she was down for his funeral, but it felt like rubbing her face in the fact he was dead by leaving it all out like that. Like he was saying, look, it was me who had to be here when it finally crashed on the rocks, you got to avoid it. Sighing, he packed it all off to his computer room. He still hadn't decided what he was doing with all of it, maybe he was even keeping it, but it shouldn't be left in the living room like a beacon announcing Cole's absence either.

He was just checking himself in the mirror and putting on some antiperspirant when the doorbell rang and Doc exploded with barking. Jim gave himself one last once over and decided that he still looked pretty rough around the edges, which would have to do, he looked like that all the time. He concluded looking for new ugly deformities before making for the door. The doorbell had just rung again as he yanked it open and stepped out. Standing there was Pamela, her Facebook hadn't lied, she still more or less looked like the Pamela that had been living in his mind all these years aged with just feather touches of maturity. Before he got a chance to say anything she had already flung her arms around him to give him a hug.

"Hey!" he said stupidly, exuberance threw him off as a rule.

"Hey yourself!" she said into his shoulder before finally releasing him. She had an enormous smile on her face when she followed it up with, "So happy to see you!"

"Umm...you too! Sorry! Come in, don't just stand out there, come in!" he said as he kicked back at Doc to get him away from the door.

Jim walked her into the living room along with Doc who was sniffing vigorously at her. "You live here by yourself?" Pamela asked.

"Yeah...I mean before...and now...well Doc here keeps me company," Jim fumbled out. She hadn't meant that as a trap, it had been polite conversation, but it yawned like a chasm.

"Oh Jesus! I'm sorry, I wasn't thinking. I mean I know why I'm down here, but...the place is nice. It's hard to think of it in conjunction with everything."

Jim smiled, "Well at least you think the place is nice. Put your coat anywhere. Doc there at least knows that he gets in trouble for jumping on coats, can I get you something?"

"Well, what do you have?" she asked as she removed her light coat.

"Fair question. What in the hell do I have?" Jim paused to think about it for a minute, "OK, I'm pretty sure I have some filtered water, some juice that I don't trust, milk, ginger ale, beer, wine, and a weird n/a malt beverage I like from Germany that tastes like that old '70s apple soda mugged an O'Doul's. Oh yeah, I think I have some scotch, but that's real scotch from Scotland so please I beg of you, don't ask me to put water in it."

"What kind of wine?" she asked already making herself comfortable on the couch.

"I'm pretty sure it's Mateus, so rose."

"Wine it is then," she smiled.

Jim smiled back and went out to the kitchen to get their drinks, Doc stayed right where he was getting to know his new friend which Pamela seemed happy to oblige. He got himself one of the weird malt beverages he'd first found in a Korean grocery of all places and poured her a rose. He was happy to note, it still had some fizz to it, which meant he'd done a good job corking it. That was half the point of even having a rose in his mind, like real wine and soda had a baby. It had taken him a minute to find the wine glasses since he never used the things. If he wanted wine, he just poured it into whatever he had handy, he didn't even remember where in the hell he'd gotten actual wine glasses from. He'd picked the wine up a couple of weeks ago because Cole had said he'd never had the stuff before.

They'd both had a small glass and into the fridge it had stayed until now.

Her smile reappeared and took on an almost mischievous character once he'd handed her her glass, "All right, who wants to go first with the, 'What have you been doing for the last thirty years' life saga?'"

Jim grinned back, "Guess as the host, it's on me to start. Two kids, divorced, my fault, job that is dull and uninteresting but I like the people, and to offset that a band I enjoy quite a bit."

Pamela nodded, "Well that's right to the point but it leaves a lot to unpack, doesn't it? I mean why was the divorce your fault, boys or girls, what type of job...."

"The divorce was my fault because I'd gotten bored of everything I was doing, which allowed me too much time to worry about my childhood and all the bullshit that had happened to me after that instead of worrying about making today not suck. So, I engaged in a slow-moving self-righteous suicide which made every today suck balls for me and everyone who had to put up with me. Somewhere along the way, I decided I was actually not enthusiastic about fucking off just yet, but the damage had been done. It gave Cindy a chance to see that even with my head straight our life goals didn't match anymore. Part two is girls, I love them, they.... well, it's hard to tell with adult girls, isn't it? But I think they at least like me."

"Quite a bit of self-flagellation in there you know," Pamela pointed out.

"Naw, I mean I've done plenty of that already, sure. It's just a cold assessment of the facts. She had a degree that could make boatloads of money and wanted all the things that came with it, I still view people who have boatloads of money as extremely suspect. It worked when we didn't have the ability to have nice things. When I was a drunk trying to kill myself in the midst of all the nice things, not so much."

"But you have wine here, beer..."

"I don't drink too much, so it isn't like the sight of it is going to set me craving it. I know it's there, and I don't really care. Look, I'm not saying there's anything wrong with AA or people who need to quit cold turkey, they just drink for different reasons than I did. Enough hobbies and a lack of being suicidal and occasionally I have a few beers, I might even get a bit slammed on a very rare occasion, I just don't like to do it often. It's time-consuming and I've got a bunch of time I wasted to make up for. Call it the difference between a drunk and alcoholic if you want, or go with, everyone's on a different journey in life," Jim said, shrugging at the last bit.

"Like how often..."

"Actually buzzed?"

"Yes, that."

"Unfair, more than two beers gets me fuzzy these days, but think I went a full year last year. Having Cole around made it a bit more often, but only a bit, sometimes we'd like to have a few when we sat around talking, so it was a social thing. I just don't think about it too much. So tonight, since I'm excited to see you and want to appear moderately human and likable and most importantly not say something stupid, I'm forgoing whatever dubious pleasure a beer might give me. Anyway, that's me, how about you?" Jim changed the subject. He didn't do it out of any embarrassment from anything in the past, it was what it was, but frankly, he was bored already about himself. As much as she wanted to hear about him, he wanted the same thing back again.

"The quick recap is, I own a small gallery outside of the city. No kids, thank Christ, because my ex-husband left my house with about a grand that he had stuffed into his pockets to buy meth with. I had a restraining order and his shit out on the sidewalk by the next morning. I shudder to think that I'd have to deal with him for visitation rights," she replied like she was rattling off a grocery list. She had probably gone through the list enough times, it was as boring to her as his story was to him.

"Ah, and now here we are washed up on the shore by a wake," he said. "So, how's the art brokerage business?"

"Well, I could live in the city if I wanted to, let's put it that way. I just don't want to, there are better things to spend money on than a prestige address. Most of the same people who have them have homes outside of the city as well anyway, as do all of my clients, almost nobody seems to live in Manhattan anymore. They just keep places for 'when they're in the city', like to show off that they have a Manhattan address. So, how's the life of a rock star?"

He chuckled, "More like weekend warrior. It's not exactly Anarchy if practice can be put off for a family cookout." Jim pointed to the TV, "Hey why don't you pick something out from the Blu-rays that you've seen a million times, so we have some background noise we can talk over."

She got up and headed over to the rack of discs and paused, she looked over to Jim taking him with an intent expression before she said in a quiet voice, "Am I going home tonight?"

Jim had been taking a sip of his malt beverage and almost spit it out, "Jesus! Where did that come from?"

She walked over to him and leaned in smiling, "No pressure, but you still look pretty good you know, and frankly, I'm at an age now where I can't stand flirting. If you're dead set against it, that's fine, we can be friends, and pretend I never said any of this. If you don't want to do anything but talk the sun up, that's fine too. But I'd like to know if I should have another glass of wine and settle in for the duration now without all the awkward pauses and fumbling about it later."

Jim looked at her in shock. He thought about it exactly long enough to almost make it uncomfortable. She looked like she was about to apologize for her abruptness when he said, "The night's young, there's plenty of time to get to know each other again first, right? Call me crazy, and I probably am, but maybe there's still something here other than hormones. I mean, it feels really wonderful to see you and talk to you right now. Don't get me wrong, you look great, and if all you want to do is naked twister, I'm enthusiastic, but I think I missed you."

She leaned over and kissed him lightly on the forehead, "OK then, talk and hangout first, then naked twister."

Chapter 8

It appeared to him that Pamela had thought about what she was going to do before she'd ever gotten there. She checked out of her hotel the next morning, and by some complete coincidence had all of her bags in her rental car ahead of time. It could have been habit, he didn't ask, Jim frankly didn't care much. She'd known her own mind and had gone about getting what she wanted. While it might seem weird to him that it was him, there was no accounting for taste. Whatever he had on his Facebook profile had combined with the heady whiff of nostalgia to tell her that she at least wanted a fling out of this visit. Once he'd gotten over the shock, it wasn't like he'd complained much either. If anything, he couldn't help but respect and appreciate her forthright nature, people fucked around way too much in life. Time was short and getting shorter by the second.

The weird thing was that it quickly felt less and less like a fling. Jim's entire romantic life had been rooted in being available as a fling, he knew what their life cycle was and this was different. In the days leading up to the funeral, they more or less spent as much time together as his work allowed. Considering he was slotted days off, that meant most of the time. Where he had been going in to work as some macho way of saying that he wasn't crippled by pain, now he found himself resenting work for cutting into the time he could spend with her.

Pamela had a sense of humor, she liked a lot of the same things he did, Jim just enjoyed his time with her. It felt like a natural relationship had been there all along, and all that it needed was to be jump-started by her forthcoming nature that first night. She was a salve on the wounds of the week if nothing else. He liked to think he was doing the same for her, she'd been friends with Cole recently, talked to him a lot online, he'd even stopped by to visit a few times when he'd been in New York. Both of them were mourning their friend, rediscovering each other at least provided yin to that yang. If nothing else, this felt the closest he'd come to an actual relationship that he felt in any way invested in since before the divorce. Nothing about this felt soulless and contrived, it was refreshing to have an intimate relationship with any actual sincerity on anyone's part.

On top of that Doc adored her. He trusted the dog's opinion more than his own some days.

They were lying on the couch together watching a film after an evening of showing her some of the tourist sites, along with going out to dinner at a Chinese place he liked. The movie was the old Bowie film, *The Hunger* which they had both agreed they'd seen enough times to safely ignore it, with the added benefit of having Bauhaus doing "Bela Lugosi's Dead" at the beginning of it.

"Can I ask you something?" she said as she leaned her head back against his chest.

"Shit, nothing good ever comes of a question like that," he replied chuckling.

"If I asked you to come to New York with me after this was all done, would you?"

Jim didn't respond at first. Would he? Just pack up his life and go chase his ex-girlfriend back to New York? A place that had completely changed since he'd lived there, even if it wouldn't be in New York proper and she lived outside the city. "Yeah, I suppose. I mean I could come down for band practice, my job is just a job. We're not broke children anymore, it's not far."

"Just like that? No demands, no manly wanting things your way? I mean you own a house here; you've got a life here...."

"Yeah, but I don't think I'd enjoy it as much if I let you walk twice in my lifetime. Why does anybody have to 'win' in something like that as long as we're happy together where we are?" Jim shrugged.

She was quiet for a little while, he wondered if she was paying attention to the scene on the TV showing Susan Sarandon in a lab coat. Finally, she said, "So what if I moved here? I only rent a place to live and I'm only in the studio a few times a week and for premiers... I mean it's not that far by turnpike really, hour and a half one way, and there's this wonderful thing called the internet that handles most communications. I could even move the studio closer if I have to, I mainly make money on commissions for finding pieces anyway. So how about sharing your house with me?"

"Better question, do you think you could be happy here?"

She rolled slightly to look at him better and smiled, "Do you have any idea what I waste on rent a month? It's not even a very big apartment!"

"So, I'm the penalty you're willing to pay for not having to pay rent, is it?"

"Well, it is nice to sleep next to something you can warm your feet on that you don't have to take walkies first thing in the morning."

"Woof."

Doc looked up at them from his spot on the floor.

"Howard, I'm still not sure about this," Jake said.

Howard paused in watching their men drilling with wooden sticks and plastic shields. He leaned back in his chair and replied, "Jake, buddy, do you know why I leave you so much autonomy? I mean most of them boys out there wouldn't piss and shit without my say-so. You, you're almost a free man, you know why that is?"

"I assumed...."

"Don't assume, know things, or don't, uncertainty is what I prey on."

"Well, you need me to deal with reality on the outside of the compound. You need someone you can trust dealing with things," Jake replied.

"That is true, I do need those things done, no doubt about it. But the reason I DO trust you Jake is that you believe in the cause. No matter how we got here before you walked in the door you would have laid down your life for the white race," Howard replied.

"True, you ain't the first leader of the movement I've known," Jake shrugged.

"So, you want the race war to happen while the odds are still on your side, right? I mean before this country is finally overrun and we're the minority?"

"Course I do."

"So, what do you think is gonna happen when I send tens of our boys into the heart of the South Bronx and North Philly for an unlicensed and unannounced demonstration of the supremacy of the white race?" Howard raised an eyebrow.

"I think those animals will tear them apart. That's the damned problem Howard!" Jake replied his face earnest with concern as to his leader's plan.

"Yeah, but the thing is, you taught me how immediate the world is these days. Those images are gonna be streaming live on the internet even as it happens. White men all over this country are going to see those savages assaulting our foot soldiers, they will be incensed. Militias are breaking out everywhere, angry white men all over this country just looking for a reason. Shooting those guns all day in the hills and on the plains wishing it wasn't just a target. All they have been waiting for is the clarion call and for a place to aim. Things are close Jake, as close as they've been since white men really did run this country, not just rich men, white men. It won't take but a little thing to push it over. Once the video of this gets out, militias all over this country are going to be marching into them slums packing serious heat! The war will be on!"

"But we're building an army here!" Jake protested.

"Buddy, without public sympathy, that army will be swarmed under in ten minutes by the authorities, and with the public securely in favor of it. We need to finally push the latent distrust into full-blown hostility and violence. That's what this has all been about, find that one public push to get the ball rolling so fast no one will ever be able to stop it," Howard smiled beatifically at his second in command.

They were silent for a moment, both of them turned back to watching their "troops" training again. After a few minutes, Jake said, "So how many of them do you think survive."

"If we ever see two of those boys again, I'd be shocked. But what of it? They have all just been part of the hive since they sat down at our table, does the hive die because every worker bee doesn't return from gathering pollen?"

The day of the funeral dawned. Jim was legitimately thankful to see Pamela in the bed next to him when he woke. Setting up the whole thing the way it really should be for Cole was a trial, today was the last climb up the hill, and he was grateful to not start it alone. The funeral home just wanted to slam Cole in a box, play some canned crappy music and get their money for the whole thing as fast as fucking possible. When he went into the whole thing, he had thought that was what he wanted too, but once it got down to particulars Jim had fought them every step of the way.

The first argument was over the suit, Jim wasn't having it. Cole had probably only worn a suit for court appearances and weddings the length of his entire life, no fucking way was he spending eternity in one. Jim put his foot down hard on that point. Then there was the music to arrange, the place said they had music that people found soothing, Jim told them to stick that as well. Instead, he put together a collection of .mp3s from all the bands Cole had played in that he could get his hands on, including three new songs that Cole had written that the band had managed to record in the short month he had been with them. After the service was over, as people were filing out, "Coffin Cruiser" by the Skulls would be playing, which seemed perfectly fitting to Jim. The parlor was not happy, Jim didn't give a fuck that they weren't happy, it wasn't that much harder for them, and this wasn't for them, it was for Cole's friends and more importantly Cole. As far as Jim was concerned, he was paying, and they could suck a dick if they didn't like it.

When they got to the funeral parlor, with no family present, Jim was forced into the role of host and adult in charge, and he sure as shit wasn't comfortable with it. He was Cole's bandmate and his roommate but he didn't think that qualified him for this part of the festivities. He had no idea what Cole had been like as a little boy or what kind of grades he got at school or much of Cole at all outside their shared experiences. Usually, these things are for the grieving family, and while Jim felt like he was indeed grieving, he sure as shit didn't want to be here in this role. He didn't want condolences, which always struck him as fake anyway, it was just something people said to fill the empty void. Oh, you're so sorry? Well, fucking resurrect him! Do something! Jim was doing all of this for other people not so other people could make him feel better. One fucking family member having an ounce of human decency and he wouldn't be stuck in the grieving next of kin seat to receive the, as heartfelt as a fart, condolences. Condolences and flatulence both had the same value, both were involuntary and automatic. People were here mainly for the same reason there was a funeral to begin with, to feel they'd done right by a friend by showing up, nothing more, nothing less. They would feel better for knowing they'd come.

He turned in his seat occasionally to acknowledge people as they filtered in while he held Pamela's hand the whole time. Jim wasn't aiming to announce a relationship as much as he was just trying to remind himself of her continued soothing presence. Like none of this mattered enough to get upset over, it would be over eventually and she'd be with him when it was. Every time he had to look up and make the proper observances towards the other person's ritualized sorrow, instinctively his hand flexed in hers. Every time, she gave a reassuring return pulse to remind him that this wasn't going to last forever.

She grasped even harder causing Jim's eyes to go wide for a minute. When he turned to see who the latest mourner was, he understood her reaction completely. Jazz was standing there next to the pew with Alison in tow. Jim's first impression was, "Wow they got old." Then he reminded himself, so had everyone it seemed, except maybe Pamela who had matured and Cindy who was preserved. He looked up and attempted a weak smile for his former bandmate as

Jazz got close enough to talk, "Hey."

"Hey," Jazz acknowledged back. Jazz had always been a lightning-quick conversationalist.

"Umm thanks for coming and all. Look, I'm gonna have a few people back at my house after, as sort of a less formal memorial sort of thing. Let me text you the address and directions. Hi Alison," Jim added at the end as a complete afterthought. It made him happy, it had been an afterthought, look at him! Look at him, letting things go that didn't matter anymore.

"Cool, we'll be there. I got a check I'm going to have to force you to accept anyway. C'mon Hun, let's find a seat," Jazz managed a small smile as he led Alison away.

As soon as they were out of earshot Pamela leaned in and whispered, "See, that wasn't so bad."

"Now if only we could leave right now, I'd say it had gone swimmingly."

Eventually, everybody was there that was going to show up. A few people had asked to speak, and Jim saw no reason to tell them not to, the longer they talked the less he'd have to. Most of them talked about how they knew Cole, mostly from music but not all. Some of them had managed to get their shit together and were people he used to hobo with. Jim would love to know those full stories, how you went from trying to old-time ride the rails to being outside of Philly in a suit and tie. Who knew, maybe if they friended him on Facebook or Twitter it would come out eventually. The band all had something to say about the time he'd spent with them, Benji managed to even pepper a couple of jokes into his anecdotes. It shouldn't have come as a shock then that Benji was the one that was crying as he left the podium.

Once everybody had their shot at it, it was the part Jim had been dreading for days now. He needed to get up and read the final eulogy before they went to the graveyard. He got up slowly and haltingly, it was funny, he could yell and scream in front of hundreds of people and not bat an eyelid, but the concept of actually standing up in front of people like this scared the shit out of him. Suddenly every nagging ache and pain that came with being alive this long flared up and told him to sit back down and shut up. Jim felt like this was like being naked, there were no stage antics, no band to hide behind. You had to be there by yourself and say what you felt to a room full of people, most of which he frankly didn't even know.

Jim made his way slowly to the podium like a death row inmate going to meet "Ol' Sparky," which wasn't far off from how he felt. He let out a big gusting sigh before he leaned in a bit towards the small microphone to say, "Well, first off, I'd like to thank you all for coming here. It's gratifying to see Cole touched so many people during his time on this earth."

He had brought up a bottle of water with him in one hand and a 45 record in the other, he took a sip before continuing, "I guess now we get to the heavy part. I'm not going to say I wasn't mad at Cole for how he died. That would be a lie and I really don't think I can afford to lie to a room full of people. I'm also not going to say I don't understand either. It may seem contradictory, but it isn't. I can be mad at my friend for leaving me, we're always mad when someone leaves, especially if they had a hand in it themselves. At the same time, I can also see how easy it is to slip when it comes to addiction. That's all it was, by the way, a slip, he'd been clean the entire time he'd been staying at my place, his guitar work with the band was top-notch, he was at work every day, he just slipped. I think every one of us in this room has experiences with addiction, either watching someone struggling with it, or fighting the good fight for ourselves. So, everybody here knows, not everybody wins that fight. Often our experience with addiction ends with a scene like this one right here. Keeping that in mind, I'd ask all of you, watch out for each other, watch out for yourselves. Nobody wants to be standing here doing what I'm doing right now."

Jim didn't even realize tears were running down his face as he spoke, if he had he wouldn't have cared at this point anyway, he needed to speak his piece, he'd gone too far to stop. He felt like he was on the home stretch and could see the finish line, "I've known Cole for a very long time. From when, all those years ago, we found out we could write music together, to the joy we felt recently when we discovered we still could. We spent a lot of that time apart but when you have something magic, I guess you need breaks from it, I mean why make magic commonplace, right? You won't appreciate it that way. He was funny, he was my compatriot from one city to the next, and when the two of us were on stage together we were always in sync. It is almost impossible to replace those types of people in your life when they leave for good. You don't stop, and what you come up with may be just as good if not better, but it will never be the same So, I have no problem mourning here today."

Jim turned to the casket, looking at Cole's remains. That's all they looked like, remains, a Cole doll propped up in there. The makeup they put on the body to make him seem "life-like" clashed with his normal, worn-out clothes. Jim reached into the coffin and placed a copy of their ep from all those years ago carefully next to Cole. He whispered in a husky voice, "Bet you didn't have a copy anymore, did ya'? Well, there you go."

When Jim sat down to recover himself, Pamela leaned in, "Nicely said, Babe."

Jim could only grunt, he was spent from the whole thing and there was still more to come.

The most important part of what remained was when

people started to get up. Jim got up and walked directly over to where Jazz and Alison were sitting. Jazz looked a bit shocked to see him come up, directly the wrinkles around his eyes vanishing as they widened. Alison's eyes were worried, maybe she expected Jim to cause a scene because of old bad blood. Seeing he had Jazz's attention he just said, "Hey, favor to ask."

Jazz was taken aback, whatever he'd been expecting, it wasn't this, "Yeah...uhh sure. What do you need?"

"Well, two of the guys from a doom metal band he played in, in Pittsburgh are doing it. The rest of our band are doing it, but that's only five. It leaves us one short," Jim replied. Seeing the look of non-comprehension on Jazz's face he quickly added, "Well, it would seem only right for you to be one of the pallbearers."

Jazz's face went through a few emotions quickly, surprise, then his eyes narrowed a bit as he considered it, finally almost a smile drifted over his lips as he replied, "I'd be honored. Yeah, you're right, it's only right."

The drive to the graveyard was almost a welcome break. A distraction from everything, more importantly, everyone, despite being part of a funeral procession and in theory part of the whole funeral experience. You had to pay attention to your driving, and since Jim seldom drove the speed limit, let alone slow, it took quite a bit of concentration on his part to stay at a sedate pace. Stupid habit of middle age that it was, he had the stereo turned down the entire way so he could concentrate. Pamela didn't seem to mind, maybe she needed the mental break that paying attention to the scenery gave her and didn't need music for the experience.

The gravesite itself was like walking into a movie scene, you felt like you didn't belong here, this wasn't for you this was something other people did. But now that you were here you still knew that you had to hit your marks and deliver your lines on time. It was supposed to be all solemn, but they'd more or less done all the important grieving during the viewing. It felt like an unnecessary epilogue, the book was over and this added nothing. What was left was just a bunch of people stuck having their personal thoughts, trying to be solemn, while wondering when they could leave in good taste and get the hell out of these clothes. This was the end of the line, he'd done the best he could to see right by Cole, his duty was done. That didn't mean it was over for Jim yet, he'd still had to entertain people tonight, which was almost as out of his comfort zone as everything else today. Not as many people, sure, still, he usually only had one or two people at his house at a time, it was stressful for him. But the part where he acquired a legitimate final resting place was finished.

The grave itself and the small headstone Jim had bought, along with the box that was suspended over its final location, none of this meant anything right now. The coffin was closed, Cole was already gone in Jim's mind, all they were doing here and now was staring at a tastefully made gray box. Maybe later he'd want to come here and talk to Cole, maybe maintain his grave for him, but that was for another day. Not now, now it was just the last piece of business until the formal part of this whole horrid thing finally ended.

People came up to him by the grave and offered condolences again before going on their way. Some of them he'd just be seeing again in a couple of hours, which only served to highlight what an empty ritual this was. It didn't matter, it was the proper thing to do, so they were doing the proper thing. Jim instinctively hated anything like this, all the little things people just did without any thought because it was supposedly the right thing to do. It was fake, right at its heart. Parts of today had been legitimate, people talking about Cole, putting together the pallbearers, his eulogy, all of that needed to be done. This part was just making observances, going through motion without meaning. Who knew, maybe it meant more to someone in the dwindling crowd, it was a possibility. Judging from their faces though, probably not. Everyone looked to be just as ready as he was to get on with actually living. Nobody wanted to rush off because they wanted to avoid being insulting, but that was still where their heads were. If it was insulting to want to be gone from here, all of them were wearing that insult on their hearts if not on their sleeves.

At last, it was just him and Pamela left, even people with invites to Jim's house later had found better things to do. Jim nodded to the gravediggers who were standing by. Turning to look at the coffin one last time he just whispered, "Later days," before turning to walk Pamela to his vehicle so they could leave.

Thank Christ they got home with a couple of hours to spare before people started showing up. Jim needed the time just to take a shower and unwind a bit. Doc needed that time to be walked, and to spazz out because they were finally back. On a plus, Jim's faithful puppy would be mellowed out by the time guests got there. They could have tried to take a romantic shower together but the nice thing about having tried it enough times in their life, both of them knew how awkward it was and said bluntly that they could probably afford to take a pass. There was an entire rest of the house to be romantic in and those parts had cushions instead of hard porcelain and cold steel to recommend themselves.

After he got out of the shower Jim just air-dried. Pamela glanced up at him when he came out of the bathroom, "Forgoing a robe are we?"

"You kidding? I plan on greeting our guests later like this!" he replied enthusiastically.

"Oh my, am I going to have to teach you polite party etiquette?"

"Polite? Aww geez Mom, I thought we wuz only having friends over!"

She smiled with a tilt of her head, "Well, at least you still have a sense of humor."

Jim grinned, "God told me I could only have two extra senses so I went with that one and direction. Common was just left out in the cold."

"I'm going to get my shower. Since you claim to be lacking the sense to do it, I should remind you, get dressed bucko. Not that I mind the view, but we have guests coming. Also, the AC is on, you might catch a cold."

Time to play host. Jim tried to remember how to do it from when he and Cindy used to entertain, as he stood in the bedroom looking for clothes. He caught himself, the funeral was over, everybody who'd been invited over were old friends, they knew where the damned fridge was, they didn't need him much for this. He had put this together so everybody could hang out, tell stories, mentally get everything out of them so tomorrow they could face the whole universe again. To celebrate their friend so the last thoughts they had of Cole weren't of him lying in a casket as part of a bizarre human ritual. He put on a t-shirt and jeans. He put Doc in his bedroom after taking him for a lengthy walk to pee him out, so he could introduce the dog to people after they were in the house, and one at a time so the poor spazz wouldn't freak anybody out with his enthusiasm. Any latecomers would have to deal with joyful pit bull as their punishment for tardiness.

The two of them had gotten everything done and had just settled in when people began showing up. The first to arrive were Billy and Alicia which was nice, they could start off with people Jim was comfortable with and who Doc already knew. As the steady stream of people showed up Jim was relieved to discover that while Cole might be the reason they were all here, it wasn't a depressing moping crowd. The mourning part had been left at the grave where it belonged. People were drinking a bit, telling stories, having fun. More than anything that had happened so far, this was what Cole actually would have wanted. He'd have wanted the Irish wake. Doc was certainly thrilled once he'd been released from puppy jail, he was getting pet, and food fell on the floor, this was heaven for him. Jim envied that positive attitude, and not for the first time, Doc could also lick his own balls.

He hadn't had much time to talk to Jazz and Alison. It wasn't that he was avoiding them, or not being civil, or anything like that, it was just hosting sort of demanded you be a social butterfly. He had noticed that Jazz had a few beers already, so as soon as he got a chance, he was going to suggest that they stay the night. He made sure everybody knew the invite was open, nobody was leaving here unsafe, leaning on Jazz to stay had the added benefit that maybe they'd get to talk some.

When the crowd had thinned a little Jim made his way over to Jazz where he was sitting idly by as Alison talked to somebody. Jazz had never been much of a talker, so Jim figured this was probably their normal party positions. She talked and he stood nearby to be handy in case she needed anything corroborated. Jim stood next to Jazz for a moment, not interrupting, but making his presence obvious. When Jazz finally registered him, Jim said quietly, "Hey, can I talk to you for a mome?"

"Yeah sure," Jazz nodded, probably glad to get away from a story he'd heard a million times before anyway.

Jim put on his best smile, "I was wondering, you and

Alison want to just crash here tonight? That way you don't have to worry about having a few more beers and shit, we ain't seen each other for 30 years...it'd be nice to catch up a bit. You can use one of the spare rooms, girls live with their mother most of the time anyway."

Jim winced internally at the way he worded that, he worried that Jazz might take it like he had suggested that he'd been drinking too much, like he was being judgmental. Jim didn't mean that, he had just wanted to suggest that maybe he'd had enough beer that driving was not his best option, but you could never tell how someone was going to take that. Instead of getting pissy, Jazz smiled, "Would you believe we've got clothes and stuff out in the car just in case?"

Jim smiled back, "Cool, I'll tell Pamela you're staying."

Jazz's eyebrow went up, "You two a thing again?"

Jim shrugged, "Really, it's too soon to tell you what we are right now. Right now, she's down for the funeral, of course, she has heavily suggested that she might stay and I told her I'd like that. So... I can only give you an emphatic 'Sort of, I think' and leave it there. We play footsie a lot so I think that's a definite maybe."

"Cool, believe it or not, Alison will be happy about that. What with the divorce.... she was worried about...."
"Told you, man, it's a long time ago, water under the bridge. Not only that, the bridge itself has fallen down from neglect and age."

Chapter 9

By midnight it was just the four of them still up. Teddy and his wife Melissa were snoring away in Sarah's bedroom, leaving Amber's for Jazz and Alison. Doc Gonzo was asleep over Jim's feet on the floor. Pamela snuggled up next to Jim. He didn't dare say anything but he was beginning to feel claustrophobic with everybody leaning on him. It was cute, but close. Jazz and Alison were on the lazy boy together, which was if anything more confined. There was a Troma film on, but nobody was paying any attention to it. Troma's film output was great for parties that way, the jokes were broad and crude enough that they didn't need context, you just paid attention when you could and could catch up from there.

Out of the blue Jazz turned to Jim and Pamela, "Hey Rat, can I ask you something?"

Jim chuckled, "Well, it's weird to be called Rat anymore, but sure."

"Did Cole tell you about...." Jazz paused, like now that he considered what he'd been about to say, it sounded so crazy he wished he hadn't brought it up.

"That maybe it was happening again," Jim finished for him.

Pamela had been drowsing but her head popped up, "What is happening again?"

Jim sighed, "The first night Cole was here.... what happened in New York....the craziness. He told me he thought it was happening again... I kind of blew him off at the time..."

"At the time kind of sounds like there might be a 'but' attached to it," Pamela said sitting up.

"Yeah, it does... I thought.... well with the funeral and all we'd just deal with one crisis at a time," Jim shrugged.

"I kind of figured you might know. Cole and I talked a lot by PM, so if anything, I might know more about it than you do," Jazz interjected.

Alison interrupted, sliding off the chair onto the floor. "Wait, I want to be clear on this. You all agree on what happened in New York? Jim never told me about it when we were dating. Jasper said you'd all agree with him...I didn't think he'd even bring it up tonight in all actuality." Alison had been drowsing but she was suddenly alert as she settled into a cross-legged position on the floor staring at Pamela and Jim intently.

"Lessee if I can summarize, bizarre demon was killing people, feeding them to other people to control them in the hope of starting wide-scale riots. That the gist of it guys?" Jim said with an almost resigned, weary voice, like somehow deep down inside, no matter how hard he tried, he'd never get away from what happened and this was all overdue to come up again.

"Yeah," Pamela agreed quietly.

"Yep," said Jazz.

"And your buddy Cole thought he found it happening again?"

"I read through his notebook," Jim replied. Everyone looked at him so he shrugged, "I missed him, it was all I had left. Anyway, judging from what he wrote, he found something. I mean maybe not the same thing, there are some fucked up people out there, but it seemed the same to me. It seemed the same to him too. Either way, I was going to go up there and see if I could find enough to take to the cops at least."

Pamela looked at him pointedly, "When were you going to tell me about this?"

"Well, I'm kind of telling you now. Really if we weren't having this conversation now, we probably would have had it tomorrow when we were alone," Jim said earnestly. Jim reached out and grabbed her hand, "Look, all my thoughts this week have been on the funeral, and us seeing where we stand with each other, but... I mean, you can understand that right? I can't just walk away and pretend this isn't happening, that's what lets shitty people get away with stuff in the first place, when good people ignore it."

Pamela looked thoughtful for a long moment, the kind of moment where you know someone is contemplating either telling you to go fuck yourself or say they understand completely, before she said, "You're going to let me read that notebook right?"

"Huh? Yeah, sure. I mean if you want to."

"If you're going up there, I'm going with you," Jazz interrupted.

"Hey look...."

"No, you look, this is unfinished business. Cole and I talked about this a lot.... like you said, shitty people get away with shitty stuff because good people fuck off and mind their own business. I need to do this, just to feel good about myself," Jazz said in a total neutral tone of voice, almost like he was reading legal wording on a document.

"Are you all right with this?" Pamela said looking at Alison.

Alison chuckled, her blond hair, touched in spots by gray, falling into her face a bit as she did, "Trust me, we've had this argument already and he won."

Pamela turned suddenly and grabbed Jim's face turning him to look at her, "Are you sure about this? I mean really sure?"

"Won't know for sure until we get there, but Cole wasn't delusional. He wasn't street mindfucked yet. He lived here for quite a while and never acted off, like someone who is about to go around the bend, except about this. And we know this isn't as delusional as it sounds. I'm almost sure there's something up there before we even look. I have an idea of how to fix it, I think. Maybe I'm fooling myself, but I know I have to try. Not just for myself, and not even for the people that this might hurt, but for all of us, cause tell me this hasn't haunted all of us all those years," Jim said looking her in the eye the entire time. It was unusual for him to do that, sociologists say children who are abused have a hard time looking people in the eye, Jim would have made a good case study in that normally. He was muscling through here to drive home how important he thought this was.

Pamela sighed, "You know, I can tell just looking at you... If you're in, well I have to stick around at least to make sure you don't get hurt, I'll call the gallery and tell them I'll be a little longer. Call me crazy, but this time I'm interested in keeping you for a while and you getting killed would screw that up. So now that we're going to play heroes, what's the plan."

"You know, my camera has a damned fine zoom. We all have phones... Maybe this time we get evidence first, for ourselves if nothing else. So, we don't sit around ten years from now wondering if we're crazy like we've all spent the last thirty. I don't know if you did it, but I sure as shit did," Jim replied.

"I did," Jazz said quietly.

Pamela looked at Jazz and then back to Jim, "Yeah, me too."

"This time we get some proof it happened first. Then we'll see about doing something stupid and possibly heroic."

Jazz and Jim sat crouched on a hillside in the woods. Jim figured this couldn't be the same spot Cole had sat at. He knew deep down that Cole had been taking risks getting closer to the place to see better. Jim figured he knew why. When you're really deep into an addiction you feel like a worthless piece of shit, even when you're clean. You do things that nobody can prove are suicidal but definitely are on some deeper, psychological level. You figure you're dying here and that it's just a matter of time anyway. By that point, all you want to do is figure out how to make your last run cool in some way, noble, or bad assed. Jim only hoped that Cole had some of his self-worth restored to him while living with him, maybe it wasn't enough to fight off temptation...it would have been nice to think that it at least salved some parts of his soul before the accident. No mistake, Cole dying was an accident, it was a relapse, not the full throes of an addiction in swing. It was "shit happened" not "I meant for that to happen."

They had been taking turns looking through Jim's camera all day. It had only been marginally eventful. They got some photos of the weird zombie-like training going on, which was worrisome on its face because it made you wonder what they were training for. Not only that, but it was creepy like it was mainly going through the motions in case of arrivals. Speaking of which, there had been some guests that arrived during the day as well, they made sure to get photos of each of them, especially since Jim was positive he recognized one of them from some White Power march that had happened a while back. It was something, but none of this was what they needed. Playing dress-up and hanging out with assholes were not arrestable offenses, the jails would be full otherwise.

"You know something I just realized," Jim said leaning back against a tree as Jazz scowled at the camera screen.

"What?" Jazz asked not looking up.

"We're going to have to do this in shifts or something. It's stupid as fuck both of us out here like this. We have to eat and sleep, we'll miss shit, and it could be the important shit."

"Fuck!"

"What?"

"You're right. You know Alison is going to bitch if we split up, right?"

"Yeah, I can't see Pamela being pleased about it."

"That reminds me, you and Pamela, how'd that happen?" Jazz looked over with a small grin on his face.

"Honestly, she more or less told me so and I thought it was a swell idea," Jim shrugged.

"Huh, will wonders never cease."

"No shit."

Jazz's face turned solemn, "So, what was Cole like when he stayed with you, I mean really."

Jim thought about it for a minute, "You know how it was at the homestead before shit hit the fan? Just living together?"

"Yeah."

"Like that, but older and less crowded and more responsible. Really, him dying was a fucking shot out of the blue. I sincerely did think he had his shit together. Reading through his notebook, I guess he did until the moment he didn't," Jim said with a sigh.

"I wish it had been the same for me."

"He stayed with you a bit?"

"Yeah, but he was still using. Money went missing, not much, but enough. I had to kick him out, it kind of broke my heart," Jazz wasn't looking at him anymore but back down to the camera as he spoke.

"Yet he stayed friends with you and talked to you on Facebook. Kind of shows how close he was to putting it down. He wasn't blaming others for his bullshit; he was at least owning that much."

"Sucks he just didn't leave it alone a little longer."

"Yeah.... we'd be able to break this up in three shifts for one," Jim may have cracked a joke but his voice was wistful as he did it, without any humor.

"That'd be nice." Jazz agreed solemnly.

"Since we're doing shifts, we better work out where to stash the camera or the card at least if something happens and whoever's watching has to get out in a hurry. So the other person can find it."

"You mean if something happens TO one of us, don't you?" Jazz replied solemnly.

"Yeah, but I didn't want to say it that fatalistically."

After a few days, it was hard to not get frustrated. Jim was pretty sure that Alison had started leaning on Jazz to return home to New York. So far Jazz had resisted, but Jim had to wonder how much longer that would even last. Jazz hadn't complained, but Jim would have to be an idiot not to know something was up just from what Alison said when he saw her. It wasn't like they could play Scooby-Doo forever here; they were supposedly adults and bereavement leave was running out for him and who knew how much longer Jazz could afford to be an absentee owner of his landscaping business without any consequences. They were rotating camera cards and when each one came back each day, they were loading tons of incriminating stuff onto the cloud. But those photos of various politicians and alt-right leaders would only be REALLY incriminating if they actually got shots of something illegal happening in the compound. Calisthenics by bald kids playing dress up as army men sure as hell wouldn't count. History had proven it repeatedly, embarrassment and humiliation barely even slowed Nazis down, they didn't have a shame gene.

Jim was sitting with Pamela. Alison was thankfully out shopping which at least was an activity that bought Jazz some time to get back. Jim's eyes were glued to the clock he had in the kitchen. Jazz was late and he hadn't called in yet. Maybe it was nothing, broken phone, bad signal, traffic, there could be all kinds of perfectly good reasons why he hadn't called in yet. Jim didn't believe a single one of them. He had tried calling Jazz's cell but had only gotten voicemail. Normally they met up at a diner between here and there and handed over the camera. But every day before today Jazz had called to let Jim know he was leaving so Jim could get a head start. Not today.

"Fuck this, I'm heading up there," Jim said getting to his feet. As he was making his way to get his keys his phone pinged.

He stopped and looked at the message. It was from Jazz.

"*Hly Sht! Thy drug in black womn and son throgh gate at frnt. Got it on film. Thy klt her, prbly going to kill son too. I gtta go in. Camera is hiddn in usl spt- Jazz*"

"Not only am I heading up there, fuck the ticket for speeding, I'll pay it later."

Pamela was already on her feet, "What's happening Jim, you're freaking me out."

Jim hesitated, his instinct was to try and protect her, to not tell her exactly what had happened so she wouldn't worry. He also knew that instinct was wrong and that she wouldn't appreciate it later, if there even was a later after something like this. Instead, he just handed her his phone with the message open. He watched as she read it, her eyes growing wide as she put the missing letters back in place.

She handed his phone back carefully and slowly with an exaggerated caution as if she didn't trust herself not to drop it, "All right then, I'm going with you."

"But..."

"Fuck you, Jim, I am not just going to sit here and worry about you like some fucking housewife on an old TV show. I know what this is, and I can see what Jazz told you and you want me to sit here? Fuck that, we need to find out what happened and we need to find out now! Two of us stand a better chance than just one of us, at least it doubles our chances of getting word to the authorities if we need to."

Jim tried to go through all of his reasoned arguments as to why she couldn't come in his head. He also knew that why she had left him before was that she didn't WANT a knight in shining armor protecting her. He might as well break up while he was at it if he wanted to continue with that line of thought, it'd save the later heartbreak. He looked at Pamela carefully trying to make a decision. Finally, he just said, "Fine, I don't have a gun but I do have some brass knuckles and plenty of knives, grab something you like and let's go."

The ride up was understandably tense, Jim kept looking at the phone tucked between them, willing it to buzz with a message from Jazz. Pamela was quiet, which was natural in a situation where they didn't have all the information, but the information they did have was frightening. He tried to think of a conversation to start just to distract himself but he kept coming up empty. He had no idea what they were getting into here, what they'd find when they got there and those thoughts crowded out everything else. At this point, he'd be happy to talk about the weather if it wasn't for the fact that the weather was more or less normal.

He couldn't believe this was coming down to him. Jazz was always the dependable one back in the day, hell that was probably what Alison saw in him. He reeked of being a future "good provider," whereas Jim had often reeked of vodka and malt liquor. It wasn't like him to leave a message like that and vanish. For the first time in his entire life, Jim wished he had a gun, even if it was stupid to think it would help now. Those psychos were armed to the teeth, and if Cole was right about what was influencing them, you couldn't even take a hostage to try and get them to take you to the source of this evil. Anybody in the thing's control would happily give their lives to protect their master.

"What are we going to do?" Pamela finally broke the tense silence.

"Well first off, we're going to where we've been watching them from. From there, fucked if I know," Jim admitted.

"Should we call the cops?"

"And tell them what? Our friend hasn't gotten back yet from spying on people?" Jim snapped. A second later he sighed and said, "Look, that came out wrong, I'm just wound to the gills. I've been running over everything we should do, trying to come up with a plan, and frankly until we get there anything I've been able to come up with is bullshit because I have too little information to work with."

"My, you have grown," Pamela replied with a slight smile.

"Huh? Where did that come from?"

"An apology right after snapping at someone, the young pup I used to date has gotten to be a much smarter old wolf," she chuckled.

"Well, you fuck up enough, you hope you learn something from the experience of getting your nose smacked with the rolled-up newspaper."

They had been parking in a little pullover off a rural highway to make these trips. It was wide and there were often other cars there, which provided some cover from the curious. There must have been some kind of natural feature like a stream or something that attracted people for the spot to be carved out of the woods like this. As they pulled in they immediately spotted Jazz's rental car parked there the last rays of the sun glinting off its hood.

"Fuck," Jim spat as he put his vehicle in to park and got out.

"Fuck," Pamela quietly agreed as she got out to join him.

Jim crossed the country road, leading the way to where there was the beginnings of a trail from him and Jazz walking out that way. At least it was only a bit of one from where they had to move through the high grass and weeds before it opened out into open woods and began to climb. It wasn't an amazingly rugged hill, it was still eastern PA, but for Pamela who had spent most of her life either in the suburbs or the city, it got strenuous quickly. She silently cursed the Stairmaster she used at the gym for leaving her unprepared to conquer anything more rugged than a fifth-floor walkup.

Jim was sweating in the heat of the day himself by the time they got to the top, and he had been doing this hike every day this week. Pamela was past sweating and was gasping when Jim finally stopped. Jim put his finger to his lips and stood for a second listening. He nodded to her to let her know it was OK. Jazz wasn't anywhere to be seen anywhere near the spot that they'd been using to spy on the compound in the distance.

When Pamela got her breath she asked, "So now what?"

Jim pointed down the hill to a barely visible fence line surrounding some buildings, "See that down there? That's the white power compound. That's where Cole thought it was the return of our old friend from the city. If what he wrote actually happened, he was most likely right. Gimme a minute, let me see if Jazz stashed the camera."

Jim walked over to a tree; he moved a flat piece of old shale at the base to reveal a small hollow where the tree's roots had split above the ground creating a little empty space. He reached in and a moment later he pulled out what he was hoping for. "Well, that's something at least."

"What is?"

"They didn't sneak up on him, he had time to put the camera away before he headed down. Let me see what's on this and see where we are after that," Jim explained as he powered up the camera. He went through what was on the card carefully, his face getting darker by the moment. When he stopped, there were tears in his eyes, "All right, change of plans. You are taking my keys and getting the hell out of here."

"The hell I am!"

Wordlessly he handed her the camera. At first, the photos were relatively standard, shots of the men doing training, close-ups of various people coming and going. Then in the later afternoon the nature of what happened inside the brightly lit front of the compound changed. So did the shooting, Jazz had put the camera on movie for this. The gate swung open and two of the camouflaged clad men came inside, it was what was between them that immediately put a lump of fear in her throat. Being dragged along were an African American woman and what was most likely her son, a boy of around ten, maybe younger.

What the film showed next was brutal. The woman was pulled apart from the boy and struck by numerous men inside the compound as the boy struggled to get to her. It ceased suddenly when the door of the central cabin in the complex opened. Out of the doorway strode an older man, sixties at the youngest. Another much younger man walked up next to him, probably a bodyguard or a second in command. There was a discussion between the woman's captors and the old man. He nodded and said something to someone behind him.

Another man stepped into the frame. In an instant he had a rope around the poor woman's neck and pulled the noose it formed taut with one foot in her back. Her son screamed as the old man drew out an enormous blade and showed it to him. The camera had even picked up that he was making a point of being sure the boy saw the blade making it all the worse to view. Then he turned back towards the woman whose struggles had slowed as she suffocated.

Pamela turned off the camera when she saw what happened next.

"Dear God that's.... they...."

"Gutted her right in front of her son like some old-time lynching," Jim said tightly.

He reached out and grabbed the hand that wasn't holding the camera placing his car keys in it. She looked at him her eyes full of tears as he spoke, "Even if it isn't what Cole said it was, and what I do think it is. Even if it isn't, the best thing you can say about the people down there is that they're vile murdering racist pieces of shit. The thing is, if I was up here, I would have tried to sneak in to get the kid out, so I'm betting Jazz tried the same thing. This camera has to go to the cops or the local papers and it has to go NOW before they do anything else to anyone. Not in a little while, it has to go now. And the thing there is, I can't leave Jazz down there if he got caught. Hell, if the kid is still alive, I can't leave him down there either. You know I can't, and you wouldn't be able to look me in the eyes if I could. What's already happened defies what I can even consider happening in this life, just like last time. I can't lose Jazz to that."

"I don't want to lose you to it damn it!" Pamela whispered.

He smiled, it had no mirth in it, it just was, "Then drive like all hell. Because if I can't get them the fuck out of there, you getting that footage to the authorities might be the only chance I got!"

"You're a dumb ass, and even worse, I think I might love you all over again," she said quietly.

"And I think it might be mutual, and I wish that was enough so I didn't have to do this. Trust me I do not plan to die today, it's not on my to-do list anymore. But if shit goes haywire, I'd feel a lot better knowing they won't be able to hurt anyone else after this. Hell, if the cavalry is on the way, I can probably stall. The last one liked to gloat, something about being a powerful demonic being, you gotta act like an ass about it."

"I hate when you act all noble."

"Imagine being me having to do it."

He smiled again, "Yeah, I'm not fond of it either."

Chapter 10

Pamela had held him for a long moment, kissing him deeply before she was willing to relent to leaving. Now that she was gone Jim was faced with the next big challenge, getting into the compound without getting shot or captured. He looked at the problem from multiple angles for a while before doing anything. This was not a, go running in all guns blazing situation, especially considering he didn't have any guns, it required a bit of planning. After a few moments spent mainly hoping for a miracle, Jim had thought of something, he just didn't like the only solution he was seeing. Most of the place was surrounded by tall wooden fencing which would be almost impossible to scale, even more so without getting detected and possibly deceased. There was only one clear way in that didn't have the high wooden slats, through the pig pens in the back which had probably been left more open to ease in removing waste. Jim had seen Snatch and had Bricktop's speech about what pigs could do to a person ringing in his ears as he crept forward.

By the time he reached the pens, he was sweating

hard again, not from exertion this time. He wasn't what he'd consider one of life's great stealth operators, the stress of trying to do it had his heart rate through the roof. He kept waiting for a voice to cry out, "Hey you!" and for this little adventure to fall apart before it had even gotten started. Thankfully, there was nobody in sight anywhere near the pens which made sense, who would want to hang out near a pig pen? Which only left the massive concern as to how to get through the animals without injury or discovery.

Looking over the area he found one pen that wasn't particularly full, so that was a start at least. It was only about thirty feet across to the other metal fence on the far side, but to his eyes that seemed like a filthy, muddy mile. He tried to rationalize, someone had to come in here to clean the worst of it up, to get pigs out for slaughter, how dangerous could they be? It wasn't a piece of rationalization that made him feel particularly good though, it would only take one of them to decide to not be good and then he'd find out how good a set of brass knuckles really were against a hungry, angry animal. He wondered to himself how thick a pig skull was. Normally animals, even wild animals, didn't spook him, but he had to go the full way across this snorting swirling mass to get inside the wood fencing of the main compound. The pens were built sticking out from it, probably to keep the pigs as far away from where the people here lived as possible, and over the low metal fence on the far side was the only way.

He had to remind himself that Jazz was probably in there and might need his help. Not to mention that the boy he'd seen on the video was in there absolutely needing help and both of them were more important to Jim than his fears. His fears had never done him any favors anyway. Taking a deep breath, he clambered up the metal farm gate and swung over into the pen. He landed with a squelch as his Doc Martens sank into the muck below him. He winced a bit at how hard that would be to clean off before he got moving. Jim kept his path to the far left-hand side of the pen, away from where the animal's feeding trough and water were situated, reasoning that if they were likely to get territorial it would be near where they got food.

By the time he'd traveled a third of the way he felt like an idiot, the pigs were for the most part ignoring him entirely. There were a few snorts and some hopeful eyes but other than that his presence was greeted with mainly disinterest. These things were fully domesticated and people neutral it appeared. Jim had worked himself up to this great big scenario where he'd have to sprint across the pen and here he was working his way along the somewhat less disgusting ground to the far side without so much as a nudge. He was so focused on being disgusted with himself that he almost put himself right on his ass slipping over the fence on the far side as he climbed to the top.

On the other side of the pens was a small open area that led to a building that had been built to surround the grassy area in front of the pens. It made sense, this way the pigs were completely out of sight from the living area, which Jim could easily see as being desirable. It also kept them still penned if they managed to slip out when they were being fed. He could only suppose the hogs were butchered inside, he wondered where they were actually slaughtered, he doubted it was right here next to the other animals. Jim wasn't relishing the idea, but he'd have to go through the abattoir if he wanted to get into the compound proper. There were three doors, two wooden ones and a dull steel one. Jim assumed the wood ones led to the slaughter area and the feed and equipment area, both of them promised to be more visible and open to the other side than the processing area itself which would need to be chilled. Like it or not, the butchering area was probably the best bet to get into the compound undetected.

The metal door swung smoothly towards him leading into a darkened large room that was heavily refrigerated, causing goosebumps to pop up on his sweaty arms instantly. The only light was sunlight dribbling in from two smallish windows, one in the front door and one in the back near where he entered. But even in the dim illumination, he could see enough to confirm where he was. Jim could see the gleam off of various steel butchering implements laid out and around tables between himself and the far door. Worse, he could see the silhouettes of bodies hanging from the rafters waiting to be chopped up and processed the rest of the way to meat. He moved slowly and carefully through the room, stepping into clouds of his own breath towards the door on the opposite side, desperate to not disturb anything. Jim could see through the window from where he was that there was an open area between this building and the next one that was swathed in shadows. He couldn't see anyone standing there but he certainly didn't want to cause any noise that might draw attention now.

He was just working his way past the swine bodies when against his better instincts he turned to look at them. Jim's hand clapped over his mouth to prevent himself from screaming. Hanging among the meat for butchering was the woman from the video! Fuck! Fuck! Fuck! It all flashed back to him, he was in a kitchen in the Lower East Side again, staring at a human being reduced to a collection of steaks and chops. He was almost positive now that Cole hadn't been wrong, this was caused by the same monster they'd killed all those years ago. Different ideology, different manipulation of a different tribe, same sickness that makes a society feed upon itself. The same horror trying to get what it really wanted, people at each other's throats, so maddened by its manipulation and magic that they had no real idea why they were even killing one another anymore. All it took was taking control away from a seed group, a small band who unbeknownst to themselves, had eaten the most delicious forbidden food. A sacrament that had given them the respite from having to make their own decisions. Something that so many drugs, religions, and political philosophies only promise, yet never deliver, absolution in the service of something higher.

He gawked at the woman's face as she hung there on a hook that was tied by a rope to the rafters. Her eyes almost seemed to plead with him to save her, even though opened up the way her torso was there was no soul left in there to do the begging. Her face said she had died hoping for something to rescue her and death had been the only answer. Except even the reaper wouldn't save her body from further desecration, death wasn't the end for the poor thing. Jim bit back another scream, this time one of rage at what had happened to this innocent bystander to evil. In front of what was most likely her child no less! With nothing else he could do for her, he did the only thing he could, Jim slowly reached out and closed her imploring eyes, the skin stiffly moved in the cold under his fingers.

Everyone who had a single thing to do with this deserved to die, just his shitty luck he didn't have an army at his back to come riding in like a righteous wave of retribution. He made his way the rest of the way to the door trying to content himself with the hope of at least saving two more victims of all of this before it was too late. Hopefully, Pamela would have gotten the evidence to the cops and it would be their problem, he was just here to prevent further bloodshed. If they believed her that was, they were in the hinterlands up here. Some of the local force were probably fellow travelers to these maggots. As lightly armed as he was and by himself, he would have to just be content in the role of rescuer and forgo the more desirable role of avenger, no matter how much it hurt him inside to leave it there for now.

At the door, Jim put his face against the glass and looked as far as he could both ways out the window. The area in front of the slaughterhouse was cloaked partially in shadow, sitting as it was between two buildings. What light got back to here was on the other side of the door only, as it peaked over the rooftop of the next building. He carefully and slowly turned the knob and pushed, sticking his head out, and let out a breath he hadn't even realized he was holding when he realized the coast was clear. Jim quickly stepped through and eased the door shut with a click that made him wince. The slaughter area was right behind the cabin they'd seen the leader of this madhouse exit. It made sense, considering what went on in the building at his back, he'd want to control visitors' access to the place. That cabin was where he was sure Jazz would be if they'd captured him. At least Jim hadn't seen him hanging on a butcher's hook, so he had to keep hoping that Jazz was still alive.

Jim tried to hug the side of the building to take advantage of the shadows to cover the distance so he could look in the rear window of the cabin. He had to stand on tiptoes but he was just able to see under the curtains of the window in the back of what looked like one of those prefab cabins you saw sometimes. It seemed to open into a tidy unlit bedroom. The door was open though and he could see down a hallway into a larger room in the front of the house. Jim's heart raced, tied to a chair in the distance near the front door was Jazz! That wasn't good, but it meant he was alive. Now Jim just had to figure out if he could save him without getting killed himself. No, scratch leaving it open to failure, he was going to save him, simple as that. The alternatives didn't bear thinking about. He'd seen the alternatives in the Lower East Side years ago.

The only question at this point was, how in the hell was he going to get to him without getting caught? He sure as hell couldn't even consider going out front, he could hear the mindless drones out there doing drills even from where he was. If Cole had been right about what this was, Jim knew the slaves weren't the fastest reactors to new stimulus, but exposed like that, how fucking fast did they even have to be? No, he'd have to find a way through this window. Jim sank back down and looked around for something to stand on.

He scanned the area in a hurry. Nothing presented itself in the dim little grassy area. He ran through mental images of everything he'd seen since he'd gotten here, there had to be something he could use on the window up there. He felt an internal relief when a moment later he remembered that there had been a large feed bucket next to the pigpen that might just about be able to do the job. It wouldn't be perfect and he'd have to balance, but it seemed like the best game in town at this exact moment.

Carefully and quietly, looking everywhere as he went Jim made his way back to the door to the butchering area. Before he went back in, he took a deep breath to steel himself for what was waiting in there. Taking one last glance around to make sure nobody had spotted him, he opened the door and slipped back inside letting the cool air greet him.

He moved quickly through the stainless tables and the bodies trying not to look at the last victim of this nightmare hanging there. Jim kept telling himself he wasn't being callous; he was keeping his resolve up to make sure nobody else had this done to them. If he stopped and looked at her too much his emotions would go off the fucking rails. He'd do something stupid, and that wouldn't help her son any. Hell, for all he knew that was exactly what happened to Jazz. Jim couldn't say he blamed his former bandmate for that at all for that matter. It was all he could do to not run back out there yelling a battle cry to attack the first person he could get his hands on himself. But that way ended up with a chair next to Jazz at best, at worst he'd be hanging in here right next to her. Probably both, a little torture tied to a chair, followed by being the main course for the next meal to look forward to.

It was with relief that he found himself back outside in the warm air, which was a strange feeling to attach to being next to a pig sty. Part of him just wanted to bolt, to leave this nightmare behind and forget he'd ever been involved in anything like this. That wasn't what he listened to. Instead, Jim grabbed the feeding bucket, which was a massive plastic thing covered with feed and feces from its use, before turning back to go back through the building. He was forced to move with exaggerated caution back through the butchering area. Something large like the bucket was so easy to lose track of, to not pay attention to completely. So easy to knock something over right now, to attract attention. He paused on his way as he eyed the stainless-steel rack containing the tools of the butcher's trade. Jim smiled grimly as he decided to add a massive knife to his meager arsenal before continuing on.

Jim froze.

He saw the shape of someone. Not fifteen feet from the door a goon was walking by! Jim ducked down automatically. Of course! For appearances if nothing else they'd have someone making rounds including back here. This wasn't some squat in New York where nobody went in that wasn't invited in, they were out in the country, people got nosy out here, meth heads stole shit. This place had to maintain at least the appearance of being an armed complex, people like politicians and movement leaders came here. They expected to see something efficient and military, you couldn't just have everybody passed out in a couple of rooms until you needed them like last time.

Jim was almost amazed that he had begun to sweat

again as he crouched there in the chilled air. He couldn't think of any reason for anyone to come in here right now, but that didn't mean anything. Maybe it was part of the routine, maybe part of it would be to check the pigs. He clutched the knife in his hand, pushing the bucket off to the side into the shadows in case the guard looked in. Ducking down directly under the window he held his breath as he waited, like a child playing hide and seek when his playmate gets close.

The light falling on the floor was invaded by a shadow. Someone was standing right on the other side of the door looking in through the glass. Jim clutched the knife so tightly his hand began to shake. He needed to be ready the second the door started to open to stab the newcomer, at this point the morality of doing it had gone out the window. He not only needed to do it, he also needed to do it so fast and so fatal that whoever it was didn't have a chance to make a sound. If these were drones like New York, threats wouldn't work, the fucker would start screaming loud and proud to protect the greater whole, even knowing it would get him killed. He needed to remind himself of that over and over again so that if the moment came, he wouldn't hesitate. Hesitation would surely cost Jazz his life, and maybe Jim his own.

Jim was almost stretched to the breaking point when just as suddenly the shadow vanished from the floor. Jim slowly exhaled the breath he'd been holding that entire time, making sure his breath went down so it wouldn't accidentally fog the window. He waited for as long as he could stand before he peaked his head back up to look through the window, just in time to see a retreating back go around the corner of the cabin in front of him.

Jim let out another great gusting breath before sucking in a deep breath and getting back to his feet. His knees throbbed a bit as he stood from staying in a crouched position for even that long. No one could be seen anywhere near the window when he took a better look. If he was going to break into that cabin and get Jazz, he needed to move, that lack of people clearly wasn't going to last. Opening the door again, he rushed across the gap. Once he was back at the window, he quickly set the bucket in place and climbed onto it, his knees protesting even more as he went. Looking through the window he could see Jazz more clearly, he was tied to a chair looking down at the floor groggily. Jim only prayed he'd be able to get him coherent enough to run once they were clear. He reached up and tried to push the window up. It moved just a little bit before it stuck.

He set the knife down on the sill and tried to use both hands. With a slight noise, it moved a little further this time. It was stiff and swollen in its track, the pressed wood that they made these places with must not have been treated right at the factory and it wasn't moving easily, he needed better leverage. Jim hopped off the bucket and moved back towards the other building, hoping to find something, maybe a pole or something to use to get a bit more leverage to get it open.

Sliding back into the abattoir and looking around the other building he quickly spotted what he needed, a broom sat in the corner. He should be able to use it to at least lever the window open enough that he could get his hand under and push. Jim snatched it up and rushed to get back, he was so close now. The sooner he got Jazz out of here the sooner he could put this whole nightmare behind him.

Jim yanked open the door and stepped back out into the bright light. As he took a step towards the window a voice to the right of the door behind him said, "Hey, asshole!"

Jim didn't even get a chance to turn before he felt a sudden thudding pain, the world went white for just an instant before it went black.

Jim heard voices talking out of the darkness behind his eyes. "I don't see why we don't get this over with," said one.

An older male voice said, "Jake, you have no sense of drama or intrigue. Also, because I don't want to, which ought to be enough you know."

"I know," said the first voice flatly. Jim kept his eyes closed as coherent thought came to him. Let them think he was still out, no point in letting on any more than he had to, it wasn't like he was fully online yet anyway. All he knew for sure was that he was seated on a high-backed chair; he could guess that he was tied up.

"Trust me, this has to be different. And hey, you got it your way, killing that woman in front of her whelp. I told you this one would be along behind the first one, didn't I? I know exactly what I'm doing here. And now, it looks like he's waking up. Up and at 'em Rat my boy, no point in playing possum!"

Rat?

Jim's eyes snapped open. Standing in front of him was a man a bit younger than him, next to him stood a smiling older man wearing wire-rimmed glasses. Behind the older man he could see a large antique desk placed like this was an office, finally at the rear of the room was some sort of flag on the wall. He didn't recognize the flag specifically, but he recognized the basics of the design. It was some sort of white power thing, all hard angles, and lines done in black and red. The old guy, who he recognized from watching the place, had a shit-eating grin partially hidden by his mustache.

"Who the fuck are you?" Jim mumbled.

"There's my boy!" the man said delightedly smacking down his hands on his thighs. "No, I don't suppose you know who I am anymore. But I damned well know who you are bucko, and I've been waiting thirty years to see you again, and here you and your buddy walk right in my back door. Ain't that a bitch?"

"I don't understand...."

"Where's the other one and the girl? Should I have someone else watching the pigpen for when your other friend gets here? How about the girl? I mean we have your address from your wallet, I suppose if you're protecting her by keeping her there, we'll just have to have Pamela picked up. So, when can I expect Cole to come along as part of your dazzling plan?"

Jim looked around, the first thing he noticed was that it was fully dark outside, he must have been unconscious for some time now. Jazz was next to him tied to a chair, as well as a small African American boy that Jim recognized from the film. That meant that this was the cabin. Both of them had duct tape over their mouths that gleamed in the light of the overhead bulb. They were conscious but both looked a bit out of it.

Looking back at the man, Jim laughed ruefully. He knew who this was now, specifically, there was no doubt in Jim's mind. "I wouldn't hold your breath on that one. Cole's dead."

A look of consternation flashed over the old man's face before he replied, "Still, no matter I've got you two and if the girl's at your house, well, woman now I suppose, lady even, I'll have her too. It's a shame Cole isn't here, but at least I get to torture you and Jazz while we wait to see if I get the clean sweep of the survivors."

"Andy? Can I still call you that, or do I need to learn a new fake name?"

"Hey look at you being brighter than you look! Course that wouldn't be too hard."

"Why did he call you Andy?" the other man, who

must be Jake asked.

"It's a long story Jake, you know what I am. I've been called different things in different times. Jake, do me a favor? Step outside and make sure I'm not interrupted for a while," the old man said smiling. He held up the knife that Jim had on him before he got knocked out and flicked it back and forth catching the light, "If anyone asks, tell them I'm entertaining old friends."

"I don't like it, Howard, we should just kill 'em and cook 'em. Better yet, feed 'em to the pigs so if someone comes around asking, we say they were never here," the man called Jake said before he made for the door.

"Your complaint has been registered, trust me, I know exactly what I'm doing here."

Jake slammed the door on his way out to lend emphasis to his displeasure.

Jim glared up at Andy or whatever he was calling himself, "So what now?"

The demon chuckled at that as he stepped behind the desk, "Well you did kill my previous vessel, so forgive and forget is kind of out of the question ain't it? I had toyed with the idea of putting you three losers out on the road. Restraint and Control as a Nazi band? Now that would cause a bit of upset and chaos right there all by itself. Might still do it, don't know if it's the same without the third wheel." He smiled again, "So what would you do if you were me? And don't say let you go, cause we know that ain't fucking happening." It was almost fascinating to Jim to watch this refined-looking man curse like a street kid, but he could see why it was so happy to revert to that patois, it's more fun for one thing.

"I have no idea what something like you would do," Jim replied with a glare.

"Now keep in mind," the creature said as he reached into his desk, "I don't think you brought along these party favors to talk about old times with me either." One after another he set down on his desk the knife Jim had grabbed from the abattoir that he'd had in his hands, Jim's brass knuckles, and finally a gun.

"I didn't bring a gun."

"No, Jazz brought that, seems he was quite upset about something. You know what I think would be swell? I think what I'm gonna do is feed you to each other. First, I'll feed the boy to Jazz, since that's what got you all into this mess. And then after he's fully turned, I'll have him kill himself while you watch, then you can have yourself a big ol' Sloppy Jazz sandwich. Either that or the band thing, still some serious traction left in that idea, I haven't made up my mind yet. Heck, I can use the kid to get both your minds, right? His Momma's in the cooler, maybe keep him alive to make sure you eat up. Then if the band thing is a wash, I can always make you eat Jazz later. And lord what I can have the both of you do to your lady friend. She called me some seriously mean names back in the day, and that deserves some comeuppance."

"You are still seriously fucked up; you know that right? No matter what you are, you are a few bananas short of a bunch," Jim grunted.

The creature, either whatever his name was or Andy, it didn't matter what it was calling itself, turned and hobbled over to the flag. The moment his eyes were off of him, Jim tested his bonds. He almost made a noise when he realized how poorly they'd been tied. It was like a child learning to tie his shoes, loose and sloppily done, and more importantly, easily undone. He moved his hands around and began tugging at the big loop of the knot while desperately trying not to make any noise.

"Even if you had succeeded it wouldn't have mattered you know," the old man said over his shoulder staring at the map.

"Why the hell not? You're dead, end of story, right? Just like last time."

"It won't matter because this time I was smarter. I got true believers to pad out my little army. Some of those dipshits out there already believed in race wars and all that other crap to make their mundane failed existences bearable. There isn't one man out there that didn't look at his own useless frailties and shortcomings and didn't decide to blame a minority for it. Most of them walked in the door wanting to believe, the only difference is controlling them keeps them out of trouble. Last time, yeah, the riot happened, but it wasn't riots, I misjudged the mood of the nation. But the thing is, there are a lot more out there like they were before they got here, and they just want one last push. Tomorrow, whether I'm here or not, two busloads of them are going to the heart of their perceived enemy and they are starting the race war. Jake, the one you saw, he has faith in the mission, he'll make sure it happens."

While the demon yammered away at how perfect he'd planned this, Jim felt his bonds fall away from him. Jazz's eyes got wide causing Jim to quickly put a finger to his lips. Jazz nodded as did the little boy who had looked almost resigned to everything at this point. The kid had been through the wringer and his eyes betrayed his exhaustion. Jim lunged to his feet and in two quick steps, he was across the room grabbing the gun. The old man never turned from looking at his flag the entire time, almost like he had known it was going to happen and didn't care. Something important niggled at Jim's brain, something about last time this had happened, with him trying to get over being knocked unconscious, it just wasn't getting through to him though.

"It doesn't matter Rodent; you're not getting out of here alive and you can't stop what I've done this time. So go ahead" Jim moved behind the old man and placed the gun at his head. "Is killing me going to bring back that kid's Momma? Is it going to stop Jake from shooting the three of you once you step outside that door? Face it, you're better off just eating the kid and being on the right side of the revolution!"

Jim's finger tensed on the trigger; it would be so easy to send this thing back to hell. It would feel good, it would feel like justice! His teeth gritted with the effort to remain calm and think it through. The tense moment was shattered by the sound of a bullhorn outside, Jim couldn't make out what was being said but the response with undeniable. A shot rang out. Followed a second later by a scattering of more. The cops! Pamela must have gotten to the cops!

That moment was when it all became clear to him in that instant. The thing wanted Jim to kill him. If he had walked up behind it with a gun last time, well he wouldn't have even made it, the thing could clobber him with a lamp or something any time it wanted to just using its mind. It had crushed him to the ground like a bug under a boot last time, but here and now it had just let him walk right up. It was giving him a free shot. It had done all it could in that old and feeble body and it knew it. Whatever mischief it had done, was already in motion, it was at the top of the roller coaster, it couldn't go any further at that age. It wanted to be set free so it could find a new body and formulate a new plan!

"Sounds like visitors," Jim said.

"It's not important."

"Fuck you! You act like you're some amazing creature, so much smarter and better than us, pulling our strings and manipulating us to do terrible things. The thing is, I've got you figured. You don't come up with shit, you don't create shit. All you do is stoke our own fires, we do the fucked-up shit, all you do is convince us to do more of it. Even worse you gotta make people zombies to pull even that off, you ain't even bright enough to be a real cult leader. You aren't some master-mind, you aren't even the demonic equivalent of the little shithead on the playground getting the other kids to fight by talking shit! If we actually figured out a way to be decent to one another, there wouldn't be shit you could do about us. We don't need to fight demons we all need to go to fucking therapy for a while!"

"Look, I-..." whatever the demon would have said next was cut off by Jim bringing the gun around and bashing it into the side of its head. Howard Calvin Fillmore slumped to the ground in a heap. Jim checked his pulse, unconscious but still alive, just like he hoped.

Jim moved quickly, grabbing the knife off the desk before going over to Jazz and cutting him loose. As Jazz was standing up rubbing his wrists to get feelings back into his hands, Jim went over to the boy. The poor kid's yellow t-shirt had a happy face on it, there was a smear of brown caused by dried blood directly across the front. Jim couldn't help but think it looked like a punk record cover. The boy's eyes gaped wide at Jim as he came over holding the knife, but he didn't struggle, perhaps over the length of his ordeal he'd lost the ability.

"Look kid, after what you've been through, I wouldn't expect you to trust anyone who looked like me ever again. So, it kind of sucks that I have to ask you to trust me. I want to get us all out of here but you're going to need to be quiet and do what I say. Think you can be brave for me just a little bit longer?"

Jim almost gasped with relief when the little kid nodded.

When they were all free from their bonds Jazz asked, "So where next Columbus? Or didn't you think that far ahead? I don't think I would have. If I thought ahead, I might not have needed the cavalry like this."

"There's a window in the back of this place. When we

get to the building behind it, we run through the butcher shop and the pigpen and the fuck out of here."

With Jazz helping it was a ton easier than opening the window than from the outside. Jim sent Jazz out first, who got his feet on the bucket which was thankfully right where he'd left it, "OK, kid, what's your name anyway? I feel stupid calling you kid."

"Kalen," the boy replied in a hoarse whisper.

"All right Kalen, I need you to go out to my buddy Jazz and he'll set you on the ground. Then I'll come out and we'll get the hell out of here. We have to go through another building, but we're going to run through that, OK?"

"Yessir"

Kalen crawled gingerly out of the window and into Jazz's arms. Jazz hopped down, clearing the way for Jim to come through. Jim was just getting his feet down on the bucket when they heard the front door to the cabin slam open. They heard Jake's voice down the hallway, "Howard! We got... What the god damned hell?"

Jim looked at Jazz as he was jumping down off the bucket, "We better run like fuck!"

As the door slammed again, Jim scooped up Kalen, who was surprisingly light, before running for the slaughterhouse. When they were through the door, he made a point of shielding the boy from the sight of his mother as she dangled there. It was bad enough he had seen what he had; he didn't need to be reminded of it. Hell, it was bad enough Jim had to look at her again as they fled.

They barely even paused when they reached the gate to the pigpen. Jim handed the boy to Jazz and slid over the fence after them. Once Jazz had handed Kalen back and was over himself, they hurried along the edge as Jim had coming in. The pigs seemed a bit more agitated, but let them pass without more than a few snuffles at their legs as they pushed their way through. Jim could only assume that they were upset by the sounds of gunfire which still seemed to be coming sporadically from the front of the compound. The defenders and the police had probably reached a stand-off until heavier ordinance could be brought to bear on the situation.

As soon as they made it into the woods Jim stopped, turned back towards how they had come before dropping to a knee, partially shielded by a tree.

"What the fuck are you doing?" Jazz hissed.

"There's a guy, who is probably armed, right behind us. He won't be able to see me in the woods and I have a gun, what in the fuck do you think I'm doing?"

"Give me the gun Jim," Jazz said quietly.

"Why?"

"It's my gun, I'm a better shot with it."

Jim had to get control of his temper; he wanted a shot at the guy. But Jazz was right, what in the hell did he know about guns? Silently he handed over the gun, "All right, me and Kalen here are going to slip a bit further back behind a rock if that's cool."

"Iceberg."

Just as Jim was pulling Kalen behind him to slide deeper into the woods to hide, the door to the abattoir slammed open. Even in the dim light provided by the one security bulb in the area, Jim could easily see that it was Jake. The man looked around for only a moment before heading straight for the pigpen. It wasn't a surprise in any way, it was the only way out of there, especially with what was most likely every State Trooper in the county out front. It was the only direction the three potential eyewitnesses to all of this could have gone. He paused before he climbed over the fence. The man must have seen a glint or something because in one fluid, practiced motion he pulled out his gun and fired!

Jim felt hot burning fire erupt in his shoulder. He'd

never been shot before, but he didn't have to have had previous experience to know he'd been hit. Jazz whirled to look back at him and hissed, "Jim, are you all right?"

"Fuck! I don't know I've never been fucking shot before; I think I'll live," Jim managed a gasping whisper as he pulled Kalen further back away from the light. "Do what you're gonna do already so we can ask a doctor to make sure huh?"

Jim remembered a CPR class he'd taken once where they talked about wounds. The important thing was direct pressure, he quickly stripped his t-shirt off and wadded it over the wound, feeling the blood making the shirt moist as he pressed down on it. While he did first aid on himself the man who had shot him slowly worked his way through the pigs coming inexorably closer. Soon he might even be able to see Jazz hidden in the shadows of the trees. Jim had to hold his hand over Kalen's mouth to keep him from making noise. He found himself willing his friend to fire already while at the same time being forced to keep quiet. He could hear the pigs grunt as the man pushed through them.

Finally. One shot rang out.

They could see Jake stumble. Both hands slammed down onto his leg where he'd been struck by the bullet. Jake looked up, it seemed like he was looking right at them. One hand began to go slowly to his side to pull the gun again, but he didn't want to spook his prey. Before he could pull the gun from its holster Jim heard a squeal from inside the pen and Jake let out a yell. This was followed by a grunt and another bark of pain from Jake. Jake started to try and limp forward with some urgency as the night air began to fill with squeals and grunts. Jake let out a scream of pain as he continued to try to muscle forward. The pigs parted briefly letting Jim see why the Nazi had been screaming. The blood must have excited the pigs, who were already riled up, and sensing food they were attacking Jake, biting and tearing at his bleeding leg. Jake let out another grunt and stumbled down to his knees. That was the last they saw his hateful face before a moment later the pigs swarmed him over. They could briefly see his hand in the swirl of pink and brown bodies until even that vanished from view.

There was no sound now but the grunts squeals coming from the pen as the feeding frenzy took over down below. Jim said very quietly, barely audible over the noise, "Nice shot."

"I was aiming for his balls."

"Let's get the fuck out of here, while I've still got some blood left."

Epilogue

There was no hope of it being "their secret" this time. Especially after they ran into the cops while trying to work their way back to Jazz's car. Hell, they'd almost gotten shot for their troubles. Suddenly, there was this bright flashlight and a young cop screaming, "FREEZE FREEZE FUCKING MOVE AND YOU'RE FUCKING DEAD!"

"Dude!" Jim called out, "we're who you're here to rescue. Ease off the trigger, we snuck out the back when you guys distracted them up front. Also, the pricks kinda shot me, so, little help?"

After that, it was chaos for a long while. Jim was given some rough and ready first aid before he and Jazz were cuffed and taken to the hospital.

"Why didn't you kill him?" Jazz asked on the ride.

"He wanted me to. When we ran into that fucker before he was able to move things, he almost choked me out at one point. He knew I was behind him; he could have stopped me at any time. Whatever reason, he wanted out. Anything he wanted, I wasn't giving, now do me a favor and stop giving evidence with Mr. Officer up there. It's not incriminating, but god damn it, you gotta be smarter than that bro," Jim explained as patiently as blood loss and exhaustion would allow.

They were silent until they got to the hospital where Pamela confirmed that they were not actual Nazis but the guys who rescued the kid from the Nazis, as in the heroes and stuff. By then those selfsame Nazis had started to surrender anyway. With Fillmore out cold, and Jake rapidly turning into pig shit there was no one there to control their heads and give orders. Most of them reverted to what they were before it had all gotten serious, dumb kids who had resorted to being offensive and playing dress-up to express their anger at the world. Not the type of people who really wanted to be in a firefight with armored SWAT vehicles.

Hell really broke loose when the grounds were searched. Especially once they found Kalen's mother. It turned out that she was a local lawyer named Alicia Johnson. She hadn't been a civil rights lawyer or involved in any litigation with any of the white power networks that were going to be exposed thanks to the photos they had taken and Cole's notes. Alicia's sole crime against their "movement" was to be African American and to have her car break down a quarter of a mile from the compound at night. A better fanbelt and she would have been fine, that was one of those sick twists of fate life provided that would bug Jim for quite a while.

Jim ended up in surgery, the bullet hadn't passed clean through and needed to be removed. They were able to do it with local anesthetic. So, while not bright-eyed and bushy-tailed, he was awake when they wheeled him to discharge and into Pamela's waiting kisses. Jim had thrown up a warning hand when she came running over, "No hugs OK, other than me possibly bleeding out, which I clearly didn't, it didn't do major damage. That don't mean it don't hurt like fuck."

"I will be gentle with my big tough hero," she grinned.

"And not at all condescending about it," he grunted.

"Not even a itty bitty bit snookums," she chuckled.

"Somehow, I don't believe you."

Despite not wanting to be, Jazz, Jim, Kalen, and Pamela became famous for a little while. People notice headlines like, "PUNK BAND MATES RESCUE CHILD FROM CANNIBAL NAZIS!" Jim weathered it as best he could, Jazz had it a bit easier, he could go back to New York where at least it wasn't wall-to-wall coverage. Alison was useful here, she suggested an agent, actually, she told Jazz bluntly to get one. When they protested that they weren't stars or anything, she explained carefully that at the moment, yes, they were, and if they were going to get hounded like stars they might as well have an agent to keep people out of their hair. Oh, and get paid for their troubles, if someone was going to be making money off of this, and she pointed out that a lot of people were, they probably should as well. It was one thing to be non-materiel and noble about it, it was quite another to let yourself get ripped off. More importantly, it was unforgivable to let other people make up a story about your life and to tag your name on to it without your permission while they cashed great big fat Hollywood checks off it.

Donations poured in for little Kalen's upbringing, therapy, and college. Including quite a bit from Jazz, Jim and Pamela, and Cindy as well once she had the whole story of what had happened. It made it a bit easier to sleep at night. Maybe one day the kid would want to talk to them, but Jim suggested they give him as much space as he needed to heal as much as he could.

Howard Calvin Fillmore was sentenced to life in

prison. After hearing the sans demon version of their story, and Jim's suspicions that Howard would be thrilled to die, he was put under suicide watch. He was eventually committed to the state mental hospital where he resides today. Visitors are not encouraged.

Finally, it all settled back to normal. Even that was for a given value of normal since Jim no longer lived alone. To his surprise Cindy approved of the new situation wholeheartedly, she told him that she worried about him living alone and she thought Pamela seemed nice, whatever the hell "nice" meant in that context. Even the girls liked Pamela, they even stayed over at the house more often now that she lived there. Jim wasn't sure how to take that, but the thing was, they were girls and he had a tendency to be a morose old man left to himself. Maybe Pamela just lightened the mood, or maybe they felt it was easier to be friends with her than him. They had never seen her at her worst, neither had he for that matter, but they'd seen the hell out of his worst. Either way, it was nice to see them more often.

With Alan finally mended the rest of the way, Hates of Gray were back together. Pamela was even cool about band practices; she even sometimes came along to listen or watch. Not full Yoko Ono or anything, but if Benji's wife was dropping him off she'd come and the two of them would hang out as an audience of two.

All of which had led up to tonight. The big return to the stage for the band. Jim had to threaten the promoter repeatedly to make sure that none of the fliers mentioned one fucking word about what had happened with the Nazis. It was just a return gig for a local favorite that had been on the shelf for a while due to health reasons and nothing more. The kid wasn't happy about losing a major draw point on the fliers, but he still managed to make them the headliners even if one of the other bands was technically bigger and from out of town.

He was out front with Benji and Pamela hanging out by the merch table. Most of his friends had come by to say hi already, so now he could just hang out and watch the opening act. It seemed from what he could see that there was a pit, and it was what he would consider a fun one. Not one of the toxic macho ones you got sometimes, this was just kids flailing about, getting all their anger and their energy out before they had to go home tonight and face reality.

As the band onstage finished their last song he turned and said to Pamela, "That's what I still love about punk, it knows."

She looked at him wide-eyed like he was out of his mind before responding, "What are you talking about old-timer, it knows what?"

"It knows how fucked the world is, but it doesn't run from it. It knows politicians are hanging out with Nazis and banks are fucking us and wars are happening but it looks it right in the eye and it says, 'Not me, I am not a part of this.' It yells it, it screams it, it is a screaming denial of everything that's wrong with this world. You know why you still talk to people from the scene online and not people you went to high school with? Because they saw it too, they were there with you when you said, 'This is bullshit' Meanwhile your high school friends all said, 'Mmmm mmm yummy delicious bullshit.' Punk rock knows and it faces its fears."

"Very poetic, you should write it down," she smiled.

"Naw, I can't rhyme it and I'm not much of a writer," he smiled taking her hand in his.

About the Author

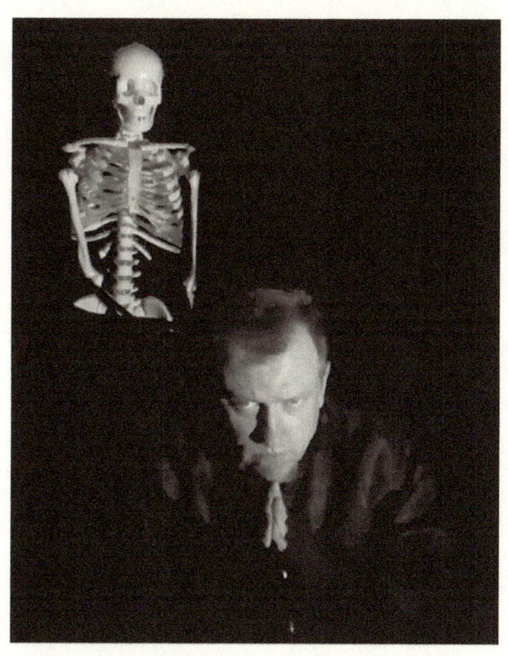

Paul has lived all over the country before settling in Appalachia over fifteen years ago with his wife Leslie and their son. He also has two adult children living in his native Pennsylvania.

He is the author of numerous novels and collections and more on the way.

Paul is a member of the Horror Writers Association, appearing on the panel for horror comedy at the 2021 Stoker Con.

He has a dark and serious horror side, but he has also never answered the question, "Is everything a joke with you?" correctly once in his entire life.

OTHER HELLBOUND BOOKS

Brat Out Of Hell

John Milton, some famous dead guy, once wrote that it was better to rule in Hell than to serve in Heaven.

What if you weren't too keen on either?

That's the position in which Danasdius, demon prince, grandson of Lucifer finds himself.

In fact, what he'd really like is to have a nice, normal life on Earth.

So, he does the only thing he can think of: he runs away from Hell.

Decades later, his unobservant, often absentee father, Moraspus, has noticed the palace is a bit quieter than usual and decides to get Danasdius back.

Can Dan and the friends he's made on earth make sure he stays a BRAT OUT OF HELL?

The Wet

In the quiet seaside village of Sable, something is stirring. Reclusive artist Jason Harding has retreated there to recover from a past trauma.

Lifeboat man Rob Woodhead returned because Sable is his home.

Disgruntled weathergirl Vicky West is on her way to interview windsurfers for her satellite TV channel.

All three will be brought together by a freak storm, one that remains stationary over the ocean and seems almost alive.

What happens next will rock the entire community to its core…

The Wet is the very first novel written by #1 bestselling, award-winning author Paul Kane (The *RED* Trilogy, *Before, Sherlock Holmes and the Servants of Hell)*.

Penned in his early 20s and recently uncovered, this terrifying curiosity, influenced by those genre-busting '70s and '80s pulp horror novels, will shock and surprise you to the very last page.

Published for the very first time, *The Wet* is certain to cause a splash!

"Paul Kane is a first-rate storyteller, never failing to marry his insights into the world and its anguish with the pleasures of phrases eloquently turned." (**Clive Barker** – Bestselling author of *The Hellbound Heart, Mr B. Gone* and *The Scarlet Gospels)*

Snow White in His Glass Coffin

This Southern gothic, psychosexual horror story follows siblings Chastity and Jonathan Caldwell throughout their terribly troubled lives…

From spending their grim childhood in a ramshackle trailer with an unstable, cruel mother who prostitutes Jonathan out to fund her meth addiction, through a brutal murder that permanently alters their relationship, and into their adulthood, where Chastity begins to take increasing sadistic joy in controlling and tormenting her poor brother.

Told from Chastity's unique perspective, *Snow White in His Glass Coffin* dares you to empathize with two deeply disturbed people who commit and attempt to rationalize their unspeakable, brutal crimes.

A gut-wrenching tale most definitely not for the faint of heart.

Road Kill: Volume 9

Road Kill: Texas Horror by Texas Writers, Vol. 9 is packed with harrowing depredations, grim manifestations and terrifying implications. Suggesting this historic anthology is just a regional horror collection is like calling Frankenstein's monster a simple misstep in medical technology.

Road Kill is no longer just an annual anthology of horror stories. It's a serial collection of some of the most serious voices in Lone Star literature. It's a chronicle of Texas terror, and Vol. 9 is eerie, edgy and feral. It will haunt you long after its first reading.

It's as fine a selection of horror fiction as you'll find today.

It's alive!

With stories of exceptional horror from:

Mario E. Martinez, L.H. Phillips, Lucas Strough, Aimee Trask, Armando Sangre, W.R. Theiss, C.W. Stevenson, Jae Mazer, M.E. Splawn,Kathleen Kent, Andrew Kozma, Julie Aaron, Robert Stahl, William Jensen, Todd Elliott, Lewis B. Smith, Derek Austin Johnson, Juan Perez, Bev Vincent, Lawrence Buentello, & Bret McCormick

Flanagan

"*Straw Dogs* meets *Fifty Shades* - heart pounding, gut-wrenching, sexy as all hell and with a twist you'll never see coming!"

Meet the Sewells, your typical, all-American couple; happily married for ten years, respected high school teachers, still crazy about one another and with a secret, shared dark side.

During their annual Spring Break vacation to recharge their batteries and reconnect as a couple, they are waylaid by a perverse gang of misfits in the one horse, North Texas, town of Flanagan.

Taken hostage as the focus of the gang's twisted games, the Sewells are brutalized into performing increasingly vicious physical, sexual and emotional acts upon one another, until events take an unexpected turn - triggered by an unintentional death.

As their circumstance descends into the worse nightmare imaginable, the Sewells find themselves involved in an altogether different situation...

Ted's Score

From the author of the movies *Lake Dead*, (After Dark Films' 8 Films to Die For) and *Farmhouse*, Daniel P. Coughlin's Ted's Score is a shocking, suspenseful tale of a depraved, ax-wielding serial killer.

When beautiful Jules Benton, a seventeen-year-old senior, goes missing after the spring formal dance in the small town of Watertown, Wisconsin, her father, Richard, becomes suspicious of Jules' boyfriend, David Miller, and his involvement with her disappearance.

When Richard confirms his suspicions, the brutality of his capability consumes him, and soon David will find out what that means...

Unbeknownst to David or Richard, a serial killer by the name of Ted Olson has more to do with Jules' disappearance than anyone might suspect.

As Jules' whereabouts unfold, the truth begins to bleed from a dark place, and the authorities begin to smell the criminal acts committed.

Murder and mayhem catch up with the slow pace of this ordinary Middle American town when evil, perversion, and death mislead these simple folks into a disastrous wave of crime that spirals out of control.

All the while, Ted collects his score…

**A HellBound Books Publishing LLC
Publication**

www.hellboundbooks.com